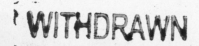

W9-BQM-372

Valerie Sayers
WHO DO YOU LOVE

"BREEZY AND KNOWING." —New York *Daily News*

"MISS SAYERS HAS A GIFT FOR VOICE AND THE HONEST, GRITTY COMMENTARY ABOUT HUMAN BEHAVIOR IN STRESSFUL CIRCUMSTANCES. SHE WRITES CLEARLY AND FORCEFULLY, WITH HER OWN VERSION OF THE HUMOR THAT SOUTHERN WRITERS FROM EUDORA WELTY TO FLANNERY O'CONNOR TO REYNOLDS PRICE USE SO TELL-INGLY." —*The New York Times Book Review*

"A UNIQUE VOICE AND VISION . . . A NOVEL THAT FULFILLS ITS MISSION." —*Chicago Tribune*

"SAYERS'S PROSE HAS VERVE AND HUMOR, HER VIEW OF SOUTHERN LIFE IS CLEAR-EYED, AUTHENTIC, AND GEN-EROUS. HER COMPASSIONATE UNDERSTANDING OF THE STRAINS, WORRIES, AND MISSED COMMUNICATIONS OF MARRIAGE GIVES THIS BOOK DEPTH AND STAYING POWER." —*Publishers Weekly*

"ABSORBING AND WISE AND FUNNY . . . SAYERS IS THE REAL THING, A WRITER WITH THE IMAGINATION TO CRE-ATE A GENUINE SOCIETY AND THE CRAFT TO PEOPLE IT WITH THOSE ABOUT WHOM READERS WILL FEEL DEEPLY." —*The State* (Columbia, S.C.)

"VALERIE SAYERS IS A POWERFULLY GIFTED WRITER, AND THE TOWN OF DUE EAST IS A RICH VEIN TO BE MINED." —*The Atlanta Journal & Constitution*

"ANOTHER STRIKINGLY WISE OBSERVATION OF HUMAN NATURE AND A CONUNDRUM: WHO STEALS YOUR HEART AWAY, ANYHOW . . . THE PLAYER OR THE PLAY?" —*Kirkus Reviews*

WITHDRAWN

WHO
DO YOU
LOVE

Valerie Sayers

LAUREL

127390

A LAUREL TRADE PAPERBACK
Published by
Dell Publishing
a division of
Bantam Doubleday Dell Publishing Group, Inc.
666 Fifth Avenue
New York, New York 10103

Book design by Anne Ling

If you purchased this book without a cover you should be aware that this book is stolen property. It was reported as "unsold and destroyed" to the publisher and neither the author nor the publisher has received any payment for this "stripped book."

All of the characters in this book are fictitious, and any resemblance to actual persons, living or dead, is purely coincidental.

Copyright © 1991 by Valerie Sayers

All rights reserved. No part of this book may be reproduced or transmitted in any form or by any means, electronic or mechanical, including photocopying, recording, or by any information storage and retrieval system, without the written permission of the Publisher, except where permitted by law. For information address: Doubleday, New York, New York.

The trademark Laurel® is registered in the U.S. Patent and Trademark Office.

The trademark Dell® is registered in the U.S. Patent and Trademark Office.

ISBN: 0-440-50441-4

Reprinted by arrangement with Doubleday

Printed in the United States of America

Published simultaneously in Canada

March 1992

10 9 8 7 6 5 4 3 2 1

RRH

For Virginia Sayers and Elizabeth Dowling Sendor

Acknowledgments

Grateful thanks to the Writers Room, New York, where much of this book was written; to Julie Zachowski and Dennis Adams of the Beaufort County Library, South Carolina, for their gracious assistance; to Esther Newberg; and to Casey Fuetsch.

Lines from "Who Do You Love" copyright © 1956 (renewed) by Arc Music Corporation. Reprinted by permission. All rights reserved.

Lines from *Either/Or* by Søren Kierkegaard, Volume I, translated by David Swenson and Lillian Marvin Swenson. Copyright 1944, © 1972 by Howard A. Johnson. Published by Princeton University Press.

Lines from *Summa Theologica* from *Basic Writings of St. Thomas Aquinas, Volume One,* edited by Anton C. Pegis. Copyright 1945 by Random House, Inc.

Lines from "Easter 1916" by William Butler Yeats from *Collected Poems* by William Butler Yeats. Reprinted with permission of Macmillan Publishing Co., from *The Poems of W. B. Yeats: A New Edition*; edited by Richard J. Finneran, copyright 1924; renewed 1952 by Bertha Georgie Yeats.

Lines from "Danse Russe" by William Carlos Williams from the *Collected Poems of William Carlos Williams, 1909–1939, Volume I.* Copyright 1938 by New Directions Publishing Corporation. Reprinted by permission of New Directions Publishing Corporation.

Lines from "In a Wife I Would Desire" from *The Complete Poetry and Prose of William Blake.* Edited by David V. Erdman, Commentary by Harold Bloom. Copyright 1965, 1982 by David V. Erdman. Published by Anchor Books, a division of Bantam Doubleday Dell.

What is youth? A dream. What is love? The substance of a dream.
—Søren Kierkegaard

I'm a old woman's wish and a young woman's dream.
Who do you love?
—Bo Diddley

CONTENTS

NOVEMBER 1963

RED SATIN NIGHTIES

It was a dreamy Thursday in Due East.

Dolores Rooney stood on the bluff overlooking the Due East Bay and daydreamed, for once in her life, shamelessly. She was not a woman for standing still, but it was one of those delicious soporific warm fall days and it would have been sinful not to bask in it: this was a day to stop awhile, to be a Mary, not a Martha. The bay below was a broad still coruscating mirror, and it released one of those almost-salty smells that teased her memory in the vaguest way. Every now and then an enlisted man drove by with his convertible top down, his radio whispering some too-slow song by some bleating boy singer, Paul Anka or Bobby Vinton.

Dolores Rooney saw a gawky crew-cut young man making

his way across the bluff to talk to her, and she considered fleeing. She wasn't at all sure she could bear a conversation with an earnest fellow whose glasses, from a distance, resembled two miniature television sets flashing light.

Dolores Rooney did not have a good history with young men passing through Due East. She recognized this one as that reporter from the New York *Times,* in town for the court-martial ("Drill Instructor Forces Recruits on Harrowing Swamp March; One Marine Dead"). He probably meant to interview her, to ask her how the community reacted to this tragedy—as if there were more than one way to react to a mad drill instructor and a dead teenage boy.

But when the reporter drew near he only said: "I think I've landed in paradise," and Dolores Rooney smiled the most noncommittal smile she could scare up. Behind the glasses the boy's eyes were a watery pale blue, but his stare was more intent than she would have predicted, and his high forehead gave him a slight—oh, just the slightest—resemblance to Robert Kennedy. The crew cut spoiled *that,* though.

The young man said that the military court was in recess today, that he'd spent the morning ogling the long funereal procession of old River Street houses, and the big easy curve of the bay, and he meant (as soon as he'd filed all his court-martial pieces) to write an article about this town for the travel section.

"I think I've fallen in love with Due East," he said, and he sounded as awestruck as if he'd just seen the Sistine Chapel for the first time. "I think a perfect little town like this just deserves to be written up. And photographed—I'm planning on taking plenty of shots framed with this Spanish moss." Dolores Rooney did not have the heart to tell the young man that the little town *had* been written up, and photographed, in *Holiday* and *House & Garden* and some of the Sunday supplements: she

4

had a feeling it would be like telling him that the pretty girl he'd just danced with was a girl with a reputation.

"How long have *you* been here?" the reporter asked, and Dolores Rooney's smile widened. He thought she was a tourist.

"Oh, about seventeen years, I guess it is now," she said.

"My, my." The words didn't sound easy on the reporter's lips: the only grown man who could get away with saying *My, my* (and then hammering out a slow cluck of his tongue) was a man who'd spent his whole life in a town like Due East. The reporter was just doing what all visitors to the South did after a day or two, imitating the accent without even knowing they tried. She'd done it herself, she supposed, for a while.

"I can imagine staying here for seventeen years. Getting out of the stream of traffic, just parking my car for a while."

Another noncommittal smile: Dolores Rooney realized that the young man was flirting with her. He seemed to possess a little more grace standing still. His features were as neat and precise as the quarter-moon eyebrows he popped up over his glasses: tidy little nose, heart-shaped upper lip.

"I've been trying out titles all morning," he said. "For the travel piece. I thought maybe I'd call it 'Time Stands Still on the Carolina Coast'—but then, the editors always change the title no matter what you call it."

The reporter didn't seem to catch the disdainful cast to Dolores Rooney's eye—she, who'd never in her life published so much as a letter to the editor, could have come up with a title that wasn't a cliché—but she was grateful that he couldn't see her disapproval. Poor earnest young stranger in town, lonely enough to be flirting with *her:* she was three months pregnant with her fifth child, and though she wasn't wearing maternity clothes yet she was sure she was as wide across the hips as the Due East Bay. Her fingers were swollen already, and she'd eased off her wedding ring three weeks ago. Her pale skin was mottled over with pale freckles that merged into smut during pregnancy, and her sharp chin, she was horrified to see, was beginning to sag.

The reporter gestured toward the big old tabby house behind them, its stone the same airy gray as the moss hanging down from the trees, its steps crumbling the same amount that they'd crumbled last year, and the year before, and the hundred years before that: slow, slow decay. "Look at those houses! Now I guess some people would call them a little shabby, but to me they look, well, elegant. Don't you think? Isn't that elegant for a little burg off the beaten track?"

A little burg: oh, this fellow was so very very young. There was only one way to scare such a young man away:

"My husband always says just exactly the same thing."

The reporter smiled that smile of the defeated—so he *had* been flirting—and said that he'd better be heading back to the motel to type up some of his notes.

"Good luck with the travel piece," she said, but already he was looking at her in a different way (maybe he'd noticed that her hips *were* as wide as the Due East Bay). He shuffled off, his feet unconsciously imitating the slow gait of the town. He didn't do the walk much better than he did the *My, my.*

Well, it wasn't the first time that some reporter or artist or tourist from Chicago or New York or Boston had stopped to talk to Dolores Rooney, picking her out as surely as if they wore radar and she beamed signals that said: "Outsider. Stranger Just Like You." And on this dreamy Thursday she'd been standing under one of those live oaks that dangled long streamers of moss in the most careless way—she could well imagine why the reporter thought she was a tourist. The old tree was almost embarrassing, as outsize as a pipe organ in a roadside chapel: it could have been a picture postcard. In fact, it *was* a picture postcard, six for a quarter at Calvin's Pharmacy.

Dolores Rooney was supposed to be having her three-month checkup at Dr. Black's across the street, but the doctor was stuck over at Due East Memorial with a baby who was stuck too, unwilling to leave a dreamy womb even for dreamy Due East. All the white patients had left when the nurse announced that she could not at all say for sure when that little old baby would let itself be borned, but the colored waiting room was still full (some in Due East were more accustomed to waiting than others). Dolores Rooney thought that she would just wait too, wait on the bluff for the doctor's big sedan to come into view. She stared out past the rows of Sunfishes and Sailfishes stacked down below in the parking lot.

If she leaned over far enough, one hand on the imposing old tree, she could just see the end of the new bridge creaking open, and she could daydream about the way this bay and those white houses behind her (mansions, she'd called them once) had looked the day she and Bill Rooney drove through Due East for the first time, seventeen years before. Dolores Rooney had taken one look at the Due East Bay, at the low palmettos sprouting here and there, at the old docks slipping back into the marsh, and she had felt the most acute shame. Up to that point in her life she thought she'd been living—*living*—in New York City.

No: seventeen years before, she'd decided that she hadn't been living at all, not in a city colored brown and gray, not in a city painted the colors of shit and ashes: she'd seen all at once that human souls were meant to live in towns like Due East, towns where light and air and trees and moss melded into one floating, gauzy canopy. She had decided on that first drive—and Bill had decided too: when you were crazy with passion you thought with one mind—that Due East was the place to raise children, the place to settle in forever.

And now Dolores Rooney was thirty-seven years old and

pregnant with her fifth child and Due East was, if anything, more beautiful. Never mind the trailer lots on the way out of town, or the tacky cheap gas stations on the highway; never mind, just for the moment, the mean little plumbingless shacks on the islands, where they painted the doors and window frames blue to ward off evil spirits; never mind the rednecks five miles up the road.

At just this dreamy moment Due East was so sublime that it was almost a spiritual, not a physical, place: even the brown marsh grass, squatting in brown mud at low tide, was beautiful. *This* brown yielded life. The bridge was limping closed under a gathering of gulls.

There was a time when that halting closure of the bridge, when the slowness, the thickness, of everything in Due East— the mud down below, the hovering birds, her own husband— had made Dolores Rooney hate the little town with all her soul. There was a time when the shuffling of the waitresses in the Ocean View Cafe, the false slow drawling of every lawyer and banker in town, seemed calculated to drive her right out of her mind. But she'd lived through that time, and past it: she'd over- come first the irritation, and then the dislike, and then the ha- tred. She had been very very young herself. Now she could stand on the bluff in the sunlight, a stranger in town after seven- teen years, and let her eyes fill up in the dazzle of sunshine. She tried to picture the new baby plunked down in Due East, but no image appeared.

All of a sudden the light sweater she'd been wearing all morning oppressed her with its warmth; she was embarrassed to peel it off, big as her breasts had swollen now. She peered down River Street, but Dr. Black's car wasn't coming into view—she hadn't really believed it would be. He was still at the hospital, still wrestling with that reluctant baby: maybe the baby had heard that time stood still in Due East.

Dolores Rooney gave up on seeing the doctor before evening office hours. She crossed over to the big wide sidewalk that would take her home, and she said a quick Confíteor, for thinking so little of that poor sweet reporter—barely older than her own sons, and eyeing her that way—and for dismissing the baby from her imagination. Someday soon she would just have to concentrate on this child she was bearing.

□　　□　　□

Katherine McGillicudhy Teresa of Avila Rooney dawdled on her walk home from Due East Junior High School. It was seventy-nine degrees out, which it wasn't supposed to *be,* not at the end of November, not even in South Carolina. Her sweater was as cumbersome as a coat of wet smelly dog hair, but she couldn't take it off if anyone was watching—she had only half ironed the white blouse underneath: only the Peter Pan collar and the thousands of little pleats in front. The back of the blouse was as wrinkled as a sea turtle's hind legs, and splotched over with faint lipstick imprints shaped like hearts (late at night Kate painted her lips with a hidden tube of Hearts on Fire and practiced kissing. The lipstick stains on her blouse didn't come out in the wash.)

Praying for privacy, Kate Rooney walked along Lee Street, the back way. All she needed was half a block to slip her sweater off and rearrange it so that it dangled from her shoulders, hiding not only the blouse's wrinkles and stains but the fact that she was the only girl at Due East Junior High School, so far as she knew, who had no horizontal bra strap showing through the thin white cotton in back. The only sixth-grader who would never have a boy come along and *thwang!* pull the back strap of her Maidenform. It wasn't that she didn't have *breasts*—they were already the size of peaches and anybody not

9

legally blind could see them growing there—it was just that she didn't have the kind of mother you went and asked for a training bra.

But she wasn't going to get a chance to slip her sweater off, because the cars were zooming by (it might as well be Darlington as Due East), and not ten paces behind her she could hear a boy and a girl, seventh- or eighth-graders, gaining on her.

The boy's voice was coarse and mealy. "It's on one of them back streets, Prince or Duke. I mean to tell you, they got so many beds in there you'd think it was a hospital."

"But the chief of police would shut it down! Wouldn't he?" The girl's giggle, as sweet and false as a pink plastic rose, trembled as she walked and flirted with the boy. Kate Rooney didn't need to turn around and look the girl in the eye to hate her. She imagined the girl behind her in some cotton shirtdress perfect for a seventy-nine-degree day: something madras, something by the Villager, something the girl and her mother shopped for together in Savannah or at Amanda Loring on River Street. Kate and her best friend, Franny Starkey, called the shop Amanda Boring, and had sworn a solemn vow never to wear anything madras, anything by the Villager, anything cute or faddish or conventional. Franny Starkey never breathed the word *conventional* without then sticking her finger down her throat and gagging.

Now the boy's voice cracked and pitched higher behind Kate. "They got jarheads lined up around the block some nights. And the colored girls wear red satin nighties."

"Oh! Hush." They were so close behind her that if Kate turned around the girl's hot breath would meet her own. "You lie like a rug with that dirty talk, Bubba. I don't believe a word you say." The three of them, Kate and the girl and boy behind, were passing by the fading sloping brick wall of the Episcopal graveyard, and the girl giggled again.

That giggle—now slurping, now soughing—acted on Kate as a prod. She heard that giggle every day in the halls of Due East Junior High School: the giggle of Southern belles in training, of future sorority sisters at Carolina. The giggle of a little *lady*, in her perfect cotton shirtdress. Kate pictured the girl behind her fingering perfect round wooden buttons, and felt her own shoulders hunched under the weight of the damp sweater.

Actually, Kate's maroon sweater bore a Villager label too, despite the solemn vow taken with Franny Starkey, and so did the blouse with the Peter Pan collar (Franny had sniffed the outfit when Kate first wore it, as if she could smell a conventional label). The sweater and the blouse were hand-me-downs from her sister Maggie, and Maggie bought whatever the saleslady said looked *darlin'* on her. Maggie wouldn't know conventional if it bit her behind. Right now she was off in New York: she'd promised the Maryknoll Sisters that she would go to college for two semesters before she entered the convent. And then for the rest of her life, Maggie wouldn't have to worry about clothes, but would be covered in a black missionary's habit: a white one if she was shipped to the Congo. Just now her sister was supposed to be testing her resistance to boys and coffee-houses, but Kate's father said there was fat chance his plain sweet Maggie would meet any fellow with trousers covering his dickey bird while she was being watched over by Yankee nuns at Mount St. Martyr's. (Bill Rooney actually *said* that, about trousers and dickey birds, in front of Kate—while her mother smoldered at the coarseness of it.)

The boy behind her said: "It's true. Swear to God. I swear on my grandmomma's grave that Due East has got its own little—"

"Don't you say that word to me. My momma'd dip ammonia down my ear with a Q-tip she thought you said that word to me."

11

Kate slowed up. What word?

WHAT WORD?

The boy let out a long, patient, worldly sigh. "I was just going to *say* that Due East has got its own recreation center right in the middle of colored town."

Kate had the distinct impression he didn't mean recreation center at all.

"And what are you going to do about it then, Bubba?" the girl said. "Are you gonna go *see* it? Are you gonna go *visit* it?"

That was enough. That was plenty. Kate cut off Lee Street and back to the last block of big old waterfront houses on River Street after all. Her cheeks were flaming from the conversation —any driver passing her would see one crimson-colored eleven-year-old girl passing through the cold proud shadow of a white antebellum house: a slip of a girl red from her hair to her burning ears to her sodden Villager sweater, red probably underneath her stained white blouse, red at the tips of her peach-sized breasts, certainly red from her waist below. Sweat drooled down her thighs.

It didn't shame her that she knew exactly what they were talking about, the eighth-graders behind her; it was her ignorance that shamed her. When she begged Franny Starkey to please God tell her all she knew, Franny hid her face: which meant that Franny had an Irish Catholic mother herself and could no more ask her than she could quit going to Confession on Saturday and Communion on Sunday. Hadn't it taken Kate two weeks to get up the courage to ask her mother to sign the permission slip to see the movie *Your Changing Body, Your Changing Life* when it was shown to the fifth-grade girls last year? Her mother and her sister kept the blue Kotex box hidden behind so many towels in the linen closet that you could hear them rummaging late at night, like coons going through the garbage, to dig it out.

No. Her mother floated above her own flesh. She could not ask her mother: her mother was interested in books and politics and music and poetry: not the function of genitals. Kate had stumbled over the word *genitals* in the dictionary—it was a *guide* word—but eighth-graders walking casually down Lee Street were already talking about colored girls in red nighties on Prince Street. Since September, when they'd moved the sixth grade to the junior high school, Kate Rooney had stepped up the dictionary word searches and had long since gone beyond guide words. She'd found *intercourse: intercourse* meant *copulation* and *copulation* meant *coitus* and *coitus* meant *intercourse.* And then there was a new one, *onanism,* which had jumped right off the page when she wasn't expecting anything much better than *ovaries* from the O's; and *onanism* was maybe the strangest word, because it was only half a column from *oneiromancy,* which sounded dirty but wasn't at all: it had to do with dreams and it was strange that it should be there right under *onanism* when these things seemed to come to her most clearly in her dreams, not in her waking hours when she could figure them out. But she'd figure out the house on Prince Street if she had to go there herself and peek in at the windows, the way she'd spent years peeking into her own bathroom door when her brothers thought they were taking their whizzes in private.

Meanwhile, she'd just offer her ignorance up, the same way she offered up wearing hand-me-downs. It was too bad if Franny Starkey thought her blouses were conventional. Franny—who'd had to change her name from Fanny last year, for obvious reasons—didn't exactly look like Joan Baez herself. Kate could offer up her disdain too. She would offer up wearing hand-me-downs, her best friend's contempt, and her sexual ignorance. All in one package. She could only hope it was not offensive, because she fully intended her sacrifice to add extra weight to her prayers that Tim and Andy wouldn't peek at *her* while she was stripping for a shower. (And that the Peace Corps would be such a success that Russia and America would destroy all their atom bombs; and that John F. Kennedy would be able to bear the grief that weighed him down—you could see it in his eyes— since his baby Patrick died; and that Maggie would not be murdered by Mau Maus if she went ahead with this missionary madness.)

Now she had passed the first row of shops on River Street and was almost up to her father's plate-glass window—Rooney Realty, home away from home; she was expected to stop and blow a kiss at least. Her father was in the perfect spot for gossip, between Friedman's Department Store (only one room, but plenty of departments, Mr. Friedman said) and Adamson's Barber Shop (two pool tables in back). Bill Rooney loved the sound of his own accent, and lured in as many passersby as he could, prospective customers or not. Her father had been threatening darkly to move to a cheaper place, off River Street, but Kate thought that was just his usual carrying-on. How could he sell such a building? The gold lettering on the glass that said William T. Rooney Realty had taken J. C. Smalls two whole days to finish painting. (J.C. had spelled out Reality first, and her father hadn't even noticed. It was her mother who called Mr. Smalls to come back the second day. He was just spelling it the way everybody in Due East pronounced it, her mother said: real-ity.)

Kate watched her reflection in her father's window: concave shoulders, long stringy red hair. She felt she had pushed through murky water on her walk—she looked like some big-eyed tropical fish that had propped itself up against the window. It occurred to her to stop squirming and squinting at herself, and then she waited for her father (talking on the phone as usual) to notice her: she waved in and blew him the expected kiss. She'd have to wean him from it gradually, embarrassing as it was.

14

Kate was the baby, and Bill Rooney's favorite.

She watched her father sit up straight at his desk and wave an enormous big-shouldered wave. He mouthed: "Hey there," and then "Love you, baby."

The other fathers of Due East were tight-bellied Marines; or they were lawyers or bankers or planters, with soft accents and Northern educations and big houses; or they were weary-looking mechanics or colored farmers embarrassed to stand on line in the bank with their fingernails so gummed up from grease or soil.

But Kate's father didn't come from Due East, anyway, and he hadn't been stationed there by the U.S. government. He'd chosen Due East. He'd grown up on a farm inland from Charleston, near a town called Shining Star. Shining Star was hot and dry and dull, Bill Rooney told his family: it was Due East that sparkled, the town and the islands and the ocean out beyond. When Bill Rooney set up shop on River Street, he made a systematic study of the local habits. He learned to wear a hat, and to buy a few good suits in Savannah whether he needed them or not. He spent an hour, at the least, in Ralph's every morning, stretching his fifteen-cent cup of coffee into a tutorial on the subject of crops (Due East rose and fell with tomatoes and cukes) and hurricanes and defense buildups (they had three military installations in the county, by the grace of God and Congressman L. Mendel Rivers). He'd told Kate a dozen times that if you meant to sell real estate in a town you had to *know* the place, had to sense what was coming the way you could sense a lightning storm coming on a summer afternoon. He kept a thick notebook in his desk labeled "What's Coming to Due East" in black block letters, but after seventeen years he'd stopped recording the information he got at Ralph's in the morning.

Kate knew that that first hour of his day in Ralph's, though it didn't start until nine o'clock, was Bill Rooney's dawn: the time when he and the other men in town let their eyes adjust to the light. He made himself large in Ralph's, and his beefy six feet allowed him to claim plenty of leg room. Her father drew attention to the Rooneys' Catholicism—you should wear it like a red sash across your chest, he told his children—but he played down his wife's politics, and he never mentioned that she read the *Catholic Worker.* If they'd heard about Catholic Workers, it would only be because they saw those pictures in *Time* magazine of the starry-eyed earnest young fellows burning their draft cards in New York. *Not* what Bill Rooney brought up as casual conversation in L. Mendel Rivers's congressional district.

He bragged and he clammed up about his children: Kate had heard him do both in the same conversation. He'd rev up on Maggie, say, remind the other men that she'd won a National Merit Scholarship at sixteen, and boast that she was such a modest child that she'd used it for a rinky-dink school like Mount St. Martyr's because that was where her mother went— and then somehow the conversation would come round to the drinking and the hot-rodding after the Due East High School Junior-Senior, and Bill Rooney would be reminded that Maggie hadn't gone to the dance in her junior year *or* her senior year, and he'd stir his spoon round his cup in silence.

He sometimes got gruff if one of the other children showed up—you could see him eyeing their mismatched clothes, or their slouches—but Kate could count on having his thick arm drawn around her. Her father loved Maggie, but Maggie was plain and intense and serious and going into the convent next year, where she'd pray for her father's drinking and temper; and her father loved Tim, but Tim was goofy enough to answer his father back, the two of them ending up in shoving fights more often than not; and Bill Rooney loved Andy, Kate supposed, but Andy couldn't abide his father, especially if he'd hit Tim, and Andy made his revulsion *real* clear. Kate's sister and brothers had all skipped a grade—Tim skipped two—but Katie's birthday was late in the year, and her mother, who'd been doing some looking into educational theory, put her foot down. So Kate didn't skip a grade at all, and school at the proper level was effortless despite her profound indifference: all the teachers had to do was see *Rooney* on the roll book and she was home free.

Bill Rooney knew that, and knew that Kate wasn't as out-of-step, as strange, as uncomfortable in their own skins as the rest of his children were. Her temper was as bad as Bill's, or Tim's, but she could run into her room and lock the door faster than any of them. She wasn't pretty—her face was a bland oval peppered with big dark freckles, and it only took on angles when she turned her profile forty-five degrees to the mirror and pulled her long sharp nose up. But she wasn't as lumpy as Maggie, or as gangly as Tim (Tim's pants always ended up way above his ankles), or as sullen as Andy. She knew how to say *hey* to the men at Ralph's without blushing. She had friends.

Kate Rooney was almost normal, and Bill Rooney loved her for that, so she would have to blow him kisses for a few more months, anyway. It was kind of pathetic, the way her father waited for her passing every day. He blew back a kiss that smacked even behind the plate-glass window: its *thwack* must have sent a shiver through whoever was on the other end of the phone line. Katie lingered, watching him swing his feet up on the old battered file cabinets before she moved along on River Street.

She couldn't imagine that Tim and Andy had ever asked their daddy about houses with as many beds as hospitals. She had a horrifying suspicion that Maggie, age seventeen, resident at a Catholic girls' college, still didn't know.

What a strange family she lived in: other families, Episcopalians and Presbyterians, probably talked about copulation and coitus right at the supper table. Maybe not Baptists and

17

Methodists. But Marine families always had a pile of *Playboy*s down in the TV room, and they let their children thumb right through them. They let their seven-year-old boys put their chubby fingers right on the Playmates' single-scoop cherry-topped breasts, and squeeze the paper.

Other people just didn't live the way the Rooneys did: they didn't say the Rosary every night, on their knees; and their children didn't spend their summers taking catechism classes at Camp Our Lady of Perpetual Help; and they didn't call boys' things dickey birds; and they didn't kiss the backs of blouses at night either, or have to go scrounging through the dictionary for sexy words. She didn't even know what word that boy had been about to say to the girl behind her, the word for houses where girls wore red satin nighties.

She considered cutting down the alley past Friedman's to stare at the river, but the riverfront was bald and depressing now without the docks. The last hurricane had taken care of the last planks, and there was no more Ocean View Cafe (there'd never been an *ocean* view from that restaurant, anyway—it had squatted right on the river, and the ocean was five islands and five bridges away). It was too hot to be in the sun wearing a damp maroon sweater: and so she trudged down River Street, down to the Point, to make her way home.

She would spend her afternoon at number 7 O'Connor Street in the shade of an old ramshackle frame house, her mother and her brothers reading and practicing under the same roof; and she would have hours to find *that word*—that word that meant another house, a house enclosing sweat and lamplight and colored girls in red nighties—lying innocent in the dictionary, somewhere beyond *coitus* and *copulation*.

Without even closing her eyes she could picture a dark interior corner of that other house, the one on Prince Street: there was the girl in the red nightie propped up on a cot, her dark heavy thigh—a door on a rusty hinge—swinging open and shut.

She walked faster now toward her own house, willing away the image, but as she neared the triangular park at the end of River Street, the afternoon light streamed off the seawall and the girl in the red nightie's thigh reappeared, caught in a shaft of mustard-colored lamplight. And there was the lamp, perched on a tomato crate in the corner of the bedroom on Prince Street, its shade fringed and yellowing. The lamp reeked of the same musky odor as the rest of the house.

Now Kate could hear music in the background too: a worn-out needle was scratching out a raspy high whining voice, and a saxophone played low behind it. Oh God: this was the occasion of sin she spent all her time chasing away now. She blinked her eyes, and the dream disappeared, but still she could feel her nipples stinging underneath her white cotton shirt.

If she ran, she wouldn't picture that house and she wouldn't feel her own body tensing: she rounded the corner and broke into a trot at the same instant. But her books slid off her binder and tumbled to the street, and there was nothing to do but squat in the middle of the road to gather them up.

A cook from the Golden Apple sat on the big restaurant's kitchen steps opposite her, smoking a cigarette and casting a pleasant smile in her direction as she scrunched the books and papers together. She passed him most afternoons, and usually they connected: their eyes at least. He was a plump middle-aged man, drawing his smoke in with a weary cheerful air.

She couldn't seem to stop herself: first she was returning the cook's smile, all innocence, and then, her eyes still on him, she was imagining the *cook* showing up at the house on Prince Street, his hat in his hand and a tired expectant look in his eyes. She imagined him listening to the low saxophone and the high whining voice on the record player. She imagined him bending down to squeeze under the low doorway that led to the yellow lamp and the dark thigh and the musky smell. She imagined the girl beckoning him to the cot with a crooked finger. She imagined his heavy step on the gnarled worm-eaten floor. She imagined him growing taller once he stood in the shaft of lamplight: now he was beefy, like her father, and he slid his belt out of his pants the way her father did when Tim was driving him crazy.

Her papers were mangled and stuck themselves out of the books every which way, but she had them collected at last into one package she would be able to carry down the street. She smiled a guilty goodbye to the cook—where did these temptations *come* from?—and he crooked his fingers into a single compressed wave.

If those eighth-graders hadn't been walking behind her, riling her up, she would have had time to say the Glorious Mysteries on her way home instead of drawing pictures that shouldn't be drawn. Instead of involving innocent Negro cooks in her own foul imaginings. She could say a quick Act of Contrition, anyway, before she crossed O'Connor Street: she breathed out "O my God I am heartily sorry" and then the missing word came to her in a hiss.

Whorehouse: the word ended on a stream of sibilance. She didn't even know she knew it—no one had ever breathed the word *whorehouse* in the Rooney family—and it had entered her consciousness as suddenly as that picture of the house on Prince Street. A word in dim light, in mustard-colored lamplight. A heavy footstep on the floor.

A word from a dream.

□   □   □

Bill Rooney swung his legs down off the filing cabinet, hitched up his pants, and went to stand on the sidewalk and

stare after his daughter's red head, bobbing now along the end
of River Street. Katie was a ball of fire, orange on maroon. He
should have put down the phone and run outside to give her a
hug when she stared in all googly with those huge turquoise
eyes: she was cute as a pickle, and she had no idea what was
coming on in her life. Lately he felt this same sentimental pro-
tective wave rising up in him every day of the week at three
o'clock, when she was due to pass by.

"Hey, Bill." Solly Friedman, hungry for gossip on a slow
Thursday, exited his department store and came to stand by Bill
on the sidewalk: he had a habit of craning his neck up to speak,
birdlike, though he couldn't have been more than three inches
shorter than Bill.

"Hey is for horses, Solly."

"Awhhh. Pffff. 'Bout hot enough to throw the air-conditioning switch, huh?"

Bill squinted at the sun, three quarters of the way down the
horizon, slapped Solly once on the back, waved, shuffled, and
retreated to Rooney Realty without another word. Affable Bill
Rooney, the man with the golden and unstoppable tongue, had
nothing to say lately. He *liked* Solly Friedman, but he didn't
have the patience for him in the last few weeks: he didn't have
the patience for anybody downtown.

The trouble with the shopkeepers on River Street was that
they had no worries. Business was good on the weekends: all
they had to do was pass the time on the five days leading up to
Saturday. They were all so bored, these balding irresolute pusil-
lanimous men, that they checked the thermometers on the
backs of their buildings three times a day to see if it was time to
throw on the big air-conditioning units they'd gone out and
bought in the last five years. Air conditioners that shut out the
breeze, air conditioners that shut out the reason people moved
to Due East in the *first* place. Weren't all the big houses built by

plantation owners from upriver, rich men who wanted a place closer to the sea, a town where they could sit on their verandas and catch a breeze they didn't get inland, a breeze as soft and strange and fresh as the touch of a baby's skin? But the air conditioners started going in by the mid-fifties, and they were still going in, and the shopkeepers were still checking to see when they could cut them on. Even in November they checked.

Bill Rooney shut the door of Rooney Realty and sat himself down in unconditioned air. It wasn't *hot*. Solly Friedman had just come home from visiting relatives in New York, from seeing a few musicals on Broadway, and he went on and *on*, reminding people of his own sense of smallness back in Due East. Dolores did the same thing when she came back from one of those "vacations," one of those trips to her family that were supposed to be medicine and ended up as poison instead, poison that rose up in vaporous gases from the sidewalks of upper Manhattan and worked its way into Dolores Rooney's lungs and heart. It wasn't *hot* in Due East: it was hot as hell in the wilds Solly Friedman visited. The jungle his wife visited.

He'd had it with people calling Due East small, with his own children's derision for the town he had chosen. Due East wasn't small at all—what overwhelmed him lately was its galloping rate of growth, seven thousand nine hundred souls abiding in the city limits, last count. What overwhelmed him was the realization that he'd been back at the snack bar, fetching himself a beer, when the Due East horses took off. Now he wasn't even sure exactly which race he was watching, but he knew he hadn't placed a bet.

The phone rang again, and he was almost disinclined to answer. The last caller had been a Marine sergeant looking for a three-bedroom house to rent for under forty-nine dollars a month. Bill would spend Friday driving him around to a dozen hot little boxes, matchbox houses on flat bleak streets in flat bleak subdivisions out by the Naval Hospital or the Air Station, and the Marine would eye the big holes in the chain-link fence and decide he'd be better off buying a trailer he could set down on a big low plot of land on the beach road, under an oak tree that swished Spanish moss. Bill wouldn't have a plot of *land* to sell the Marine. He'd put most of his capital into the little houses, and he had so many of them vacant he couldn't even rent them out to coloreds if he'd wanted to. There were more and more recruits coming through on their way to Southeast Asia, or maybe to Cuba if things heated up down there again, but recruits didn't rent matchbox houses—and when their families came to graduation it was the motelkeepers who were getting rich, not the landlords. Bill had had a chance to buy a motel out by Parris Island ten years ago, and he'd laughed out loud at the notion: pain in the behind, he told Dolores, running a motel. Not to mention the carryings-on. He didn't want his children dropping by one of their daddy's ventures and *hearing* what went on at two o'clock in the afternoon in a motel room close by the base. So he hadn't invested in a motel, and he hadn't invested in much land, and as Due East expanded, his income contracted.

It was slow, this failing.

It was so slow and so solitary. It wasn't like the failures of his father's generation: there was no mass burial pit, the way there'd been in the Depression. This was a lonely failing, a slow slide down into his own narrow grave; and all the while he was sliding, he was still grabbing out at other men to tell them that at least he hadn't been wrong about what John F. Kennedy—by God not just a Catholic President but an *Irish* Catholic—would do for the economy.

"See," he would gloat in Ralph's. "WhudItellyall? The Democrats are holding those taxes down after all." Or: *"See?* Due East is a boomtown. A boomtown!"

And all the while he was pretending to Ralph, to the shop-keepers, to the other real estate men, to his own family, that he stood firm on the steady ground that John F. Kennedy was guarding. But he knew better. He was sliding. All the while he was pretending and sliding, new realty companies dotted the two highways coming into town and the beach road too. Hilton Head was gone—it had never even occurred to him to get a piece of *that* action.

Suddenly, for the first time in his life, he understood God's mercy in sending hurricanes and earthquakes to wipe people out. Better that sudden swipe of the Lord's hand than the slow ulcerous disgrace he was enduring. He'd listed his own building on River Street: he was willing to sell his own storefront (not that there was anyone to buy it) because he'd come to a dead end in Due East. And it was one hell of a time to be sitting in a stalled car facing a roadblock.

There was a new Rooney on the way. After eleven years, a baby.

He was still in shock from the news, still gray-faced and tight-smiled when he met the shaving mirror in the morning, and the only concrete action he'd been able to take was to pull out the Sales book and painstakingly print: "101 River Street. 2 stories. Top floor unoccupied, good for storage or rental. 800 sq. ft. No basement."

How else but by selling the building his own business sat in could a thirty-eight-year-old man come up with the money for Baby Number Five? Hadn't his pockets been picked clean enough with Maggie traipsing back and forth down the coast? And they still didn't know whether Tim would win a scholarship as big as hers. Dolores wanted Tim at Columbia. (When she'd first mentioned it, Bill had said: "Sure he'll go on up to Columbia. Carolina was good enough for me, wadn't it?" Then his wife had straightened him out: Columbia Uni*ver*sity. Tim's teachers

24

said he could probably go to Harvard or M.I.T., but Dolores wanted him close by her mother, at a school with working-class sympathies. Thomas Merton had gone to Columbia. So Bill had said: "Well then, how about Notre Dame?" and Dolores had hooted with derision. "Tim doesn't play *football*," she said. How could you even answer such a snippy crack? How could you even say, once she was so pigheaded and snooty about the whole thing, that Timmy was just a *little boy*, for the love of the sweet Lord Jesus, and could do with some watching over by hard-nosed priests better than he could do with being set loose in New York City?) He'd lost *that* battle before he'd even come up with a strategy.

And Andy would be graduating two years after Tim. If Maggie backed out of the convent—and he couldn't see why any daughter of his *wouldn't* back out of that grim life—he'd have three in college at the same time, Kate nipping at their heels.

Dolores was three months already, and they hadn't even told the kids. He didn't want to think about what kind of shape Dolores was in: later, when she'd pulled herself together, he'd be able to face that. Right now, all he could think of when he saw his pale anemic wife was the trench that she'd dug deeper and deeper down the center of their bed, the irony that after eleven years of increasingly infrequent visits to that no-man's-land on her side of the trench, *now* she was pregnant. For eleven years they'd assumed that the early fecundity was drying up along with their early passion.

For eleven years Katie had been the baby. She'd be furious when they finally let her know; she'd be revolted when she imagined her parents conceiving the baby. Besides, they'd had eleven years to spoil her rotten. But who could blame any of them for spoiling her? Katie radiated the same jangling energy, launched the same furious assault on the world that her mother had launched when she was twenty years old and pregnant with

25

Maggie and determined to pick up her diploma and then leave
New York forever. The same need to crash through the underbrush that he himself had possessed when he found Due East
and decided to start his family there.

The Rooneys had needed one child full of herself, one little
girl all charged up. They needed to remember the way they'd
once charged at each other: Bill and Dolores, lustful and giddy
and young.

He picked up the phone, but at the sound of his voice answering there was a click, and then the receiver droned out the
dial tone.

□　　□　　□

"Katie? That you?"

Kate ripped off the clinging sweater—her mother, who had
more important concerns than dirty laundry, wouldn't even *ask*
how lipstick stains imprinted themselves on the back of her
blouse—and threw it down on the piano bench before she followed the disembodied voice past the dining room.

Dolores was calling from the kitchen. When Kate threw
open the swinging door, her mother smiled up from the table, a
thick book open before her.

"Hi there."

It almost frightened her, seeing her mother in such a static
state—it *had* frightened her a few weeks ago, but now she was
growing accustomed to the pale image. Her mother had been a
color photograph last month, and now she was black and white:
a shadow. For eleven years, right up until Halloween 1963, her
mother had been a whirlwind, a terrifying spin of energy consulting lists she'd jotted on scraps of paper Scotch-taped to the
walls and the icebox and the phone; a month ago her mother
was tearing off, to the library or the hospital or down to the

26

Center to teach catechism, just as Kate was coming in from
school. A few years ago Dolores Rooney had even gotten herself
involved with the Democratic Party of Due East County, despite all her misgivings: anything for integration if Kennedy was
really going to do it, her mother said, even consorting with
those career gals and their shellacked hairdos.

But on Halloween night at nine-thirty, when the last of the
colored boys were knocking on the front door (last to the ban-
quet: the same boys who sat in the colored balcony at the
Breeze Theatre and threw down popcorn one lonely kernel at a
time), Dolores Rooney put her head down at the kitchen table
and said she could not be kind to one more child; and lately
when Kate came in at three-thirty, her mother was a languid
shapeless form sitting in the kitchen with a book or—even
worse—lying on the couch fingering a paperback. Her lips were
fish-scale gray in the afternoon light, and Kate had seen suddenly how her hair sprang out pale yellow, not red, from her
temples, and how the new-colored hair sat loose and damp and
hopeless in its French twist. She'd never thought of her mother
as *old* before, but now when she smiled an extra chin threatened
to dangle, and there was a distinct bulge pressing through her
smocks. Kate saw her in the bathroom late at night tweezing
whiskers from her chin.

"Tell me about your day, Kate."

Kate considered, and pulled out a chair. Her mother might
have aged and thickened and dimmed overnight, but she still
meant for her daughter to deliver a full report. If she hadn't
been in such a slump, Dolores would have been darting around
the kitchen while she listened to every word Kate breathed,
starting half a dozen tasks, finishing none of them, all the while
leaving dirty measuring spoons and yellowing recipes and newspaper clippings and more lists behind on the counter. Dinner
was an agonized pale lump of meat and potatoes and vegetables

boiled into yellow stringiness or broiled into dry shards, the mess of it covered with some new floury milky sauce. Dolores would have been attending to more important things than the recipe.

For a millisecond Kate imagined reporting the house on Prince Street, but now she was sitting face to face with her mother, and her mother's face was serious and kindly and interested. Kate said: "We had the same old integration-segregation debate in social studies. I swear some of the kids—"

"Some of the—?"

"Children. Oh, Mommy, nobody says *children* when they mean *kids*. Children go to elementary school. Whuduhya call children who go to junior high?"

"You call them wise guys."

Dolores was forcing a merry smile, but Kate let out a long *phew* of disgust. Her mother knew all four children idolized her —Kate imitated the way she fingered strands of hair escaping her French twist, the wordless way she threw up her hands when Bill berated her, even the way she ate a *shrimp*—but this loveless formality about every little word was going to drive her children into the nuthouse at an early age.

"Mommy—" Come to think of it, nobody she knew said *Mommy* either. There was something very Old World and Catholic about saying *Mommy*. Kids—white Protestant Southern loafer-wearing kids—said *Momma;* and they said all the other words forbidden to the Rooney children: *y'all* and *ain't* and *reckon:* the words Bill Rooney used when he wanted to rankle Dolores. "Oh, forget it, Momma."

But her mother wasn't even looking at her anymore, and had released that forced ghoulish smile. Dolores's eyes were sinking back down to the book in front of her, and upside down Kate read the page headings: "St. Thomas Aquinas" and "Summa Theologica." The new pastor, Father Berkeley, had been piling on the readings for her mother's discussion group. Bill Rooney said Father Berkeley and the readings and the discussion group were "Doo-doo! What's he trying to impress us with? You act out your faith, anyway."

But Kate's mother had been coaxed into becoming group leader (as if her mother needed coaxing), and talked about quitting the Democratic Party work now that the readings and the note-taking consumed her. Kate had seen Father Berkeley sit wordless in their parlor, watching her mother with slow-drifting eyes. It had even crossed her mind—she *knew* this was evil, not to mention completely disloyal to her father—that Father Berkeley, in his seersucker priest's suit, with his serious courtly manner and his Charleston accent, would have been a much better match for her mother than Bill Rooney. One night after her father swung a baseball bat around the dining room, trying to rout out Timmy, she'd even gone up to bed and fantasized her mother running away with Father and going up to Greenwich Village to live with him as an outcast. Father Berkeley would say Mass on a fire escape, for the neighborhood waifs. *Introibo ad altare Dei,* Father would say, and the children would call back: *Ad Deum qui laetificat juventutem meam.* The Rooney children would all get to pick which parent they wanted to live with, and they'd all pick their mother (though they would write to their father every night, and ache for the memory of the Point). They would catch sight of Bob Dylan and Joan Baez on the streets of Greenwich Village.

She'd let that fantasy go so far—way beyond an occasion of sin, all the way to savoring a vision of Father Berkeley kissing her mother's freckled cleavage—that she'd had to confess it, though not in so many words, of course. Not to Father Berkeley. She said she'd "wished something bad would happen to her father," and her penance had been ten Our Fathers. Naturally.

"So how's the Thomas Aquinas?" She rose to read over Dolores's shoulder:

As regards the individual nature, woman is defective and misbegotten, for the active power in the male seed tends to the production of a perfect likeness according to the masculine sex, while the production of woman comes from defect in the active power or from some material indisposition, or even from some external change, such as that of a south wind, which is moist, as the Philosopher observes.

DO WHAT? The words *sex* and *male seed* shimmered up from the page. Kate read the lines again, twice over.

"What's all this stuff about the south wind?"

"Oh, Aquinas had—quaint ideas, I guess you'd say—about biology." Her mother didn't sound embarrassed, only vague and flat.

"Then what's this about woman is de*fec*tive? And everything's *per*fect in the male sex?"

Her mother squeezed her hand in distraction, but kept her eyes down on the page. Maybe she was reading it over, and maybe she wasn't. It occurred to Kate that perhaps it was Thomas Aquinas who had her mother down these past few weeks. Dolores Rooney was a paragon of control, but she had a high temper when it came to *principles:* she told the woman who came calling for the private school association that she had no patience for that nonsense, for running away from integration when it was not only inevitable but right and decent and long overdue; she'd managed to lambaste the woman without ever raising her voice or letting her small pleasant smile fade. If Hartley Dinkins—the county Democratic chairman she called Hardly Thinking—sneered at her Yankee ideas, she just laughed and said: "You mean *twentieth-century* ideas, Hartley." She had a gift for speaking easily through her anger, whether it was Bill Rooney or Hardly Thinking she was rebutting, but how was she supposed to respond to St. Thomas? Being at a loss for words in a contest with a saint could account for how distant and weary her mother had become.

"Mommy, I can't be*lieve* he says this."

Now her mother looked up and smiled at her and said: "Oh well, times change. People's understanding changes. But he's still *St.* Thomas. Even in this muddle about the south wind he's teaching us about the difference between men and women. It's not a south wind that makes the difference—but men and women are made for different purposes. We're made with different personalities."

Kate held her tongue in imitation of her mother's control. That cool kind detached thinking of her mother's was as irresistible as the moon's pull.

"Guess what. Miz Lovelace said in English class today that she never wanted to be called a woman, she always wanted to be called a lady—so Franny Starkey raised her hand and said she didn't like the sound of *lady* because it sounded frilly, like lacy underwear, and everybody was laughing so hard Miz Lovelace thought they were making fun of the *lace* in her name and comparing her to underwear, so she called Franny a right saucy little tart—a *right saucy little tart, can you believe it?*—and sent her down to the principal's office." Franny's father was assistant principal.

"Which will hardly slow down our Fanny. Franny. Just see you don't get sent to the principal's office with her, Katie. You won't have a father there to bail you out. Just see you're more circumspect: and no disrespect!"

"Yes ma'am."

"But I'm not one of your teachers, darling. You don't have to call me *ma'am." Ma'am* nettled her almost as much as *y'all.*

"Yes, Mommy. Momma."

"So which would you rather be called?"

"You mean woman or lady?"

"Yes. Woman or lady."

Katie snorted. "Oh. Woman, of course. Jiminy cricket! *Lady* is like, is like—" She had a picture of who they were, a group photograph, but she couldn't put a single caption to the serried faces. They tended the azaleas downtown for the Garden Club. They met the first Thursday of every month to discuss Mary Cassatt's sweet paintings or Emily Dickinson's sweet poems, and the *Courier* reported which of them officiated at the tea table. They sat in clusters on their verandas, gesturing with frosted glasses in their hands, and news of their house parties appeared in the "People You Know" column in the paper (if L. Mendel Rivers or Strom Thurmond had been at the house party, there was a snapshot on the front page). They were slender and breastless. They wore short little green golfing skirts, and bouncing white pompons peeked out from the backs of their tennis shoes. If they were not born into money, and hadn't managed to marry enough of it, then they taught school, like Mrs. Lovelace, and took out their frustrations on Franny Starkey. They were false simpering treacly mindless pandering sycophantic grown-up little girls, and they got married to self-satisfied men who drove big white Cadillacs and let their bellies grow as big as their cars' V-8 engines.

"Never mind," her mother said, and Kate stopped reaching for one of their names. "I'd rather be called woman too."

Kate could have drawn her head down close to her mother's breast and let herself be held there, all the afternoon, but her mother had already pinched out a cigarette from her pack of Kents and lit up. Kate studied the tilt of her mother's head, and memorized the way she shook the flame from the match. Her mother smoked a cigarette advanced enough to have a

Micronite filter, an elegant prop between her fingers, and she guided its plume of smoke as if she were conducting a symphony. She understood perfectly that business about the ladies, without goading or dismissing for a minute. Sitting at the kitchen table with her hair twisted back, Dolores Rooney was as regal as Princess Grace or Jacqueline Kennedy, and some of the color was surely back in her cheeks.

"I think I'll go study." Kate turned her face away so that her mother would not see written on it that *study* meant search the dictionary for dirty words. Princess Grace and cigarettes: coitus and copulation.

"Lily's upstairs. I think she's doing the bathrooms by now."

"Okay."

"Don't forget to say hello."

"I always say hello to Lily!" Her mother thought she'd forget the maid—and wasn't that the whole *point* about the difference between women and ladies? But once again her mother had drifted back to the book, drawing the cigarette lovingly to her mouth as she scanned the page. She wasn't reading, Kate was sure. Her mother wasn't even reading the lines.

❑   ❑   ❑

Dolores Rooney fought the fatigue with another cigarette. Standing on the bluff, she'd forgotten how tired she was; sitting at her own kitchen table, she struggled to stay awake. At least the nausea was gone for good (first morning sickness since Maggie: she was getting old), but the weariness was a wave that threatened to pull her down in a single tumultuous rush. And she could not, *could not,* let the wave so much as grab her ankles. The old trouble, the trouble that began when she was pregnant with Tim, overtook her when she gave in to the weariness, when she took a nap first once a day and then twice a day and sometimes even three times a day while poor Maggie—still a chubby toddler—crouched under the kitchen table and pulled out drawers and sang sad lonely songs to herself.

But she had done better when she was pregnant with Andy, and she'd been a model of virtuous pregnancy with Kate: she had concentrated on the principle of *control*, and control would get her through this pregnancy too. Every morning, controlling her urge to dive backwards into a dream, she breathed deeply while Bill still slept beside her; and then, controlling her desire to sleep away the day, she heaved herself up and stretched her feet down to the cold wooden floor; and then she ran the water in the kitchen until the brown stream ran clear, all the while controlling the urge to forget that she was bearing a fifth child (poor little thing, so disregarded by its own mother. She could control just about everything but her utter lack of connection to this baby.)

This time around—seventeen years after coming to Due East and finding it Eden; sixteen years after deciding that Due East was Eden after the fall, after deciding that she'd been buried alive in the moss and the cloying low-country air; fifteen years after she betrayed her husband and her first child, her Maggie—she could pray. Or maybe not pray in the truest sense of the word, but certainly read the books and mouth the words and promise the child she was bearing this time that she would not, *would not*, give in again to a depression so deep that she'd not only been unable to go to Confession fifteen years before, she'd been unable, at first morning light, to focus on a tall young husband bending down to kiss her good morning.

She'd not been able to see her husband clearly or fill in his outlines or look him in his gray eyes, that second pregnancy, when he was such a stranger to her. When Bill Rooney was not at all who she'd once thought he was. He was not a gruff light-hearted musician full of bad jokes and woozy Southern charm:

he was a businessman now, and once they'd settled in Due East, he'd accelerated his drinking, and he'd become ignorant and intractable. She'd detested him, and she'd been pregnant with his second child, and she'd been cheating on him too, for the first and last time—she was spending Maggie's nap time with a funny rich boy on summer vacation from his doctoral studies at Columbia. A blond pale wraithlike boy who stayed with his aunts, the Mansard sisters, in their big brick house, and loped up her front stairs when he knew it was time for a little girl to be asleep in an upstairs bedroom, time for a boorish husband to have gone back to work after lunch.

Now, fifteen years later, it was hard to remember who that fierce young woman could have been, a woman hateful enough to cheat on an unsuspecting husband, cowardly enough to slink away from an affair into a depression so deep that it left her catnapping all afternoon in the shade of the house on O'Connor Street. A young woman who'd memorized, when she was nine years old, the virgins of the Church: January—St. Prisca, St. Agnes, St. Emerentiana, St. Martina. February—St. Agatha, St. Dorothy, St. Apollonia, St. Scholastica.

Now Dolores Rooney, sitting (no, slumping, or sliding) at her kitchen table, remembered Walker Mansard sitting at that same table, and felt a little charge of current course through her. Her snapshot memory of the boy—wispy blond beard on narrow chin, hazel eyes averted—was in itself a weapon against the threatening fatigue. She didn't need another Kent. She stubbed it out, and saw in the cigarette's last gasp an image of Walker Mansard calling on her at nap time to demonstrate his latest meditation techniques.

She had met him when she walked Maggie out on the green in the cool mornings. Walker Mansard, dressed in a tie even on his holiday, even in Due East in July, strolled across the little field to pay his regards to the toddler and her mother. He had that easy Due East conviviality, but it was borrowed: his father, brother to the Mansard sisters, had grown up in Due East, but Walker Mansard was raised in some soft Long Island suburb. He was a year older than she, but there was something so innocent in his taking things for granted—his aunts' cloistered existence, the tuition checks—that sometimes Dolores thought she could have been his older sister. She might have run into him at Columbia if her mother had let her use the Barnard scholarship, but they never would have talked the way they did in Due East. He would have been rollicking in some fraternity house while she was taking the subway uptown to her mother.

What Walker Mansard said to her the first morning was: "I'm studying Zen Boo-dism and I have to have somebody in this god-awful town to talk to." (To think that fifteen years later there were Buddhist priests setting themselves on fire in Saigon.) But back then, Dolores Rooney had let loose a real girl's giggle. If somebody visiting Due East was studying Buddhism, there was hope for her existence there. She feigned an interest—all her semesters studying theology had not introduced her to an Eastern philosophy—so Walker Mansard volunteered to bring her books. He made social calls to the kitchen after lunch, meditated on meditation in five-word aphorisms, giggled himself, and once, in his fast-paced breathless way, confessed he didn't know how she could bear living in this godforsaken segregated reactionary state. She remembered shaking her head. In 1948 she was twenty-two and pregnant, with a useless degree in Italian from a third-rate Catholic women's college. She was pretty well buried alive.

What was scariest was not how easy it had been to suspend everything she believed while Walker Mansard was calling on her in the kitchen (for the longest time she'd been capable of entering a whole other realm of consciousness when it came to sin): what was scariest was how Walker Mansard knew that she was capable of it. He must have guessed from the start that she was in love with him—oh, not in love, but infatuated with his Zen, and pitying of his boyishness and his skinny white frame. He actually understood there was not another soul like her in Due East, South Carolina, in 1948; and they had code words— "Henry Wallace" or "Hiroshima"—that made them both wince together.

She was not a danger to him, pregnant as she was. She wasn't the sturdy red-haired girl with big loose breasts ("devil-woman," a drunken colored man called her on the A train back home) who would have frightened a young graduate student away. No, it was easy enough to fetch him one cup of tea after another, and to smoke cigarettes together all the afternoon. It should have been an enormity when he slipped up behind her one day while she filled the kettle; she should have been filled with terror when they laughed about the big belly that intruded when he pulled her around to kiss her. Bill was right downtown. Her baby girl Maggie was upstairs. She was pregnant.

But there was nothing enormous or frightening about it— she suspended guilt, Catholicism, the litany of the virgins: everything. Bill never would have even suspected it of her, smug as he was with his growing business and his growing family.

No, Bill wouldn't suspect it of her and Walker Mansard wouldn't be frightened off by her. He actually thought she was a spiritual companion for a while. She only scared him once, lying on the scratchy rug in the parlor—oh, she couldn't even picture it now: not naked, not with the baby upstairs and the venetian blinds half cracked—when she bubbled up with her suspension of belief and told him that he took the place of the priest in the confessional for her.

So she must have known what she was doing after all. The graduate student's bearded jaw had poked out rigid at *that* bit of looseness, and then Walker Mansard, Zen-studying Episcopalian from Long Island, told her in an unwavering voice that perhaps it would do her good to tell a priest in the confessional what was eating her.

So. So some prep school boy dabbling in Eastern mysticism knew what her husband had never guessed: that there was plenty to confess, that there were childhood sins festering away, sins unnamed close to ten years. Walker Mansard's seeing through her was enough to make her rise naked from the rug and tug the venetian blinds tight. It was enough to make her skip Maggie's nap altogether the next day, to take her down to the Piggly Wiggly instead. It was enough to make her disregard Walker Mansard's rapping at the door the next afternoon, and to walk Maggie away from the Mansard house in the mornings.

On his way out of town Walker Mansard sent her a vase of scarlet roses flittered through with baby's breath (oh, the *possessiveness* of rich boys; she had to bury the roses in the trash so that Bill wouldn't find them). But three days later, she took that stiff advice about the confessional. She drove all the way to the cathedral in Charleston one Saturday afternoon to kneel in a faceless priest's confessional and she said, in a voice as plopping and unhurried as the drip of the leaking toilet Bill never got around to fixing:

"Bless me Father, for I have sinned. I committed adultery. For a few weeks.

"And when I was thirteen I slept with my cousin. For a year. For a little over a year."

It had taken her almost ten years, a marriage, two pregnancies, and a Zen-studying graduate student to say that to a real priest.

After the confession, she skimmed the narrow highway back from the cathedral in Charleston to the house in Due East and thought the car might lift itself aloft. She'd been making bad confessions for years, leaving out the one important sin, and every time she kneeled at the Communion rail she'd sinned again: she'd been living in the haze of rationalization since she was thirteen years old.

But at thirteen she hadn't even possessed the right word to name her sin. How could there be a word to describe her cousin Tim's hurried groping in Aunt Brigid's apartment? She'd tried to confess it as a child, really tried, but she had to grab hold of words more precise than "I sinned against the Ninth Commandment, Father"—and not those playground words flung around the streets of Inwood. When she struggled to visualize the words in the confessional, the words disappeared in darkness, and she left the black narrow booth feeling she'd escaped her own grave: she thought back then that a priest might excommunicate her if he knew what she'd done. There wasn't another Irish girl in all of Manhattan who'd lost her virginity by the age of thirteen— and if she were excommunicated she would never be able to receive Communion again.

Oh, she could close her eyes and remember *that* fear, remember how unthinkable it was that a little girl sleeping with her cousin could go without the sacrament: she'd given in to sweet Timmy the same year her father left her and her mother for a big blonde with an apartment downtown. She'd lain in her cousin's arms and felt the thrill of anger that came with picturing her black-haired, blue-eyed, charming drinking womanizing father. She *had* to have Communion.

And she remembered too how clearly she felt that what she did, if she couldn't confess it, couldn't be a sin. Timmy—sixteen years old, a senior at a good Jesuit high school downtown— wasn't confessing it either. She knew he wasn't, because every Saturday at confession time she and her cousin were sitting down to dinner at Aunt Brigid's, and every Sunday their eyes met on the way to the Communion rail. Every Sunday she watched the priest genuflect in rustling vestments, and closed her eyes when the moment came for him to raise the Host and breathe out *Hoc est enim Corpus meum,* and knew that no matter how it compounded and blackened her sin, she had to walk down the aisle and kneel at the altar to receive. Hoc est enim Corpus meum. For this is my Body. If she did not open her mouth and thrust out her pink needy tongue for Communion, something—someone—would die: her father, in the arms of his new blond sweetheart; her mother, in the clutches of her new poverty and feigned jollity; or she herself: she—first in her class at Blessed Sacrament, thirteen years old, cut off now from giggling with the other girls about kissing and silk stockings and forbidden lipstick and when they would be allowed to go dancing—would wither and die from that deprivation.

And Timmy would not deprive himself either. He was a strapping shy black-haired Sodality-joining teenager who had picked up from somewhere (surely not the Jesuits) the information that he could buy condoms in seedy rest rooms. His gaze, in the aisle at Blessed Sacrament, was as tentative as his touch in Aunt Brigid's apartment. He must have confessed it finally after she stopped slipping off to the bedroom with him, after she'd pored over enough psychology books in the Forty-second Street library to realize the enormity of what she was doing. He was ordained the year after she was married, and hugged her close at Aunt Brigid's reception—so he must have found his peace before she found hers.

She'd kept it a close secret, even from Bill, all that time. In high school she'd felt sometimes that she was standing at a stove using both hands to hold down the lid on a steaming pot, and sometimes she thought the tough wiry neighborhood boys looked at her as if she were a succubus who would float into their dark narrow beds in the middle of the night, singeing them with her hot touch. What had made Timmy know—she'd *al-*

ways been such a good girl, just full of high spirits, full of beans, her father said—that she would be the one who would let him put his arms around her (under his bed! in a two-bedroom apartment in upper Manhattan that held Grandma, Aunt Brigid, and five other cousins listening to the radio in the next room)?

What had made Walker Mansard know that she needed Confession after all these years?

Dolores Rooney, three months pregnant with her fifth child, lit another Kent. She'd confessed it after all, and now when she was conscious of her good breasts and her wide hips and her own fierce need, it never occurred to her to flirt with young men who approached her on the bluff of the Due East Bay, or to go to sleep in the middle of the afternoon, or even to despise her husband anymore. Now she could fight off the waves of weariness. Now she wakened at six o'clock, and walked to Our Lady of Perpetual Help in time for seven o'clock Mass; now the whole family lined up for Confession every Saturday afternoon, and the sin she listed most wasn't adultery, but pride; now if she felt herself slipping she picked up Teresa of Avila's *The Way of Perfection,* and forced herself to read the harsh words over and over, until they registered.

Katie had even picked Teresa of Avila as her Confirmation name, to please Dolores. (But no matter how she teased her daughter, Kate would not read *The Way of Perfection.* She demanded summaries of the saint's life from her mother, and Dolores—who would never have given in that way to Maggie or Tim or Andy—provided them. Kate was able to answer with a self-satisfied, confident air when the bishop picked her out of the crowd for questioning.)

Kate herself shored up Dolores in this pregnancy: her carelessness, her sureness—Franny and Kate calling themselves

41

women, not ladies!—were reminders of her own brashness somewhere back in that other life called girlhood. Last year Kate had
presented with utter indifference a permission slip for a movie
the school nurse was showing. (When she was Katie's age she
would have forged her mother's signature—as if they would
have been showing such films at Blessed Sacrament. At Katie's
age there was not another female she'd have confided in: girls
had to leave her out of their playground talk—she knew what
they didn't want to know yet—and women, once they married,
gained weight and grew chins and let their ungainly breasts
heave down, and then their husbands left them, and they pretended that men's infidelity was just another trial in this vale of
tears.)

Katie was more full of beans than she'd ever been. This year
her breasts had flowered, all at once, and she carried them
around without a brassiere and without apology. Dolores
wouldn't force her daughter into those Playtex confinements
(the way her own foundations-obsessed mother had forced her)
until Katie was good and ready.

She meant to save Katie from the agonies of sexual ignorance too. She'd had Maggie—patient pliable too-good Maggie
—to practice the talk on, and soon it would be time to sit down
with Kate. Though she suspected that Kate and Franny Starkey
had already figured everything out, had already pored over their
own psychology books, and that Kate would pay bored attention, feeling sorry for her mother.

At least she'd see to it that her daughter had some sense of
the gravity, the enormity, of sex, because anyone could just
look at Kate, nipples showing through her half-ironed white
blouses, and see that it was smoldering away, somewhere just
below the surface. Now Kate was the boiling pot. Poor little
girl: only eleven and already so steamed up. What would Teresa

of Avila say to that? What would Thomas Aquinas make of *that* female defect?

She stared again at her book, cigarette smoke obscuring the lines, and the corners of her Aquinas formed a frame. Without closing her eyes, she could picture that other Dolores, Dolores McGillicudhy, slipping into a dim hallway seeped with the smell of cabbage and carrots and potatoes. She was sneaking out into the night, the slim big-breasted girl, her black convent-approved pumps in one hand and her white gloves folded into a shabby handbag. She could see the sad gentility of her mother's scrubbed walls, of those apartment house corridors painted a brown the color of dried blood, and she watched the girl—one hand on her faded black hat, always holding the lid, always containing herself now—tiptoe until she reached the stairway, and then slide down the banister.

She was eighteen years old. She was on her way out to meet new friends—college girls, girls who would never suspect she'd lost her virginity in her last year at the parish school—on the A train platform. She'd be riding downtown with other convent-educated scholarship girls who had slipped away from their own dark hallways.

She was on her way to the jazz clubs. The college girls with the white gloves knew that Fifty-second Street was filled with G.I.s home from war, G.I.s who congregated in smoky clubs the nuns would never approve of. She was on her way to sipping martinis so dry they'd make her lips pucker (in Inwood it was only Guinness, or Paddy's), on her way to giggling with other girls who let her giggle now, who didn't know that she was holding the lid on a steaming pot.

Girls who didn't know that she had a weakness for boys, for men, that the meanest of them could remind her, after a martini, of her black-haired cousin Tim, of her black-haired father.

Girls who didn't know that she was fighting the urge to rest in someone's arms again: oh, warmth and pressure and dissolution.

She was on her way to leaving her mother's sour-smelling apartment for good.

She was on her way to meeting Bill Rooney.

SINS AGAINST PURITY

Kate, still sticky in her woolen skirt, toiled up the stairs to her bedroom. Through the open windows, upstairs and down, came the sounds of her brother Tim's high rhythmic singing—all down O'Connor Street Tim's song would be floating in, unbidden. Oh God, it was humiliating. How could Andy bear to walk home with him? The bus dropped her brothers off at Due East Elementary and then they had to crisscross six blocks together, Tim hollering out "Love Me Do" all the way. (Father Berkeley had taken a trip to Ireland and England over the summer, and brought Tim back the 45 and a clipping from the *Daily Mail*. Father said the Beatles would be taking America by storm too; they had a way of channeling nervous energy into a tune you could actually hum. They'd be bigger than Elvis, Father said, and then he'd crossed himself and lifted his eyes to heaven in what Kate thought was a perfect prayer.)

But of course Father Berkeley was safe in the rectory over on Division Street—*he* didn't have to listen to "Love Me Do" all the livelong day. Tim sounded as bad as their father did when he'd had a beer and made fun of rock and roll, only Tim wasn't making fun. Other high school kids drove cars—little Corvairs or their fathers' old Pontiacs—and played the radio loud, and had their girlfriends sidle up close on the front seat. But not Tim. Tim went by foot, and sang himself. Last year he'd put together a band, the Daydreamers, but after a couple of talent shows and one dance at the high school (the only dance Tim ever went to) the other guys drifted off. In shame, Kate was sure, that they'd ever been associated with him. He was a fifteen-year-old senior, and such a celebrity that he didn't care what anybody on the Point thought of him. He certainly didn't care if anybody at Due East Junior High School found out that he was her brother.

Kate scuttled into her room, locked the door against her brothers, kicked her loafers off. And then realized that she hadn't said hello to Lily after all—how did her mother know her so well? Well, she *would* say hello to Lily, but not that very minute: the dictionary, an irresistible temptation, was open where she'd left it, and she had a word to look up.

She stood at Maggie's old desk and flipped the thin pages, familiar as her own skin, open to the H's. Hoarhouse? Horehouse? *Hoary* was there at the top of the page (oh God, her mother wasn't getting hoary, was she?), but no *hoarhouse,* no *horehouse,* no *hoorhouse*—not in a decent dictionary. She was sure she had the right word. Its absence was probably a sign, clear as her mother's reminder, that she'd better say her hellos to Lily after all.

She creaked open her bedroom door just as the front door

downstairs slammed shut. Tim would be sitting down directly at the piano—now he was going to *play* "Love Me Do"—and Andy would be making his way to the kitchen, ready to deliver his own report on the day. If she was quick, and quiet, neither of them could come to torment her.

She stopped outside the bathroom.

"Lily?"

The cleaning woman, a garish yellow bandana wrapped around her head, was bent over the toilet. She dropped a rag in the white foamy water and looked up, waiting.

"I just wanted to say hi." Lily was so hard to read. Her father had been threatening that they'd have to let her go, that they didn't have the kind of money other people on the Point had, and sometimes—from the way Lily glided around the house so soundlessly, as if she were waiting for some word of dismissal—Kate figured Lily knew she was expendable. There were girls at Due East Junior High School who had maids closer to them than their own mothers, maids they confided in, but Lily wasn't part of the Rooney family. Her mother said Lily deserved her privacy.

"Hey baby," Lily said.

"Well. I better get back to studying."

"You study good." Lily was already bending back down, her tiny frame cradling the toilet.

"I will. Bye then."

Lily grunted with the effort of swishing the rag round the brown rings. "I done put you pitchers on the dresser."

"My pitchers?"

"The pitcher book."

Her *album*. Kate colored as red as she'd flushed on River Street. She kept the album between the mattress and the inner springs, and every Thursday she moved it to her bottom drawer so Lily wouldn't fish it out when she changed the sheets. But

47

this morning she'd swaddled herself in the sheets, hiding from her father's bickering with Tim downstairs, and she'd forgotten it was Thursday, and

"Thanks Lily."

She ran to her room, praying that her mother hadn't come in after Lily cleaned. She'd sworn she needed those *Life* magazines for social studies class—her mother hooted at the notion that a child of hers was going to learn anything of social value from *Life* magazine—and if Dolores found the pictures culled from the pages of *Life* she would have found Kate out; she would have caught her lying about the money for the magazine subscription and much worse—much much worse: her mother would have caught her being corny and mushy and oh, *please* let her not have come in.

The dresser top was bare. And the tube of Hearts on Fire lipstick had been wedged in the bedding too.

The album wasn't in the closet, wasn't in the bottom drawer. Now she could hear Tim playing something new downstairs, some icky forties swing music he practiced in the afternoon, then played at night to appease their father. The swaying sweetness of "Heaven Can Wait" made her want to kick out at air. *Where was her album?*

She tiptoed now, going back down the hall, and found Lily still on her knees but advanced to the rings in the bathtub. The water ran full-force, drowning her out when she whispered: "Lily?"

Kate slipped into the bathroom and tapped the old woman on the shoulder: Lily started from shoulder to knee, as if an electric shock ran through her, and then turned to grin up at Kate, her front tooth shimmering gold.

"Oh baby. I *knew* they wasn't no ghost in here."

"I'm sorry Lily. I couldn't find the picture album."

Lily swiped away at the porcelain, considering.

48

At least Tim and Andy hadn't found the album. That would have been worse than her mother finding it: her brothers would never let her forget until the day they left home that they knew she kept a secret Kennedy scrapbook. And it wouldn't be the pictures they'd taunt her with until they went off to college; they'd memorize the lines she'd written underneath the Scotch tape, lines like: "He's worried here. The eyes." Or—oh she could die from shame or throw up thinking of it—the pages near the back where she'd drawn three hearts. You should never ever put your truest feelings on paper, you'd always be found out and misunderstood. Tim and Andy would never in a million years know that the three hearts were for J.F.K. and his wife and baby. They'd think she had a crush on him—it would never occur to them that she'd drawn the three hearts there when her parents had made their restive peace over Kennedy, when her mother had admitted that J.F.K. was a man with a conscience.

But now Lily was heaving herself up and brushing past, talking to herself. Kate trailed just behind, but could not make out the words. When Lily was not skimming soundlessly through their house, she was mumbling or humming snatches of hymns or berating one of her long-gone children. Now she seemed to be offering up some prayer to find the album—the word *Jesus* rang out—and Kate was reminded that she herself should have asked St. Anthony in the first place. Then she would have found the album directly.

Lily searched the same places Kate had searched—closet, drawers—and then swung her arms akimbo and laughed at herself. "Lordhamercy. Looking like this when I puts the thing back where I *finds* it." She raised the flowered bedspread, lifted the mattress, and there, in the exact spot under the pillow where Kate replaced it nightly, was the dark plastic cover floridly inscribed with a single white word: Memories.

"Oh Lily, *thank* you."

49

"I puts the lipstick inside so's you don't lose it."

"Oh Lily, thanks."

Lily held the bedspread up for Kate to retrieve her goods, but the little girl held back and the spread fluttered back down over the bed.

"We all got to be keeping secrets: oh init the truth."

Kate sat on the bed. She could have cried.

"Oh baby now, don't you be looking so blue. Your own momma she keep Dr. King on the dresser."

Kate hung her head. Martin Luther King had divided her parents again. Her mother said he was a saint the Kennedy brothers weren't paying enough attention to—the Alabama speech was good, her mother said, but it was the very least Kennedy could do; and how could you even compare it with the March on Washington? With "I have a dream"? How could you compare any of the fluff that had been ghostwritten for Kennedy with King's letter from the Birmingham jail? Her mother had found the letter in a Quaker magazine, before everyone else made such a big deal of it, and she read the whole thing to the children after dinner (her father excused himself, in a high snit). Her father said King was a troublemaker riling up innocent peaceful folks (including those gullible Quakers) and probably red underneath his black skin. How could she look Lily in the eye?

"Now baby. We all women, ain't we? Got to have some romance in our lives. That President Kennedy got lots of women crazy for him."

"Oh Lily, I don't *like* him. He's going to get the schools integrated—"

Now Lily was turning away. Her mother was right: she'd stepped over the line Dolores said they shouldn't cross.

But Lily was chortling to herself, her yellow bandana bobbing up and down—laughing at Kate keeping pictures of Kennedy? At the notion that the Due East schools would ever contain colored and white together?

"How old you be now, Kate? Twelve? Thirteen?"

"Eleven."

"*Eleven!* And the size of that chest?"

Kate crossed her arms over her white blouse.

"Oh baby. I be fourteen years old, fourteen years *old* when my momma get me married the first time. You keep that pitcher book. You hold on good to that."

Kate had not exchanged so many words with Lily in all eleven of her years, and her lips were streaked with little white surges of panic: maybe it was better not to know Lily'd been married at fourteen. But Lily was laughing away harder than ever and now sat herself down, full of hilarity, next to Kate on the bed. Another line they'd never crossed. They never so much as sat at the kitchen table together.

"Fourteen." Lily smoothed out her old print wrapper and then slapped her knee in remembrance. "I beg my momma. I say I don't know nothing about no mens, but din't she send me into that bedroom when I wanna hide away. He come into that room and I be hiding under the bed. I be hiding under the bed. That man be *grown.* Uhnuhn. I don't wants to know nothing 'bout *that.*"

Kate peeked over at Lily—they were just getting to the good part—but Lily had quit her laughing and remembered her cleaning. She was already rising, her short legs, swathed in heavy black stockings, already stretching down to reach the bare floor. She was a skinny unlined woman, her wrists as thin and smooth as a girl's, and she grinned at Kate when she reached the door.

"Thanks Lily."

"You aks your momma now."

Kate looked around in dismay.

"You aks her please tell you all she know."

"Yes ma'am," said Kate. "Yes'm I will."

"All right baby. All right. You ain't got to hide under no bed." She shut the door tight behind her.

What was *that* all about? And Lily had looked through the book: not just found it, but looked right into it and found it was Kennedy and—oh, there was no place to hide in this house. Not even under a bed. She threw herself face-down onto the pillow and fought the urge to pull out the album, to run through its pages until she found the one that reminded Lily of a wedding night when she hid in a dark corner. Fourteen. Kate tried to picture Lily smaller than she was now, skinny and trembling before some big tall stranger. Some thick man, a man dark as his own shadow, his stern mouth a slash across his face. He stood in the lamplight in Lily's girlhood room, his very presence a demand; and now the saxophone wheezed again on the scratchy record. Now the man squatted down in mustard-colored lamplight to pull Lily by the arm from under the bed. Now Lily's little bony face appeared, her eyes screwed shut.

"KATIE. OH, MISS KATARINA."

That was Tim, hollering up the stairs. He'd want her to play a duet just so he could berate her slow right hand. Well, she wasn't going anywhere for Tim. She was going to lie right here on her own bed, her head above the album, until they left her alone. She was going to lie right there and figure out what on earth got into Lily, telling her that.

A rapping on the door.

"We know you're in there, Katie-poo."

Oh *Tim.*

"Come out and play, little Katie."

"Go away."

"We know you're in there reading 'bout romance."

Oh Mary sweet mother of Jesus, they couldn't know already, could they? Lily couldn't possibly have told them about the album?

"Come on Kate."

That was Andy: serene remote Andy. "Come on Kate, we've got Father's camera and we're going to shoot the last scene. Come on. It'll be dark in an hour."

Andy and Tim were making an eight-millimeter movie down by the trestle. It was all Tim's idea, naturally, and Father Berkeley was willing to loan them the means for their madness. Tim wrote out a script he wouldn't have dared to show to their mother: Andy played a demented teenager who set fires in the woods (they'd already shot those scenes, thank God), and they wanted Kate to play the little girl Andy threw off the bridge. She'd said no, of course (what she'd said was *You two probably WOULD throw me off the bridge*), but Andy had bribed her; he said he'd sit down right next to her on the piano bench every afternoon for a week and play her scales for her.

She'd made them swear that they'd shoot the scene where the trestle met the rocks, so it just looked as if she were dangling over the water—but she was not about to have Andy pick her up and throw her anywhere today. She was not in the mood to have anybody *see* her with her brothers today. What if you could see through her blouse when the film came back from the drugstore?

Now came the scraping searching sound that meant her brothers were poking a nail into her door lock.

"Get out!" She was screeching in what her father called her fishwife's voice, but the handle continued its turning, and when the door was finally pushed open, Tim was gone: the only good sense he ever had was the sense to disappear when his little sister was ready to throw a loafer at him, heel first. Only Andy faced her, looking sheepish underneath the dirty dark bristles of his latest haircut, and Andy only said:

"Hey Kates."

"Get out."

"Katie Tim's got to have the film in for his English project next Friday and the drugstore said they can't get the reel back from Savannah unless we give it in tonight and just think he's sending off his application to Columbia and if he has an F in English he'll never get into college and then you'll have to live with him for a whole nother year."

There were times Andy could have convinced her of climbing into a space capsule and orbiting the earth with John Glenn. He had that way of casting his eyes down while he was apologizing that made you think you could trust a boy every once in a while. Their mother said Andy could do with a Jesuit education: he'd wind up a Supreme Court justice, the way he had of conniving with people, and he might as well learn from the masters.

"Y'all could have *told* me you were going to shoot this afternoon."

"We didn't know. We didn't know until this afternoon when we stopped by Calvin's and they told us it takes a whole blame week to get one bitty roll of movie film developed. Hey, Kate, you ought to come with us and see what's going on at Calvin's. They're moving out the whole soda fountain."

"You said I could have as many cherry Cokes as I wanted if I was in your stupid movie. You're just trying to get out of it."

"No I'm not. Swear. We'll have to buy you a cherry Coke down at Ralph's."

"What are you *talking* about? Why would they move out the soda fountain?"

"Why you think? Didn't Momma say so?"

Silence. Her mother had said there would be worse to come the day the Klan marched down River Street and congregated in the triangular park, jostling each other like schoolchildren on line. Four Rooney children rode their bikes down to the water to laugh at them—grown men dressed up for Halloween—but Kate shrank back behind her handlebars when the Grand Dragon began his harangue in a high-pitched Cracker accent, and Maggie had to comfort her: "Don't worry, Katie, he's not a dragon, he's just a silly rooster parading out here." She'd led Kate back down to O'Connor Street and played her three games of chess to get her mind off it.

"You mean we can't get a cherry Coke at the drugstore anymore just because—"

"Just because if the Freedom Riders come to Due East and go into Calvin's there won't be any place for them to sit down! There won't be any soda fountain to integrate!"

"But they aren't even doing sit-ins anymore. The Freedom Riders aren't coming to Due East, Andy. They went to Mississippi. They went to Alabama." Hadn't her mother told her the night of the Klan march that they were blessed to live in Due East, where there was plenty of progressive thought—look at Father Berkeley, she said; look at the Historical Society and the Literary Society and the Little Theatre—and where the sheriff and the mayor had enough sense to let the Klan go ahead and march and make fools of themselves? Hadn't the whole Rooney family looked at Chet Huntley's pictures of Birmingham, of the bombed church and the little coffins of the little girls, as if they were being beamed from another continent, or another planet? Due East wasn't like the rest of the South.

"Well, you're right there," Andy said. "They're not going to come to Due East now. Mr. Calvin just wanted to make sure."

But Mr. Calvin was the pleasantest of old men, dapper in his white druggist's coat, elegant in the way he shook hands with little girls, as if the little girls were their mothers. He told the salesgirl behind the cosmetics counter to let the Rooney Redhead have a whiff of Chanel from the atomizer anytime she

55

wanted. It was cologne, not perfume, but still: *Chanel.* "Oh no. Andy, shut the door."

Her brother made no move, and she lowered her voice. "Andy, don't let Lily hear."

A shrug. "You think Lily's not going to know the minute she walks downtown? Anyway, Katie, get your bike. The light's fading. We'll ride down River Street and you can see for yourself."

Kate pictured herself twirling the red-seated stool around Mr. Calvin's soda fountain, Maggie and Tim and Andy twirling beside her, while some blonde from Due East High School, gum snapping behind her red lips, poured Coke syrup into the big machine.

Already Andy was backing out her bedroom door, sure that she would follow. He'd just made that up about the soda fountains—hadn't her father said at the supper table that her mother shouldn't be passing around the silly gossip she heard at party meetings? Her mother was always trying to put Due East down, Bill Rooney said, always trying to convince her own children that folks were small-minded here. Well, they weren't small-minded. They voted for Kennedy, didn't they? And those were white votes that carried the county, white Protestant votes. Didn't they have the first colored officeholder in South Carolina since Reconstruction right here in Due East, sitting pretty on the County Council?

No one had to get so crazy, her father said, as to shut down their biggest money-making ventures. It was going to take years to get integrated, he said, and Kennedy was doing it the right way, taking his cue from Lyndon Johnson and watching out for Southerners' feelings. He wasn't going to emasculate Due East (whatever that was supposed to mean). He wasn't just going to steamroll things through the way Martin Luther King and his ilk wanted him to. If Dolores thought they were going to start shutting down soda fountains, did she think they were going to shut down Ralph's? Did she think no one was going to eat chicken chutney at the Golden Apple on Sundays anymore? No, her father said, it was going to take years—and they couldn't possibly be taking the soda fountain out of Calvin's because her brothers had *promised* her as many cherry Cokes as she wanted if she would be in their movie.

She heaved herself off the bed and checked the bedspread—smoothed over the depository in the mattress, the way Lily left it—before she moved to the dresser to find her stretch pants. Her brothers were tricking her, and once again here she was, following after them.

❑   ❑   ❑

At four o'clock, Bill Rooney was a happy man once more, and he tilted back his big wooden desk chair twenty degrees. At three forty-five, out of the blue, Coramae Ruttledge had called to say that she wanted to take a look at the old Levinson place in Hundred Pines. He'd been listing that house for nine months, the same amount of time Max Levinson had been safely buried underground. Max's nieces and nephews in Savannah were asking fifteen thousand dollars more than they should have been asking, but they had all the time in the world to liquidate the estate—and coming from Sava*nn*ah, that Southern seat of sophistication, they had no inclination to listen to the advice of a Due East real estate agent. He hadn't shown the place since the September rush, and he'd long since quit fantasizing what he'd do with the big commission. Now, in the space of an hour, he was calculating once more that the five percent would see him through December and January, if the deal closed fast.

And he was pretty sure that Coramae Ruttledge would close *real* fast, because this meant that the rumors about her pretty daughter Maisie, seventeen and the cheerleader at Due East High School with the longest brownest legs, were true. Tim had announced it at the supper table: "Maisie Ruttledge's in the family way," and Andy had chimed in: "Got a loaf in the oven," and he'd had to rise from his place and take a swipe at the two of them. Where in God's name had they dug out *those* old-fashioned phrases? Besides, their own mother had had a loaf named Maggie in the oven when she married him and came down to Due East.

Well, it was too bad Maisie Ruttledge was only seventeen; but if Tim and Andy were right it was Tooty Barnes who got her that way, and even if she would begin life as Mrs. Tooty Barnes—what a waste of long brown legs—the two families between them would see that the newlyweds didn't suffer much. Tooty would probably go off to Carolina to study business while Maisie stayed home with the baby, watched over by the two clans; and the biggest problem for all of them would be to see that Tooty didn't get some new brown-legged cheerleader up at Carolina pregnant too. Maisie and Tooty would be starting their Due East life in a refined little four-bedroom pine-shaded house on the water; and you could hardly shed any tears over that, especially when you knew that in four years Tooty would come home and be vice president of his daddy's bank. He and Dolores had started *their* life in Due East in a two-room apartment in the back of Mrs. Twoomy's dark house on the John C. Calhoun Road, and Mrs. Twoomy had decided, once she could see Dolores was pregnant, that she couldn't bear the noise of a baby. Gloomy Mrs. Twoomy.

Tomorrow, anyway, he'd be driving Coramae Ruttledge and her engineer (that woman wasted no time) over to Max's place. Business was looking up, and so was his afternoon; *now* Bill Rooney was in the mood for holding court. Jack Calvin had dropped by just after the phone call, fleeing his own drugstore renovations. (You had to hand it to Jack: he was too much of a diplomat to even hint that he didn't want to integrate the soda fountain. What he said, instead, with a smile unclouded by ambivalence, was that he needed more room for the cosmetics display cases. Dolores would have had a fit if she'd heard his prevarications, but what could you expect the man to do? Why should Jack Calvin, who'd never expressed a political opinion in his life—who'd never joined in the hysterical rantings on the subject of states' rights, who wasn't trotting out the Bill of Rights every time someone brought up the subject of integration—why should Jack Calvin be called on to be the test case for Due East? And it wasn't just Jack Calvin. Everybody was running scared: he'd seen Jack's face in the *Courier* photograph of the audience at the private school meeting, but hell, he'd seen *every*body's face in that audience; and of course Dolores was right—of course you should stick it out in the public schools, and why should our kids have music class and Latin and a decent chemistry lab when their kids didn't—but he wasn't entirely sure that he, married to another woman, a Southern woman who understood the subtleties better, wouldn't have listened to Jack's argument at the least. He was certainly not going to cast judgment, the way Dolores would be sure to cast her judgment tonight at supper. He only hoped she was planning to make her condemnation of Jack Calvin short, because there was something about the way the Rooney children looked at her in the middle of her pronouncements, something too close to idolatry, that made it hard for him to sit in his own dining room.)

At least in his office he could talk to Jack Calvin—who was a decent fellow even if he was a coward—without apology. At least in his own office he could gather his company around him. This afternoon, after Jack Calvin sat himself down in Rooney Realty, J. C. Smalls followed him in, because Jack was the only man on River Street who would laugh at J.C.'s jokes; and then Solly Friedman followed them both in, because Solly Friedman could tell a wasted afternoon was coming on the way a worm could tell a tomato was fixing to ripen on the vine.

There they sat, the four of them: Southern gentlemen all, though each of a different stripe. Maybe a sign painter wouldn't pass for a gentleman, but even J.C. was a craftsman at what he did—his angled script would have pleased Sister Mary Immaculata at the Cathedral School—and his signs had a classy look that belied his outlook on life, which you'd have to define, if you were defining it, as coarse. J.C. had told Bill once that when he was a kid out fishing the trestle, the colored boys used to call him Jesus Christ Smalls, and Bill believed it. He wouldn't have put it past J.C. to *tell* the colored boys his name was Jesus Christ. J.C. spent a good portion of his day collecting Gullah jokes, and Bill spent a good portion of the time he was listening to J.C.'s jokes wondering what Dolores would say if she heard them. It was hard to say who he'd be more embarrassed for.

Right now J.C. was cupping his hands behind his head, measuring out the words for his latest story with the same care he measured a plywood signboard: "All right now. I got me a good one."

Jack Calvin said: "J.C., all your jokes start with that line. 'I got me a good one.'"

Solly said: "No, Jack, unhunh. That's not true. Sometimes he says 'I got me a funny one.' Sometimes he says 'I got me a *hysterical* one.'"

"Thank you, Solly. Thank you kindly for that vote of confidence."

Bill settled into his chair. There was an easiness in his office that he didn't find in his own home. A Jack Calvin and a Solly Friedman and even a Jesus Christ Smalls could drop by here without so much as a rap on the door—but who ever rang the doorbell on the Point anymore? Here there was a give-and-take, a bridge of cordiality that spanned the chasm of difference between them: Lord, could J.C. and Solly possibly have *any*thing in common? But here they put up with each other. Here there was none of the sniping at each other's decisions that went on under his own roof. Here they sat, obedient as schoolchildren taking their turns in reading group, each letting the other say his piece.

"All right now," J.C. said. "I can't take the credit for this one. I got this one off Buddy Miles."

"J.C. You can get on with it now."

"O.K. Joke courtesy of Buddy Miles." J.C. fanned his hands out, defining his joke-telling territory. His hands were small enough to be a woman's—they looked right on his dark compact body—but they were gnarled tough workman's hands, and he worked them into his jokes as if they were props.

"So. There's these three paratroopers up on their first jump. All scared enough to pee in their pants." J.C. stood, crossing his hands in front of his crotch in terror, to do the paratroopers. "There's not a one of them ready to *jump* out of that airplane. But the captain says: 'Now look here boys. You just do what I tell every soldier fixing to jump for the first time. You just put your faith in the Lord. He's not gonna let you down.'

"So the first in line to jump is a Catholic boy from New York City, and he does him a big"—J.C. mimed—"whatuhya-call it, Bill?"

"Sign of the cross."

"He does him a big sign of the cross and he says: 'Father Son and Holy Ghost, I never did eat meat on Friday and please now keep me safe.' So a voice booms out from above saying: 'Jump my son. You are in my hands.' And the mackerel snapper from New York City jumps and his parachute opens and the rest of them see him floating down safe and sound." J.C. fluttered the small tough hands.

"Now the next soldier stands at the open door. This one's Jewish." A wink at Solly. "He stands at the door looking up to heaven and he says: 'Oh God of Abraham and Moses I never did do a lick of work on Saturday and now please keep me safe.' And the voice from heaven says: 'Jump my son. You are in my hands.' And the Jewish boy jumps and his parachute opens right up and the captain says: 'See there? I knew the Lord would keep y'all safe.'

"Now we're up to the last soldier, and it turns out this last soldier's a colored boy from Savannah, one of them boys you see with a dew rag wrapped around his head, you know, dealing cards out on the street corner Saturday night." J.C. couldn't resist: now he mimed a man shuffling the deck. "Now idn't this colored boy the scaredest one of all? He's never even *been* in a plane 'fore this. So he's wringing his hands, and wiping his brow, and the captain says: 'Go on now, son. You just do what them other boys did. You just put your trust in the Lord.' So the colored boy leans out the door and he looks up at the sky and there's light streaming out from behind a bank of clouds. And the boy gets kind of dreamy-like and he says: 'Oh Jesus. Oh Jesus,' he says. 'You ain't give me such good breaks in life Jesus, you ain't give me no daddy and you give my momma a passel of chidrun.' He says: 'You ain't give me such good breaks in life but I goes down to Grace A.M.E. every Sunday, now ain't I Lord, and I sings in that choir, now don't I Lord, and now I prays just this once you keep me safe. Just this once, Jesus.'"
J.C. took a respectful pause at the conclusion of the prayer—
—but revved up again with a volume that rivaled the Baptist preacher's: "So what you think happens? The light streams through this break in the clouds like the colored boy and the captain never saw before. And now the voice from heaven

booms down and says: 'My son, have faith in me. You are in my hands. Jump. Jump." J.C. looked especially pleased with his imitation of God, which involved climbing on his chair to call down from heaven, and gesturing in wide circular motions as he implored the paratrooper to jump.

"So the colored boy jumps, and his parachute won't open. He's tugging and he's tugging, and the captain's shouting from up in the plane to pull the 'mergency, and the boy's pulling the 'mergency, but *that* one won't open neither. So the boy falls faster and faster down to earth, and sure enough he goes splat on the ground, and the captain just can't believe it. He just can't believe it. He says: 'Oh my God.' And the voice from heaven comes down and says—"

Big pause: J.C. could have used a drumroll.

"The voice from heaven comes down and says:

" '*Stupid nigger.*' "

Bill shifted again in his chair. Jack Calvin laughed the way he always did, a laugh so good-natured and broad it was hard to believe he was faking it; but Solly Friedman ran a hand through his sparse hair and said:

"I don't know, J.C. I think that's what you call *in bad taste.*"

J.C. let out a big guffaw. "Now when'd I ever tell a joke in *good* taste?"

Solly squirmed his mouth around, right and left. "You got me there, J.C. I can't say I ever remember your telling a joke in good taste."

Jack Calvin said: "Well, least it wasn't a dirty joke. I'd say your dirty jokes are in the worst possible taste, huh Solly?"

Solly Friedman looked at Jack Calvin with what Bill would have called a flicker—the barest trace—of annoyance and said: "I guess I better get on back and count out my money." Was that a flicker of sarcasm in his voice too?

Solly rose slowly enough, and then he walked out of Rooney Realty, slowly enough, and when the door clicked shut after him, Bill found himself shifting yet again in his chair. There was an acrid smell to the air in his office.

Jack Calvin raised his eyebrows ever so slightly. "You don't suppose Solly was—offended, do you Bill?"

And Bill said: "Who, Solly? Aw no, I don't think so. He's been acting distracted ever since he got back from vacation."

J.C. rubbed the little bristles on his chin with his little hand. "You know I wouldn't hurt Solly for all the money in the world. And I've told plenty of Jew jokes before, right, Bill? You ever get bent out of shape about a Pope joke?"

"I send 'em right on to Rome," Bill said. "I write up all your Pope jokes and mail 'em straight to the Vatican."

"Well, it's the damndest thing," J.C. said, "because when Buddy Miles told me that joke he made it Catholic, Protestant, and Jew—you know, he put a Jew at the end of it, and God says that'll teach *you* not to believe in my son—and here I go switching the joke all around so I won't touch any of Solly's nerves. And now he acts like I just pinched his grandma's *be*hind."

"I wouldn't worry it," Jack Calvin said, but Bill could see Jack's eyes already shifting out to the street. Now Jack would find an excuse to leave. Now Jack would say he had to go back to the drugstore to supervise the workmen; and then J.C. would leave, and he would be left alone again in his office to run the joke through again and to let his irritation prickle up.

And his irritation wouldn't be prickling up at J.C.—J.C. was a boy with his jokes, a boy who could use a whipping for having so little sense as to tell that kind of joke to Solly Friedman (so little sense he'd go out the very next day and tell the joke to somebody who'd like it even less. He'd tell it to the colored man packing his bags at the Piggly Wiggly). No, his irritation would be prickling up at Dolores. At his wife.

At the woman who imposed her presence on him even in his own office, who was whispering to him now, while Jack and J.C. still hovered (and her voice was so distant, so soft: softer than a conscience, but pitched ever so much higher). Dolores was telling him that he should have seconded Solly, that he should have stood by Solly when the joke was over, that Solly—wispy-haired, skinny, bird-beaked—had more of a spine than he did. That Solly had done the right thing to walk out on that joke and that he—he, the one Dolores had picked out in New York City as the Enlightened Southerner—had once more sat silent, a co-conspirator to the J. C. Smallses of the world and their coarse childlike jokes (you'd think he was a Judas!).

Now Jack was rising, just as Bill thought he would be, to leave. "I best be getting back. See whether those boys are knocking over my magazine racks and ripping up my linoleum."

And J.C. was rising after him: "Me too. My old lady's ready to whip my tail she finds me playing hooky one more time!" A gleam in J.C.'s eye at the picture of his wife whipping his tail.

Bill didn't bother to rise after them, or see them to the door, or look out behind them on the street to see what other excitement he was missing on this warm slow Thursday. Better to sit for a few minutes. He was filling up with that gas-in-the-belly that made him feel like one of the bedroom radiators just before it spewed out steam. This disgust for his wife was sudden and passionate, but it wasn't unfamiliar. She had been trying to hoist a two-ton load of guilt onto his back for a long while now.

He slammed his fist down on his own desk. A man told a joke, and Bill Rooney could only think of his wife.

Everything was black and white for Dolores (ha! an apt description given the context: civil rights had long since overtaken her own family as the front-runner for her attention). Dolores wanted everyone to see the world as a spiritual dichotomy. She made their own children sit in an auditorium with a wide aisle down the middle, and then she paraded people and ideas across the stage. The children had to choose which side of the aisle to sit on; and what happened when he—uninformed insensitive Bill—had to waltz across the stage in front of his own kids?

There were nights at the dinner table when he wanted to take notes, or record her conversation on tape, and then play it back to her so she'd know how she sounded, so she realized the cruel game she played with her own children:

"Who do you love, boys: do you love Martin Luther King or J.F.K.?" Oh Momma Momma if you love Martin Luther King best then so do we.

"Who do you love, Katie: do you love the Freedom Riders or the druggists ripping out their own soda fountains?" Oh Momma Momma if you're fighting for integration then so am I.

"Who do you love, children: do you love your momma or your daddy?"

Who do you think? And then Dolores would correct him: No, Bill, it's *whom* do you love. It's *whom* do you think.

He saw Katie's red head bobbing. Tim hunched over the piano to play him Gershwin. Maggie leaving for New York from the train station at Yemassee. Andy spitting disdain.

He was so weary of having his family life directed by her latest moral infatuation, her latest reading crush. Bad enough when she was pregnant with Tim and letting that excuse-*me* Columbia boy sit in *his* parlor smoking *his* cigarettes, making fun of *his* town. If she hadn't been pregnant he would have suspected the kid of trying to literally seduce Dolores instead of just simpering around with a spiritual seduction.

And it only got worse after Katie started first grade. Sometimes it seemed to him that her packages of books were arriving daily—the Kierkegaard she hadn't read since college, when she was getting permission every other week to read books on the

Index; the Marcel recommended by somebody in *Commonweal* —and that the kitchen knife slitting open the brown tape on the box of Dolores's new books might have been slitting open his own marriage.

But she would never slit it open by leaving him—no, her father's leaving her mother was the worst sin she could imagine, and she'd never repeat it. Her cleaving would be done with the latest reading program she'd set for herself, the latest political program.

And the programs she'd set for her children. She was forever bothering Maggie and Tim—Tim who, for God's sake, should be spending his teenage years learning how to sail a boat or at least drive a car, like every other boy in town: the rest of them went down to take the test the day they turned fourteen, but not Tim. No, Tim's mother was sitting him down at the kitchen table to discuss with him whether maybe Thomas Aquinas wasn't just the first existentialist after all, as if that was what a teenage boy was hungry for.

He slammed his palm down again, harder. Poor Tim. Slam. Tim. Tim climbing into their bed night after interrupted night. Bill would have let the boy curl between them, at least until his breathing slowed and the nightmares receded, but night after night Dolores walked Tim back to his own bed: "We don't want him to think he's incapable of facing his own fears."

Incapable of facing his fears. When what the boy needed was warmth and the pressure of his father's body next to his. Dolores was all talk. *All talk.* She could spend an entire dessert lecturing the children about following their consciences; she could tell Katie that they did not have to be frightened about the Klan, not when they could act as witnesses against the Klan; and exactly where was Dolores Rooney acting as witness? The Democratic Party of Due East? Where she tweaked Hartley Dinkins's nose? Bill had suggested, in the heat of one of

67

these steam attacks, that if she was so *committed* (so goddamn committed) to civil rights she could just hop on a Greyhound— she didn't have to go so far as Alabama or Mississippi, she could go right on up to North Carolina and sit in a lunch counter there; she could drive the car right down to Savannah for God's sake; but hadn't she said: Oh, it wouldn't be fair to the children? It wouldn't be fair to Katie if I had to spend the night in jail. That you had to *choose* your actions. And what actions exactly did she choose?

The ones that would estrange his own children.

The ones that would paint the halo round her own head.

After he finished taping Dolores's supper table conversation, he'd love to tape Lily Lightsey's conversations with one of her church friends. He'd love to hear Lily telling some wizened stooped-over colored lady how embarrassing it was to work for a white lady who *kept a picture of Martin Luther King on the dresser,* who thought she was the great white savior of the colored population of Due East County. He'd love to see Lily's lips part—not in disgust, she was too kind a woman for that— but in merriment at Dolores's self-serving folly.

He'd love to watch Dolores put her face to the mirror and see:

And see:

Dolores twenty years ago. Dolores sitting in a smoky cramped audience, elbows on her knees, staring up at him with such intensity that he stared back from the little stage and let the piano play itself. It was one of his own tunes:

> *You're making me dream in colors*
> *In hues I've never seen before.*
> *You open my eyes by daytime*
> *And at night you make me walk the floor.*

He wasn't much of a lyricist, but he couldn't have written a better line for *her*. She was the most vivid girl he had ever seen —not pretty: vivid. Her skin was a shock of white mottled through with freckles, and her mouth was painted crimson, and her green dress shimmered even in the dim club-light: it was either very cheap or very expensive. She had piled her red hair high on her head, and a little white veiled hat—all wrong for a club, right for church, maybe—perched there precariously, trying to contain the willful hair. Her lips were parted as she watched him, not with the judgment and scorn that came later, but with anticipation. She did not even know her mouth was open.

And Dolores McGillicudhy *floated* on the music. On his music. He was in love, from the stage: all right, wary love, or just lust. The dress was cheap, after all, and the hat was peculiar— but the size of her breasts under the shiny material! That open mouth.

She still opened her mouth that way sometimes. Even without the funny hat and the garish dress and the youthful unlined skin around her eyes, she still managed that look of anticipation from time to time. Only now the look was cast on the children, and not at him at all. Now it was Maggie's music, or Tim's, that moved her. Now if the boys came in downcast from high school, from that world where they fitted in as poorly as the veiled hat had fitted her own head, she comforted them the way she had once comforted him. She brought them round to their small glories, to their grades and their honor societies, the way she'd once brought him round. She lifted them up, he had to admit it. And it was the way she'd lifted him up once, and pushed him on, to find a new place to live, to start a business out of air.

Out of air and sunlight. He'd never have found Due East if it hadn't been for Dolores. He would have ended up playing honky-tonks in Newark or Baltimore, drifting down the coast

69

with the knowledge that he'd never really be a musician, that his heart wasn't in it any more than his heart had been in the accounting classes he fled when he went to New York.

He missed that gaze of Dolores's. Now and again there were still moments when he was in her favor. Now and again she would put a hand to the back of his neck and squeeze, barely, and say: "Everything all right, dear?" Dear. Not honey or sweetheart or darling, but that Old World word, that word of her mother's—a word with the look of the veil on her white hat —and he would be so grateful for her sudden sweetness, so resentful that the sweetness came his way so seldom, that he sometimes did not even answer her.

Everything all right, dear?

No, Dolores. No, I'm weary at the end of the day and I have no patience for these piles of mail you've set out for me. The sanctimonious mission appeals. Dorothy Day's opinion of the real world. I think I deserve Huntley-Brinkley and a beer as much as any man in Due East.

No, Dolores. No, I don't want to join a discussion group with Father Baloney Berkeley. The Douay-Reims Bible is enough philosophy for me.

No, Dolores, no I won't drop J. C. Smalls whether he makes your hair stand up or not. You think we could actually live in Due East without one J.C. or another?

No, Dolores. No. You cringe if I open a second beer on a long night.

He slammed his hand down again, just to see if he could work his passion up, but there was no resonance in the plop of palm on wood. He was already imagining the way she would look when she pulled on the old fussy maternity clothes, faded after all these wearings. The way her skin would go sallow and her breasts would heave down. The way she would stare at him, past him. Beyond him.

The way she would hold herself completely alone—tall, shoulders straight as a drill instructor's—shutting herself off not just from him but from every other woman in Due East too, the other mothers she could have made friends with if she weren't so contemptuous of their yacking at the garden clubs or their stiffing the colored maids. *She* had a maid! She loved digging in the flower beds as much as they did (the sweet springtime pattern of a quarter inch of dirt under every one of her short fingernails)—so why did she put on these airs?

She'd gone so far out on her righteousness limb that even that loud New York City crowd—those smart gum-popping girls from Mount St. Martyr's—wouldn't have climbed out on her branch to join her now.

Oh Blessed Jesus, was he pitying *her?* Worse, a thousand times worse, than his own self-pity. To be thinking of her breasts heaving down like her mother's, when once he'd spent delicious guilty hours squeezing them in his imagination.

He shifted the hands that had once squeezed his wife's great white breasts, hands that rested now on the desk of a stranger, a failing real estate man. He didn't recognize the stranger, didn't recognize the desk, didn't recognize the hands. Sparse dark tufts sprouted from his fingers, and the dark wiry hairs called back to him the look of his father's old barbed-wire fences on the farm in Shining Star.

The memory shook him free. He rose to stuff the barbed-wire hands in his pockets. No more thudding those hands down on the desk. No more time to waste.

Tomorrow he was selling the Levinson place, and that sale would be a sign that could have been painted in J.C.'s big careful script, a sign that things were looking up.

That they wouldn't just get by with a new baby coming. They would flourish, the Rooneys, the way the Ruttledges and the Calvins flourished in Due East.

□   □   □

Dolores Rooney heard her daughter shut the front door—*thudud*—and she shut her own book, *dud,* in imitation. She could hardly concentrate on St. Thomas's dreariness when the air was drifting in cooler now, waving scents of pine and moss and giving the kitchen itself a bosky smell.

Four-thirty. From the back yard, Kate called in with the cool air that she was off on her bike to the trestle. Her daughter was trying her best to contain a quiver of excitement, but her voice was still pitched high. Dolores went to stand at the back door and swallowed back a grin, watching Kate pull her bike from behind the kitchen stairs. So Tim had asked her to be in the movie after all.

"Watch out for rattlesnakes! They're liable to wake up on a warm day like this." Actually, she wasn't sure, after all these years in Due East, whether the rattlesnakes were supposed to hibernate in November.

Kate grunted, without looking up.

"Get off that trestle if you hear the *hint* of a whistle!" Now Kate condescended to stare up and roll her eyes, and this time Dolores couldn't help smiling. They both knew that the freight train came bellowing down the tracks at exactly six-oh-seven and that every child playing on the trestle had taken up a place on the rocks or in the ditch at six-oh-five. Any danger to Kate wouldn't come from the train, or the woods, or the water: if there was danger, it would come from her brothers and their crazy movie scheme.

Dolores watched Kate mount the old Schwinn as if it were a beloved horse, and then she watched her daughter pedal off for eight-millimeter-movie stardom, trailing a goodbye wave. Kate would catch Tim and Andy down the road, and Dolores pictured the three of them bickering on bikes as they rode down River Street.

She had finally read the movie script two nights ago, when Tim left it out on the kitchen counter: an unspoken invitation, she figured. She'd stood there rubbing cigarette after cigarette out while she read the lines through, and she'd felt herself go mushy and sentimental. Tim's script was so *bad*—so childish and boyish and downright silly—that it moved her deeply. She never would have thought, not since Tim entered Due East High School at the age of twelve, that he could have conceived of such piffle. His essays were just the opposite now—polished and reasoned and sometimes almost sophisticated—and yet the same intelligent boy, *her* intelligent boy, was capable of complete twaddle. Tim's hero was a lonely teenage boy setting fires in the woods and speaking pathetic monologues while the flames went up.

She'd stiffened, of course, when the little girl entered the picture, when the lonely teenage boy killed the girl and then himself—what mother wouldn't find her throat closing at *that* sort of invention? But the lines of dialogue Tim had written were as gawky as his walk or his hangdog expression, lines like: "How can I go on, without love?" and "I am saving her from the life of anguish she will surely lead if I do not rescue her." Dolores could not imagine lines like *that*, lines written up as title cards and flashed on the screen between scenes, being adolescent cries for help. Besides, the movie murder was in lieu of a paper contrasting the murders in *Billy Budd* and *An American Tragedy*. Tim had shown her the mimeographed assignment sheet and she'd stamped her foot in agreement with his vexation: "It's hard to believe," she told Tim, "that Miss Elayne Kindle has even *read* the books, much less gotten the point. Does she think she's teaching sociology?"

Anyway, as long as Andy didn't really drop Katie when he

73

held her over the water (that scene was why Tim had left the script on the counter—so she would give her tacit approval—and she guessed she had), she was glad to see the three of them working together again. Without Maggie, Katie had soured like milk left on the counter, and the boys pinched their faces in distaste when she turned down their schemes for plays or operas. You'd think *they*'d be the ones getting too old for a little girl—good Lord, they were in high school—but it was Katie lately who disdained it all. She'd been spending far too much time in her bedroom, alone, and it was good to see her biking after them instead of disappearing into the little cell upstairs.

Dolores had never been allowed time in a bedroom, alone, when she was a girl. After her father left them, she and her mother Rose had moved to an apartment half the size of their old one, and the one narrow bedroom in the new place was barely big enough to contain the double bed where Dolores McGillicudhy now took Andrew McGillicudhy's place nightly. When she'd tried to escape to that bedroom in the afternoon for an hour's privacy—when she'd tried to plop on the bed or read a book or daydream—her mother's cheerful voice had drifted in from the kitchen: "Idle hands, Dolorey. The devil's workshop. Come help me peel potatoes."

Dolores never invented chores to call Katie away from her privacy. But this September, when she went into her daughter's bedroom with the clean clothes, she'd surprised Kate buck naked, prancing like a wood nymph around the bed, and she'd had to go back out in the hallway for a good horrified laugh. Soon she'd be finding cheap steamy romances under Kate's mattress the way she found the *Playboy*s under Tim's when she went to help Lily change the sheets. Poor Tim. A *Playboy* under the mattress and a sad Blessed Virgin Mary—a framed reproduction of a Raphael Madonna, a gift from Father Berkeley—over his bed. No wonder he still had sleepwalking episodes. She pictured

Tim down by the trestle, trying to look like Orson Welles, Father Berkeley's little camera perched on his shoulder like a bird.

Four thirty-five by the kitchen clock. Dolores made her way back through the house and saw in the bathroom mirror that her hair had curled up a little earlier, in the heat of the day. The combination of the damp air before and the cool air later had left her skin whiter than ever, a moony blue-white, but now her full lips had darkened and taken shape again: for most of this pregnancy, white mouth had bled into a white chin. Now she was getting her face back. Bill always said, round about her fourth month, that she was beautiful pregnant, and he was so corny ("A vision," he'd say. "I *mean* it. You take my breath away") that she'd almost believe it, and spend the middle months sneaking glances at her own reflection in windows and toasters. Her strange pale face smiled back at her from under her, serene under a French twist, but she pulled the pins out, helter-skelter, and let her hair float free.

She'd intended to clear up some of the kitchen mess, but the sight of her own contented face made her decide to walk out into the afternoon instead. She could see if Dr. Black had freed that stuck baby—and if he had, she would take it as an omen of hope. She smiled one last smile at the mirror, and saw herself walking down River Street in the hour before dusk. Carpe diem! (Sister Agnes, her favorite, eighth grade.)

What a cruel trick the body played on pregnant women, slowing them down just when they were so desperate for the light and air and company of the world outside the house. For three months she'd felt as if she were pushing through a sundae glass of Jell-O. Now it was as if she'd worked her way up to the top, and she thought she might just let herself float on the cream awhile.

Outside her front door the afternoon light was as blue-white as her skin had looked in the mirror, and the cool November air buoyed her. She *was* ready to float down the block. Next door Mrs. Rapple was out, sitting as uncertainly as an unclaimed package on her own front steps. Dolores never could remember her next-door neighbor's first name, though she thought it might be Faith or Hope. A virtue, certainly, but maybe a more tedious virtue, like Constance. Mrs. Rapple looked so bedraggled and hopeless and wispy and vague that Dolores was moved to call out:

"Hello there." And then added, to stretch it out: "Isn't this cool air delicious? After that hot midday?"

Mrs. Rapple looked startled—the young Rapples often stared clear off in another direction to avoid greeting any of the boisterous Rooneys—but managed a tight smile. "Yes indeedy."

Dolores waved goodbye, but Mrs. Rapple went on, almost as if she were calling her back: "I *needed* this fresh air today. I surely did."

Dolores tried her best to look sympathetic. She'd called on the Rapples once, canvassing for Kennedy; the husband had been polite and evasive, but the wife couldn't hide her disapproval: "Oh no," Mrs. Rapple had said. "I like that Nixon."

The Rapples had the nervous look of a couple afraid maybe they'd swum out a little farther than they'd meant to. The husband was a car mechanic who looked uncomfortable in his own house, which was a big simple two-story frame built in the twenties, like hers. The house had belonged to the wife's family, and the Rapples had been there for three years; in those first three years of their marriage they'd lost two babies—far along too. Dolores would have wagered from the size of her that Mrs. Rapple had been all the way to six months with both of them.

The woman couldn't have been more than twenty-two or twenty-three. Dolores had a prickling sensation that Mrs. Rapple's saying she needed fresh air was her way of saying she was pregnant again—and sure enough:

76

"I don't know why they call it *morning* sickness. Me, I'm sick the livelong day." She colored and looked down.

"Well! Congratulations!" Dolores didn't even have to force heartiness into her voice: the poor woman looked as beaten down as an Okie in the Depression, with those drooping shoulders. She deserved a child as much as any woman did, and Dolores had the feeling that a baby might lighten her up.

She was almost moved to tell Mrs. Rapple that she was pregnant too—from the looks of her, and the talk of the morning sickness, they'd probably be delivering close together—but the idea that the girl might ask her for advice or suggest that they share walks through the streets of the Point, the two of them pushing baby carriages, filled her with dread. "That's grand news," she said instead.

Mrs. Rapple nodded her thanks and held her right hand up. "I've got my fingers crossed, I tell you. You like to give up hope, y'know, after you lose one."

Dolores had never had so much as a six-weeks miscarriage, not even in punishment of her adultery. She could hardly imagine what it must have been like for this young woman, who'd lost the first one right in the living room, before the ambulance or her husband came to help. Chlotilde Jackson, on the other side of the Rapples, told everyone up and down the street what a heartache it was to see a perfectly formed tiny child, covered in the blue mess of childbirth, perfectly dead. Hyaline membrane, Dr. Black said—the baby wouldn't have lived even if he had made it to term.

"I'll say a prayer for you," Dolores said. "Good luck, my dear."

Good heavens. She must sound like a grandmother. But Mrs. Rapple smiled a grateful smile and said: "Thank you kindly," and Dolores walked down O'Connor Street saying a prayer not for Mrs. Rapple but for herself: another Confiteor.

And once again the sin she confessed was pride—she could have broken down and *mentioned* her own pregnancy. Mrs. Rapple probably guessed it anyway, probably wondered why Dolores Rooney should keep something like that, something they shared, such a secret.

She hurried away from Mrs. Rapple and turned down Welty Street, a street she and Bill had once driven down with their breaths held, back when they were so tight for cash it didn't seem possible that they would ever own a house. On Welty Street the houses leaned over the road in proprietary fashion: they were old frame houses built a century before her house was built, houses with verandas upstairs and down, with big brick bottoms to hold them up from the river when it overflowed. No one was out on Welty Street, and Dolores floated again in her solitude.

Welty Street went right up past the Golden Apple, a big tabby building painted yellow—not apple yellow, but mustard yellow, an almost ferocious color against the washed-out blue of a sky that met water just behind the restaurant. These days the Rapples could only afford to eat at the Golden Apple once or twice a year, but when she and Bill first moved to Due East they would take the last of the grocery money and sit in one of the dark cool dining rooms on a Sunday afternoon. The two of them—she was pregnant with Maggie then—would make wagers about which of the doddering old gents really controlled Due East. Which of the tottering old women trailing pearls.

At first it seemed to Dolores that none of those sweet blue-haired old ladies, none of the old men patting her hand so insistently, could possibly *control* anything; but Bill said no, those liver-spotted hands wrote big checks. They made important phone calls. They knew what other hands to shake. And take a look at the old coots, Bill would say: they had no compunction about asking the waitress at the Golden Apple for a bourbon.

Bill was right; they'd both seen the highball glasses brought to those tables, the martini glasses. But when Bill inquired about a scotch the waitress said: "Oh no sir. South Carolina's a *dry* state for restaurants." Dolores had had to kick him under the table to stop him from pushing it any further.

At first, Dolores looked on the Golden Apple Sunday brunch as her chance to be a contestant on the local quiz show. Name That Social Standing. She thought she could tell after two minutes of conversation whether the old ladies were Episcopalian (sweet and modest, a little pixilated, old money) or Presbyterian (newer money, and more of it, less inclined to chat) or Baptist (younger, flashier). But she would invariably find out later that she was wrong, that she'd had all the categories confused.

Besides, Bill was so nervous around them that the conversation, like Tim's violin when he was lazy tuning it, always yielded a false note. If an old couple stopped at the young Rooneys' table to tell Dolores about their latest trip to New York, Bill flinched. Later, in bed, he would replay the conversation:

"How'd you like the way that old bat says 'Where'd you say your mother lives, honey?' And then when you say 'Inwood,' her eyes glaze over."

"Mrs. Swenson. Oh but Bill, she couldn't possibly know Inwood. A working-class neighborhood."

Bill would pounce. "Exactly. Couldn't possibly know, couldn't possibly care. Didn't you *see* how she walked off right after?"

"She probably walked off because she was getting hungry for her deviled crabs."

"Hungry for more important people to talk to, once she'd decided you weren't a *sophisticated* New Yorker."

Sometimes she thought she could feel Bill trembling in bed at the thought of the indignities they suffered as newcomers to Due East, and after a while she stopped trying to comfort him.

Bill Rooney wasn't one to buy his way into the country club—
not that they'd ever have the extra money for *that*—or to sniffle
around the local politicians, hoping to be noticed. He was just
one to lie in bed at night, trembling over their invisibility.

Thank God he'd found a place for himself in the mornings at
Ralph's. And a different place, Saturday nights, at the Knights
of Columbus. Thank God he'd discovered a house on the Point
in such bad shape that they could manage asking his parents for
the down payment without groveling. He'd driven her round to
O'Connor Street the day after she came home from the hospital
with Maggie, and she'd sat weeping dry tears in the front seat of
their old Chrysler, a diaper draped over her open blouse, the
baby squeezing her nipple so hard it stung. She could have wept
at her sore nipples. Wept at the hormones that gushed. Wept at
the sorry state of the house. Wept at Bill's kindness.

Her mother, who'd taken the train down to Yemassee two
weeks before her due date, leaned forward from the back seat
and put her hand on her daughter's shoulder. "He's a good man,
Lorey," she whispered, both of them watching Bill's proud dash
up the front steps. "The size of this place! What a good man."

He *was* a good man to get them out of Mrs. Twoomy's, and
not as stupid as she'd convinced herself: else why would she
have married him? Anyone who could play the piano the way
Bill did—sitting down with a lewd shake of his hips, half closing
his eyes, showing off his trills and honky-tonk riffs, then closing
his eyes completely and tiptoeing through "Für Elise" or a Mozart sonata—anyone who could do that wasn't stupid. Anyone
who could walk into a strange town and start a business with a
big grin and a hand thrust out and a knack for drawing out a
long slow conversation, even while he was trembling at the in-
dignity.

When she'd first taken to confessing pride—when she'd
cleaned out the old dust balls of adultery and fornication and

moved on to new sins—she'd had in mind the way she let Bill think it only bothered *him*, this being new to Due East. She'd done such a good job pretending that eventually, after the nightmare with Walker Mansard, she'd accumulated company. Not the old Due Easters, not the other mothers: but she was less restless anyway talking with Father Berkeley and Sister Dominica, who'd had two years of graduate school and was really quite intelligent. Dolores Rooney was content with the company of her own children. And with the bases so close, there was always someone moving into town: now it was a young Navy dentist in the discussion group. It was obvious from the first that his wife had dragged him along, but once he'd suggested they read some Catholic magazines: "Why we could read the *Catholic Worker!*" he'd said, and Dolores had nearly fallen out of her chair. The rest of the group always wanted to read Fulton Sheen, or Cardinal Spellman, and liked to pretend that there was no Vatican Council going on at all.

Dolores Rooney rounded the corner of River Street. Four forty-five by the bank clock. She walked another block and hesitated. She was coming up now on Bill's office, and Bill would be sitting in the dark watching the passersby through his plate glass. Bill would be trembling, as he'd once done in bed after the snubs by the town swells, only now the trembles would be set off by his fear that he'd never sell another piece of real estate. She didn't believe *that* for a second; but she went over the budget every night now, after Bill's fourth or fifth beer. After he and Tim had finished their nightly potshots. Bill slept, heavy in the armchair, and Tim studied in an angry fervor upstairs, and Dolores toted up the overdues at the kitchen table once again.

It wasn't the baby who worried her. A baby could sleep in a dresser drawer lined with a towel. A baby—her baby anyway, even in this day of powder formulas—drank from the breast. A baby could wear its brothers' T-shirts cut down to diapers if it needed to. No, it was Tim. He'd win a scholarship and pay his own way through Columbia. But what would he wear once he landed in Morningside Heights? Poor child: it would come to him all at once in New York City how awkward he looked, and if she knew her son, he'd develop a taste for gray flannel trousers and double-breasted blazers.

And how would they pay Tim's train fare back and forth? They couldn't even manage Maggie's now—she wouldn't be coming home for Thanksgiving. Bill said if she had to send Tim off, well then he'd have to stay with her mother for the holidays; but Dolores's mother would be no match for this Timothy, any more than her mother had been a match for her cousin Timothy. Her mother wouldn't know that Tim drank a beer or two himself. At age fifteen! And he smoked: Dolores was sure he smoked. By next year, if he bought himself the flannel trousers, he'd be sneaking girls—maybe not Barnard girls, maybe high school girls—into that very same double bed she'd shared with her mother. And her mother would never in a million years think to say to *Tim:* "Idle hands. The devil's workshop."

When she sent Tim off to New York, she'd be sending off a child, a boy just turned sixteen. It would be like setting him down in the water in a rush basket, and she didn't have *that* kind of faith. If Rooney Realty's business didn't pick up soon, she would have to come up with some other plan for financing that child's trips back and forth from Due East. Some other financial plan: she winced. As if she were in a position, pregnant as she was, to find a job. She'd never had a paying job in her life —when you grew up in an Irish neighborhood, even the babysitting jobs were scarce, with grandmothers and aunts and older sisters always hovering. The other girls went off after high school to answer phones on Wall Street, their high heels clicking down the streets of Inwood on their way to the subway, but she'd been fingered by the nuns, to her mother's dismay, and lined the scholarships up herself.

Back when she was still a student, when she and Bill were sneaking visits in his hotel room, she had planned vaguely to teach Italian one day, though she wasn't sure about graduate school: she was starting to go to clubs, and she loved to dance. She couldn't picture herself in horn-rims. But Sister Andrea was certainly urging her on: by 1944, she was the only Italian major left in the modern languages department. Her mother thought she was out of her mind, majoring in the language of the Fascists—LOREY, THEY ARE THE ENEMY (and she didn't just mean in the war, Dolores suspected; she probably had in mind some childhood snub by a good-looking dark-haired girl in the Bronx). It was useless trying to describe to Rose the sensation she felt when she first picked up Dante: *"L'animo, ch'è creato ad amar presto, ad ogni cosa è mobile che piace, tosto che dal piacere in atto è desto.* It means the soul is roused to act when it's moved by pleasure,"* but Rose found it gibberish in English or Italian. It was useless trying to explain about sound or rhythm, about a language that took as many climbs and swoops as the roller coaster at Coney Island. *Cara mamma, do try to understand. I don't want to be a nurse.*

Besides, she told Rose, it didn't bother her that there was a war on, that she couldn't go hear Italian in Italy. The Italy she imagined tramping through had shaped itself back into the country of the visionaries (and now she had Bill to imagine with her. Of course Bill wanted to go to Europe, as soon as the worst was over. Bill was a *musician:* he wanted to spend time in Paris and Rome and even Berlin, if it came to that). What appealed to her was Florence, which she knew—by heart, as if she'd walked the streets herself—from *Romola* and *Room with a View.* What appealed to her was hiking over from Florence to Siena (Catherine was the most sublime of saints). What appealed to her was Assisi—she thought she could imagine the violet sky over St. Francis's head. She would do without Venice and Naples and Sicily: what appealed to her was Rome.

Of course she'd never made it to Italy or to Europe at all; she'd gotten herself pregnant instead. And the closest she'd ever gotten to teaching Italian was the odd lesson or two she'd try to give Bill in his hotel room at three in the morning: *"Penso che egli parli troppo"* or *"Egli non è como suo padre."* Bill's stabs at Italian, in that lowcountry accent, sent her off in spasms of laughter (and he would clown, shamed at how bad he was with languages: "I like-a you sweet melons, mamma mia!"). After they moved to Due East, it was a joke between them, her teaching Italian in a town that wasn't even big enough for a parochial school, much less a high school that could offer more than French and Latin. (Lord knew what languages they offered at the colored high school. She'd banned J. C. Smalls from the house after he said English was a foreign language to colored kids in Due East.)

Bill would have hated her working anyway: even teaching. Even when they'd been their poorest, when they'd poked through the ashtrays to find cigarette butts long enough to smoke, even when they'd looked at each other smoking butts and laughed until they choked the smoke down, even at Mrs. Twoomy's when they were eating black-eyed peas out of a can for supper every night—ugh, with a little fatback the way Bill liked it—even then he would have flushed with shame at the thought of her working. And she would have been ashamed if he'd ever suggested it.

She'd been standing on the corner for a minute at least, wavering about whether she should go by and rap on the window of Rooney Realty, or dangle out a breezy wave while she floated by on her way to Dr. Black's. She'd been picturing Bill, dingy sheet up to his chin in a crummy Manhattan hotel bed, smoking and spluttering: "I like-a you sweet melons, mamma mia." She'd just been staring—what a strange day, how unlike her to just *stand* there on River Street, to spend all this time daydreaming—at the plate-glass window that said

Rooney Realty

(Rooney Reality?) in J. C. Smalls's careful hand.

◻   ◻   ◻

Kate found her brothers opposite Calvin's Pharmacy, straddling their bikes and grinning like circus clowns on River Street. Calvin's twin front doors were propped open and funneling out swirls of dust.

"See," Tim said.

Kate coasted to a stop beside them. Across the street, colored workmen were carting out the chrome-and-red-plastic stools from Calvin's soda fountain—the red stools she'd spent a whole *lifetime* sitting on—and lining them up on the sidewalk by the gum machines and the **Your Weight • Your Fate** scale. Calvin's was a carnival.

"I can't believe Mr. Calvin's doing that," Kate said.

Her brothers shrugged at each other. Andy said: "Look who he's got carrying the stools out."

"You can carry it, son," Tim said, "but you can't sit on it."

Then Tim and Andy shrugged at each other again, and Tim, jockeylike, leaned forward on his bike. Andy gave the signal: "Let's go!"

Her brothers sped off in unison, Tim singing out: "Come on Katie, we've got to catch the light," without so much as turning to look at her. She was poised to follow, but her kickstand jammed; by the time she'd hammered it back into place with her foot she saw her father stick his neck out of Rooney Realty's front door.

"Hey Daddy," she called, but Bill couldn't hear her across the street. Just then Mrs. Coramae Ruttledge was passing by, and her father had his attention on Coramae.

Katie took her foot off the pedal. Coramae Ruttledge was a name she could have put to her photograph of ladies in Due East: a lady who always wore fussy suits, rose or powder blue, and little bone-colored pumps, just to walk down River Street in the middle of the afternoon.

She watched her father leave his doorway and sashay down the street toward Coramae Ruttledge, arms open. Bill and Coramae greeted each other by grabbing one another's forearms —it reminded Katie of one of those nature film strips Mr. Digby liked to show, a little dance of the predators—and then Bill put his big affable arm around Mrs. Ruttledge's shoulder and started promenading her down the street.

Kate felt she was standing in shadows, or sneaking a look through a peephole, though her father wouldn't have put his arm around that woman any differently if Katie had been right beside him. It was the same way he hugged every woman he could get a squeeze from on Sunday mornings, at Our Lady of Perpetual Help. Right on Division Street, right in front of Father Berkeley. Right in front of their husbands, he'd cradle them close. Right in front of Dolores.

It gave Katie the creeps, because she couldn't imagine that it didn't *really* bother her mother, no matter how blank or even cheerful Dolores looked while Bill was doing his flesh-squeezing.

And it especially gave her the creeps to see her father cuddling Coramae Ruttledge on River Street, with her mother nowhere around, because she'd always assumed that her daddy squeezed ladies' arms just *because* Dolores was there. Just so Dolores would see that he could still make ladies look up at him and bat their silly eyelashes. Katie imagined from across the street that Coramae Ruttledge wore blue eye shadow as fake as the rose-colored suit, and after a minute she even thought she could make out smudges on those Ruttledge lids as Coramae did a slow wiggle with her father.

Bill walked Mrs. Ruttledge down to the bank, where she minced off on her bone pumps, waving a sweet little bye-bye. Then her father skipped back down the sidewalk like a boy, and dodged into Rooney Realty.

He never did see his daughter.

Kate took off, pedaling as fast as she could past Rooney Realty and speeding through downtown. Then she started hollering. The light *was* starting to fade, if ever so slowly, and more than she hated seeing her father with his arm around a woman on River Street she hated walking through the woods to the trestle when there was even a hint of darkness.

Once she was past the courthouse, she had her brothers in sight, down in front of the junior high where River Street curved and Union Street took over.

"TIMOTHY. ANDREW. WAIT UP, HEAR?"

Her brothers gave no sign of hearing: Union Street was swallowing them up. And hadn't she told them the last time that she would not, *absolutely would not,* be in their movie if they ever again ran off and left her in the dusk, to find her way alone past the creepy trailer? But had they paid her any mind?

Once she crossed the John C. Calhoun Road she had to tack down Union Street, swinging past obstacles, and she lost all hope of finding them. This stretch housed Marine families, mostly, and the children and the dogs and the tricycles always found their ways to the middle of the road. At the big intersection she'd crossed a line as clear as the one separating colored town from the rest of Due East—the houses on Union Street were small shingled boxes cut from a pattern and painted in pastel colors. Neglected dollhouses. It was hard to imagine that whole families squeezed into them. Since the hurricane, their roofs were clashing plaid patterns of whatever shingles the Due East roofers could get their hands on. The roofs and the houses had a mildewed droopy look, and so did the children who played out on the street in front. The bases let out at four-thirty, and now Marines in fatigues and drab tan uniforms were pulling old sedans into their driveways, waving away the children who tumbled over to greet them.

It looked like fall on Union Street with the scattered brown piles of leaves and nuts under the pecan trees (the pecan trees that were *left*, after the subdivisions were put up and Hurricane Gracie had her way). A block before the dirt road and the patches of woods she slowed. A little field stretched out to one side, desolate and overgrown in the fall light. In the spring and the summer the field was awash with unruly black-eyed Susans. Now, barren, the field reminded her that she was alone.

There, on the dirt road just past the field, were Tim and Andy's bikes. But there was no sign of Tim or Andy.

The creeps.

Kate coasted in, dropped her bike beside theirs, stamped away from them, came back and kicked all three bikes, one at a time. She gave Tim's bike a second kick. They *knew*. They knew she didn't want to walk through the woods to the trestle alone.

Well, she wouldn't do it. She just wouldn't go through the woods. If she had to, she'd go by the tracks—though that could be even worse than going by that man's trailer, because the colored boys went by the tracks and now when she passed by they stared right through her, as if she were invisible, when just a year or two ago they would have said "Hey" and showed her what they caught or told her not to bother fishing today, the tide was too low. It was too creepy for words, the way they ignored her now. What had *she* done? Was it because her breasts showed through her blouse?

But if she didn't go by the tracks, there was no other way to the trestle but the woods, unkempt woods that were a quirky mishmash of oaks and low shrubs and vines on the other side of the marsh. The dry dirt road she was standing on would narrow and dampen as she followed it down through marsh grass: in spots the mud, dotted through with fiddler crabs' holes, would be the color of dried blood. Sad refuse—gray stumps and gray limbs and gray moss—would litter the ground. And there was that man's trailer.

She stared up at the tracks, stretching out atop a little dirt hill scattered through with stickers and sour grass. Droopy wisteria vines climbed along the trees, overtaking them. Sometimes in the summer, she and her brothers were so hot by the time they got their bikes here that they could go no further. They stopped, and sat at the edge of the tracks, and pulled out Indian grass in slow motion. Sun-drugged, they peeled the grass in an ecstasy of languor, one string at a time, sucking the measly trickle of sour juice as if they'd reached an oasis or found one of their father's beer bottles with a trickle still in it.

She'd just decided again that she couldn't possibly face the dark marshy woods—it must be close to five o'clock, and that ghoul would be sure to be in his trailer—when Tim and Andy sauntered out of a neat clump of pines, Father Berkeley's camera perched on Tim's shoulder.

"You retards."

They grinned up at her.

"WHAT ARE YOU TRYING TO DO, SCARE ME TO DEATH?"

"Hey Kates," Andy said, "you *told* us you didn't want to walk back through the woods alone. We waited up."

"We had no intention of leaving you behind," Tim said.

Kate snorted. "You just wanted to scare me."

"You shouldn't kick the bikes, Kate," Andy said, mild and not even looking in her direction. They had been watching her.

"You definitely shouldn't kick the bikes," Tim said, and handed the camera over to Andy without another word. He stooped in the dirt by a tire print and then, a bird plucking a worm from the earth, he pinched up a cigarette butt. It was a good fat one, half unsmoked, and Tim pulled matches from his pocket to light it.

"Oh Tim. Yuck."

Tim lit the butt.

"It could be that guy's," Kate said. "You could get T.B. Or polio."

Tim took his first majestic drag. "You don't get polio," he said, "from smoking somebody's butts."

Kate put a hand to her hip. She bet she looked like Dolores, not willing to take any lip from either of the boys. "You sure of that, Timothy Rooney?"

Andy grinned, but he couldn't handle grinning and smoking together: he choked.

"Fairly sure." Tim grabbed the cigarette back. "Polio? Definitely not. T.B. maybe, but them's the chances you got to take in life. Here Katie, you want to learn how to inhale?"

"I most certainly do not." She was dying to smoke. "You know, Momma's getting suspicious. You guys shouldn't leave her packs half empty like that."

Tim spluttered. "WHY YOU THINK WE'RE SMOKING BUTTS WE FOUND IN THE DIRT?"

Andy said: "Here Katie, last chance. It'll be gone. It's a *menthol*. That's the easiest kind to learn on."

Kate wavered, too long. Andy held out the smoldering little butt; but his proffering arm—chunky, covered with dark freckles and sparse dark hair—called back a picture of Andy reaching out a hand to

to

lift up her *nightgown?*

It was the kind of sudden image that flashes for a second—Mr. Digby's filmstrips, force-fed through the projector—and then disappears. She couldn't grab hold of it, and she was so very small in the picture she was chasing that maybe it wasn't a real memory at all. Maybe it was like those dots that floated in front of your eyeballs when you scrunched your eyes too tight in the sunlight, and then floated away.

Andy pulling up her nightgown? *Andy?* Maybe it was like one of those stories the family told over and over about something that had happened long before she was born. The story became so familiar that eventually she could see herself in the picture—and then she could remember the story better than anyone who had actually been there could remember it. Like the picnic at Hilton Head, when the alligator came slinking up right behind the tree stump where Maggie sat. The version Maggie told was plain and bland—oh, there was never really any *danger*—but when Katie borrowed the story, she could not only picture herself rigid on the fat stump, she could feel the gritty palmetto bark scratching the sunburned backs of her legs. She could feel her daddy's big red hands scooping her up, his fingers digging into her rib cage hard enough to leave pale blue bruises under her nipples.

And if she could remember that about Maggie—if she could *become* Maggie, remembering—then she could be making up this memory of Andy reaching out his chubby little hand and pulling up the summer nightie with the eyelet and the bedraggled ribbon and letting his hand crawl up her thigh while she stood perfectly still. It was in the dark. The vision hovered for another second. It was in the closet, it was in *her* closet: she was standing on a little pair of blue leather sandals, and she was bending their edges over with her bare feet.

Andy stubbed the cigarette out in the dirt. He was two or three inches shorter than Tim, but he was so much more solid (two or three inches broader across the shoulders) that he always looked the older brother.

Maybe she didn't imagine that floating moment. Andy flashed on the screen again. First grade. A whole year of her life washed down over her, and she was *sure* this picture was real. She had written it down on the little Sins list she had saved in her top drawer for First Confession. If you wrote it down, that meant it really happened, and she had printed *Sin Against Purity*.

Andy had told her to lie on the bathroom floor (the white tiles were clammy-cold) and to pull her panties down so he could poke around with bobby pins. Tim, crashing through the door to take a pee, caught them just as she wriggled her legs, and cried: "No, dope, give her some *privacy*."

Their mother must have heard Tim. Dolores charged up the stairs with a purple cry, snarling like a wildcat at the sight of the bobby pins and Kate pulling up her drawers. She grabbed the two boys by the ears and dragged them out of the bathroom, Tim shrieking in protest. If she was in first grade, he would have been ten. Tim ten, Andy nine, Katie six. Six years old.

Dolores would have none of Tim's denials: Kate cowered in the linen closet, scrunching underneath the bottom shelf, listening to her mother bless out both the boys in their bedroom. When Dolores was done with them, she pulled Katie out of the closet, and drew her into the bathroom—the only door with a lock when they were small—and said:

"It's not that they meant to do anything so bad." Dolores's

voice still trembled. Kate had never seen her mother so *confused.*

"Is it a mortal sin?" Kate had whispered. She still got them mixed up, mortal and venial. The only sins Sister Agatha was willing to categorize definitively as mortal were murder, bank robbery, and going to see movies on the Condemned list.

Her mother stamped her foot and clenched her hands and closed her eyes and said:

"No."

Then she kneeled, Katie's height, and grabbed her shoulders and said:

"No. No. No. No."

Her mother's breath was warm and smoky. Maybe she wouldn't be able to stop saying it. No. No. No. No. No. Maybe she would go on forever. Kate hugged Dolores round the waist. This sin (even if it was only venial, which she doubted) was definitely going to have to go on the Sins list. What on earth was she going to call it?

"Tim didn't—"

At least her mother had stopped saying *no.* Dolores held Kate close and started to speak—"Tim just doesn't . . ."—but she never finished. She never finished what she had to say.

Andy was still grinding the butt out with his sneaker, crushing it in his meticulous way. It was impossible to imagine that dark solemn Andy—the same Andy who defended Tim against their father, the same Andy their mother said was as eloquent and handsome as J.F.K., no, handsomer—could have ever wanted to poke around her with *bobby pins.*

Now Andy said: "Tim. You're not going to finish that movie we don't get *out* of here." And Andy took off down the dirt road at a trot, motioning Tim and Kate to follow him.

If Andy was nine when it happened, he must be able to

remember the whole thing. And if he remembered the whole thing, how could he possibly look at her now, much less be in a movie with her and pretend to throw her off the bridge? He would grab her wrists with his dark thick fingers.

"C'mon, Katie-Kates." Tim was hanging back for her. "Oh *now*. What's the matter?"

Kate threw up her arms. She would never be able to look Andy in the eye again.

"C'mon Kate. You scared of that man in the woods?"

Kate nodded.

Tim flexed his muscles and mugged and said, in his deepest Orson Welles voice: "I'll defend you against any who would seek to besmirch your honor, m'lady."

Still Kate hung back.

"Hey Kate, he's just a nut. Just a nut likes to live back there alone in the marsh. He wouldn't *hurt* anybody."

Tim hadn't been so solicitous in a long time. When he said: "He wouldn't *hurt* anybody" all the mugging muscles of his face straightened out and he was just red-haired, freckled Tim, the male version of her and Dolores. A boy so wispy his father could have *blown* him away. No wonder Andy defended him.

Tim crooked his finger and wiggled his hips the silly way their father did when he was feeling good, and Kate followed. Setting out on the dirt road—watching it sink down, watching it moisten and darken like a spreading stain in front of her—she found herself saying another Act of Contrition, for being ashamed of Tim all the time. For hoping nobody found out he was her brother.

The road swooped down through the marsh, and the light was bright again off the pools of water. But when they reached the woods on the other side, it wouldn't be a road anymore: it would narrow to a path. Usually Tim's long legs could walk twice as fast as Kate's, but now she felt him shortening his stride beside her.

"O my God," she repeated to herself, crossing over from road to path. "I am heartily sorry." Not only had Timmy tried to stop Andy, that day with the bobby pins, but he'd given her the name for her sin.

Kate stopped at the edge of the woods and turned around to watch the light surge one last time.

"C'mon Katie."

She and Andy and Tim had stayed in their rooms all afternoon that day Dolores found them in the bathroom, though Dolores had not told them to. Dolores didn't believe in silly punishments. The house was eerie and quiet without the sounds of their mother in the kitchen or bustling up and down the stairs.

Finally there was a step on the stairs, and then the clap of the back door opening and shutting. Kate saw from her bedroom window that Timmy was wandering around the back yard alone, tending to his shrines. He'd set three of them up in back: one in the flower beds, one under a pecan tree, one way back in the corner, hidden by tall grass from the neighbors' Protestant eyes.

Kate slipped down the stairs and tiptoed through the kitchen to follow Timmy. Her mother didn't seem to be anywhere: was it that bad, what they did?

Tim was standing by the far shrine, his back to her, when she ran up behind him. The blue plastic Virgin was his latest, and he'd hauled a ring of driveway stones to circle her, and woven a crown of pine and sweet grass for her head. The crown was falling apart.

"Hey Timmy," she said, and he looked around startled.
"What Kate?"

"Timmy Sister Patrick says Maria Goready—"

"Maria Goretti. St. Maria Goretti."

"St. Maria Goretti was killed because she wouldn't do something bad that a man wanted her to. What do you call that? That bad stuff?"

And Tim didn't even look away. He said: "You call it a sin against purity."

"Timmy is it a mortal sin?"

And when she stared down at her feet—dirty feet, in blue leather sandals—he said:

"Naw. Not until you're ten. Not for you and Andy. It just hurts our Blessed Mother."

And seeing the panic on her face, added:

"And it hurts *our* blessed mother," and pointed back at the house.

She followed his long pointing finger and saw Dolores's profile in the kitchen window, back where she belonged. Then she saw that Tim was smiling, and so she smiled too, and then Kate and her older brother were laughing like loons together.

In another minute she'd climbed into the swing and her big brother was pushing her, way too high, so high she thought she'd fall off the world, but she couldn't find the voice to tell him to stop. She could only laugh and swoop, up and down, laugh and swoop, and picture throwing up when she finally came down.

Now he was ahead of her: now Tim's pace had quickened, and she almost had to run through the path to catch him. Already through the woods she could see the antenna poised, a spire on that man's trailer.

"Tim. Wait up. Wait up."

He stopped and turned, one hand on his hip. He didn't look annoyed, but he said:

"C'mon Katie. We've got that movie to make."

So she hurried along behind him, and wondered if he knew he was just like Dolores sometimes, bustling around with his projects. Throwing one hand on his hip. Correcting her pronunciation of saints' names. Telling lies about mortal sins.

SAINTS

Dolores had decided, after all, not to pass by Rooney Realty on her way to see Dr. Black. Bill was jealous of the doctor (years ago she'd made the mistake of saying how much she liked him), and he was jumpy and acid on her appointment days. No need to rub salt in the wound. Dolores strolled along Lee Street instead of River.

The doctor was like Bill, actually, with his own thick accent and corny jokes—Dr. Black was the only man in town who could call her *sugar* and get away with it. He had a raucous laugh, and he made all the visits gossipy, even the gynecological ones. Especially the gynecological ones. He was a good old soul, and he'd delivered all four of her children, and someday soon she meant to prod him again about those segregated waiting rooms of his. Last time he said, "Dolores sugar, this is not New

York City. We all like the way we live here. You couldn't *pay* the nigras to sit in y'all's waiting room." She wouldn't be able to bring it up again until after she delivered the baby: men, even doctors, thought you went brain-dead when your belly got big.

Dolores pushed open the door to the white waiting room. The green plastic chairs stared up at her, empty, a sign as clear as a posted notice that the doctor was still at the hospital with the stuck baby. But she rang the buzzer for Sharmayne, anyway, to ask about the baby's progress. She'd been hoping for an omen.

Sharmayne, with her black beehive and bad skin and grape jelly lipstick, answered the inner door in full white uniform. Sharmayne always made Dolores feel a little shorter, or a shade paler: she could have been carrying water from the well on her head, the way she balanced the weight of her hairdo. She smiled her efficient smile at Dolores.

"He's *still* down to the hospital."

"That baby's not out yet?"

Sharmayne sneaked a pointed glance at Dolores's belly, but gave her the news anyway, with restrained relish:

"No ma'am, that little old thing didn't make it. Dr. Black's with the momma now. She's in pretty bad shape."

Dolores shuddered. "Anybody I know? You don't think of women having trouble with childbirth anymore, do you?"

Sharmayne shook her head, disappointed at Dolores. "No ma'am, I don't mean the momma's in danger. I wouldn't have told you *that.* I mean she's blue now she's lost the baby. After a C section too. The doctor called about an hour ago, after she woke up, said he best stay and hold her hand. Some colored woman from out by Frogmore? I don't guess you'd know her. The midwife drove her in when it started looking bad—I think she'd been in labor 'bout seventy-two hours."

"Three days!" Dolores found herself eyeing the stacks of

National Geographic and *Good Housekeeping* on Dr. Black's table, trying to imagine what words of comfort the doctor would summon up for a woman he'd never seen before he sliced her open and delivered her baby dead. She couldn't think of a single phrase that would do. Another little shudder, for this doomed baby and for Mrs. Rapple's doomed babies, shimmied down her spine.

"I'll work you in early tomorrow, Miz Rooney," Sharmayne said, her voice edging toward tart. "Only don't mention the baby to Dr. Black. He dudn't like me to tell pregnant ladies about the ones who don't make it. Course I know *you're* not going to get all nutsy about it. As many's you've had."

Sharmayne was perfectly right. No matter how bad an omen it was, Dolores Rooney wasn't nutsy at all when she went back out in the light, which had taken on a golden cast. She crossed River Street and stood on the bluff, just as she'd done that morning, and she watched the clouds billow up and drift over the water. It was the same sky the mother at Due East Memorial would see if she looked out her window: the same frothiness, the same effortless suspension. One of those skies she'd thought she'd see in Italy.

Dolores Rooney found herself, every now and again, staring up at the Due East sky for comfort. Growing up, she'd had to strain and crick her neck to see blue from the courtyard of an Inwood apartment building. But in Due East, the sky imposed itself: she'd learned that as soon as she moved down and accustomed herself to the hurricane watches all summer and fall. Not many hurricanes came ashore, but they were always threatening and teasing, and when they were passing close the sky demanded attention.

She hadn't liked the way it looked before Gracie, in '59, and though everybody in town was bragging about hurricane parties —"I bring the whole family down from Atlanta, and they get a real thrill riding it out. We drink champagne 'til the electricity goes, and then we tell ghost stories"—she'd watched with a chill. Twenty-four hours before Gracie, when they were still waiting to see if the storm wouldn't change her mind, the sky was an angelic pastel blue, a child playing so peacefully that the mother began to worry. By the time Due East knew Gracie wasn't just threatening (Huntley-Brinkley showed footage of the fighters at the Air Station clearing out for higher ground), the sky resembled an infant enraged at a late feeding, its little purple face puffing up. When she finally hit, her tantrum went on hour after hour. Gracie caved in the junior high school roof, and then she blew out the Wises' west wall, so you could see clear into their living room. She left the Rooneys' front yard a snake-filled swamp.

After it was over Dolores had waded through her driveway, picked her way around the lumberyard O'Connor Street had become, and walked down to the water's edge to stare up into the peculiar lavender sky, the very same sky that enclosed miles of destruction all around her. They'd watched the water seep through the kitchen door: if Gracie hadn't come calling at dead low tide, the Rooney house might have floated away. She'd thought her fear of the hurricane—her terrible resentment of God for torturing them with the wind's buffeting all those long hours and taking away even *Bill*'s gabbing—would last for days. But looking up at the strange sky, pastel again even behind the nasty dark clouds, Dolores Rooney had felt perfectly content. As weightless as the clouds. All around her mad birds perched on light poles and seawalls and chattered out their relief. The storm was over.

Just behind her a car horn tooted, and when she swung around she was startled to see a stranger pull his long black sedan over and jump out, waving his arms as if she were about to flee. He was familiar: white shirt, navy tie with awful zigzag red stripes, no jacket. Square black glasses.

Glasses flashing light like a television set. It was the New York *Times* reporter who'd sought her out that morning, and he'd caught her dreaming again.

"Mrs. Rooney?"

Dolores started again—she couldn't remember telling the reporter her name—but couldn't help smiling at his flapping arms and flapping tie. Tom Prince. They *must* have exchanged names.

"Mr. Prince."

The young man waved his hands yet again as he drew near. "Sorry to pester you twice in one day," he said, "but I've got this rented car out of Savannah and I'll be darned if I can figure out what's going on with it. The alternator light's blinking like a sign for the Kit-Kat Club, and now it's starting to shudder. I was about to pull up to the first stranger I passed, and then I recognized you standing here on the bluff. Don't suppose you know of a good mechanic in town?"

Dolores considered. It was one of her nightmares that her own car would break down, on the beach road or out by Yemassee at night, when she was alone.

"My neighbor's a mechanic," she said, and she made a point of smiling at young Mr. Prince. "At Hogan's gas station on Lady's Island."

"Which is just over this bridge?"

"That's right. You keep straight on the beach road and you'll see it on your left. It's a—what's the one with the orange and blue?"

"Gulf."

"Right. It's a Gulf station. The mechanic's name is Rapple. He seems a decent sort."

The reporter smiled his thanks and turned to his rented car.

But Dolores called him back: "Only, it's getting on to five o'clock. And even if he's there, how will you get back to town if he needs to work on it?"

Now Tom Prince considered. "How far are we talking about?"

"Oh, maybe two miles."

He laughed. "Jeepers, I walk two miles just getting to the subway and back every day."

The man said *jeepers*. She couldn't even remember the last time Tim said *jeepers*—when he was ten?

"But you might break down," she said, "and get stuck by the side of the road. Look—"

and she stopped because this was not the sort of thing she did; she'd spent a lifetime in Due East avoiding just this sort of offer to young men with dirty-blond crew cuts. But there was something touching after all about the way he said *jeepers*, something sweet about hearing a voice that wasn't slurring at the end of every word—

"look, why don't I pick up my car and follow you out there? I can introduce you to Mr. Rapple. And if he's not there, why you can come back to my house and wait for him to show up next door."

"I couldn't put you to all that trouble."

She spoke to him the way she'd speak to Tim, or to Andy: "No trouble at all. You need the car to get to Parris Island, don't you? Besides, you can tell me about the trial. I'm hungry for conversation."

After he'd opened the passenger door for her, she grimaced at that last line—*hungry for conversation?* How could you reveal that much of yourself to a total stranger?

"My husband parks the car on River Street. An old blue station wagon," she told him, and looked sideways at his cheek, which was, just as she'd thought, dotted with irregular stubble.

Too young to even have a decent beard. Face to face in a dark car, though, Tom Prince was not so gawky as he'd been out in the sunlight. He had a good firm jaw and a small straight nose and, like most men, he looked more sure of himself behind the wheel. He stretched his long legs out and wiggled his shoulders until they settled.

But there was no sign of the Rooney car on River Street, and Dolores saw by the bank clock that it was five past five—unless he was showing property, Bill made a ritual of locking up as the big clock struck the hour.

"Not a sign of it," she said. "We'll have to pick it up at home. But I'm only a few blocks away." Bill would probably insist on driving Tom Prince himself, and be annoyed with her for having made the offer just as he was opening up his pre-dinner beer.

"I really feel bad about all this trouble."

"Nonsense. Just go straight through this light. You make the left at the end of River Street, and then down two blocks to O'Connor." They were coming into sight of the Golden Apple, and Dolores saw at once that Tom Prince hadn't driven back through this part of town yet. He perked up, and reminded her of a dog on the trail of a new scent. One of those shaggy Walt Disney animals.

"What's that?" he said, pointing. "Hotel?"

"It's a restaurant, mostly. It has a few rooms, but I think you have to book them five years in advance. Or be somebody special. I'm surprised the *Times* didn't put you up there."

He snorted. "Looks a little pricey for the *Times*. They count how many cups of coffee I drink in a day. That's some yellow, though. That's some yellow they've painted that place, Mrs. Rooney."

"Dolores."

He smiled a little smile. "Dolores. I'm Tom."

"Right."

Tom was turning down O'Connor Street now, with a flourish, and Dolores was conscious for the first time in a long time how the street must look to someone who'd never seen it before. It was a hodgepodge—the crumbling back side of the slave quarters; the little pond with the cattails; the big white Percy house, a sentry standing face-out to guard the end of the block. The other houses lining the north side of O'Connor Street— hers, the Jacksons', the Rapples'—were ordinary old houses, smaller and more likely to need a new coat of paint. They didn't have what the Percys and the Mansards and the Dinkinses had: they didn't have gardens set between brick walkways and they didn't have two floors of verandas clinging to the front façade and they didn't have shutters painted Charleston green, green the color of a nighttime swamp. The shabbier houses had been built on the Point as an afterthought. She and Bill hadn't hired anybody to paint *their* shutters since Maggie's Confirmation, when they'd offered to serve the bishop and the old pastor, Father Sweeney, their Confirmation night supper. That would have been eight years ago, and in eight years the salt air had scraped away at the house until it looked as smudged and neglected as a child with busy parents.

"We had a bad hurricane a few years back," she said. "Everybody had to use the insurance money for roofs—I believe I read that ninety-five percent of the roofs in town were damaged —so anything *under* the roofs has been left a little shabby."

Tom Prince sighed. "It's just right. Just shabby enough. I can sure see the attraction of this place."

Why had she apologized? She waved him into the curving driveway, but there was no sign of the station wagon. "Oh dear. I'm sorry—he must be out showing some property."

"Well, see there." Tom Prince braked the black sedan directly in front of her steps and threw his right hand out, palm open, all in one smooth motion. "Must be a sign that you've gone to too much trouble as is. Let me see you off here. With thanks for the effort."

Dolores couldn't say why this Tom Prince seemed more intelligent this afternoon than he had in the morning—the way he threw his palm open? or the way he said *With thanks for the effort?*—but the sight of her empty house egged her on.

"I just don't feel right," she said, "about sending you out all alone to Lady's Island at this hour. Why don't we call the station and make sure somebody's out there?"

He turned the ignition off. "All right. I won't say no to that."

She let him come round and open the car door for her; waiting, she eyed her own bare freckled legs and wondered what the reporter would make of them. She was the only woman in Due East to go without stockings in November (sometimes, seeing the scarves and gloves and long rayon sleeves in church in August, she thought she was the only woman in Due East to go without stockings all summer long). If her children had been home, Tim would have been hanging out one of the upstairs windows, watching a stranger sneak a peek at his mother's pale naked legs.

Inside, she didn't even offer him a cup of coffee—Bill would be home any minute. She handed over the thin little phone book, and Tom Prince, after he laughed at the size of it, cased the kitchen while he ran his finger down the numbers. Now that he was eyeing her cabinets and counters, Dolores saw the kitchen the way she'd seen O'Connor Street: the way the breakfast dishes lingered, chipped and encrusted, in the kitchen sink. The way Tim's violin case sat on the counter, wide open. Tim hadn't rosined the bow in a week. A honey jar next to the sink trailed wormy golden globules.

"I'll call," she said. "What's the number?"

She thought it was Mr. Rapple who answered the phone out at Hogan's—a man's voice mumbled: "Gulf"—but then she was cut off. She *thought* he'd said Gulf. She shrugged and smiled an apology at Tom and dialed again.

This time the ringing clicked off before she made the connection, and then an angry high-pitched bark sounded.

"Strange," she said, and held the receiver out so that Tom Prince could hear.

"Sure you don't have your phone tapped?" He grinned.

"Tapped? You mean wiretapped?"

The grin widened. "The F.B.I. have any reason to listen in on you? Or Hogan Gulf?"

Dolores smiled too. "I'm pretty sure they're not interested in Hogan Gulf. But sometimes my husband gets nervous *somebody* from the government's going to ring the front doorbell."

Tom perked up, doglike again. "No kidding. You involved in politics?"

She shook her head: "Just the Democrats. My *heart*'s with the civil rights movement, but I don't do nearly enough. Oh, I've got a million excuses."

"No kidding," he said again. "Well, I was just joking about the F.B.I. I'm sure they're not interested in Due East Democrats. They save the wiretapping and stuff like that for the big boys. For Malcolm X and Martin Luther King."

Now Dolores felt herself perking up. "You don't mean to say they listen in on Martin Luther King's phone calls. They wouldn't dare."

Tom Prince looked gleeful enough to slap his knee, but he held back and brought her the open phone book. "Sure they'd dare."

"Oh Lord, I guess I've been down South too long. I'm getting so naïve."

"You and everybody else," Tom said. "We're all too naïve. They say Hoover's got a file on the President."

A reporter for the *Times* should know what he was talking about—she *had* been in Due East for too long. In college she would have made it her business to know about this wiretapping business. Now she did her best to keep her eyes from widening like a girl's.

"Here, let me try that number." He took the phone right out of her hand, dialed, and held the receiver out. The same barking. "You suppose this is a sign?"

Dolores smiled. "It's a sign I'd better drive over to Hogan Gulf with you. Make sure you have a way back to town. Make sure Mr. Rapple hasn't been murdered over there."

"Don't tell me you get murders in Due East. I mean, outside of Parris Island."

"Oh, I don't mean it about Mr. Rapple. But sure we get murders! Had an ax murder last year—in fact, it was the other Gulf station, the one downtown. I suppose that's what made the words come out of my mouth."

"Such a civilized-looking town. Ax murders?"

Dolores shrugged. "And every few years there's a rape down some country road: you know, high school kids are out parking, and someone glides up to the car, out of the dark of night. Holds a knife to the boy's throat, and tells him to get out of the car."

"Someone Negro?"

She gave him a sharp look, but he stared back with a blank reporter's face, his dogginess vanished.

"Well," she said, "those are the ones you hear about. Naturally. But the truth is coloreds in Due East have more to fear from whites. My boys come home from the high school repeating what other boys—oh, this is really dreadful, I don't believe it happens, just teenage talk—"

Tom Prince watched her.

"—just what other boys say. The ones who've grown up hunting, with guns always around. Sometimes they brag the way boys do and they say they're going out over the weekend to get themselves some niggers. I don't think that really *happens*, in Due East." She was embarrassed she'd even told such a tale: Bill said she made the children fearful clinging creatures, giving credence to such nonsense. "How many times did I hear the word *jigaboo* on the streets of Inwood?" he would boom. "There's no more prejudice here than there is up there, only here people know what the rules are! We don't deal in that New York hypocrisy!"

Tom stared down at his shoes. "I wasn't any too keen on this assignment. No predicting how the locals are going to feel about the New York *Times.*" He looked up at her again and smiled. "But Due East isn't at all what I thought—"

"No," Dolores said. "No, it's not. Actually—but maybe you know this already—actually they say Martin Luther King might make a visit down here. Not that we'd read about it in the *Courier.* They squeeze that stuff onto a separate page for colored people. Half a page. And they certainly won't want to give any extra space if Martin Luther King shows up at the Friends Center."

"I've been meaning to run out there and look around. I thought maybe I could work a sidebar in. But how the heck am I going to make the connection between a Marine court-martial and a Quaker school for Negroes?"

How the heck.

"It's more than a *sidebar.* They've got the farmers starting co-ops," Dolores said. "They train midwives."

He smiled, indulgent of her passion. "You must spend a lot of time out there." She could picture him, in a few minutes, pulling out a notebook to take down all the background information she could provide him. This morning on the bluff she would have put him in his early twenties: Mrs. Rapple's age. Now she would say he was thirty.

"I drive out there from time to time. When they have a talk or an open house. But it's . . . a little awkward, to tell you the truth. I mean. They don't need *me*. They've had plenty of Quakers come down over the years—they don't want any more white women poking their noses in, I'll bet." And then she added: "I've never seen Dr. King."

"That would be something."

"That *would* be something," she said. "You've never met him?"

Tom Prince looked down at her through his glasses again. "No, I've never met him. To tell you the truth, Mrs. Rooney—Dolores—I'm just graduating from Metro to National. This is my first honest-to-God on-the-road assignment, and you know, I think they would have had a stringer covering it if I hadn't made such a pest of myself."

"Congratulations."

He waved her off. "Oh," he said. "I'm like you. I should be doing more. I should be quitting my job and joining the Peace Corps. But I'm too darn comfortable. On my way up at the New York *Times*."

"Surely you can do tremendous good with that!"

He dismissed her with a wave of his hand, and now he didn't look boyish in the least. "You get lazy," he said. *"I* get lazy, anyway. It's funny you brought up Martin Luther King, though. That's who I think about when I think about what I *should* be doing. The man puts us all to shame."

"The March on Washington."

He nodded, and a droning memory buzzed.

The nod. Walker Mansard. She would say *Henry Wallace*, and Walker would bow his head in silent communion.

Tom Prince was still nodding. "To tell you the truth, I was anticipating rednecks down here at the trial. I didn't think I'd be in Due East, South Carolina, talking to a white woman who admired Martin Luther King."

"I think he's a saint," she said, and then could have swallowed the words back whole. Bill always said that she couldn't stop *blithering*.

"I don't know if he's a saint," Tom Prince said. "But he's a good man."

If she wasn't careful, she'd have herself convinced that she hadn't had a talk like this in fifteen years. And that wasn't true: her own children, Maggie and Tim and Andy, even Katie, could have been carrying on this very same conversation with her. For all she knew, that dentist in the discussion group was interested in civil rights. And Father Berkeley tuned in on what she had to say. Mae Pryor, at party meetings. Dr. Black, pretending to prejudices he didn't even hold.

She realized in the stretching silence that she was rubbing her belly with both hands, circling and spiraling inward, a motion she wouldn't usually be making until the last months of a pregnancy. And here she was, a month away from the quickening at least, stroking her little bulge. Like a guilty child, she thrust her hands behind her back.

"You're pregnant, aren't you?"

Amazing how this young man had aged standing in her kitchen. Amazing how she had thought him awkward and gawky at first.

He beamed while she reddened: "I didn't see that at first, you know, this morning. In fact, I thought I might ask you out to dinner."

"I'm glad you didn't," she said. "My children would never forgive me if I started going out on *dates.*"

"How many children?"

"Four."

"Four! And this will be five."

"This will be five."

"You don't look nearly old enough," he said; and now *she* smiled so he would see that she was grateful for that last line. Not that she believed it. Anybody who'd seen her in the sunlight had seen how deep the crow's-feet went now.

"You must be Irish then," he said, "with five children and that red hair."

"Well of course."

"You know, some people think the birth rate's going to go way up, with Kennedy in the White House."

"I don't think my pregnancy's a result of the election."

Now the reporter was embarrassed: Bill said she was as snooty as a Mother Superior sometimes. Sharp as a serpent's tooth.

"I didn't mean that."

"No, I know you didn't. But it's funny, isn't it, it's my parents who were really *Irish*—my father came over as a boy—and they didn't have a big family. I was an only child."

"Me too," he said. "Not Irish. An only child."

And then it was apparent—the two of them standing the way they were, with no place to put their hands and nowhere for the conversation to go but down, down into the intimacy of childhood or belief—that it was getting late.

Tom Prince checked his wristwatch (big and black; *it* looked like a TV screen too) and feigned surprise. "I better get a move on," he said.

"Let me drive on out there with you. I feel obligated, now I've kept you so long."

"Oh no, you don't. You didn't keep *me*. This has been a pleasure, Mrs. Rooney."

"Dolores."

"Dolores. Really, I've enjoyed the talk. Haven't enjoyed a talk so much since I got to Due East!—oh my God, have you ever tried to conduct an interview with a drill instructor? Yes *sir*. No *sir*. Anyway, you'll have four children running in here any minute looking for their dinners. I'd better get out of your way. I can't even begin to imagine what it's like, with a big family."

"Let me run out there with you, and you can stay for supper. You can see what it's like." She panicked the minute she'd said it: she'd been meaning to stretch a pound of ground round steak into meat loaf, and Bill complained long and loud when she crumbled cornflakes into it. There was nothing but beer for him to drink.

"It's a nice offer," he said. "Tell you the truth, it's the first home-cooked meal I've been offered since I landed in Due East. Will you let me buy you a bottle of wine?"

He could have said a pound of caviar. There hadn't been a bottle of wine at the Rooney dinner table since the last time Father Berkeley brought one over.

"It's a deal. But we have to hurry. Can't buy wine after sundown."

He laughed out loud when she said that, and she laughed too. From the time she'd first come to Due East, buying a drink was as complicated as local politics. Who got served whiskey in the Golden Apple? What time was sundown?

And buying a drink had been crucial when they first came to Due East: Bill was used to the clubs. She'd tapered off—she was pregnant then and had to slow down—but Bill couldn't go a day without. He wasn't one of those dramatic alcoholics who had to have a drink in the middle of the day. He didn't black out and forget what jokes they'd told at the K. of C. He just had to have his beer at night. And he was a big man. Four or five beers slipped right into his pocket.

"I'll get my handbag," she said, and scooped it up in the hallway. Tom Prince put a hand to her shoulder while he held the front door for her. They could have been a married couple stepping out together.

The sun wouldn't go down for another forty minutes, but it seemed to Dolores that the light was going fast in the shadows under the oak trees. Standing next to a New Yorker in the driveway, she found herself picturing city sidewalks in the twilight: a long stretch of upper Broadway in early evening, the light over New York dwindling as it dwindled in Due East. Tom opened the car door for her, and she slid into the front seat, watching him watch her swing her bare legs.

"You look a little dreamy," he said, starting up. "Hope I'm not taking you on a fool's errand."

"Oh," she said. "I'm just relaxing." But as they drove off in the black sedan she leaned forward, not back—it was what she'd been thinking all day, that it was strange she should be so *dreamy*—and though Tom Prince was telling her about the trial she wasn't really listening to him.

She was listening to traffic. She was standing on the sidewalk on that stretch of Broadway that had appeared to her in the driveway, and now she reached out for her cousin Tim, who would have stepped into traffic before he'd have taken her hand. He was humiliated to be walking with her; he was using his own right hand to tug tight blue uniform pants away from his crotch.

She was ten years old, and the light was fading. Her mother sent her next door to fetch Tim because it wasn't right for a little girl to walk into a bar unescorted to fetch her father home. Rose could not accustom herself to legalized liquor, but at least Andrew wasn't slipping off to a speakeasy downtown anymore. At least the bars kept him away from the docks, where he used to think he could cadge a flask of Bushmill's.

And kept him back in the neighborhood, where Rose had the bright idea to send Dolores after him. The faster Tim loped on ahead, the closer Dolores shadowed. The A train was still spilling out, and Tim pulled away, trying to lose himself in the crowd: "I don't know why *I* have to go. He's not *my* father." Tim's father was long gone.

But Dolores's father was still hanging around, in those days, and Rose McGillicudhy discovered that sending Tim and Dolores was a foolproof way of getting Andrew home for his dinner. After a week doing the errand, Tim walked at Dolores's pace; and after a month he wasn't embarrassed to be seen with her. He quizzed her on her catechism: it was Confirmation year. "You've got to be prepared!" her cousin said. "Or the bishop won't slap you."

When they reached the dark glass with the gold lettering that said

LENEHAN'S

Timmy opened the door for her—a good parochial school boy— and they let their eyes adjust to shafts of light, light spilling down from dusty white lamps, light swirling up the mists of cigarette smoke. Together they stared at the sawdust on the floor (going to Lenehan's was a little like going to the circus) and then Tim pushed her forward to her father's tall wooden stool, its seat worn white under Andrew McGillicudhy's big backside. Her father always sat at the same stool.

Dolores brushed against her father's leg, wordless, and he feigned great surprise at seeing her there: "Mother of Mercy! Do they let little girls into places like this?" Then he hoisted her up on the stool next to his, and she clung to the brass rail while he curled his big hand around to brush the hair from her eyes.

The palm he used was calloused, but his cuticles had all been pushed back (oh he spent hours in the bathroom seeing to his hands) and he trimmed his nails so meticulously that you would have sworn he went to a manicurist. Black hair sprouted up over his knuckles, coarse curly wires, and sometimes Dolores put her own small hand on his and pressed both hands—the manicured and the chewed—down on her cheek and held them there.

Settled. Her father called Tim over and they drank one last round—White Rock ginger ales, with speared cherries, for Tim and Dolores—while Andrew showed off in his booming voice, educating the bartender on the rights and duties of the working-man.

"Murdering Micks," he'd say. "I'm ashamed sometimes to call myself one of them. They've all gone for cops when they should be out striking like good Wobblies."

"For God's sake Andrew." The bartender had heard it all before. He winked at Dolores. "There's something *unorganized* about the Wobblies that doesn't appeal to an Irishman."

"Oh and it's a shame too isn't it. Unorganized. Were we organized in 1916? Or were we willing to let our passions carry us along?" He straightened his shoulders to recite.

> *"We know their dream; enough*
> *To know they dreamed and are dead;*
> *And what if excess of love*
> *Bewildered them till they died?"*

He swung his arm out to indicate he was overcome and could not go on, but the truth of it was that he didn't know more than a few lines of any poem. He always chose the lines well, though, Dolores had to admit. "A terrible beauty is born," she whispered, and he squeezed her shoulder tight. He saw to it that *she* memorized the whole thing.

"Easter 1916," Andrew sighed. Of course he'd been long out of Ireland by 1916: he left as a baby of two, and any brogue that slipped out after an afternoon of drinking was strictly affected. "Now enough of such seriousness. Did you hear this one, John, about the girl who leaves Cork for Liverpool?"

"A thousand times, Andrew. Why don't you tell it for the rest of the patrons then?"

The blowsy brunette on the other side touched his hand. "Go on, I haven't heard it."

"All right then. See, there's a poor girl in Cork City, the eldest of thirteen, who sees that her family can't afford to feed her anymore. So she sets out for Liverpool, her heart aching already for dear old Ireland, and she finds that the picture's pretty bleak in England too. There's no work, she doesn't even have the boat fare home, and she's starving. Finally, in desperation—knowing no other way to save herself—she offers her services to a madam. (Close your ears there, Tim and Lorey.)

"Well, she makes a good living as a working girl, a fine comfortable living, and after a year she wants nothing more than to go home to see Ireland and spread some of the wealth around her family. Off she sets. Her old mother meets her at the train station, and at the sight of that decent honorable woman, the poor girl, in all her finery, bursts into tears.

" 'What is it?' says her mother. 'It can't be that bad now.'

" 'Oh, Mother,' says the girl. 'Oh, it's very bad indeed. I've become a prostitute.' And she wails louder than before.

"Her mother turns gray as ash. 'Sweet suffering mother of Jesus,' she says. 'Tell me, daughter, that I didn't hear you right.'

"The girl is keening into the night. 'It's true, Mother, it's true. I was starving and I became a *prostitute.*'

"Immediately the mother bursts into a merry laugh and pulls her daughter close. 'Is that all?' she says. 'You had me very worried there, my darling girl. I thought you said you'd become a *Protestant.*' "

The girl on Andrew's right wiped mascara-blackened tears off her cheeks. "Oh, you're a card," she gasped, and Andrew, in order to make a triumphal exit, left his drink half finished on the bar. Half-finished drink, half-smoked cigarettes in the ashtrays at home, half a poem memorized. For Dolores's room he'd made a lovely set of bookshelves, half sanded.

Andrew was an electrician and a union man, of course. Somehow (and the somehow was charm, Rose always said) he had not missed a day of work during the Depression. He loved the Wobblies and the I.R.A. and Franklin D. Roosevelt and, unlike everyone else in Inwood and Blessed Sacrament parish, he saw no harm whatsoever in the communists, and no contradictions in his passions. "You have to have a big heart," he told his daughter. "You have to love them all. Anybody for the workingman. One and all."

He liked to spend his lunch hour in Union Square when he could, and came home once with a copy of the *Catholic Worker*, which gave Rose the heebie-jeebies. So he took Dolores and Tim downtown to see a Catholic Worker soup kitchen—"I won't have you cowering like your mother"—and they stood on the sidewalk across Mott Street watching the down-and-outs file in for a meal. "Now *that*'s the work a church should be doing," Andrew told them. "You remember that the next time you hear the Rosary beads clacking on into the night. The next time you see the old ladies mooning over the holy cards. You remember there are Catholic *workers* too." Dolores asked if they shouldn't go in to help out, but her father said oh no, *that* wasn't necessary. They had plenty of big strapping single young people for those jobs. And then he had Tim escort Dolores home, while he went off for a drink.

Andrew's drinking consumed Rose more than it did him. He only stopped at the bar every evening—but Dolores's mother offered prayers at daily Mass, at the Rosary Society on Tuesday nights, at the Legion of Mary on Thursdays, at her dusting and her sweeping and her dishwashing. Prohibition ended in New York, but it was still effective in Rose's apartment, on the pastor's advice. Andrew didn't even object: there was more room in Lenehan's Bar, anyway, for an expansive man.

Over the years his hours at Lenehan's lengthened, but then her mother's resignation lengthened too. Having Andrew out of the house every night gave Rose extra time to visit with her sister, and she was down at Blessed Sacrament four nights a week, often as not bringing Dolores with her. After she'd stopped sending Dolores and Tim to fetch Andrew home (Dolores reached an age to be the one who was embarrassed, and Tim was off with his high school Sodalities), her father made his own way back to the apartment, and long past twilight. Sometimes when Dolores was wakened by the sound of his key scuttling in the lock she could hear her mother offering raucous prayers of angry thanksgiving in the bedroom. But by morning her parents were once more two cheerful souls: her mother rose at five-thirty to make her father a decent breakfast, and sometimes they reached out and squeezed the little rolls of flesh that had accumulated on one another's middles.

Her mother didn't breathe a word of fear about other women until Andrew started going to Mass. Dolores was twelve by then, and in her lifetime had never known her father to strain for more than the most casual attendance at church ("Oh it's pay pray and obey: a church for old ladies"). Suddenly, though, he walked to Blessed Sacrament with them every Sunday and stumbled through his rusty Latin:

Mea culpa
Mea culpa
Mea maxima culpa.

His eyes were watery at Communion time, but he didn't receive. When the pastor announced that he needed more men of the parish to sign up for ushering, Andrew was the first in line. Rose asked her daughter if it didn't seem a little strange, at this time of his life, if she'd noticed anything unusual about her father. Dolores said she'd noticed that he stopped parting his hair on the side.

After the eleven o'clock Mass she stayed to help him stack the missals. Andrew wore his blue serge suit, shiny at the cuffs, and now he combed his black hair straight back with brilliantine. Sometimes, if he stood under the light angling through a stained-glass window, she could see a red patch of hair sprouting up from his widow's peak. That coxcomb on his black head was his connection with her.

He told them after one of those ushering stints.

He walked Dolores back home and on the way he picked up a half dozen sticky buns to have with a pot of tea. Not a word of warning, and he made it a full confession, right in front of his daughter: he was in love with another woman. He made leaving them sound sacrificial—something about having their welfare in mind, not letting his two sweethearts go on living with such a miserable low scummy creature—and he cried profusely. Dolores held a sticky bun in one hand and considered hurling it at him, but her mother stared out the kitchen window.

"So that's why you came back to Mass," she said. "I suspected as much."

Her father sobbed.

"We just genuflected at the altar. Don't you know it's a MORTAL SIN?" The sticky bun crumbled in Dolores's fist.

"Lorey." Her mother's voice was blank and soft. "You can't talk to your dad that way, no matter what he's gone and done."

It seemed that the other woman had written her mother. Rose had had months to brace herself. And a year later, her mother confessed to Dolores the relief she'd felt when those months of waiting, those months of walking to Mass with Andrew, the warning letter smoldering in her pocketbook, were over.

"Oh Lorey," she said. "There had to be a woman. All those hours he was gone. Didn't you suspect it too, now honestly?"

No, I didn't see it. "It must have been *excess of love,*" she said, but her mother did not know the line.

"And I never cared for those political harangues. Any man courting communists and anarchists is bound to be courting other sorts of immorality! But he's been good with the money, Lorey, you have to admit. Pretty good anyway."

Dolores stared hard at her mother.

"Oh, but he was a handsome man." Her mother brushed away one of the tears she allowed herself on Sundays only. "A big good-looking Irishman. It's pathetic, really. The way men think they have to do that. Chase after women. There's never a moment's peace for them—I thank the Lord I was born a woman and not slave to *that.* It's the drink of course."

And, seeing her daughter's face:

"It's like they've got ants in their pants, huh, Lorey?" She laughed out loud, and busied herself clearing the table. "They can't stay in any one place too long. Don't you worry. He'll be moving on from that girlfriend's too. Like as not he'll be back here asking when his suit'll be pressed for Mass."

Ants in their pants. Her father sent her a scrawled and grimy note asking her would she like to come to Schrafft's with him and Lorene. He'd buy her an ice-cream sundae, he said, or whatever she liked. Dolores mailed the pieces of the note back to him, thinking of the times he lost his temper and threatened her with the back of his hand, but by then he'd moved out of Lorene's, and the letter—the pieces—came back to her. The checks stopped altogether.

She was finishing high school when her father died of a heart attack at Lenehan's. Her mother swore she hadn't known he was back in the neighborhood. Twice a day, for months after, Dolores passed the bar and tried not to stare in through the dark dusty window. It was hard to remember what he'd looked like, how broad his face had been, whether his chin had been pointed. She was only really sure of that patch of red hair in the light.

When the union called her mother to come down, Rose met Lorene and Andrew's next wife, Patti.

Rose told Dolores that her mouth had fallen open wide enough to fit a cabbage inside. "Wife?" Rose would repeat the whole scene for anybody who cared to listen. "I'm his wife. We were never divorced. We're *Catholic,* you know."

And Lorene and Patti, having no idea, were blank with rage. "Very attractive," Rose said with dignity. "But cheap. *Dyed hair,* the two of them." Andrew had married them all—he'd been married to three women at once—but of course Rose got the money. And there were no other children.

Dolores was the only child.

Her mother said he was a good man, after all, not to put her through the agony of a divorce. He was somebody *trying* to be good. Rose had a Mass for the Dead said—they were too late hearing the news to bury him—and a line from the service, like a radio jingle, stuck in Dolores's head and repeated itself for days: *My heart like ashes,* was the line. *My heart like ashes, crushed and dried.* Crushed and dried and, she would have added, ready for a good stiff drink. Ready for a double to fling at his grave.

Dolores looked across the car at the stranger with the black glasses, and saw that they were already crossing the bridge. Tom Prince had stopped trying to talk to her and was staring ahead at the Lady's Island Road, a road that pushed through the water and then curved around it, like a father's hand pushing his daughter's hair back off her cheek. It wasn't yet time for the sun to set, but it seemed to Dolores Rooney that the dusk was already swooping down through the trees.

◻︎   ◻︎   ◻︎

Bill Rooney knew he'd forgiven Dolores (before she ever knew in what contempt he'd held her) when he found himself humming "Take the A Train" and tapping out its sway while he tidied up the office. Coramae Ruttledge had said on River Street: "If that house is near as sweet as I remember it, Bill, you've got yourself a sale. Maisie's getting married, did I tell you? Now don't look at me that way, I *know* she's way too young, but she's not listening to her momma, and her daddy and I figure we best set her up just as comfortable as we can. Might as well have 'em in a good house—that first year of marriage can be a living hell!"

And Bill, walking with his arm around her, had squeezed her shoulder tight in agreement with her last words, even though she was dead wrong. *His* first year of marriage had been heaven, even if his paradise wasn't eternal.

Coramae was as manipulative and flirtatious as a woman got, but he still admired the studied delicacy of every word she spoke. Look at the way she had outfitted herself to walk down River Street on the day before the whole town would know what sort of trouble Maisie was in: jaunty little rose-colored suit, the skirt just a tad shorter than the usual Due East matron's skirt; kicky little high heels; her cheeks rouged up just past the point of natural but not all the way to theatrical. She had even lined her eyes in black, the way you saw skinny English fashion models on magazine covers doing it now. There was something about Coramae's look that was old-fashioned and forward-looking at the same time, and the perfumed gloss of her sun-streaked hair and her walk and her words tweaked him with the fleeting regret that Dolores didn't put a little more *style* into her dressing or her hair. That decade-old French twist. Dolores's ghostly white legs, often as not bare. Other women shopped for stockings in shades like Suntan or Palm Beach Bronze.

But he wasn't mad at Dolores anymore. If anything, he couldn't wait to lock up and get home to celebrate (oh now Dolores, *don't* start in on counting your chickens). She had been putting up a good cool bluff about the money—infuriating little speeches about lilies of the field, about how *rich* her family made her feel—but she made a beeline for the books every night. She'd lighten up when she heard about a good sale. A big commission would put the color back in her cheeks.

And it wasn't just one sale anyway: something like this, like running into Coramae after he'd talked to her on the phone, was more in the line of an omen, a sign. He allowed himself a three-second visualization of a baby, but it gave him a pain in the small of his back, as usual. He could smell the diaper pail, but he couldn't recall a single word he and Dolores had exchanged about this child who would be making its appearance in six months.

Four fifty-five. He was scrupulous about not locking up early (way too easy to sink into the quagmire of laziness when you ran your own business), and he had five minutes to do hip-swaying variations on "Take the A Train" with pencil as drumstick and desk as drum. "A Train" had been a standard for the Carolina Gamecocks. (They'd named themselves after the university team, not because they were athletic—no musician Bill ever knew was athletic—but because they thought the word *gamecock* had sexy overtones without being too tacky. *Every* musician Bill knew thought in sexual terms.)

He dropped the pencil and let his hands range over the desktop. At home he might go weeks without playing, but then he had his older boy to do his practicing for him. Tim knew every song in the Gamecocks' book, but if his father gave him a word of advice—"Slow down Tim, we've got too many speedboats out in the bay as it is"—the boy would stomp off from the piano in a rage. What did Timmy want, unlimited praise? He was a fifteen-year-old boy, trying to play a man's tunes, songs swinging with a sexuality that was only now just pushing through the surface in Tim. Maybe he could flutter through his thirty-second notes, but he couldn't drive out a four-four bopping rhythm yet.

He, Bill, evidently didn't have Dolores's gift for criticism—she gave the children, all of them, long lists of pointers about their playing, and they never stomped off. But her words were cool and technical. He got steamed, telling Tim what was lacking, but shouldn't you ought to? With music? Thank the Lord Tim had calmed down, and it didn't come to grappling anymore. The shoving matches that drove Dolores crazy—that made her actually threaten to leave him—were in the early days.

He sat, now, at the piano-desk and remembered Tim at seven or eight, already leaving his sister Maggie behind in the piano dust. They couldn't afford to pay Lydia Mansard for two children's music lessons, so Bill made the most monumental mistake of his fatherhood and decided to teach Timmy himself. The little boy (gawky-looking even then, his shoelaces always untied and his hand stuck in his pants) used to fume at some simpleton piece Bill had him play over and over (what was it now? The cool elegance of the minuet from *Don Giovanni*, de-frilled for a child's little hands, suddenly stepped into Rooney Realty on buckled shoes.) Tim, unable to visualize a minuet, had whizzed through that one. Bill remembered one night's endless lesson, remembered making a fool of himself *showing* the boy a minuet, remembered telling his son—who was obviously ready for harder pieces but already a wild man who *needed* the discipline, for God's sake—to count the time, slow down, count-count-count. When he insisted, after twenty minutes of this, that his son play it *one more time, counting, for the love of the sweet baby Jesus,* Tim rose from the piano so fast that the bench overturned.

He *had* shoved his son too hard for doing that—he'd gone to shake him by the shoulders and had somehow kneed him in the gut. He could still remember Tim's look of little-boy horror, the slow motion of it spreading down from his white eyebrows to the thin strip of his mouth as he regained his breath, the one thing that day that had finally slowed down. But Dolores (who rushed into the room, a police-spy mother) acted as if he'd beaten the child up, when he had only had the bad luck to connect with his seven-year-old in the solar plexus and take his breath away. Did Dolores think he'd slept any better than she had (on the floor, in Maggie's bedroom, for crying out loud, as if *that* sort of statement to her own children was any less vicious)? His act had been spontaneous, when she'd had all night to reconsider hers.

A sigh (but only a small swift one. It was depressed men who squeezed deep self-pitying sighs out of their chest bellows, and he was not a depressed man anymore.) Four fifty-nine. Four fifty-nine and thirty seconds. Four fifty-nine and fifty seconds.

The bank clock chimed, and Bill Rooney turned his key in the Rooney Realty lock. Heading for the car, he thought he might celebrate with a six-pack of ale (a step up from beer); but then it occurred to him that Dolores would really be tickled with a bottle of wine. Champagne? No, that *would* be counting your chickens. Wine would be the ticket. Wine would get Dolores sleepy enough to fall in bed with her husband at a reasonable hour for once. She wouldn't have books to pore over until midnight tonight.

Down at Monck's Liquor Store, at the end of River Street, Bill settled on Christian Brothers sherry. Luke Monck only had ten brands of wine to choose between, the most expensive a French wine which would have brought his father some pleasure but left Bill indifferent, the cheapest a bottle of Richards Peach Wine, one of South Carolina's own. In between were the sherry and the Manischewitz, and Bill knew which one would bring on Luke Monck's joshing. Still, he felt fussy buying a bottle of sherry and made it clear that it was his wife he was buying for— "If it was up to me I'd be coming home with a fifth of Jack Daniel's." Luke Monck smiled an irritating knowing smile and wondered aloud if the Christian Brothers were monks.

"Like my family," he added, tickled with himself.

Luke Monck was a cretin. Bill said he didn't think they were monks, but you could count on the Christian part, by golly. Anyway, he said, you had to ask the women about that business of which wineries were run by monks. Just the sort of thing women liked to keep track of.

"Now my wife, Luke," Bill said, "she could tell you whether a Dominican likes pickles with his meals, or why a Franciscan wears sandals on his feet. Before I could teach my boys how to tote up a batting average she'd taught 'em which priests wore skirts and which priests wore beanies and which priests wore jockstraps."

"Which priests wear jockstraps, Bill?"

"The ones at Notre Dame and Holy Cross!"

Luke Monck, always polite, slapped his counter. "That's some religion y'all got there, Bill. Some *powrfl* religion."

Bill always knew when to tread lightly in Due East, and he backed out the door with a good hearty wave. "Got a lot of respect for *your* church too, Luke," he said, though he didn't have the vaguest idea whether Luke Monck was Baptist or Episcopal or Holy Roller or Masonic Temple. There were more Protestant churches in Due East than there were intelligent people, he told his children. "And if I catch you stepping foot in one—"

"You'll what, Daddy?"

"I'll make you sit in front of a Billy Graham crusade on the television every night of the week!"

"Not that! Oh please not that!"

They were just teasing him anyway—his children didn't *really* want to walk down the aisle of the Baptist church, giving scandal. He'd taught them to stick their chests out and strut when it came to being Catholic: it was the only way to survive in a place where the other kids called you mackerel snapper and asked you were the nuns bald under those habits. "You tell anybody who asks you that Sister Agatha grows roses where her hair should be, but only Catholics are allowed to see!"

"Bill," Dolores would admonish, but she'd smile too. She'd learned real fast what outsiders the Church made of children in a little town like this.

Bill put the sherry next to him on the front seat of the station wagon and patted the bottle the way he would have patted a dog if he'd had one. Were the Christian Brothers monks?

Now he allowed himself a good hearty sigh. *His* family came from Charleston, where there were at least as many Catholics as there were plans to rekindle the War Between the States. The Catholics in Charleston were a classy minority who fielded a

128

pretty good football team at Bishop England High School and threw some pretty good cocktail parties at the other Bishop's. Catholics in Charleston didn't have to apologize for themselves, the way they did in so many little Southern towns.

But he hadn't been raised in Charleston—his father's real estate business (commercial, not at all like this Rooney Realty) folded in 1929, before Bill was even old enough for school—and his family had retreated to a farm they owned thirty miles west of Charleston, way out in the country, where Catholics were as rare as Republicans or colored men registered to vote. He'd been raised in Shining Star.

Bill reached down to pull papers off the floor (Dolores used the car as her personal garbage dump) and swooped up a three-month-old copy of the *Catholic Worker*. This he read column by column and with a bemused sympathy that would have startled his wife, who—smart as she thought she was—did not have the sense to recognize that she and her husband operated on what was, after all, the same moral plane. Of course Dorothy Day was a *nut* (but a bigger-hearted and less conniving nut than Dr. King, Bill would have said) and he could hardly swallow this stuff whole. Pacifism! Anarchy! It was a joke—but it seemed to Bill that it was a well-focused joke with a good punch line, and it never wavered. Which was the point about Catholicism to begin with. He was big enough to read the *Catholic Worker*. In the privacy of the car, he could take it for what it was worth without being treated to one of Dolores's personal lectures.

Arguing with Her Worship's column, he lost track of the time and was startled to see from his watch that it was already twenty past five. And this was the night he finally had news to share. He folded the *Catholic Worker* in a neat rectangle, then a smaller one, started the car, and headed home with his sherry.

Overhead the polio banner strung across River Street ("We Can Stop This Scourge Together") twisted itself in the wind, and then straightened itself back out. The big oral vaccine campaign was coming to its triumphant conclusion this weekend, when every doctor in the county would be set up in an elementary school lunchroom, handing out sugar cubes dosed with the miracle serum. Ninety-five percent of the white families in Due East had signed on, but the Rooney family would be staying home.

Bill had mixed feelings about turning down the new vaccine —it pretty much put the Rooneys on the same footing as the islanders who felt they didn't need to consult *medical* doctors when they were already consulting Dr. Buzzard for their spells and their roots—but Dolores was adamant. She remembered every magazine article on medical disaster she'd ever seen, and a few years back she'd read about a group of first-graders tested with some vaccine (tetanus? whooping cough?). Two children had died.

"No thank you very much," she said about the new polio campaign. "Let someone else's children act as guinea pigs. We'll stick with the old one until we see the lie of the land. If it's safe after all they can take it in a year or two."

A fierce old she-bear about her children. Let someone else's children try it. Funny, with all the checks she wrote out for mission babies, Indians and Congolese and Vietnamese. You wouldn't think she'd want other kids to be the guinea pigs either, but she was willing to have them taste from the poisoned cup before her own children drank.

Like his own mother that way, though of course Dolores wasn't nearly as overprotective. He squirmed in discomfort at the linked subjects of his wife and his mother and disease, and he patted the sherry bottle again, almost for comfort. He was tempted to unscrew the cork with his teeth while he was driving and help himself to a little nip, but the drive home took exactly two minutes and twenty-five seconds, and Dolores might look out from the house and see him pulling in, trying to *re*screw the cork with his teeth.

O'Connor Street already. Bill pulled into his driveway and bounded up the front steps to let Dolores know the good news.

"Honey, I'm home!" (It was his routine at the K. of C. hall too, where his Desi Arnaz imitation slayed some of the guys.)

No answer. The house had the same empty lonely feel it so often had at five twenty-five.

Pulling his bottle along by its neck, Bill checked the kitchen (a hellhole! How an intelligent woman could let her son leave an open violin case out next to an open honey jar was *way* beyond his comprehension.) Then he took the stairs two at a time, still clutching the sherry, hoping for Kate or Tim at the least. No one: the children's doors were shut tight, and when he pushed them open their unfamiliar order, the order that meant Lily had done the upstairs today, discomfited him as much as the silence. The kitchen was filthy, but the upstairs was done. So Dolores, despite his protestations ("She's already the best-paid colored maid in the state of South Carolina!"), was persisting in the notion that Lily could only handle *either* the upstairs *or* the downstairs once a week, but not both in the same day. So the Rooney household never had a chance at being clean all at once, even if he could afford to keep Lily on. Again he pictured Lily with her friends, swearing on the Good Lord's Book that the crazy white lady ("You know the one keep the picture of Dr. King on the dresser") actually thought that three bedrooms and a bathroom constituted a day's cleaning.

He didn't know what point Dolores was trying to make.

Downstairs he poured himself a coffee cup full of sherry and swigged it. It was disgusting medicinal slag, but it did give an efficient buzz—by the time he'd finished the bottom of the cup he imagined that he felt the effects of the first sips.

Thursday was *Courier* day, and he began chucking up piles

of papers and books off the counter, hunting for clues as to where Dolores might have left the Due East paper. Then he poured himself another cup of sherry and took it with him while he went to search the parlor. Dolores had left the Savannah *Morning News* out (on the piano. This made no sense to him either. Did she play and read at the same time?), but there was no Due East *Courier.* He didn't know why he was so determined to find it—around this time of year it wouldn't be listing too much more than the winners of the Rooster Crowing Contest at the Due East County Fair—but he was hungry for news of the Ruttledges or the Barneses. A little item on the society page mentioning a trip to New York or Paris, a house party honoring the lieutenant governor. Some reassurance that the Ruttledges and the Barneses were the kinds of customers who'd have plenty of cash and would close the deal day after tomorrow.

But there was no confirming *Courier.* No Dolores. No kids. He was used to this of course—Dolores didn't know how to stay *in* the house—but most nights he looked forward to his first beer in solitude. Tonight was different. Bill grabbed up the little brown coffee cup and went back out the front door. He didn't know exactly why he was standing there (it wasn't as if he expected his family to come trotting up the block), but he noticed after a minute that his neighbor Mrs. Rapple (a brown little paper bag of a woman. Dolores called her a turnip, for some reason) was sitting on her front steps and she seemed to be inclining her head toward his, as if she wanted to make conversation but didn't know how to start it. He'd be damned. How many times had he called out *Hey there, young folks,* only to be ignored or run away from?

Faced with talking to Mrs. Rapple or retreating from her, he chose to bring his coffee cup of sherry into the station wagon with him, and once he was sitting in his station wagon with a coffee cup full of sherry he decided to drive around town looking for his missing wife. He peeled out of his driveway without so much as a wave to Mrs. Rapple, and his little spitefulness felt *good*.

He didn't know exactly where he was going to hunt for Dolores, but he couldn't hold his news. It had been a dry fall, way too dry. Besides, he was going to drink all the sherry if he stayed in the house alone, and he'd bought it for her in the first place.

□   □   □

Hogan's Good Gulf was shut up tight and had been since five o'clock, according to the sign on the office door.

"Only in Due East," Dolores Rooney said, and caught a glimpse of herself in Tom Prince's sideview mirror. You couldn't see the crow's-feet in the dim evening light, but she was sure there was an extra chin hovering. "Only in Due East would a gas station shut down"—could this man really have been meaning to ask her and her double chin for dinner?—"just when everybody's due to be passing through."

But Tom, in the driver's seat, was sanguine. "Hey, they open at five-thirty in the morning. That's phenomenal. I'll get myself out here at the crack of dawn and have her all fixed up in time to get to my court-martial at eight."

Actually, there hadn't been a blink from Tom Prince's alternator light on the whole drive, and for half a second Dolores flattered herself that this *Times* reporter had just made up his car trouble as an excuse to talk to her, to take her for a drive. Shouldn't he have called the car rental people in the first place?

In the kitchen, when he said he didn't know about Martin Luther King's being a saint, she had succumbed to liking him. Now, watching him throw up his arms to concede a cheerful defeat, she wanted to sit on these feelings the way the nuns had boys sit on their hands when they couldn't keep them still. It wasn't a simple matter of finding a younger man attractive (that was the sort of temptation a married woman was used to sitting on); no, the agony of this particular sexual attraction was the vision of her husband that followed the vision of Tom Prince, the vision of Bill Rooney finding Hogan Good Gulf shut up tight. Bill would have said: "Oh Jesus Mary and Joseph, oh *somebody* give me patience," and then he would have lost his patience anyway. He would have slammed down his fist on the dashboard, then taken out his misery the whole ride home, berating whichever of his children happened to be riding in the back seat.

She could not imagine Tom having a temper tantrum over a closed gas station. This was a beautiful town, he said, and he meant it. Martin Luther King was a good man. The gas station would be open in the morning.

"There's sure to be another station open out on the Savannah Highway, if you'd like to see to it tonight."

"Oh Lordy no. This'll do fine," he said, but this time she did not wince. He had no idea that he was affecting these *oh Lordy*s or cranking out an accent that would have been too hokey for *Jezebel* or *Gone With the Wind*.

"Will you still come to dinner?"

He nodded—oh sure, that'll be swell—and she told him that they should probably see to the wine. If you couldn't figure out what time the state of South Carolina had decreed the sun should go down and the liquor store should shut up, you weren't entitled to a drink. They had half an hour probably, but it was never smart in Due East to take a chance.

He laughed.

Mabley's Spirits was right on Lady's Island, only a five-minute drive, but the ride was interminable because Tom's presence was such a pleasant irritant now, reminding her as it did of all that Bill was not. She was beginning to think of him as Tom, beginning to imagine how Tom would irk Bill when they met at the dinner table. Tom was perfectly content to be heading for a bottle of wine in his unrepaired car, and he was humming in such a low, shy hum that it was impossible to make it out. Mozart maybe? Or Rossini? Bill would have found that pretentious. Bill would have sung right out loud in his clear pleasant tenor, if he felt like singing, and he would have drummed the dashboard and the gas pedal while he was doing it.

It set her humming herself, dream-humming, and she realized after a moment that she was humming the big rolling overture to *Figaro*. Oh that was transparent: Bill Rooney was crazy for opera and had found a soul mate at the K. of C. to furnish him with bargain-basement records from the P.X. And the very week she had met Bill in New York she'd taken him to the Met —she'd asked tentatively, because he spent every night he wasn't working club-hopping on Fifty-second Street or in the Village, but he said he'd been waiting on that first gig's pay so he could ask *her* to the opera. It was something he dreamed about in Carolina, he said. He was crazy for Mozart.

So Dolores McGillicudhy took the piano player to buy standing-room tickets for Mozart. They were standing on top of their shoes by the end of the first act, holding hands in the back of the old dark house and taking turns watching each other watch *The Marriage of Figaro*. *Oh God, if I could hear Pinza*, Bill said after, and they came back a week later to hear it again. She imagined she could understand every word of the Italian— *Non so più cosa son, cosa faccio*—and Bill closed his eyes listening to "Sull'aria." It made his head spin faster than a Mickey Finn could have spun it, he said; he wanted to see it a third time, he wanted to see *Così fan tutte* and *Don Giovanni* and *The Magic Flute*. Sometimes she thought it was the Mozart, and not her pregnancy, that made her decide to marry Bill Rooney. Any man who loved *Figaro*. It seemed almost a sign, an omen, because her father had sung along with the arias on those old Red Label records, and told his daughter he couldn't make out a bloody word but knew it had something to do with heaven. "You watch out for those Italians now, Lorey. They've developed a language to make a grown man weep." Andrew McGillicudhy wept over the music, and so did Bill Rooney when he was loaded: the music's curves and bends, he told her, were all about sex.

And now she hummed Mozart with a stranger. "You turn off there," she said, "for Mabley's."

He turned. "May I ask you a personal question?"

She jumped a little. "Ask away." She might not look girlish in the rearview, but she sounded it, and she was even sneaking glances at him, at his tie, which wasn't nearly so loud as she'd thought earlier, in the bright sunlight. In the darkness of the car, its stripes were pure bloodred slashes.

"How'd you come to settle in Due East in the first place?" He braked and pulled his key from the ignition in one smooth motion.

"Oh," she said, and waited while he came round to open the door for her, glad for a minute to compose a simple answer to such a complicated question. Now he was holding a hand out for hers and she was smiling up at him—oh really, she was such a simp, behaving like a flirting teenager.

"My husband grew up not too far from here, and the lowcountry was all he could talk about. The light and the sea."

Tom smiled.

"We came on a camping trip, actually. I'd never been farther south than Staten Island. And I'd, you know—a city girl— I thought it would be such a lark. I'd certainly never spent the night in a bedroll."

By now they were through the glass door and down the dim

center aisle of Mabley's and she felt, after the nod and the how-do to Mrs. Mab at the cash register, that she should stop her talk of bedrolls.

Though maybe the proprietress of Mabley's Spirits would not be titillated by the sound of the word *bedroll*, and maybe it meant nothing to this Tom Prince either. To her it had meant everything. When she was twenty and Bill first uttered that word, it conjured up—oh, she didn't know, it was everything, *tutto*—bohemians on the road. Walt Whitman. Making love in the Italian countryside, throwing off the bourgeois yoke of marriage. She and Bill decided to go down the coast to South Carolina two months after they'd met, a time when they were suspending the rest of their lives to snuggle in Bill's gray hotel sheets or dawdle in the shower, a time when Dolores Rooney could not believe that she was massaging a man's dark hairy back in the bathtub every morning and picking at boiled carrots with her mother every night. She could not believe, after all that agony with her cousin, that she was suspending all the rules again.

When she was twenty and in love with Bill Rooney she missed a tutorial with Sister Andrea for the first time in a year and a half. For weeks she covered her hair, and sometimes half her face, when she went up to Bill's room; but eventually she took off the blue flowered scarf and looked the elevator man right in the eye. By then she had worked her way past seediness, to the point where this illicit sex—oh it wasn't even *related* to what she and Timmy had once done under the bed—was surrounded for her, and for Bill too she thought, by an aura of innocence. Such an unlikely merging (he was so *loud*, he told such terrible jokes to complete strangers, and she still spoke in the self-deprecating intelligent voice of the good scholarship girl) resulting in such perfect synchronicity. Unsanctified though it was—and neither one of them could stop feeling guilty about *that*. They went to Mass hand in hand—such a passion surely had to be a coupling with some sort of divine approval.

If anything, she'd felt a strengthening of her faith after two months of being this unemployed musician's lover, and she resolved to make the longest Confession she'd ever made once they straightened out what to do with the rest of their lives. When Bill closed his eyes in the hotel bed, she would pull a Lucky Strike out of the pack on the bedside table and remember, inhaling, the psychology books she'd pored over at the Forty-second Street library. Their obsession with frigidity. After Bill, *she* could have taught the women of the Western world how to take pleasure. Sex was musical, just as Bill was always claiming: you had to give yourself up to it, you had to submerge yourself not only in its rhythms and crescendos but in its rests, its silences. Bill's only silences were in bed. Sometimes she felt herself stifling a sob when he rolled over, a good sob of release, and then seeing in that moment of relinquishment a sudden flickering vision from childhood: Timmy climbing down the steps to the A train, his shoulders hunched over with the weight of his books; her father shaving, with a towel wrapped around his middle, annoyed that Dolores needed to use the bathroom.

And people thought they needed psychoanalysis to make sense of the past.

Smoke a cigarette, she would have counseled all those frigid women, all those wealthy women headed to their Park Avenue analysts. Have a drink. And fall in love with a big guy, a big tall good-looking Southerner who made love like a great flapping eager bird: she was a Leda to his swan. She was reading him Yeats—she would have counseled the frigid women of America to pick up poetry and forget their studies for a while (because she herself was studying now only on subways, on the rides back and forth to see her crazy musician lover. It didn't matter at this point; she could coast and still get the *summa).* And she had been planning to take a year off to decide about graduate school anyway. She told Bill she'd been thinking of joining the Catholic Worker movement, of living in one of the Houses of Hospitality for a year to decide if she could give herself over to a life with the poor. He—wearing a pathetic mask of rejection on his face the minute she raised the possibility—asked if she could just volunteer a few nights a week and she said no, that was missing the whole idea, you had to embrace the poverty yourself, you had to put it on with your clothes in the morning and wear it on your back all day. It was a sacrifice, she told him, that she thought she was called to make. A boy from Fordham she'd been dating, an Italian boy from New Rochelle, had been asking her how far she was willing to go, and he wasn't talking about embraces. She told Bill with infinite patience that she, Dolores McGillicudhy, was called upon to act.

The truth of the matter was, at that point in her life she'd already pretty much decided that she didn't have it in her, that gift for selflessness. Twenty years old, riding the subway to nightclubs, dressing the way she wanted for the first time in her life, taking a lover, she knew that if she lived among the desperate poor she would begrudge every bedbug who suckled her in the middle of the night, that she would come to see her father's inconstancy on the face of every wandering bum who slurped a bowl of soup. She had resented every small sacrifice the war had called her to make, even as she berated her mother for complaining. The scholarship to the Dominican Academy had introduced her to rich girls who always had good cuts of meat on the table, war or no war. It was the *idea* of the Catholic Workers that appealed to her.

Bill blanched at the thought of her living downtown with the bums for a year. She'd fall in love with some other sacrificing guy—that was the panic she read in his broad face—but she saw too that he wouldn't dream of saying he'd give up a year of his life to join her. He was honest, and she was not. Here they'd been scraping together every last cent to hear music whenever they could hear it, and she was teasing him with a life that would have made no sense to a musician, a life she had no intention of leading.

"I don't think you should flirt with that pacifist stuff anyway," Bill said. "You ought to be in or out." It was easier to be out then, out of the Catholic Workers who'd opposed the war, now that they all knew about the concentration camps. Early in the war Dorothy Day herself had come to Mount St. Martyr's, and when Dolores went home that night to try to explain pacifism to Rose, her mother said: "Oh I should know enough by now to worry about it. You know how your father went on. Socialism! Anarchism! But it was all talk, in that lovely deep voice of his. They couldn't even get him to walk a picket line— oh no, his wisdom tooth was killing him, or he'd sprained his ankle. I expect you take after him in that, Lorey."

So she was not to be a Catholic Worker, then. When Bill talked about going South together to decide what to do, when he said those words *sleeping bags*, she jumped.

Now she told Tom Prince: "Anyway, he was right about the light. That first trip we saw artists out at the beach, trying to hold their easels steady in the wind, and I could understand why they'd come here to paint. The light was just otherworldly. Just stretching out forever."

Tom, paying for the wine, looked up from his wallet and said:

"See there? Otherworldly light. That's exactly why I want to do an article about this town. I could sure use your help."

Mrs. Mab counted out the change with her eyebrows raised just fractionally. "Well, *excuse* me for barging in on your conver*sa*tion," she said. She was a fat old lady with golden ringlets

140

who spoke so slowly that Dolores, in the past, had thought of her as a verbal cripple, even worse than the average drawling shopkeeper. Now she was introducing herself to Tom Prince and ferreting out who he was.

"I just want you to *know,*" she said—his apologetic mention of the New York *Times* had her all aflutter—"how de-*light*ed all of us here in Due East are that you are con*sid*ring us for an *art*icle. We *have* in the past you know"—Good Lord, you'd think she was giving the introduction at the La Sertoma luncheon—"entertained a good *man*y reporters and writers and so on and we like to *flat*ter ourselves that we are capable of a good deal of Southren hospi*tal*ity."

Tom Prince, in just the right pleasant but formal tone, said that was very kind of her.

"Well, you let Miz Rooney show you around, hear, because she has a very good out*sid*er's point of view. And of course if you ever want a real in*sid*er's point of view you can certainly feel free to call on any one of us atall. Oh my *word* but won't Mr. Mabley be tickled to hear about a reporter coming in today. I can *hard*ly wait to shut down for the night and go home to *tell* him. You be *good,* now hear, Miz Rooney, and you show this young fellow a real good *time* while he's in Due East."

In the car Tom said: "Well, *Miz* Rooney. You be good, hear?" and they laughed hard, outsiders together. She was getting used to his black square glasses, beginning to see that they had a studied aggressive quality that was probably a year ahead of Due East eyeglass fashion. She had seen him all wrong on the bluff precisely because she'd been in Due East too long, listening to the Mrs. Mableys behind their cash registers.

"I was thinking of running you out to that beach you're talking about. You know, the one everybody in Due East's been telling me I have to see before I leave town?"

She raised her eyebrows a fraction, in imitation of Mrs.

Mabley. "We might get there in time for sunset." And then, giggling again, did it in Mrs. Mab's voice: "We *might* could *get* there in time for the little old sun to set."

They giggled like teenagers: it was as if they'd tasted the wine already, or been friends for life, the way she and Tom Prince were carrying on. It hurt her belly to laugh like a girl.

"Let's do it," Tom Prince said, backing up. "Can you? Or do you have to get home to your kids?"

"Oh," she said, breezy, "they're out making a movie this afternoon. I don't think they'll be home for hours. I don't rightly *spect* they'll be home for *hours.*" But then she thought to inquire about the alternator.

By now he was moving the car forward, not backward, and he did not appear to have any intention of stopping. "I've made it this far. I don't really think we're going to break down, do you? I probably just overreacted. Would you be game?"

Of course she was game. She was connecting with another living breathing adult male for the first time in what felt like five years. Ten years. Fifteen.

"Sure," she said. "But you'll have to cheat on the speeding limit a little if we want to get out there in time to look around."

So Tom, like one of the teenage boys who went to Due East High School in a souped-up Chevrolet, gunned the gas pedal with a shy sidewards smile and they took off down the beach road. The stranger at her side began humming again, but then accelerated it along with the car and decided to hum right out loud, and he smiled over at Dolores in a way she would have described as proprietary. He was humming Mozart. She smiled, hardly conscious of the double chin that threatened to give her away. She might have been singing herself.

□   □   □

If she hadn't turned around to catch the last surge of light before she entered the woods, Kate would have caught up with her brother Tim and none of the rest would have happened. (Well, of course it would have *happened*, whether she was there to witness it or not. Her presence did not cause it to happen. She was clear on that anyway. Pretty clear.)

But the point was: if she hadn't seen it, she wouldn't have felt that terrible sickening sensation that meant she was obligated to act, that she, Katherine McGillicudhy Teresa of Avila Rooney, was morally bound to save somebody in trouble (Dr. King. Thomas Aquinas. Maria Goretti. Dolores Rooney.) And if she hadn't felt obliged to *do* something, her brothers would not have made out what a fool she was, and she could have anyway gotten a decent night's sleep that night instead of twisting and turning on the lumpiest bed any girl could make up for herself, the bed of anxiety.

But she did see what she saw, and so she didn't get a decent night's sleep that night, nor for that matter for a good many nights to come. At the entrance to a swampy wood, Kate Rooney looked over her shoulder and saw that the sunset, in three quarters of an hour, would give her brother far more spectacular lighting than he deserved for his movie. Already the sky was filtering from gray to orange, spreading out light as silky as those stockings her mother said they wore back before the war —and at the same moment Kate Rooney observed the light she observed two figures staggering up the dirt road behind her.

There was no question that one of them was *that man*: that man who lived in the trailer deep in the woods, that man she had been so determined to avoid, that man she and her brothers called the Snake Man. In his front yard—a rectangular strip of mud and moss and roots not much bigger than a gravesite—the Snake Man kept a murky pool of cut-up rattlesnake parts behind a painstakingly lettered sign that said:

I CATCH YOU TRESPASING
I CUT YOU UP TO.
NO KIDDING. HA HA.

Despite Tim's disclaimer (oh he wouldn't really *hurt* anybody), the Snake Man had chased Tim and Andy a dozen times at least, not because they dared step on his property, but only because they dared brush his property when they walked by. (Kate doubted anyway that it was his property, back in this swamp. More likely it was just a watery parcel of land some rich man forgot he owned and never came to check on, like half the marshy property in Due East.)

Kate had never actually seen the Snake Man chase her brothers, but they told of each scare with grislier details: Andy said last time, in a flat voice, that the man went after him with a bowie knife, and Tim said not only did he have a rattler's meaty body cut up and marinating in a rain pool, but he kept the rattles too. One day the lunatic ran out after Tim, waving the rattles like castanets and hollering that there was venom still in them and that he meant to squeeze it out all over Tim's sorry head. On nights when they'd been chased her brothers would come in breathless on their bikes, late for supper, and raise their eyebrows to tell her that there was a new story, a story that could not possibly be repeated in front of Bill and Dolores. Then at ten o'clock, after their father made his beery descent into sleep, they tiptoed into her bedroom (Dolores was doing the bills downstairs, always doing the bills downstairs) and amused themselves more than they did her with the newest version of their tales. Sometimes she had already drifted off, and it was hard to sort out the Snake Man stories from her dreams.

It had never occurred to her that her brothers might have exaggerated, even though she had been witness to none of it, even though she had often walked the same trail with Tim and

Andy through the same woods and had never so much as glimpsed the man outside his trailer. Once she had seen the shadow of his naked torso through what must have been his bedroom window: it was a muscular lithe absolutely white torso with black arms descending like fitted curved pipes. Tim and Andy said the Snake Man's arms were so covered with grisly tattoos that he would surely die of cancer because there was no place for his sweat to go. One day all his body's wastes would back up and his organs would explode; pieces of kidney would float inside the Snake Man the way those pieces of cut-up rattlesnake floated in the pool.

On that day when she saw the Snake Man inside his trailer, it appeared for a minute that he was waving a greeting, but Andy said: "Skedaddle Kate, he's after us," and so of course she had, outrunning even her brothers. She had been dead wrong about his gesture: a languid wave through a bedroom window was just his style of threat. That man's sign said that he wouldn't think anything of cutting them up and leaving their bodies to marinate in the murky pool. It wasn't even farfetched.

Nothing was farfetched once you stepped deep into these woods. You saw plenty, mostly glimpses of yellowing crisping magazines that Tim and Andy whisked out of her way before she had time to educate herself better on the visual meanings of the words *copulation* and *coitus*. She had caught enough glimpses, though, to know that there were women in the world with breasts big enough to make them look as deformed as carnival freaks, and that these freakish women tweaked their own nipples in such a way as to make you resolve that you would never ever put your own hand on your own breast, or certainly not when anyone could see you doing it. She had caught enough glimpses to know that the large-breasted women liked to wear leopard skin, which was about as tacky as you could get. They stuck their sagging backsides, as crinkled and crumpled as used tinfoil (only covered in leopard skin), straight up into the air. They appeared to be as old as her mother.

If Kate walked alone she hardly knew what to do when one of those magazines beckoned from off the path. Look? Pray to Maria Goretti? You could probably get worse than T.B. from touching the edges of *that* cheap soiled paper.

Once Tim and Andy were laughing so hard at a catalogue they found on the tracks that they forgot she was looking over their shoulders, and she ogled page after page of Adults-Only Toys—for the Naughty Grown-up in You. She didn't close her eyes until the climax of the book, when her brothers turned the page and revealed the plastic blow-up dolls for the grown-up men, brown plastic dolls with perfect round black holes for their surprised mouths. Two sets of mouths. Kate had worried for those dolls: well, she was only ten, then, when she saw that. The catalogue, she had no doubt, belonged to the Snake Man.

She had seen other things too, though, glimpses of the naughty grown-up in you that even the Snake Man couldn't be single-handedly responsible for: high school kids necking, the boy backed up against a smooth clean pine tree, his hands cradling those low bumps easing out from a girl's tight skirt.

And now, just because she had turned around to see the last brilliant spasm of full light before she entered the woods, she saw what she had been dreading for a year or more: the Snake Man, coming toward her down the dirt road, cutting her off at the path. Now that she had crossed the marsh with Tim, there was no way for her to get back to the railroad tracks and escape him. She wasted a long second twirling around to look for her brother—Tim, who had outrun the Snake Man so many times, would know what to do—but Tim's gangly legs had carried him far beyond her sight. All she could see in the dim woods light was woods: a tunnel of bark and moss. Later, of course, she realized that she herself could certainly have outrun the Snake

Man far enough along the path to reach Tim, and Tim would have taken over thinking for her.

But at the moment she had no such realization. She was stunned that the Snake Man was not alone: he was approaching with a Victim, and Kate was so distracted by the sight of the two of them that she could barely stop her right knee from twitching, much less plan a rational escape route. She *couldn't* leave. Now it wasn't only her own safety that concerned her. Now there was a Victim to save too.

The two of them staggered along the narrow road like a couple of drunken sailors, the Snake Man propping the Victim up, and even from thirty yards she could see from the way he gripped the girl's elbow that her walk was involuntary. Kate could have fainted from the simultaneous rush of sensations as she stood just off the path, motionless but for her right knee twitching. How grateful she was that *she* was not the Victim. How terrified she was that the Snake Man might be strong enough to propel two Victims by two elbows. And how light-headed the necessity for action made her.

She could not make out much from thirty yards, but she could see that the Snake Man wore old blue jeans that slumped down from his narrow boyish hips (hips like Tim's) and she could see that he wore rough laced work boots, the kind of brown boots her father and her brothers never would have dreamed of wearing. She imagined the weight of those boots meeting the Victim's soft flesh, on a thigh, on her belly. The Snake Man and his Victim advanced so slowly as the damp road carried them through the marsh that Kate was able to stand in perfect horrified stillness to peer out at them from behind a pine tree.

The Snake Man wore a flimsy shirt, sleeves rolled up, and she was sure she could see how dark his forearms were, dark with hair like barbed wire, hair darker than the hair on her father's arms, dark and gummed with tattoos that, for all she knew, pictured little plastic dolly girls with two sets of black mouths.

Oh it was a wonder she could breathe at all.

Finally she scurried behind a bank of pale sandy mud that presented itself exactly at the moment when she was sure that she had been struck with paralysis, sure that she was doomed to be Victim Number Two. Squatting, she was barely concealed, but she consoled herself that in the dimming light any part of her red hair sticking up would only resemble a bird's nest, or dead pine needles.

She tried to remember to hold her breath as they came closer, but breathing went on unbidden. She imagined the girl, whose high-heeled shoes (high black heels. Stilettos! She must be one of the cheap high school girls who smudged red lipstick onto cigarette butts) were now surely sinking into the soft earth near the path's entrance. The girl had looked dark, Italian or maybe Indian. She could even have been one of those colored girls Mrs. Lovelace called moo-lat-to (she pronounced it as if it were a delicate forbidden foreign word, and Franny Starkey stuck her finger down her throat every time Mrs. Lovelace brought it up, which was often that year, since they were studying South Carolina history). But it didn't seem likely that even the Snake Man would dare walk along with a colored girl down Union Street.

What was strangest of all was that the dark girl in the dark stilettos wore dark tight pants—toreador pants—that did not make her look like a Victim at all. Girls in black toreador pants wore ruffled tops that slid off their shoulders, and they slipped outside during the dances at the Canteen to sip beer from a paper bag with a boy who didn't look much more innocent than they did.

But Kate was certain as death that the girl was not walking

of her own volition. She tottered like a three-wheeled vehicle thrown off balance, and the Snake Man, an evil gardener manipulating his wheelbarrow, pushed her along. She was incapable of propelling herself. She wore a flimsy shirt too, but not long-sleeved: sleeveless in fact, like those nylon Villager shells in pastel colors every girl in Due East wore over a delicate flowered skirt (even in her terror Kate wondered why her thoughts so frequently came back to a *clothing* label). The Victim's shell, though, was certainly not a Villager shell: even at dusk and even from a distance you could tell when a sleeveless pullover was so cheaply made and ill-fitting that it was probably bought for sixty-nine cents at the five-and-dime out by the base. You could tell because the Victim's breasts, instead of waving out nicely like the bell curve on a graph, sagged and protested against the material.

An involuntary shudder rippled through Kate's hunkered body at the thought of the girl walking along in the woods at dusk, in November, in a sleeveless summer shirt. The Snake Man must have taken her by surprise, kidnapped her, grabbed her from her car or maybe from one of the poorer houses on Union Street. Maybe she was even one of those teenage Marine wives from Tennessee or West Virginia (oh, when the Marine met the Snake Man, righteous angry violence would meet terrifying murky evil violence, and then these quiet November woods would erupt).

Now the squish of their feet approached, an irregular *blug* as they came closer. Kate closed her eyes, opened them, closed them again. If only she could have fallen against the sandbank into a deep sleep while they passed.

She realized with horror that the man was humming as he dragged his Victim along, a false bass humming of some sleepy popular tune—"Roses Are Red"? The monster. Roses are red. He was passing directly in front of her now, and alongside his deep unhurried tune was the sound of the Victim's labored breathing, as if he had whipped her before and was now dragging her half-alive body along the path. Dead leaves and dry pine needles crunched beneath their feet and branches grabbed for their pants, the drooping blue jeans and the tight black toreador pants that narrowed over the tall black heels.

All noise stopped.

The Snake Man had stopped, and he had brought his Victim to a stop alongside him, directly in front of Kate's hiding place. He had seen her, just as she had seen him: he had seen a halo of red hair over the sandbank. (Oh what a fool she was to think that orange hair would pass for a bird's nest, for pine needles. It would never pass for anything but what it was and this was her punishment for being so prideful about her unconventional hair color. Now her hair would be more than her downfall: it would be the death of her.)

Kate forced her eyes open. If this was to be her death then she, her mother's daughter, could face it. Maria Goretti had faced it. St. Agnes had faced it. Katherine Rooney could face it too. She would look the Snake Man in the eye and she would forgive him, no matter how he tortured her before she died. She would whisper: "I forgive you, you don't even know what you're doing," as he tormented her; "I forgive you," as he squeezed the last breath of life from her body (she was imagining being strangled, but now remembered the bowie knife. She would say: "I forgive you," as he lightly drew his obscene markings on her skin with the knife point; "I forgive you," even as he plunged the knife into her heart.) He would laugh hideously as he murdered her, but afterward, remembering her soft words and her composure, he would be filled with horror. He would know for the first time in his life what sin was, and he would repent. He would tell the jail warden of her forgiveness, and the warden would tell the chaplain, and then the whole canonization process would be set into motion; there would be a ground swell of interest and sixth-graders, why even Mrs. Lovelace, would tell the Church about Kate Rooney's unswerving devotion to integration and social justice. The state of South Carolina, Protestant though it was, would be filled with that old Southern pride at a native daughter finally recognized for her true worth, and they would keep the Snake Man alive until he could fly to Rome, accompanied by a whole battalion of armed guards, to see the Pope declare her a saint. Even Tim and Andrew would forgive the Snake Man, because she had forgiven him, and after all, now he would have to face his own execution. St. Katherine Rooney, in heaven, would intercede for her old tormentor.

But there was no sound of the murderer approaching, no sound of the work boots coming to get her. There was no sound at all but birds taking wing farther along, deeper in the woods, and in the distance the whine of the telephone wires and the whizz of bugs and horny mud creatures. The Snake Man was toying with her, teasing her, making her wait for him to come and drag her out as he had dragged the first Victim. Would he drag her by the hair, until he held orange tufts in his hand? By the elbow, until her very arm strained at its socket?

Kate Rooney saw, in the last minute of her life, how fitting it was that she should die behind this sad bank, surrounded by the decay of wet sliming leaves and dead birds and frogs left out to dry like parchment. It was almost enough to make you believe in predestination, though of course Catholics believed in free will and not that prefab mumbo jumbo. She was reminded of the squirrels they had dissected in science class: Robin Bunter's daddy had shot the one for their group, but they could not take their tweezers to the rodent's heart, because the heart had been shattered. Her own heart would more likely wither here on this spot, where her body would lie for days after the man copulated and coitused her. (That part she truly could not imagine.) The hot fall sun would burn her white skin pink and drain all the liquid from her body.

She could have peed in her pants. There was no sound. No sound. No sound but a long chhhhhchhhhhchhhhh smmmooochch.

The Snake Man was *kissing* the Victim. The Snake Man had paused in front of her hiding place to *kiss* that poor girl who was so lost in her own terror that she could not support herself to stand up straight. Kate considered showing herself at just this instant: she could climb the bank and cry out like a banshee. HOW DARE YOU? she would say. Startled, the Snake Man would release the Victim, whose hands he had cruelly pinned behind her back, and the Victim would look up at her with trembling grateful relief and would run back up the path to the road, through the marsh, back to safety.

ON THOSE STILETTO HEELS?

No. It was not one of those moments that called for bravado, it was one of those moments that called for cunning. She was on her own; she had long since stopped imagining that her brothers would come to her rescue. They were filming their movie, and even she, one of the stars, was expendable. They had forgotten her presence, or they had assumed that she had deserted them, gone back home. She had only what her mother called her lazy intelligence to rely on. She wished her mother could see her now: at this moment there was nothing lazy about her, cunning and shrewd and cool and intending to save herself and the Victim too.

The moment of silence that meant he had quit his smooching came soon enough, but it was followed by a sound even more terrifying. His voice.

"Look here, shug."

Oh God he sounded like an *Okie*.

"You're gonna have to pull yourself together there sweetie pie and just propel your butt over yonder to that trailer."

His voice was thick as Karo syrup, and the sound of it made of him a living breathing person. Kate knew then that she would never be a saint, because she would never be able to forgive a man with that cruel voice. If the Snake Man spoke when he came to kill her, she would be stunned, a fly struck with a swatter. She would be as speechless as the Victim, who had been reduced to gurgling some floating sound, some drowning sound like

Puhleze oh puhhhllleeezzz.

"Unhunh baby I can't show you no mercy *now*. Let's us get you marching along. Let's us see you go HUP TWO THREE FOUR. HUP TWO THREE FOUR." There was a slapping sound, palm meeting toreador pants. Then he laughed.

She had never heard a laugh before that she would define so unqualifiedly as *male,* not even the laugh that sometimes escaped the gym teacher, that hairy sadist Mr. Smolinski. Her father let out deep laughs, but you could hear him *forcing* them deep for the Coramae Ruttledges of Due East, and her brothers, of course, had voices still high-pitched enough that you were embarrassed for them.

But this man's laugh—so pleased with itself, so forceful, so grainy and lewd—why it was pure gonads (which was a term she had not had to scrounge for in the dictionary but had been introduced to in that very same science class where they dissected the squirrel with the shattered heart). This gonad laugh could mean nothing but violence and cruelty: no, she would not be able to forgive him. She would probably just roll over and die, or pray for death anyway.

And so behind her sandbank she braced herself for death, as cunning and intelligent in her watchful waiting as her mother would have been. It took her a minute at least, maybe two, to realize that the sounds of the Snake Man and his Victim were receding, were negligible, were in fact—was that the slam of his trailer door way off down the path?—gone.

So he had not seen her.

So she was alive and unmolested as she had always intended to be until the day she died a white-haired graceful but persnickety old woman.

Then she began to tremble: not just her knee, which had twitched throughout, but her entire body, from red hair to red sneakers. She was not frightened, she was absolutely blank, and she could not imagine why she twitched so. She willed her knee still, which accomplished nothing, and then she realized that she had not once, at this her greatest hour of need, prayed. Automatically she began a quick Act of Contrition, which quieted her knee for a moment until she realized that she should not be asking for forgiveness but for help.

If she took ten steps she could be out of the path and out of the woods. She could be on the road, on her way through the marsh, on her way to the clearing. If she took ten steps she could escape the Snake Man forever, and when she reached her bike she could fly to one of the dollhouses off Union Street and fetch help.

But she could not leave that way, and she was not sure why. She couldn't race breathless to some stranger's house, to some housewife or Marine, and say: "He's going to copulate her!" There was another word for it—she was sure she had heard that word when those three colored boys on Lady's Island were dragged off for copulating that high school girl—but it escaped her. The more she reached for it, as she had reached for the word *whorehouse* earlier that day, the more she realized that she was embarrassed too because she harbored a lingering doubt that the Victim was truly a victim. It pained her to even let the thought cross her mind, but there it was: the possibility that the skinny girl with the sad sagging breasts had *wanted* the man to drag her along the path, to push her by the elbow to his trailer.

Now was the moment for an Act of Contrition. How shameful that she should think, even for a fleeting second, that the girl wanted such a thing to happen to her just because she wore such high heels. How often she had heard her mother say to her father:

"We mustn't blame the victim."

Though her mother, of course, was always referring to colored people and this girl . . . well she *might* be colored. It didn't matter. What mattered was that she, Katherine Rooney, was the only witness to this shameful act-in-progress, and she was called upon to go on witnessing.

And so (perhaps she was going to her own execution. Perhaps she was Lot's wife, looking on the destruction she should have been fleeing) she pressed on into the dark woods. Moss lolled down to brush her, and she forced herself to follow the path where the Snake Man had dragged his victim. Now every limb and joint twitched recklessly, and now that she had chosen to act, she began to despise the Victim for being so helpless. She began to despise herself for going on alone. She certainly despised her mother, who would have been so proud of her action, no matter the cost. She was following the moral course as she followed this path, and she despised every saint who had ever followed it.

Now she could see the trailer. She stood still in a cluster of saplings and honeysuckle to plan her attack. The path veered off at a forty-five-degree angle just past the trailer, and the trailer faced the disappearing, not the approaching, path.

By itself the tin home didn't look threatening, especially as Kate saw it, in profile: it was new, and it was compact, and it was colored an innocuous pale blue. The Snake Man must have, at some point in his recent existence, plopped down a few thousand dollars for it. (Or maybe, as Tim was always pointing out, he had won it in a card game or just flat out stolen it. You could picture a tattooed man like him walking right up to one of the mobile home lots and hitching a new trailer to an old truck, without anybody saying a blessed word—because he looked peculiar enough to do whatever he pleased, including take away a baby-blue trailer if he felt so inclined. What no one could figure out was how he even got it back here—dropped it by helicopter? floated a barge?—and what he did for plumbing and fresh water. Tim said he probably just peed right out the window, especially when an innocent kid was passing by.)

The antenna the Snake Man had set up behind his trailer might have cost a thousand dollars itself (or another card game): it certainly gleamed silver and majestic, and it made a pretty complement to the big WDUE radio antenna out behind it (DUE was home of the whole family's favorites, which meant that they played Elvis, but only the slow mushy ballads). The DUE antenna was anchored almost all the way across the marsh, on a little bald island which served no other purpose. The Snake Man's antenna pushed its way up through the gray oak that shaded his roof. There were two big live oaks, in fact, just behind the trailer, because the Snake Man had made his residence right on the marshfront, where the gray old trees liked to spread their big roots and lounge. He wasn't on deep water, of course, or otherwise whoever owned the property would never have stood for the Snake Man's embezzling the view.

The baby-blue trailer (one bedroom, Kate and her brothers had always calculated, the very word *bedroom* taking on a sinister tone when applied to the Snake Man) was more interesting when viewed from the departing path, where you could get a good view of the snake pool and the threatening sign and the mold that was already spattering out over the bottom half of the Snake Man's home. From the approaching path, where Kate hung back now, twitching even more if that was possible, there was only one side window. It was from that window that she had thought, months ago, that she'd seen the Snake Man wave a greeting one morning.

The trailer's front door was closed. No sound came from within. She knew what she was required to do.

She was going to have to crawl on her belly up to that window, so the Snake Man would not see her approach. There was no other way to see what was going on. She felt just as foolish as she would have felt if she had been required to knock on strangers' houses to tell them about this attack, but she dropped to her hands and knees. She crawled for a few steps, confused, and then stopped to check behind her. If some intruder in the woods were to catch her in this humiliating position—

Then she checked in front of her for the Snake Man, certain that he was watching her from within, holding a bowie knife or perhaps aiming a big hunting rifle at her head. The crawl was interminable, what with all the checking, but she was a spy behind enemy lines. She was taking the action St. Thomas said was required, taking the action of her own free will. (Oh she was formed by a *moist wind* indeed. Was St. Thomas watching her deformed female body now, risking all humiliation for his sake?)

Now she had to veer off the path to go directly up to the Snake Man's window. Now she had to make her way knee by fist over the gnarled protruding limbs and piles of wet fetid leaves. She thought more than once that the rustling she heard was a snake burrowing through the rich undercover, but the rustling was only the sound she herself made as she inched forward to save an innocent victim. The ground was almost flat back here, barely above the level of the marsh, but it sloped fractionally as it made its way down to the water, and she paused every few steps to hold her palm out flat on the cold

November ground and reassure herself that she was still alive and breathing.

The trailer perched on a low cinder-block base, with the bottom of the bedroom window standing five and a half feet from the ground. Kate herself stood under five feet tall, and as she forced herself to crawl closer and closer to the side of the trailer (he *had* to hear the leaves flattening out under her palm, he *had* to hear her knees snapping twigs in two), she planned how she would raise herself to window height: she would haul over a wooden crate he had left lying out beyond the trailer.

Of course, if the Snake Man was looking out another window, looking out the back side of the trailer as she went to get the crate, then her number would really and truly be up, her goose would be cooked, her fate would be sealed. She would be —what did her brothers say?—belly up. Her belly softened, and she lay flat on the ground the way she lay in her bed on school mornings.

She did not want to go.

The coldness of the earth reached out and tugged at her: she forgot her full bladder, and her need to act, and she felt instead her blood pressure lowering, her whole body shutting down into coldness. She was her mother's daughter, she was an actress about to go onstage, she was St. Katherine Rooney, and she was not even conscious of the moment she stood to carry out her mission: one minute she was pressed to the cold damp ground, and the next she was dragging the wooden crate back with her to the side of the trailer. She panted a little, but she was not frightened. Her body was on automatic pilot.

Now she rested, and calculated the passage of time. If the Snake Man had seen her out a back window, if he had heard her dragging the crate, by now he would have come to take his revenge. But he had not come.

She had to move forward. She eased the crate down for a

step directly below the window. She put her hand against the cold metal side of the trailer. She put one foot up on the crate and adjusted it to stop the wobbling. She put her other hand against the metal, her other foot up on the crate. She was on. She was balanced. She squatted there and counted to three and then, before she could stop herself, she raised herself up and found that she was tall enough to look in, but that she looked in on darkness.

So he wasn't there at all. So she had to repeat this horrible moment again and again, at every window, until she found him.

She stared in again at the blackness—she meant to memorize the floor plan, in case later he held her prisoner inside, tied to a chair and gagged—and as she stared, she realized that the room was not, after all, empty. The interior light was not black but only a deep gray, and the gray stretch of it was broken in the far corner by the small golden glow of an electric fake hurricane lamp perched beside a bed.

So what she looked down upon was the side of a bed. What she, Katherine McGillicudhy Teresa of Avila Rooney, looked down upon in the dark room that was not really dark was a cheap modern bed, the kind that would have come with a fully equipped, fully furnished powder-blue mobile home. The blond plasticized wood of the bed, routed through with gold paint, was as innocent as a baby's cry.

And what she saw lying on the bed, in the dark room that was not really dark, was the tight tense form of a naked man lying atop his own bedcovers: no, wait, lying atop squeezed pieces of dark human flesh that could be nothing but a naked girl beneath him. Kate was transfixed as she stood—no, stretched and strained—to make herself tall enough to see, to have light enough to see. To see

to see this ineffable evil. It was as if she had wakened fully now, as if her eyes were finally and truly pried wide open. Now she could see. Now she could look straight down upon them from her perch and see that the Snake Man did have tattoos on those white arms, but Tim and Andy were wrong: there were not so many. Now the glow of the hurricane lamp could have been a sun in the corner of the room. Now she could see everything. She could see that there were two tattoos on the arm facing her, and she could even make them out: a smiling tootsie in a bikini on the Snake Man's biceps; a muscleman lifting a barbell on his forearm. His skin was as white as the moon reflecting the sunlight of the lamp, even underneath the thick black hair that covered his arms and his legs and yes his hairy buttocks. His back, though, was clean, as his chest must be too, pressed against the woman's back; and she could even read his back, now that the light was so clear. Now that she could really see. In the rut between the Snake Man's shoulders was a fat frilly heart adorned with thorns. Across the heart, bold as a beauty queen's banner, were the words

MY SAVIOR

Oh, the essence of evil, the heart of darkness, that this man who was raping—THERE WAS THE WORD, just as she needed it, *of course*—this man who was raping this woman should wear on his back the words *My Savior*.

The man's hairy buttocks held Kate motionless. There was nothing to see of the girl, the girl who could just as well be Kate Rooney lying there, but her long arms and her wrists, pinned on the sheets above her head by the Snake Man, and the blobs of brown flesh, pieces of hip and thigh, which escaped from underneath the man. Kate could see that she was struggling, struggling to be free of him, and that it required all his strength to hold her down. He clenched her wrists in his fists. The sheets and the Snake Man's flesh shimmered white heat. Every muscle of his buttocks bulged.

She could not stop this by herself. All the will in the world could not stop arms that could grip so, fists that could clench so. Now that she knew the word for what was going on, there was only one course of action to follow. She had to fetch her brothers. She had to run to the trestle with all the strength that was left her and fetch her brothers back to stop this man. She had prayed that she would know what to do, and now she knew.

A long shudder of fear and thanksgiving escaped her.

And alerted the Snake Man that a little girl was peeping through his window. He tensed, then paused in this great evil effort of his. He shook his head loose, and his grip on the girl's outstretched arms loosened too. The victim beneath him was powerless to move, and Kate was frozen, equally powerless, outside the trailer. She watched him locate the sound and peer startled over his shoulder at the window.

She must have been a shadow to him, but to her he was a close-up photograph staring stupidly, an unshaven black-haired devil. His mouth was a pink length of rope: as if knowing she watched it, he opened his lips and revealed a gap where his right eyetooth should have been. His white skin, blue as it progressed up to his forehead, appeared to be stretched back tight over his skull, and she could count the scars below his high sharp cheekbones, three scars that radiated from the black shadows beneath his eyes. She felt she had never seen a man so clearly before, and she could not say for the life of her why he reminded her of her father. It was a bizarre nightmare, to see her father now as she stared at this wicked man.

Did she crave her father's help? The Snake Man seemed to register her presence, and still she was locked into her position on the box, her fingers gripping the tiny cold metal ridge of the window. She watched him lower his head the way a horse might, whinnying, and then she watched him look up at her again. He had a single thick eyebrow over his small delicate nose.

He saw her, and his arms—no longer pinning the girl's arms, palms flat now on the sheet—strained to hold him up. The fleshy mass beneath him quit its shimmying.

He saw her. He held his eyes on the window, trying to make out her dim outline, and a little smile seemed to play at the edges of his mouth. For the first time in her life Katherine Rooney looked a naked man in the eye, and though he couldn't possibly see her clearly, the naked man looked back.

Then the Snake Man winked at her.

YOU SHOULD BE
SMOOCHING

Driving through Due East, searching for his wife, Bill Rooney tried Dr. Black's first, because pregnant women spend half their time at the doctor's. Dolores didn't mention her appointments anymore. She thought he was jealous of Dr. Black because the old man was doing his gynecological turns with her (only a graduate of the Dominican Academy could think *that.* Only the nuns could come up with such a twisted idea.) Actually, what made him a little nervous at the thought of the doctor's office was not the doctor at all, but his nurse, Sharmayne.

Sharmayne wasn't really a nurse, just a receptionist, but she dressed in a nurse's uniform, and she reminded Bill of one of those busty dress-up dolls his own daughters had always scorned. She was a pair of exaggerated curves on top of a pair of exaggerated curves, and her tight shiny white uniform stretched out to a gap between the third and fourth buttons. Every fifteen minutes or so she'd come out to the waiting room to straighten the magazines. This was a ritual that didn't seem to register on the waiting women, but it surely raised the hackles of all the males over the age of six. She *had* to know that when she bent over she exposed a good three inches of garter and stocking top and fleshy thigh. Bill was sure, in fact, that she'd grazed him more than once on purpose. A nurse's little joke. She sent men scurrying into the bathroom before their checkups.

Sharmayne was the kind of woman who savored men's embarrassment when she bent over or when she stood in the doorway, sticking out her pelvis in the most un*nat*ural way and chewing on a fat child-size pencil. Her own husband was a hairy bruiser who drove a big rig all over the lowcountry and had the habit of dropping in at the doctor's whenever he was passing through. Sharmayne needed checking up on.

And he wouldn't have minded checking up on her himself today. With a little sherry in his belly, a little Sharmayne sherry, he'd be able to breathe her in and resist her all at the same time—maybe brush up against her (accidentally of course, the way she brushed against him). How many visitors did she have after work, when her husband was out on the road?

Oh Jesus, now he *knew* Dolores was pregnant. This was what happened every pregnancy. By the time her belly was showing he was ready for three cold showers a day, and not from the thought of his wife, not hardly. *Any* other woman in Due East could excite him when Dolores was pregnant: Sharmayne, Coramae Ruttledge, the homely waitress at Ralph's with the chipped tooth and the orange faded lipstick. He'd confessed it to Father Sweeney, way back when Maggie was the loaf in the oven, and the old priest had a good yuck about it.

Have you committed adultery, then?

Well no, Father, it's just that my wife's pregnant and all I can think about is other women—you know, impurely.

Oh my goodness, said droll Father Sweeney. *Oh my goodness. Is that all?*

Well yes, Father. WHAT DO YOU MEAN, IS THAT ALL? WHAT ABOUT THOU SHALT NOT COVET THY NEIGHBOR'S WIFE?

You've got to go back to your catechism then, said the priest, *and look up the difference between temptation and sin, Bill.*

It was Father Sweeney's habit of recognizing everybody's voice and then calling him by name in the confessional—the private, secret confessional!—that shut the door on *that* conversation. There was always a waiting line of six or seven in the back of the church for Saturday Confession, the entire line pretending to be lost in piety, pretending they hadn't heard a thing, when Father Sweeney's voice was so loud and contemptuous that you couldn't *not* hear what advice and chastisement he was dishing out.

Besides, the old man probably thought when Bill said *impure* that he was talking cheesecake and pinup, that his fantasies meant Sharmayne without her clothes on. But he wasn't talking naked stacked women—he wouldn't have troubled to confess *those* images—he was talking a whole whorehouse in his imagination, a whorehouse specializing in whips and chains and two women at once, one of them tied to a chair and the other one on her knees. Bill Rooney was talking maybe three women at once (oh the delicious permutations: two he could ravish at once while the third one begged for mercy. Please Bill oh please oh please I've got to have it.) The kind of fantasies he savored were real sins, not just the occasions for sin (and who did Father Sweeney think he was anyway, so dismissive of a man's mind's wanderings? Bill's own father couldn't have made him feel smaller.)

He'd brought up the fantasies again when Father Berkeley

was transferred to Our Lady of Perpetual Help, in the dim hope that the new priest would take him more seriously. He now had daily visitations, and he did not hesitate to call them sins no matter what the hell Father Sweeney called them: the later Dolores came into his bed at night, the more he indulged in his solitary visions. Solitary sins. His marriage to Dolores had lifted off with an explosion of sexual ecstasy and had come down to earth only to land in a pool of drying semen. His whole life stank of it.

But when he confessed to the new priest that he plotted ways to shame his wife, Berkeley wouldn't even give him the time of day. He gave him a piddling three Hail Marys for penance, without so much as a discussion on the sacrifice required in a marriage. Bill Rooney was the only man in Due East, so far as he knew, who had never once in eighteen years of marriage even considered cheating on his wife, who had turned down the chance of a Charleston whorehouse when he was eighteen years old, who had spent months with musicians who got laid three times a day while he, chaste, pretended he was sneaking off to see his own sweetie—but did the priests have to take it for granted that way? It was enough to drive a man to adultery.

He always trapped himself inside his own fantasies, and even the priests wouldn't help him find a way out the back door. Anyway, Sharmayne was out of the picture altogether now (well, almost out of the picture—he could still see that hunk of thigh), because Dr. Black's office was shut up tight and the sign peeking through the window said:

SORRY TO MISS YOU! THE DOCTOR WILL BE BACK AT 9 O'CLOCK!

So Bill, without even a brush against Sharmayne to console him, retraced his route through downtown. Thursday wasn't the day Dolores taught catechism class, and he was pretty sure it wasn't the day for her hospital visits either, Jesus be praised. Oh *my* she was sanctimonious when she'd been in the presence of disease and death.

Disease and death. There was the polio banner again. He pictured each of his children, deprived of the new vaccine, in leg braces: Maggie saintly, limping down the aisle as she became the Bride of Christ. Tim stomping polio legs down on piano pedals. Andy kicking out at the dog with his braces (well, if they had a dog).

Katie in an Iron Lung.

That, of course, was way too much. The minute he pictured his baby lying on her back he realized that she was *too* going to get the new vaccine on Immunization Sunday, even if he had to escort her down to Due East Elementary School himself. To hell with Dolores's superstitions. *Listen to you,* he heard himself saying to his wife, *braying like a donkey at the moon. Don't BE an old lady now, Dolores. Don't BE like your mother up in Inwood. Don't be like all those old Irish biddies.* (You're-just-like-your-mother was a sorry old routine to fall back on, but it worked. It always worked.)

A little sermon on the advances of modern science wouldn't hurt either: *Think how my life would have changed if they'd had cortisone for me! Or would my momma have been too frightened to let them try it?*

That was confusing the issue of course—the fact was, they *didn't* have cortisone when he was sick and he'd lived anyway, which weakened his argument; but on the other hand, the double whammy of being compared to her own mother *and* his mother would likely press Dolores down on her knees, from which lowly position she'd beg him to take Katie for her vaccination.

Anyway, he sometimes thought the fact that he had almost

died when he was a boy (and now tracked the progress of his old disease with the avidity of a rare stamp collector) was what impressed Dolores the most about him.

He laughed out loud in the car, and finished up the last sip of sherry. The first night he ever saw Dolores he introduced himself by talking death and disease. He went right up to her at the break, before he'd even had time to swallow a beer down (he didn't need a beer, he'd been playing like an angel). He made himself swagger up to her table—when you carried a few extra pounds it was a choice of swagger or crawl on your belly—and he said:

"I was taken for dead when I wadn't but seven years old, and now I can see why I was saved. I was saved for *you.*"

Pretty good line. She thought so too—didn't know whether to laugh or hide under the table, but must have been convinced by his accent (he kept it soft in New York, and filed down the Charleston edges) and by his good tweed jacket (hot as hell to wear while he was playing, but he had the reputation of the South to uphold while he was booked in Manhattan clubs. He'd bought the jacket off a Pullman porter, when the train was pulling into Baltimore, for fifty cents. Brooks Brothers.)

Dolores McGillicudhy laughed good and loud at Bill Rooney that night, without even checking to see if the other girls at her table were laughing too. The others waved themselves off to the ladies' room, good tactful little girls, and Dolores invited him to sit down. She knew a bit about music too: she said his playing called to mind Art Tatum, and he would have married her on the spot.

The place (the Blue Oyster) was a dive, the kind of crowded basement joint where you'd either get fried or trampled if a fire broke out, but he didn't apologize for playing it—after all, she was the one who *came* to the dive where the G.I.s would paw at her. Her friends had to run a gauntlet of soldiers on their way to the bathroom and back. It didn't appear that they were in any hurry.

He tried to keep the swagger up, sitting down, but she didn't make it easy. She fired questions at him like a hard-boiled reporter, and he couldn't tell if she was amused because she liked him or because she thought he was a hick.

"So what'd you almost die of?"

"Rheumatic fever."

Her eyes lit up. "Heart diseases are very symbolic," she said, and giggled. Pretty cute giggle. "They took you for *dead?* Did they put you in a coffin and all that?"

"Oh no no no." He was tempted, actually, to say that they'd laid him out, but a childhood memory was fuzzy enough without getting into outright lies. "It was the maid thought I died. I collapsed out of the blue. Fainted dead away. 'You better come quick, 'cause he dead,' you know. My momma thought I was a goner, but then she put a mirror to my mouth and saw some misting, so she ran to get my daddy."

"It came on just like that? Rheumatic fever?"

"Well, almost just like that. I had a sore knee, and my father said: 'Oh, send him on to school,' but my momma kept me home. I was getting out of bed to tell her it hurt worse. In fact, it hurt like hell. And then there I was, flat on my back, with Lavinia, that was our maid, weeping over me."

"Well, I already know a good deal about you, Mr.—"

"Rooney. Bill Rooney."

She smiled wider, he thought. *Some*times an Irish name helped.

"Well, I already know a good deal about you, Mr. Bill Rooney. I already know you had a maid named Lavinia!"

"And rheumatic fever."

"And rheumatic fever. This was where? Wait, let me guess. Tennessee."

169

"Tennessee!" He was more than offended. He was wounded. "No, not Tennessee. Not hardly. South Carolina. Dizzy Gillespie's from South Carolina, you know."

That stopped her for a second, but then she said:

"Well, what did your father do?"

"Why he didn't do a blessed thing. He was *supposed* to be out back cleaning his guns, but he'd slipped off into the woods for a drink and he was slouched up against a tree when they finally did find him. Probably wouldn't have shown too much mist if you put a mirror to *his* mouth."

She liked that. And he found out why, later: her daddy was a drunk too.

"Oh my gosh. So where did this leave your mother? Poor woman."

"Well, she called for the ambulance and the doctor and such, but the closest little town—we were on a farm—was called Shining Star, and it didn't have but one ambulance, which, as it happened, was out in the woods picking up my father. A little girl cutting through the woods on her way home from school saw him lying there and took him for dead."

"Shining Star! What a name."

"Well my mother had no idea what was going on or what kind of sickness had come over me. To tell you the truth now, she was always keeping me home from school because she'd already lost one son—"

"Golly. Of what?"

"Train accident. Down by the Charleston station, back when the family lived in town. My brother used to walk down there with his friends and tease the passenger trains coming in. Flirt with them, y'know? He got friendly with nearly every conductor on the Seaboard Coast Line. But one afternoon—it was never clear how it happened, if one of the other guys pushed him, or if he just lost his balance—one afternoon he fell off the platform just when the West Coast Champion was pulling in. Squish."

She shook her head. "Just awful for you."

"Nope!" He grinned. "I wasn't alive yet. It hadn't ever been much more than a story to me. My brother was fifteen years old when he died. I wasn't born until the next year. So we used to celebrate my birthday with carrying-on and weeping. I was the only boy I knew who had to go to *Mass* for my brother on my birthday."

"Were you a big family?"

"Nope. Just me."

She shook her head. The hat trembled. "You mean they had one son, and he got to be fifteen years old, and then they had you?"

Bill nodded.

"What was his name?"

Pretty sharp little redhead. How'd she put her finger on *that* one so fast? "His name was William Thomas Rooney, same as my name."

And as soon as he answered he realized that she had taken charge. *He* came over to start the game, and she was calling all the plays, turning the story *he* was telling into part of her own preliminary personality test. How many G.I.s had survived her grilling? None, he hoped. He would be the first to survive.

But she didn't ask him another question. She said: "I was an only child too." This was part of the test: instead of asking him what it was like to live in the shadow of a dead boy, wearing a dead boy's name and a dead boy's clothes, fifteen years out of date, she only told him something about her own life. And he was supposed to find their common ground and make an intelligent comment about it.

This was an *essay* test. Finally he thought he had the angle: "When I complained about being the only one, my momma always said"—oh Lord, this was not the way to start out an intelligent comment, he *did* sound like Tennessee after all—"that we come into the world alone, and we leave it alone, and we might as well get used to the solitude."

Full credit for that one. She was smiling and didn't even seem to mind the folksy stuff.

"Well, let's get back to that rheumatic fever," she said, the way a math teacher might say *Well, let's get back to those binomials.* He loved it. Snip-snap, chop-chop, no muss, no fuss. "What did your mother do, finally? Looks like she saved you."

He leaned back in his chair and stretched out his foot until it was touching her open-toed high heels. She didn't draw her foot back, and he imagined—the fantasy of wartime—that he could feel a silk stocking through his shoe.

"Well now, she held me in her arms, she says—what else could she do?—until they could track down that ambulance. The ambulance driver had the good sense just to slap Daddy on the face and send him home. Walking. So my father was walking through the back door about the same time the ambulance—which by now's gone all the way back to the Shining Star volunteer fire station and picked up the new call—about the same time the ambulance was pulling up at the front door. Daddy used to say that Momma about *heaved* me at him, she was so desperate to save me. And you can imagine that ambulance driver's face when he saw the tipsy gentleman he just woke up in the woods holding a little boy passing in and out of consciousness. They say I was screaming bloody murder while I got handed around the room."

"It's a painful disease?"

"Yes *ma'am.* Very painful. It hurt like that for days—I can still remember it, all these years later, and don't forget, I wasn't but seven years old the first time. Like somebody ran screws through every one of my joints. And then tightened them. Once in catechism class Sister read out: 'And they numbered all His bones.' I wanted to shout: 'I know what *that*'s like.' " What a mistake—comparing himself to Jesus Christ.

But no: extra credit. Now she was resting her hand on his while he lit her cigarette. He was passing this test. He was the first man to ever pass this test. He tallied back up what gained him her smiles and saw that his winning answers were:

A. Being named Rooney.

B. Being an only child.

C. Quoting Scripture.

D. All of the above and throw in being tall and black-haired and good-looking, down to only ten pounds overweight.

"How long were you sick?" The way she smoked. She drew the cigarette back to her lips as if she were reaching over to open the curtains, and then sure enough—the light streamed in and her full lips gathered up the filter and he was filled with lust all over again. To have those lips opening up and covering . . . anything. Any part of his body would do.

"I was sick forever."

That would have to stand as the answer to the objective section of the test for now. You couldn't just meet a snappy redhead with breasts like those and a mouth like that and right off pour out your sorry heart. You couldn't very well start off what you hoped would be the first successful seduction of your own twenty years (for the love of Mary he had somehow survived two weeks in Manhattan without anybody in the band figuring out that he was a virgin, despite all his father's best intentions) by telling the object of that seduction about the six months you spent in the hospital when you were seven years old. It wouldn't do to tell her you received the Last Rites a dozen times before you received your First Communion. And surely she wouldn't want to know just quite yet about the new attack a couple of years later, when you were just starting to think you were normal.

You couldn't very well describe to a brand-new acquaintance of the female persuasion—one who was using a long white finger to poke a loose strand of red hair up into that goofy little hat, one whose lips were opening again the same way they had when she was watching you play—you couldn't possibly tell someone so very pale about the way your mother carried the tray into the sickbed ("Oh now Billy, let's us *please* get our hands off our dickey birds. We don't *do* that when a lady enters the room and we certainly don't pretend that nobody can see us"); and you wouldn't want her to know that the tray was all filled up with cherry cobblers and pecan something-or-other goo (plenty of Karo syrup) and you wouldn't want her to know that six months here and six months there lying around eating cherry cobbler and pecan goo left you with breasts bigger than any of the little girls had sprouted by the time you finally did get back to school. You couldn't very well whine that your mother kept you inside the dark house in the afternoons, when before you would have been learning the woods that skirted Shining Star.

No. All *that* was too much to tell a girl you'd just met. You were supposed to be smooching with her. You were supposed to be figuring out what experience *she* had (not much, from the looks of the hat). You were not supposed to be telling her about the hissed arguments that heated up once the lights in Shining Star were stilled. You were not supposed to be giving the blow-by-blow on fights between a father who'd swallowed a tad too much bourbon ("I know puhfectly well I'm a failure, thank you very kindly Regina, you *needn't* remind me of that when the topic of discussion is whether you intend to lock up this little boy in the house for the rest of his life") and a mother who was growing wattles and a big backside. A mother who was just too old, who'd been the wife of a rich real estate man when she had her first little boy, at a normal age, and was now stuck way out in the country and taken for her second child's grandmother ("I've already given up one little boy God rest his soul and don't you think it didn't *stab* me right through the heart to think of that little angel Frank so if you believe I'm going to let you take this one, this sweet sorry little sickly fellow, out into those back woods and teach him how to shoot a *gun* with which need I remind you he could very well take off his own hand or foot or *heart* well no thank you Frank having gone through the shame of losing my house and my little sweetheart and my life as I knew it I am not ashamed to say that I may be as you choose to call it locking Billy in the house but I will take that any day over locked in his grave which is where he'd be if you had your way with him").

Eventually of course they always got back to who was really responsible for the first Bill's death, and the second Bill—he—could see how peripheral he was to their struggle. He tried to pretend he wasn't a coward, but he was afraid to jump out of the pecan tree, even with its drooping branches, afraid if his heart started pounding (always an extra little murmur in there now), afraid if the ball in the dusty Shining Star schoolyard was a hardball. He was famous for his bad jokes—if the gym teacher asked him to fetch the bats, he said the bats only came out at night—and he heard himself getting louder and racier as the years went by. "So there's this nun," he would say, to gather the good Baptists around him, "who's up at the pearly gates taking her entrance exam. And St. Peter says to her: 'Here's your question. What was the first thing Eve said to Adam?' And the nun gets all worried, and says: 'Oh St. Peter, I'm not sure that's in the Bible. That's a hard one,' and St. Peter says: 'Correct. You may enter.' "

The only good thing that ever came out of the rheumatic fever was learning to play the piano, an hour's lesson from his mother every day once he could sit up, and the chance to give *her* something to do. Because any little boy, even one with a spare tire around his belly already, could see that she was desperate for some way to pass the time now that his father had given up even any pretense at farming.

Frank Rooney had gone through cows and pigs and even soybeans, but he wasn't a farmer, he was a failed real estate man. "I've got no truck with truck!" he said, dismissing tomatoes and cucumbers. Eventually he was content to put on a coat and tie in the mornings and just take a stroll through his empty acreage. He'd salvaged enough stock in other companies, even in the middle of the Depression, to ensure that he'd never actually have to farm his last piece of property, that he could use the land instead to hunt quail and dove, birds whose soft sweet flesh at the supper table reminded Bill that his obedience to his mother, his refusal to hunt, irked his father more than the business failure ever had.

Once a month, dead sober when he started out, his father made a ritual of taking Billy into Charleston alone. They went on the last Wednesday of the month, because on Wednesdays the stores were closed and school was let out; and they had a good dinner at Harvey's, where the colored waiters called his father Mistuh Rooney (it gave him the willies sometimes, seeing how they were sitting right over the old slave market). You would have forgiven the waiters for shuffling to keep a job in those days, but they didn't shuffle, they smiled distant pleasant smiles and went about their business, bringing back illegal drinks in sugar-dipped glasses. Bill squirmed. His father never looked the waiters in the eye or thought to say *thanks* or even seemed to hear them when they said the she-crab soup was *specially tasty today sir. Spicy but not TOO devlish, no sir.* The waiters seemed to him to possess a formal grace that irritated his father more than servility or toadying ever would have. He was always waving them away, and sometimes in the process of leaving, shadowlike, one of them would catch Bill's eyes and nod.

At home his father was gracious, why even courtly, with Lavinia, but at Harvey's he was too busy making eye contact. Frank Rooney still knew everybody in Charleston (went to school with the mayor himself); all the men paraded over to their table in their bone-colored linen suits as if Frank hadn't even hit a slick patch on the roadway. As if they weren't paying their regards to a man who'd been involved in a head-on collision. As if Frank Rooney would leave Harvey's after his dinner and walk right back down to the office, taking his son along with him to sit behind one of the big mahogany desks. If one of the men said Frank was looking good—and Frank always *was* looking good, big and pink, like a well-contented blue-ribbon hog—Frank let out a good-natured chuckle and said country life sure did agree with him. His *wife* never agreed with him, but country life did! Then he raised his eyebrows, the signal to Bill that he should tell a little joke (Bill was on the joke-a-day plan, crucial for social discourse). His father would go first, to demonstrate: "So y'all hear why our new President's not ever going to appear on a postage stamp? Well sir, they're afraid people might just spit on the wrong side of a Roosevelt stamp." The men patted Frank and Bill on their backs, and the waiters glided off.

When the other men in the room had passed through the reception line by their table, his father drank too much brandy with his coffee, and pretty much ignored his son the way he ignored the waiters. Oh, sometimes he thought to say: "Sit up there now!" or "Use that napkin, *sir,*" and once in a while, if he was really dreamy, he'd give Billy's hand a rough squeeze. "I *wish* your momma hadn't taught you to be quite so fond of pie," he might say, and Billy would put the fork down, and quit his eating.

They arrived home to a mighty dose of bitterness. His mother would try a cheerful routine first: "I'm so glad my two boys got a chance for a man-to-man meal together!" but already her voice was too high-pitched. The voice would go up by octaves as the afternoon passed, and by the time the lights went out in the big old farmhouse, on the last Wednesday of the month, he braced himself to hear the falsetto litany of her regrets.

Once his mother got going, she surely could recite a pitiful history. It was not, she said, that the Rooneys were ever up there with the polo-playing crowd. No, they hadn't lost a life like that, that was a life for Protestants and pretend blue bloods —by God you'd think the entire population of Charleston was descended from people who'd signed the Declaration of Independence—and she for one didn't envy them their stables. She never would have *wanted* a wearing empty life like that, taking the train up to Manhattan whenever the mood struck you. And it was not that they would have done so much socializing with the plantation people, or the bankers: she was *glad* that it was a little business they'd lost. It was not even that they would have sent Bill to boarding school anyway *(which* Bill?). No, it was not that she was stuck way out in the country and missed her pretty garden in Charleston. You had to bear your crosses, and she had certainly tried to bear hers with a measure of good grace. But (and here her voice got as squeaky as the high notes on a violin) she didn't think that God Almighty wanted her bearing the cross of a house *puhr*meated with the smell of alcohol. She didn't think the Blessed Virgin Mary wanted her whole life *puhr*meated with the smell of bourbon and brandy until she thought she might be living in a bawdy house.

A bawdy house?

He didn't need to know the meaning of the words to know that on those Wednesday nights, and on some other nights too, his father would rear up and cry out (well, maybe it was closer to stand up and choke out):

"Bawwwdy house? No ma'am, no ma'am I don't suppose you ever *have* seen the inside of a bawwwdy house. No ma'am, I don't suppose you ever have."

The words thrilled Bill, but not nearly so much as the storming out (for the woods? No, it was the dark of night, and the Ford was cranking up out front.)

His father's exit (like an opera! like a Dock Street Theatre melodrama!) was always followed by pitiful muffled sobs. Bill hit the pillow, waiting for them—praying for them—to let up, and when it was clear that she was not going to be able to lift herself up from this vale of tears, he knocked on his mother's door. He was supposed to lift her up. He was supposed to tiptoe over to her dressing table, where her gray old head rested on her tear-soaked fleshy arms. He was supposed to put his hands on her stooped shoulders, and he was supposed to lean his chin down on top of her thinning hair. He would rather have put his face down into the dark rich mud of a Shining Star creek bottom.

"Oh plumpkin, I miss him so much." It wasn't clear whether she was referring to Frank or to Bill Number One. "But at least you're my faithful one. At least I've got my little sweetheart to love me."

At which point he would quicken his massaging fingers, so he could hotfoot it out of there after a kiss to the top of her head. He despised the sniveling and he felt a swelling of admiration for his father's flight. But she sat with him over the music with such patience; he could not desert her. She herself played with a sad ordinary proficiency, but she had a good ear, and could pick out the ragtime that appealed to him after she'd heard it once on the radio. When she played a Mozart sonata, her body was resculpted in C major, her spine straightening and her shoulders curling gracefully. Allegro, andante. His mother finally came to life, as she must have when she was a girl and played with the Orchestra Society. This was what *vivace* meant: someone who once scented love letters with her best perfume.

She was smothering him, though—his father was right about that. She said no, he could not go to camp and have sailing lessons (there was a picture of the first Bill on the mantel, a racing cup in one hand and the other shielding his eyes from the sun). She said he wouldn't get much of a chance to sail, all the way out here in Shining Star, but he knew what the real reason was. She didn't want him to drown. And worse: she'd fixed it so that he asked *knowing* she'd say no. She'd fixed it so that he was afraid to ask in the first place, afraid of a sailboat, afraid—just like her—of drowning. Afraid of hunting.

Frank sometimes looked at him in wordless disgust—if he turned down a sip from the battered silver flask, say, or declined to sneak out back to try some shooting behind his momma's back. Sometimes when his father turned away from him and shuffled off he would run off in the other direction, kicking at clumps of drying wildflowers or uprooting them, patch by patch, in the big fields. If he had gotten his hands on a rabbit he could have throttled it.

Once a brown toad, smallish and trusting, had the bad fortune to hop into Bill's cupped hands after his father had clucked his tongue at him. Bill stroked its back and then flung the unsuspecting creature against a graceful narrow pine trunk, not even turning his head at the *splat*. And sobbed all the way back home, pulling out clumps of his own hair in punishment. For the rest of his childhood, he saw peculiar damp stains on all the pine trees in Shining Star.

But his father was, after all, pretty pathetic himself, slumping out in the woods when once he'd run a business. *Owned* a big slab of Charleston. On sober days Frank drove himself to the

Shining Star library, where he sat at one of two reading tables and calculated how much longer he could let his land lie fallow.

God knew Bill had looked for ground he and his mother and his father could occupy all at the same moment. For years he rose early so he wouldn't miss Frank's reading the editorials aloud from the *News and Courier* at the breakfast table. His father read with table-thumping approval, slowly, rolling his tongue out with pleasure at every word. But by the time Bill was enrolled at Bishop England High School and driving himself into Charleston every day, his father's tirades—the union-bashing, and the gimpy imitations of F.D.R., and the craziness about colored communists—made him uneasy; and after a year of Father Fitzroy's government class (Father Fitz was an F.D.R. Democrat if ever there was one) he skipped breakfast altogether, and declined to talk politics with his father the way he'd once declined to disobey his mother.

When he went on up to the university (no question of the Army with a scarred heart. His mother said *now* she saw why they'd been tested with the rheumatic fever) he signed himself up as a business major, and that seemed to give his father a measure of pleasure. He fell in early with the other unphysical musical types (the campus was mainly *composed* of 4Fs) and he bought stacks of 78s and traveled deep into the country to hear the Carolina Cotton Pickers or over to Atlanta to hear Duke Ellington. He worshipped Ellington. Six months after he joined a quintet, he was composing on his own—derivative smooth swinging tunes. The small bands were getting work now too in small clubs, and God knew there were plenty of small clubs in South Carolina and North Carolina and Georgia. They hired the Misses Lynette and Chantelle Breyers, twin blondes who introduced themselves in a bar out by Fort Jackson, as their girl singers, and stretched themselves a little further on up the coast every weekend. Bill was glad they weren't a dance band: he preferred a small room, and by the time Lynette and Chantelle were pulled out of the band by their father he was all for the Carolina Gamecocks trying their luck in Washington and Baltimore and hell, why not, New York City. The drummer had a second cousin who was a booking agent: they might not have sounded so good, when he came to hear them in Raleigh, if there hadn't been a war on and he hadn't been so desperate for sidemen. He could get the quintet into colleges in the Northeast, he said, and if they moved to New York he could slide them one at a time into little clubs, as one-night replacements, until they got their union cards. He told them they better be quick studies, though: New York jazz was moving into a whole other dimension. They couldn't just do the old Glenn Miller shit.

Regina and Frank Rooney got a chance to rant together when Bill dropped out of college. ("New York? You deserve what you get up there, boy, and don't come crying to me about the big city.") He always wondered whether it wasn't the chance to face him down together that drew them close so late in their lives. Once he was out of the picture, it seemed to him that they actually started . . . well, not snuggling, but conversing. When he visited on the weekends his mother was sitting at the breakfast table, nodding her approval at the editorials. Frank and Regina Rooney traveled down the road from conservative to crazy together, and it seemed to Bill that the turnoff on that particular highway must have come up around a bend. He hadn't seen any warning signs: when he left home his mother was reading the *Catholic Banner*. When he came back for visits they were subscribing to newsletters that made Bill's flesh crawl and talking up Father Coughlin. His mother had said, when he was a boy: "Oh I thank the blessed Jesus I was not born colored. I don't know if I could bear such troubles." Now she said: "Mark my words, those nigras are going to cause real trouble after this war is over," and his father—my God, the bone-colored suit—nodded his head in pious agreement.

He resolved not to argue music or politics with his parents, and they forgave him—hell, an only son, did they have a choice?—after he took Dolores down to Due East and decided to start the business there. They loaned him enough to rent an office and to invest in the little rental houses, and they gave him the down payment for the house on O'Connor Street, though neither one of them ever could abide Dolores. Before they ever heard a word of her politics they thought she was pretentious. She dressed like a girl. She let her hair hang loose. She smoked *while she was walking down the street.* His mother thought she squandered the money and stayed up drinking with him half the night. Well, maybe she did, at first, but that was nothing compared to what they thought when they heard her mention Norman Thomas's name. Regina could now outdo her husband's line on F.D.R. and colored communists and unions, and she could do it in a shrill tongue. They were trying to organize the textile mills upstate! You were hardly safe in your own bed!

He smiled again, solitary in his car. His mother was hardly prepared for Dolores. The poor old woman was rusty for conversation to be*gin* with, but then Dolores—persnickety and unruffled—bore down on her: throwing a *mutatis mutandis* or a *sine qua non* around the conversation, quoting statistics she'd probably made up, generally showing off as a Yankee bitch. He didn't come to Dolores's defense either: those two could handle themselves. A couple of peahens screeching in the yard.

When his parents died—together, in a car crash on one of those narrow dark roads leading up through the swamps—they were killed (he couldn't believe it) by a drunk pulling out of the woods. Probably a colored communist union organizer, he told Dolores, but she didn't think it was very funny. Never had a good sense of humor about his parents, even after they were safe in the Charleston ground.

They weren't either one of them in too good a mood after his parents died, actually. Andy was on the way by then, and though the rental houses brought in the steady income Bill had counted on, he hadn't counted on the maintenance they needed when one Marine family moved out and the next one was ready to move in. People took the doors off their hinges. People let their kids bathe Betsy Wetsy in the toilet bowl, and were surprised when her plastic arm got stuck down the hole. People let their children draw crayon *murals* on the wall. (Actually, people let their children scrawl on the walls. It was his own wife who thought of mural projects for their children's bedrooms, and had directed Maggie and Timmy to sketch out their ideas in pencil before he—praise St. Joseph, help of fathers everywhere —saw what they were up to and brought them scrubbing brushes.)

Maybe he should have been more direct with his father. Maybe he should have told him right out how iffy business was, how the cash didn't so much flow as it did trickle. And maybe it was just ignorance of how much help Bill and Dolores really needed that made his father leave what was left of the stock to the John Birch Society, in memory of Billy Number One. (He couldn't help feeling that it was his mother who went so far as to specify the Birchers, and that they had occurred to her only after Dolores was on the scene.) His parents left Bill and Dolores the Shining Star property, which Bill could hardly bear to walk across: in its final incarnation it was mostly a field of sour grass and brambles, blackberries and black-eyed Susans. Did his parents think he'd want to move his *family* there? It took him a year to sell it, and then it only brought in enough to cover what the mahogany coffins and the burial and the big

funeral supper at Harvey's had cost. For a year he had nightmares of giant metal machines disfiguring his parents.

The nightmares encouraged him to believe that his true in-
heritance from Frank and Regina was fear. Look at him, living
in Due East, living at sea level, living in sea *par*adise, unable to
even sail a boat. Every day of his life he drove past the bay,
where down below *teen*agers played with their toy Sailfishes.

He even had a hard time if the conversation at Ralph's
turned to sports, as of course it always did. He faked an interest,
and made himself scan the box scores every day of baseball
season, but his heart (ha!—his murmuring heart) wasn't in it.
Sometimes when he was pulling into his driveway he'd see Brent
Percy tossing a football with his sixteen-year-old friends, graceful boys in oxford shirts and chinos, boys with unconsidered
easy motions and low self-assured laughs, and he'd feel once
again that he was sprouting breasts on his own nine-year-old
chest.

There *was* one asset Frank and Regina hadn't even known
was in the will. They'd left him, the two of them, with the
resolution that if he had one child he'd have a passel of them,
that if one of *his* kids ever heard a sobbing momma he could say
to a brother or sister: "Oh Lordy, there she *goes* again."

And that resolution had brought him the only real pleasure
of his existence. He didn't care if he went bankrupt and had to
take to begging in the streets. He didn't regret having four.
Hell, he didn't regret that he'd soon have five. He could have
bragged on his children twenty-four hours a day. He wouldn't
be a bit surprised if, on Judgment Day, it was his children who
brought him safe passage into paradise.

Not that he could have foreseen having four so smart when
he first met Dolores McGillicudhy. Not that he could have foreseen having children at all with her. He couldn't even foresee
getting her out of the green shiny dress and getting his hands on

those white breasts. When he told her he'd been sick forever he was picturing what it would have been like to hold a naked redhead under the sheets back when he spent his days in bed, waiting for his heart to heal. He was picturing what it would have been like to dab a little pecan pie filling onto the pale nipples of this strange girl who sat laughing at him not because she thought he was a hick—he was pretty sure of this now—but because she thought he was *worth* interrogating.

He was already anticipating her next question, because you could just tell from the way she leaned her elbows on the table that she was ready to pounce with the next one, soon as she thought it up, that she'd be willing to spend the night with her chin resting on her palms like that, until she satisfied herself that this Southern piano player in the tweed Brooks Brothers jacket wasn't just trying to seduce her.

Which, actually, was all he *was* trying to do.

Or had been trying to do.

The trouble was that every time you actually started to talk to a girl, or to one as smart as this one seemed to be, or to a Catholic girl anyway, the images of their nipples smeared with pecan goo began to merge with images of the scapulars round their necks, the Christopher medals dangling on delicate gold chains. Somewhere behind them, like faint newsreel footage on the walls of a bar, other faces flickered: the Blessed Virgin Mother, saddened by your scheming; your own mother, sniffing the air around her; Father Cuomo in senior ethics class, so off-hand and humorous about the ants in your pants but so firm, too, about the *responsibility* a young man had, the whole weight of a young girl's life in his hands. All he wanted was the whole weight of a young girl's breasts in his hands.

Girls like this Dolores McGillicudhy, no matter how cheap and shiny their dresses were, just weren't girls like Chantelle and Lynette, the kind of girls who were only too happy to shed their slinky dresses. (But for the other guys in the band, not for guys like Bill Rooney. Not for guys who could kid them—

"Hey Chantelle, what's the difference between you and a peach?"

"I don't know honey, what *is* the difference?"

"Why a peach doesn't wear its skin *near* as tight as you've got that dress on."

"And a peach isn't half as juicy neither, huh Billy?"

—guys who would never, once it came right down to it, actually make the right move.) He'd never figured out how the Chantelles of this world figured out what you wanted, and how scared you were to get it, while the Dolores McGillicudhys of this world stared up with such eagerness and innocence and— *dammit* Father Cuomo was right—such trust that they'd never even suspect what you were after.

Or so he'd thought at the time. So he'd thought at the moment he was telling Dolores McGillicudhy about his escape from disease and death, and laughing about it.

But then, of course, it turned out that he hadn't had to work at seducing her at all: she'd pretty much gone and seduced him before the night was out.

Ah me. Ah mercy me.

She left his hotel room at three o'clock in the morning with a big damp stain on the back of her green satin dress.

And now she didn't want to let their children try a new polio vaccine.

Ah mercy mercy me.

And here *he* was at the end of River Street, remembering what it was like to be nineteen and so horny you'd screw a girl you just met and rip her scapular in the process. Here he was with nothing but an empty house to look forward to for the rest of his evening. Oh, hell's bells. He made a right turn, over the bridge.

At the very least he could drive around Lady's Island. Maybe she'd hitched a ride with Mae Pryor or Father Berkeley and gone out to the Friends Center, where they'd all stick their noses in where their noses weren't wanted. Maybe the saintly Dr. King was finally paying a visit out there, the visit Dolores had been praying for.

Oh, he couldn't even have one sweet memory without irritation breaking out like prickly heat. He gunned the accelerator and watched Due East recede in the rearview. Funny how things came back to you. Funny how he'd been thinking of Dolores as a girl so often lately.

Funny how old they were getting. He looked in the mirror again, this time at himself, and wondered if maybe he wasn't growing wattles too.

□   □   □

The sun was setting behind them by the time they pulled into the parking lot. Tom stopped like a tourist—well, he *was* a tourist after all—to gape at the light, at the size and the hysterical pinkness of the sun. It was painted in some imaginary color, some color that chemists might have cooked up for powdered fruit-punch mix, and purple clouds streaked up around it as unabashed as hussies. She took firm hold of his elbow (or maybe this was too familiar? She dropped her hand down) and told him they'd really have to hurry now if he wanted to look at the sea. The ocean on a Southern shore, Bill had said.

In 1945, one week before Roosevelt died, she and Bill arrived at this beach close to sundown too, and saw the sky in pastels when they limped off the rickety Due East beach bus. They were too late to register with the ranger: the driver left them off at the campgrounds, and they trudged over the sand not knowing whether to be dazed or giddy. Her first view of the beachfront, a broad white expanse stretching down from a bank of palmettos, made her think she was on a desert island, not in Carolina. Behind the tall formal trees was the paved road they'd arrived on and behind that, they soon discovered, a deep wood full of marsh and decay and underbrush, full of snakes and ticks, mosquitoes and chiggers. Bill was at home with the cacophony, but the buzz and the hum and the whine filled her with dread once the sun went down. To her it was a lament, a dirge, and she buried her head in Bill's chest. On the other side of the island—the side where the sun was setting now—there was a treacherous inlet and then a stretch of placid salt marsh broken by one island, then another and another and another, until the salt marsh became Due East. It was Due East that had already claimed her, on that first ride through town.

Now Dolores Rooney steered Tom Prince through the dirt parking lot onto a narrow beach—Hurricane Gracie had claimed seventy-five yards—and showed him where the storm had ripped open the bathhouse. The concrete foundation rocked in the surf, strong tonight at high tide, and rusted spirals of steel swung back and forth. Usually, she told him, the ocean looked gentle here. There were two or three drownings a summer, of strangers who thought they were swimming out into a lukewarm sea as soothing and as safe as bathwater. They were carried out by an undertow usually, and sometimes they washed up a mile downshore. Since she'd lived in Due East there'd been three or four shark attacks too.

"Good night!" he said. "I'm glad you told me."

"Oh, you won't be going swimming in this chill air," she said. "I don't think you're in danger of sharks."

"Well I guess not. But I can see myself coming back here when it *is* swimming weather. There's the article to write. And now someone to visit."

She didn't answer. Tom Prince would visit their house once,

and there he would meet loud jolly Bill, and then he would see her in a different light. He would see her double chin.

She didn't know what else to show him on the beach at dusk, now that she'd shown him sand and water and trees. She pointed out the fiddler crabs, and stretched her hand out along the horizon to show where porpoises surfaced when it was warmer.

"They come in very close," she said. "Close enough to nuzzle you sometimes. And we're all so anxious about sharks that—"

"Ugh," he said. "Something big and dark brushes up against you in the lukewarm sea." He brushed her, sharklike, and then drew back.

Now they were silent together. When he touched her, her lips pursed the way they did before she spoke up at a party meeting or challenged Bill when he'd gone too far with the children. How had she put herself in this spot? What was Bill thinking, at home, while he opened one beer after another in the empty house? She hadn't even troubled to leave a note.

"Mind if we walk a little?" Tom was pointing toward the campgrounds. "What's that way?"

She should tell him that she had to get back, that she had to let her husband know where his pregnant wife was. But she said nothing, and led him along the shore the way he had pointed. How many pleasures did she allow herself anymore? Surely a moment of serenity in a young man's presence, a walk along the beach, was innocent enough.

The campgrounds would be deserted in November, she told him, but he was unconcerned and undeterred. More silence as they slogged along. The night was thickening and she was reminded of those tenebrous nights with Bill in the bedroll, the dense sound of the night oppressing her. She had been fearful in the hot South, but Bill was home and surging with eagerness: at

190

night he flapped around the sweating tent, trying to comfort her, and in the morning he went to fetch the firewood with a face as grinning and grimy as a Boy Scout's. Oh, she could almost flinch at the memory of such sweetness on Bill Rooney's face. Sometimes, in the early years of their marriage, she had wondered whether the European war brides weren't like her, if they hadn't fallen in love with some soldier's walk or grin or broad shoulders only to discover in America that they had misinterpreted all those signs. If they hadn't discovered years later, when they finally spoke the same language as their husbands, that they had misunderstood everything. Absolutely everything.

Bill was in a panic about the new music when they decided to stay on this beach. *Come with me,* he'd said, *and let's us think about what we're going to do for the rest of our lives.* He was beginning to think he didn't have a musician's soul: he'd gone to hear the new stuff Dizzy Gillespie was tooting and touting, he'd gone to hear Charlie Parker, and *I don't get it,* he told Dolores. "Oh, I mean, I get it, but I can't play it yet—anyway it seems to me the piano player is mainly sitting back for all of this and I can't *do* that. Just can't do that. Whuduhya think Ellington'll do?" He heard everything he could in New York, but when he sat in he couldn't adjust to the horns and the reeds abandoning the melody line like that. Bop. He was getting bopped. The war was nearly over, and the musicians were crowding back in from Europe. Even those college dates in New Jersey were drying up, and by the time he asked Dolores to go South with him the rest of the Gamecocks had cleared out of New York.

It didn't look as if he'd ever get his union card, much less make a living as a musician in New York, but he'd been happy in the company of musicians, in the crowd of sidemen he picked up and brought back to his cheap hotel room to suck beer from bottles and wave chicken legs back and forth while they argued about the new sound. Their language shocked her as much as the good big apartments of the Academy girls had shocked her; she was used to the prim "shite and onions" of her father, and came close to choking on musicians' conversation ("Excuse me, ma'am"). They were always drunk, of course—she understood that part—but she could have fainted dead away when Bill pointed out which ones of them (Sweet Willie on the saxophone, Ike on clarinet) had been sitting in his hotel room stoned out of their minds on heroin. Why did she think they kept nodding out like that? Oh, the late hours, she said. Incredible how innocent a girl could be.

It was awkward, new lovers crowded into a little hotel room with such dubious characters, but she liked the way Bill stretched out when there was a tap on his door. She loved the way he argued Charlie Parker's case when the old-timers said the man wouldn't know a melody if it asked him to dance. He told her he'd always had a roomful of musicians in his college dorm, just as he'd always drawn a crowd with his bad jokes in the play yard: those long days sick with no one but his mother to comfort him made him just as glad for the company of men who stuck needles up their arms as he was for the chance, for a short while anyway, to be a million miles from Shining Star. He took her to Harlem for the first time in her life.

They decided on the trip South before she even knew she was pregnant. They planned to go on Easter break; she would tell her mother she was off with a college friend. She meant to see the world. The little trip to South Carolina would only be dress rehearsals for the trips she and Bill would be taking to Italy, to a liberated Paris.

Bill found a pair of rings in Woolworth's (five years before she'd stood on the sympathy picket line in the Woolworth's strike) for their disguise as a married couple. She hardly realized that hers left a welt. She was probably pregnant by then; by the time she got on the bus she had to put away the worn copy of

Dante she'd brought with her. She was doing her senior thesis on the *Purgatorio*, but she could not even read without getting woozy. She would not be able to make her Easter duty this year either, not while she was living with Bill as if they were man and wife.

Bill didn't want to take her to meet his parents; he wanted her to see where he came from, but Due East would have to be the stand-in for Shining Star. Due East would have the same encompassing white light. She went with him to rent the tent and buy the bedrolls and realized that he'd never been camping in his life either. They'd probably freeze to death or set their tent on fire, but they were drunk with the improbability of their expedition. She was crazy for someone so crazy he'd do this— but then, he was a musician. An artist. He'd try anything. Once he'd given her a marijuana cigarette, and she'd swallowed all her horror whole to go along with it. If she had to adjust to the bohemian life artists lived, she had to adjust.

It had taken her awhile to realize the extent of Bill's innocence. At first she worried that the decadence of his life—the marijuana, the boozing, the dirty sheets, the getting up at two o'clock in the afternoon to drink beer—would shock the sweet earnest boys she'd met at the Fellowship of Reconciliation or the Catholic Workers scrubbing the floors in their overalls. Then Bill told her the story of his father dropping him off at a whorehouse on his eighteenth birthday and how stupid he felt when he realized where he was; how he had walked back home, thirty miles through the night, begging rides for a mile here and five miles there, to announce to his father at the breakfast table that it had taken him eighteen years to figure out where his old man had been disappearing to every time he had a fit of temper. It had taken him eighteen years but now, he told his father and he told Dolores, now that he had it figured out, he didn't countenance it, no sir, no ma'am, he didn't countenance it for a minute. A vow was a vow, and a marriage vow as sacred as a priest's.

Before that story Dolores had assumed, from the sure eager way he held her (as if *she* were a piano and he only had to coax the notes out of her), that Bill had been taking lovers since he was twelve. A musician. Wasn't that something Southern boys, even Catholic ones, were supposed to do? Something to do with living close to the land, or the heat. But after the whorehouse story she saw that she would never be able to confess about her cousin. This man, this boy, this Bill who'd walked away from the birthday present of experience his father had arranged for him, was too—well, what other word was there but innocent?— to hear about her own sins. This was a boy who said to her:

"Oh Miss Dolores"—rolling his eyes and clowning—"this is heaven on earth and I will never, I swear it to you, I do, I will never, no matter what kind of no-'count lowlife musicians tempt me to do otherwise, I will never in my life be unfaithful to you."

She stopped and, not knowing she did it, closed her eyes for a moment.

"You're very peaceful and quiet," Tom said.

"Just remembering," she said, "what this place looked like at first. Trying to see it through your eyes."

"Well. I think it looks the way you described it before. Otherworldly, after New York." Suddenly, out of nowhere, Tom Prince turned a cartwheel on the sand, and then another. He stumbled and righted himself in the dark, and bowed an elaborate corny bow from the waist. She clapped and smiled, then bent to pick up the black glasses that had fallen off. He was still very young.

"Thanks," he said, and then stood facing the ocean and blowing his chest out. The cartwheels had energized him. "Oh," he shouted into the wind, and she was startled that he was suddenly so loud. "It's good to get out of a car and a motel and a court-martial. It's good," he said in that new loud voice—and then there was a gulp between the words, a gulp she wasn't sure came from him or from her, at the expectation—"to be walking on the beach with a beautiful woman."

"Why thank you," she said instantly in a voice without inflection. She sounded as false and cold and efficient as a Miss America contestant answering the final round of questioning. She sounded like a woman who heard that she was beautiful every day—and surely Tom Prince knew that she wouldn't fall for *that* falsehood, not with two chins and swollen breasts and a bulging belly. She sounded almost like a *Southern* woman: she dismissed him with her answer, held him at arm's length, the way all the mincing flirts downtown held her own husband at arm's length.

He was embarrassed. After a formal silent moment he began walking toward the campgrounds again, and pulled away without seeming to know that he'd left her behind. Didn't this Tom Prince have any idea of what she might do when he said something like that?

Why did this little twerpy reporter—oh now he was fading back again into the overeager goofy-looking boy who approached her on the bluff—why did he think that she'd go to bed with him in a second? What was the matter with her? She was pregnant. She had been faithful for fifteen years.

What did she send out—rays? She heard Tim and Andy whispering in their bedroom late at night. *Easy lay*, Tim had hissed in the dark, and Andy had repeated it with a dirty giggle. *She's an easy lay.* Innocence of language was the first to go. They had no idea what they were talking about. Tom Prince had no idea what he was talking about, calling her beautiful, telling her he'd meant to ask her to dinner. Did he really think she'd have an affair with him? They were not in New York; they were in Due East, South Carolina, where adultery in 1963—if it happened, and she guessed it must have happened to *someone* else besides her—was as hidden as a duck blind in a thick swamp.

There was nothing to do but follow him as he tramped off down the beach, nothing to do but say, when she finally reached him:

"Tom, I'm sorry. But I'm going to have to be getting back now."

His eyes reflected mild surprise behind the glasses, but then he threw his arms up to concede defeat the way he had when faced with a closed gas station. Oh sure, sorry, of course. He looked away and took off for the parking lot at a near-trot—but then he slowed and waited for her to walk at his pace again. He gave a smile that was: what? Apologetic? Encouraging? He had the perfect even teeth of a dirty-blond Protestant boy—oh what the boys in Inwood, with their miserable rotten Irish teeth, wouldn't have done for such a mouth—and she set her face toward the sea. She was wrong. Reading all that into it when there hadn't even been anything there. He told her she was beautiful because he'd just done a cartwheel. He knew she was pregnant: why should he want to make love to her? He was just trying to be sweet (the look on Bill's face when he showed off the house he'd bought for her and the new baby). Tom Prince, boy reporter, had no idea who she was. She'd gotten it all wrong.

"I'm sorry," she said, "to be taking you back to town so soon. But I saw all at once how dark it was. Is."

It *was* dark. The horizon she'd pointed to was no longer visible—the ocean spread out now the way the light had spread before—and the wild pink sun was down. There was enough light to see from the pale half-moon and the early stars, but she almost tripped over a stubby piece of buried driftwood. Tom grabbed her by the elbow, then released her just as she'd released him when they arrived.

"Thanks," she said, and when she looked up at him realized again even in the dark that calling her beautiful hadn't even been flirting as far as he was concerned. It was just one of those gallantries that men spat out as easily as tobacco juice. Saying they'd been planning to ask you for a date.

"We'll be ready for a glass of wine," she said, drawing her sweater tighter. "It's *cold* out here."

"Look," he said—by now they were almost back to the parking lot—"it's getting late. Maybe you'd just let me give you the wine. I don't think I should trouble you to fix dinner so late. Not tonight anyway. It's a weeknight and all, and I know you've got your kids' homework to see to."

He thought then that her children were young, an impression she must have given him back in the kitchen. She hadn't said a word about Maggie's being away at school. Oh well: she would have a little one again, soon enough.

"Please come to dinner," she said. It didn't matter if they ate meat loaf and her husband was a boor.

"You're *sure?*"

"Of course I'm sure."

He held the car door open for her, and when she slid inside the warm air soothed her. All at once the same pregnant tiredness she felt every evening descended, but behind it was the same little surge of energy that must have made Tom Prince turn cartwheels on the beach. When he climbed in behind the steering wheel she saw that a piece of palmetto frond had attached itself to his lapel, and she reached over to brush it off for him just as the door closed and the light shut off.

Then she heard Tom suck in his breath and draw his whole body back, and that moment of confusion in the dark made her feel thirteen again. He thought she was reaching over to make a pass at him. He thought *she* was making a pass.

"I just wanted to—"

"It's all right," he said, in a peculiar confused voice.

His confusion set her off. "I just wanted to brush the *palmetto* off your jacket." The way she would have talked to Tim. How ridiculous of him to think . . .

"Oh." It was the most doubtful *oh* she had ever heard in her life.

She found herself shrinking against the passenger door and despising herself for shrinking. How old was this man? Twenty-five? "It's still there," she said. What would Bill have called her tone? Condescending? Bitchy?

By now they could see each other in the dark. Tom looked down, saw the piece of tree, had the good sense to shake his head in embarrassment, and brushed it off.

"Did you think I meant to do something else?" It was madness to make this worse, to draw it out, but by now there was steam issuing from her mouth. If he had been a foot closer to her it would have scalded him.

"No. Of course not." He was completely confused. His voice had gone high.

And she was completely confused too. "Sorry." A pause. A second to will dignity. "A misunderstanding."

"Look," he said. His favorite expression. God, she despised young men. "Look, I like you very much Dolores. But I think—" Oh go ahead. *Struggle*. "I think I'm getting mixed messages from you."

Now she was shrinking past thirteen, shrinking back into childhood. She was bothering her father as he listened to the

198

Saturday afternoon opera. Her father was shooing her away. Mixed messages indeed. She could have slammed her fist down on the dashboard just as Bill would have done. Had she really meant something she didn't even know she meant when she leaned over to brush his jacket? If Bill had accused her of such nonsense she would have said:

"For God's sake. Don't be ridiculous." And that would have been the end of it. Now she stared out of the passenger window and imagined triple chins, quadruple chins in the sideview mirror.

"Look." He'd said it *again*. "I find you attractive."

She gave her head a quarter turn and stared out ahead.

"I find you very attractive, and I've never said that to a stranger before in my life."

Sideways, she watched him. He really was struggling, and it wasn't only embarrassment. There was a physical strain in the front seat of the rented car. She hadn't invented it. She hadn't got the *beautiful* thing wrong at all.

"But I know you're married, and I know you're pregnant, and I don't want you to think that I'm—"

She burst out laughing, and turned to look him full in the face. Now he stared out, smiling a little at the sound of her laughter. How very sweet he looked in his embarrassment.

"I didn't want *you* to think," she said, and thought that maybe his shoulders relaxed. She added, throwing it off as an afterthought: "I find you very attractive too."

The innocence of language was the first to go: mixed messages. "Anyway," she said, brisk and efficient. Enough talk. She wasn't going to end up naked with Tom Prince: she was too old, and he was too sweet. "I'd very much like you to come to dinner. I'd like you to meet my children, and my husband too of course."

"Okay," Tom Prince said. "If you say so. I'd be delighted."

The tension dissipated. Tom eased the car out of the heavy sand, then gunned it when they were back on the beach road; but he did not travel quite so fast leaving as he had arriving, and Dolores slipped into the cloud of sleepiness that the dissipating tension had spread.

5

FORTY YEARS OF BAD LUCK

There were six of them at the trestle: her brother Andy, another white boy, and three colored boys clustered around Tim, the director, who was filming them as they passed cigarette butts among themselves and performed weird febrile boy-dances. Kate counted their weaving forms as she emerged from the trees and stood on the little hill that marked the path back up to the tracks. She even paused to calculate which mugging silhouetted figure might belong to a boy she knew.

Now one of the white boys was not smoking but doing a balancing act out on the trestle itself: after a moment she could see that it was Stevie Dugan, who was loved and despised concurrently by Kate's best friend, Franny Starkey. It was Stevie who all last year had put on an innocent uncaring face and

201

called out sweetly: "We all have to start at the bottom, Fanny," and "Sure hope nobody tells me to kiss their Fanny," and led Miss Frances Starkey to rechristen herself before junior high school started. Stevie Dugan was a tall pimply skinny boy with thick glasses who published his own comics and newspaper, and so *nat*urally he had picked Tim for his mentor. Kate's feelings for him were not nearly so complicated as her friend's: she despised him, clean and simple. His presence could only complicate her mission.

She was able to take this minute out, this pause to recognize Stevie Dugan and to despise him anew, because she was composed now, composed and purposeful, her heartbeat barely quickened. Calm and deep breathing had carried her through the woods and out here to the hill overlooking the tracks where she could gaze out on her brothers, who would probably help her, and on the other boys, who probably would not.

Of the colored boys she recognized two: Josephus was one of the skittish boys who had stopped talking to her in the last year, dark and pleasant and grinning with lips as pink as Bazooka bubble gum. He had distinguished himself by introducing himself as *Sephus* a few years back, befriending Kate whenever she showed up with her brothers, and then forgetting all at once who she was. The tallest of the colored boys was Jefferson Davis ("Don't say my family didn't have a sense of humor!") and the only colored boy in all of Due East whose full name she'd had occasion to learn in five years of going to the trestle. Jefferson Davis was Tim or Andy's age and often had five or six younger brothers trailing after him; the Davises were sons of the colored doctor, a g.p. whose sorry-looking concrete office stood on the border between colored and white Due East, and they were always dressed in identical pairs of ink-blue Levi's from Friedman's Department Store, jeans starched and pressed so that they rustled when the boys made a move, and plaid shirts with the tails tucked in and the sleeves buttoned up. The third boy might be one of the Davises too, though he was jockeying to put himself in the center of Tim's lens in a way that staid Jefferson would not have. As they grew older the Davis boys grew more formal and quiet. Once, at the dinner table, Kate had said of Jefferson that he spoke just like a white boy. That had made Tim crazy—Tim, who had actually been talking to Jefferson about whether he might be the one to integrate Due East High, conducting a conversation no other white boy would have dreamed of striking up, a conversation Jefferson, sidestepping politely, never seemed to take part in. Jefferson, unlike Stevie, kept his own counsel.

When she said that Jefferson talked white Tim rose from his chair with a spasm that knocked the chair down and then careened to Kate's side, where he grabbed her by the wrists and squeezed the skin there until it smarted. He said, holding her: "Don't you ever say that in front of Jefferson, hear? Don't you *ever* say that." Their mother, rising too to preclude their father's prying Tim away, said in an offhand way: "Don't dramatize Tim. Sit yourself right back down. You know Katie better than that."

Tim turned on their mother too. "Oh, you think *you* can save them. You and Katie. Don't you think they're perfectly capable of saving themselves?"

"Who, Tim?" Her mother, standing, still affected a careless tone.

"Colored people." Bang on the table, right next to Katie's plate. "Colored people can get themselves their civil rights without your talking about it day and night and Katie thinking she's doing them such a big favor saying they talk like white people. You two make me crazy the way you go on. Meanwhile people put their *lives* on the line. Colored people."

Katie wasn't surprised—Tim regularly read her out for her

moral deficiencies, and he would apologize before the night was out; she for one couldn't care less about the Oldest Altar Boy in Due East's sermons—but Dolores, they all could see, was stunned. Dolores sat and stared down at the gluey mashed potatoes and didn't seem to see that Tim looked strangely to his father for confirmation or that his father, even more strangely, tipped his chair back. Bill said to Dolores, who still would not look up: "Well, bless his heart, he's right, idn't he? They'll do it by themselves with or without the Reverend Dr. King. We don't watch out they'll do it with the help of that kook Malcolm XYZ. You're right as rain Tim, they will most certainly look out for themselves without any white speechifying—except for J.F.K., who's got to provide the moral leadership, dudn't he?— but will you, for the love of the sweet Lord Baby Jesus, will you please quit your shilly-shallying Tim and sit yourself down to eat your supper?"

Then they spent the whole night long, the two of them, Bill and Tim, smug and casting each other little conspiratorial looks. Tim and Bill on the same side. I guess we put *her* down. It had lasted all of a night, the alliance between Tim and his father, and all because she, Kate, had ventured the observation that Jefferson Davis spoke like a white boy.

Now as she stood by and planned her approach she saw that she was wasting time, speculating on which of the six boys would help her, picturing which of them, how many of them, could take on the Snake Man and his knives. Because it didn't matter after all who went with her to rescue the girl as long as two of them did: as long as her brothers would believe her and come. She made her way to the tracks themselves and hobbled along, a cripple, an old decent woman just trying to do the right thing, the worn ties below giving way beneath her feet. For years she had walked along this last stretch by the side of the tracks, the underbrush and the wild grapevines and the Queen

Anne's lace reaching out to tickle her, but one day she and Andy had seen a golden wildcat squat along that border, and since then she had taken the tamer route.

When she drew closer the air stank of the boys' cigarettes, a smell she didn't recognize as the odor of her mother's Kents or as the smell of pilfered menthols either. This was something harsher and sweeter all at once: maybe Tim and Andy had been buying singles out of an open pack at Mr. Tobias's grocery again or maybe the colored boys rolled their own. The cigarettes had a foreign odor, as foreign as the fatty dank vegetable smell of the dark drafty shacks where her mother carried clothing packages from Our Lady of Perpetual Help.

None of the boys stopped the action as she stood in their midst on the sandy pebbly bank, ten yards from where the wooden trestle began. Andy's eyes puffed up red and swollen; he was sitting now, in the dirt at Tim's feet (or at Tim's feet whenever Tim, who was prancing around with his camera, came back to home base), and he smiled at her in a peculiar laconic way. "Well here she is. Hey Katie, what took you so long? That man didn't come after you, did he?"

Andy wasn't laughing, not exactly, but there was an explosion of giggles from the boy called Josephus and from the little one, the one who might be one of the Davis boys. Andy never made fun of her. She felt herself reddening. Pulling down her drawers. *Bobby* pins.

"As a matter of fact," she began, and heard her voice trip out.

"As a matter of fact," Andy said, in his same slow dreamy voice, "we've only got fifteen minutes of good light." He stopped, and leaned his chin to his knee. "Jesus, *look* at this light."

"Andy, don't say *Jesus* like that." Embarrassing. She only wanted him to listen.

"Andy, don't say *Jesus* like that. He will strike us all down daid and I didn't get to Confession last week!" Stevie Dugan: he'd skipped his way back across the trestle and now peeked out from behind Tim, the two of them looking like one of the Hydra's double heads.

"Stevie, look I've got something to tell my brothers."

"Something to tell her brothers? Hmmm. Something Tellibly Important and Presumably Private." Stevie Dugan was a baby; what was the matter with all of them? Tim held his camera aside to grin at her and she saw that his pupils were as wide as Andy's, his eye rims red against his blond wispy lashes. Josephus and the little one had *tears* running down their cheeks, but it was hard to say whether that was their hilarity over Stevie's razzing or whether they'd smoked too many butts themselves. Stevie himself didn't look as if he'd indulged in cigarettes: just his regular despicable self. And Jefferson looked right, standing off to the side and averting his eyes. The others, though, made it seem as if Tim's camera was running in slow motion. It was all right that she had been calm and considered on her way to come fetch them, but now they had to move: right away. They had to save that girl before the Snake Man sliced her up and put her in the marinating pool in his front yard.

"Timmy, Andy, I need you to come. The Snake Man—"

"Oh," Andy said, and nestled his chin deeper into his knees to catch the view, to get a good long look at the shallow water, at the meandering marsh and the shadowy clumps of oak and southern pine out beyond. The light (it had moved from gray to orange to something pink now, something like that boy Josephus's bubble-gum mouth) was only a backdrop for the dark calm evening water. The horizon was picked clean of birds. Soon the freight train would whoosh along, clackening out the sounds of escape. It was cold, and they were not listening to her, and he could be murdering her at the very minute. "We made all that up about the Snake Man, Katie. Din't you figure that out yet?"

"Oh Gawd," said Stevie Dugan. "What y'all tell her about that guy? You tell her he was a criminal? I bet you did. A murderer? A murderer embezzler robber pilferer rapist?" Stevie Dugan knew what a *rapist* was: well, of course. He published his own comic books.

They had to get out of here.

"Timmy," she said.

Tim took his eye away from the eyepiece and stared down at her. He seemed to be considering her for the first time; she was almost drawn to his kindly stare. It was the stare of a *father*, of Father Knows Best and Andy Griffith and even Ricky Ricardo when he held Little Ricky in his arms onscreen the first time. The look on her brother Tim's face was puzzled and delighted and its effort was mesmerizing: she almost could have stood there forever, letting its paternal glow wash over her.

Almost. But that girl.

"Katie," Tim said in his faraway voice, "I had another of my brilliant wholly original ideas. I'm putting in a dream sequence. Show her what we been doing, you guys."

Stevie and Josephus and the little maybe-a-Davis performed an impromptu Looney Tunes dance.

"It's a nightmare Our Hero's having, see?"

"The movie," Andy said.

"Right, she gets it, it's part of the movie, you get it, right Katie?" They sounded—drunk. Had they brought a bottle of her father's out here?

"Look I need you to *help* somebody."

They stared at her, even Stevie Dugan, oafish and uncomprehending. Mother of Mercy, grant me strength.

She heard the whirr of Tim's camera rolling again and heard

him say, or glub, as if he were under water: "Go ahead Kate, you're in the dream too. This is perfect. This is just before he kills her, he sees her in a dream. Go ahead. Improvise. Dig into your subconscious." Oh God he had been reading *An Outline of Psychoanalysis* again, which her father had made him swear he would not ever once more discuss at the dinner table. Bill said there was more danger from Sigmund Freud than there had been from Joe McCarthy and John Birch put together. Kate heard from the kitchen that the Due East librarian wouldn't let Tim check out *The Sexual Enlightenment of Children* either, and Bill wouldn't let Dolores go get it for him. "Fifteen years old? He's still a children himself!"

"Timmy I'm not kidding. Shut that thing off."

"Go on," Josephus said, almost looking at her for the first time in a year. "We having fun."

"Andy tell him to quit. I'll get Momma to write a note to the English teacher, we'll finish the movie tomorrow. I need you guys to help me now."

The little boy said: "Don't you be shutting it off. Take *my* pitcher," but Jefferson Davis touched him on the shoulder: "Quit."

Andy said: "On the other hand you could just relax and do Tim's little dream sequence and then we could *all* go help you. What is it anyway, Katie?"

Now Andrew had borrowed the paternal gaze. She could not meet it. She could not spit out the word *rape*, not with Stevie Dugan there. They had made all that up about the Snake Man? Or did they make up that they were making it up?

"Move on out there by the tracks Katie," Tim said. "I'll shoot Andy throwing you off in a minute and then we'll be all done. No muss no fuss. Right now Katie just stand out there with your back to the water."

The old wooden trestle stretched out beyond her. Boys

fished from it all day long, but she had only crossed it once. Between every tie was black shallow water, glassy water resting over mud, and on her one trip across every step between ties had reminded her that her sneakered foot could slip right through and leave her pinned and dangling while the freight train bore down. She'd only walked over once—thinking that she'd go see what the boys saw, plantation fields, cucumbers going soft in the midday sun—but after the crossing she'd turned right around and headed back, slowly, counting the ties and vowing that she'd never do what her brothers did: run across as soon as they heard the first hoot of the evening train, beat it out, and crouch on the other bank as the big engine clanked past them, spitting out pebbles and disdain.

They had made all that up about the Snake Man? "Timmy, don't, just listen."

"That's good. Yes, my sugar lamb, this is what it means to make a movie! That's right, just shove me away like that, like I'm going to push you backwards over the water. That's part of his dream, you're shoving him away."

"Timmy, that man has got forty pieces of rattlesnake cut up in his front yard! I know you didn't make that up, or the sign neither, because I've seen it with my own eyes."

"Holy moly that's good. Wait now, stop and calm down, like you're talking to him in the dream."

"Timmy, he took a girl in there. Into the *trailer*. She wadn't much older than me." Now five boys were an audience who strained forward for her next sentence, but Tim said:

"Older than I."

"Timmy she was just a teenager and he was pushing her along. I *know* she didn't want to go and then I could see through the window—"

Hoots from Josephus. "Uh-oh. Peeping Tom. Put *you* away on the chain gang." Someone clearing his throat.

"Shut up now, you morons," Tim said. "This is perfect. Katie, you are writing the script yourself. Bless your heart, this is better than *An American Tragedy*. Hell's bells, this is better than *Billy Budd.*"

"Timmy, turn that camera off and listen to what I am telling you. That man dragged a girl in there and then he ripped off her clothes and then—"

It was Andy clearing his throat. "Oh Kate," he said in a low mournful voice. "You don't want to go on now, do you?"

He wasn't laughing at her, and Tim wasn't, and Jefferson Davis, trying to shove his hands into his starched narrow jeans pockets, wasn't laughing at her: they were none of the older boys laughing, but the other three were, not just laughing but hooting and hollering, holding their hands over their crotches to stop themselves from peeing.

"Go on Miss Rooney. What'd he tear off first?" Stevie Dugan.

"The Snake Man is raping a girl back in the woods and we've got to stop him."

It was a Moment. Stevie looked as if she'd punched him in the gut, as confused as her mother that day with Andy. The smallest boy looked to Josephus to model a response, but Josephus only smiled a friendlier excited smile.

Then Tim, offhand, lowered his camera and looked at her with the worst look of all, the pitying one. It was not that he didn't believe her. Worse. As if he were the Pope, so sure of his own doctrine that he doesn't even need to get all heated up about it, he said:

"No he's not."

The magisterium.

And then Andy echoed him while she was still able to look around at all of them, while she was still able to look him in the eye:

"No he's not Katie. He takes girls back there all the time."

Josephus and the little one clutched each other, overcome with spasms of glee, but Stevie Dugan only threw his arms up in what looked like, wonder of wonders, an offer of apology.

Tim drew the eyepiece back up to his eye and Andy carped up at him again:

"Tim, we've got to get that bridge scene done. Quit messing with that dream stuff now. Come on, I'm starving. Shoot the part where I throw her off and then let's us get on home."

Tim said: "Just give me a little more Kate. Don't worry about that guy. Say it the way you said it before, about the rattlesnake cut up in his front yard."

"Forty piece 'a snake," Josephus said. "I know what that mean, in somebody dream."

Tim pushed the button and the camera whirred. He did not ask Josephus what that meant.

"I had me a dream with rattlesnake cut up, I be counting on having me a mess of bad luck."

"That so?" Tim wasn't listening: he was concentrating on shooting his sister, who stood blank, only her little rounded belly, through the stretch pants, heaving out her confusion.

"Uh-huh. That snake cut that way mean they gonna be blood running in the street. Forty piece a snake, forty year a bad luck. I'ma tell you."

"You full of shit." That was the little one—he *couldn't* be a Davis. Jefferson shook his head in disgust.

Kate tried to mold her face into the same elegant dismissal and went to sit on the ground next to Andrew. She buried her head behind her knees; her brother reached out to touch her shoulder, but she drew away, repulsed. What her brothers meant was: that girl wanted to be coitused.

"What if you're wrong?" She knew she was hissing. "What if

he made her? What if he made all the others? And then cut them up and put them behind that sign?"

Andrew was not trying to touch her anymore, but he shifted closer on the ground and answered her in a low voice so that none of the others could hear, so that Stevie Dugan could not hear:

"I'm not wrong. I've seen them too."

Oh how could you possibly trust somebody who wanted to poke around with bobby pins to know whether a girl was in danger of being murdered by a lunatic.

Tim said: "C'mon Katie, upsy-daisy. Now we shoot the scene where he throws you off the bridge."

How could you trust another lunatic, for God's sake? Her brother Tim looked like a wild man, a rabbity madman with pink eyes, idolized by little boys who would make fun of him in a year or two. Who were probably making fun of him already. Jefferson Davis was walking back across the trestle.

"C'mon Katesie, quit your worrying. Here we go."

Now he was trying to pull her up by the wrist.

"Here we go? Here we go to hell, Timothy Rooney." She shook off his hand and rose up by herself and—she had no notion why she should do such a thing—she crossed herself, stuck out her tongue, and watched Stevie Dugan recoil from her in mock horror.

"Oh come on Kate, it'll only take a minute. Who're we gonna use for a double?"

But by the time he asked her who would replace her she had already started running, running along the rotted uneven railroad ties, her toes digging down into rocks between. She knew that by the time she made it all the way back down the tracks to Union Street the dark would be falling. The dark would be falling, and the treetops against the night sky would look as if God had taken pinking shears to them. The chill would be wending its way through the woods and over the tracks, and the freight train would be rumbling along, closer by the minute.

"If you guys won't help I'm going to get Daddy," she was calling back over her shoulder. "My daddy'll know what to do." *My daddy?*

She could hear Andrew's clear, reasoned young debate-team voice following her down the tracks:

"Oh Katie don't get Daddy. Use your head."

But she wasn't using her head—they were using their heads, using them to block out what had to be done. *She* was using her feet to carry her away from her merciless brothers and their crazy movie and the black still water underneath the tracks.

She did not look behind her, but she knew she had no echo. They weren't following after her. There was another word to look up; she'd heard them use it over the summer. *Poontang.* She seemed to be running on alone.

□   □   □

Bill Rooney, crossing his second bridge, passed from Lady's Island to Paradise Island and troubled to wonder aloud what the hell he was doing driving to nowhere.

Way out here, down half-paved rutted roads, he found himself passing first one juke joint, then another: low concrete buildings no bigger than the two-bedroom enlisted men's specials rented out by Rooney Realty, rectangular concrete dives where sweating bodies crammed on the weekend to sway and shimmy.

It wasn't the first time he had found himself driving past the Paradise Island clubs (some *clubs*). There were Saturday nights —Saturday was always, always the hardest night of the week— when Bill Rooney had his fill of the sanctimony of his house and escaped to drive out here, alone down a country road. Oh sure, he knew what he was doing, he didn't need a psychiatrist to tell him that his father always drove off in a huff when he couldn't take Regina anymore, and that he, Bill, couldn't even think of an original punishment for Dolores. It angered him that he aped his father, but it didn't make him stop. Someday Tim, if Tim ever found a girl crazy enough to have him, would tire of his young wife's reproach, and then the third generation of Rooneys would drive himself out into the night. There was something about peeling out of your own driveway that reaffirmed your status as head of household; and there was no denying that Dolores gave him more respect on a Sunday when he'd taken one of those solitary drives, just as Regina had once paid Frank more mind.

The rides reminded you that life went on outside your own walls, outside the little boxes of tension that families built for themselves. These juke joints in the country held fifty cars in front, fifty cars in a part of the county where you wouldn't think there were fifty *houses* if you didn't know how far back some of the dirt roads were set, if you didn't understand how circuitous they were, how what looked like a mud flat after a spring rain was really Star Route 64, home to a score of cabins and houses and shanties spaced out over the miles.

Miles of little boxes, miles of roads with carloads of people looking to bust out of those narrow boxes. And where did they go to escape? They crammed into another box, the juke-joint box. But there they were not so much imprisoned as enclosed, wrapped tight and secure in the music and the bodies pressing up close. They came to hear the Shirelles or Sam Cooke blaring out of a rented jukebox; but once in a while, on a warm summer night especially, Bill would drive by and hear a couple of live musicians, guitars and drums mostly: once he'd heard a sax begging for mercy in the dark night. It was a piano that finally overtook the sax—who'd have thought a piano in such a dive?

214

—and there was nothing he would have liked better, those Saturday nights, than to pull into that dirt yard that made up a parking lot and shoulder his way into a concrete box where forty-watt bulbs and coolers of beer and flasks in breastpockets and pianos—rented? borrowed from church?—were lighting up the night. Out of the question, of course, not worth even fantasizing: a white man would be the law, and the crowd would ooze itself out the back door as he pressed in at the front. What Dolores didn't understand was, you didn't just walk into a place like that. Why not? she'd said.

There was no end to what Dolores didn't understand.

Now, at dusk, he passed one of those concrete clubs, looking pathetic and stood-up on a lonely weeknight despite its recent coat of government surplus tan paint—no sign to identify it, but everybody, even white everybodies from town, knew that this one was called Moses Place. Moses Place. Jesus there were some beautiful names on these islands, names attached to juke joints and names attached to people: Ezekiel and Nehemiah, Samuel and Eurydice and Ophelia. Last week a girl named Zenobia had called for Lily Lightsey, a girl with copper skin, probably part Cherokee. Cat's eyes, with a yellow light to them, and a knife-slash on her chin. A beautiful girl with a full round rump, a Zenobia who would dance in Moses Place and get herself in trouble in no time, a Zenobia who maybe, the depth of that knife-slash seemed to say, already knew Moses Place and already knew trouble.

Leaving Due East, he'd headed for the only place out here Dolores could possibly be: the Friends Center. But when he turned off and passed the old tidy buildings under the oak trees he saw that the place was empty and dark. There was talk that they'd be sending Peace Corps volunteers down to the Center soon to train, down here where innocent idealistic city types could get used to heat and mosquitoes and tricky tidal inlets.

Well, it would give Dolores something to do, buzz around the beatific Peace Corps babies. No doubt she'd be talking of volunteering.

But just now the Friends Center was empty. He wandered down a few more back roads, past Moses Place, and found himself heading, again, in the direction of a place everybody in town (though none of them had direct experience, of course) said was a whorehouse. What did people out here call a whorehouse if they called a bar Moses Place? Mary Magdalene Place?

He had to laugh at himself, driving past what might be a brothel. Dolores, in one of her sweet moments, had admitted to the same urge herself, the desire every time she was out this way to go look it over. Even Tim and Andy—faking innocence, pretending they wanted to see a fort—knew where to go and hung out the windows like a couple of dogs, tongues dangling from their mouths. God he was glad he'd never have to be a teenager again.

From the traffic ruts down the dirt road, it was pretty clear that this need to drive past a putative whorehouse was irresistible to everybody in town. It was a good-sized house—sixteen hundred square feet, his realtor's eye told him—on a half acre, a house with its door and window frames painted blue, like so many of the other shacks out here, to ward off evil spirits. Only this wasn't a shack. There was winter rye in the front yard and on the side a fenced garden of okra and spinach and tomatoes; an oystershell walkway curved from driveway to front door; tidy azalea and camellia bushes clustered under the front window. An insurance fellow named Nickerson Bunting owned it and took so much ribbing about it—"Hey, what can I tell you, they pay the rent on time"—that he swore he'd sell it the second he could find somebody to take it off his hands. He'd even tried to palm it off on Bill. Not a chance. *Way* too much significance in a whorehouse for him to even consider it: "You'll have to find yourself another real estate man, Nickerson. Somebody without a church committee looking over his shoulder." That, of course, meant somebody who didn't exist in Due East.

Dolores said—well you could predict *this*—that the reason they all, and she included herself, the reason they all thought it was a whorehouse was because of its tidy prosperous look, the spidery outline of lace curtains in the bedroom as genteel as anything lace-curtain Irish could tack up. A sorry thing that people, and she included herself, assumed that any prosperous colored person who wasn't a lawyer or an undertaker must be involved in some shady business. The shame of it was that they gossiped over such a house while Due East County was still so crowded with colored shacks that had chickens pecking in the front yard and pigs slopping in the rear, neither the chickens nor the pigs looking any too content. The shame of it was, Dolores said, that so many of the shacks did not have indoor plumbing and that tuberculosis still ran rampant in a county with this much sunshine. Not to mention hookworm, tapeworm, pinworm, flatworm: what it all came down to, for the people infested with disease and poverty, was wormwood, a bitter potion. The shame of it was that a tidy little house she called *bourgeois* and everybody else in Due East called *right pretty*, having such a refined and delicate look, was judged guilty before trial.

But Dolores never stopped him when the boys made their innocent suggestion to turn down this way. The Rooney family, on their Sunday drives unable to resist the temptation, had never seen a soul emerge from the neat blue-trimmed house to enter the neat blue Oldsmobile parked in the driveway. But Bill, on one of his solitary outings, had twice seen a plump colored woman, white straw church hat on her head, emerge with her bosom heaving. It was this old woman, this picture of respectability, who led him to believe that everybody was right, that

217

the blue-trimmed house was a colored brothel. How he would have loved to catch a glimpse of some prosperous white man, some Democratic Party stalwart, emerging from the back door and skedaddling through the woods to where he'd hidden his car; he'd even tried, on a couple of Saturday nights, to keep such a watch—but teenage kids had the same idea, and good Lord, this country road looked like Times Square from his old hotel window, ribbons of traffic swirling off in all directions. A line of Chevrolets keeping watch on the place. No doubt any white man who made use of the services did so at ten o'clock on a Wednesday morning, when everyone else in town had some-place respectable to be.

He thought, actually, that he might catch someone out here on a Thursday night; but lately he'd taken less and less pleasure from driving by the blue-trimmed house. Lately he'd reminded himself how often in his life the same need had overtaken him: how in college he'd listened up for word of the local brothel, and then walked past it like a schoolboy, waiting for a rope of hot perfume to float out on the breeze and lasso him in. No decision required on his part. The whole notion of a prostitute, of who'd been there ten minutes before you, repulsed him and yet when he went up to New York City on the train and had a two-hour holdover in Baltimore, did he use the time to go hear music in the best jazz city on the East Coast? No, he'd bought that Brooks Brothers jacket off the conductor and coaxed out of him the information that he could meet a girl down yonder by the water. He had no doubt to this very day that the man believed he, twenty-year-old tweed-jacketed Bill, was going to relieve himself there directly, when what he'd done, as he'd done in Columbia and later in New York and later still in every city he'd had the chance to pass through, was circle the block on which the whorehouse sat, circle it round and round again.

And no, it didn't take a psychiatrist to explain *that* one to him either, to tell him that he was just replaying the night his father had tried to give him as a birthday present, just testing himself over and over to see whether he mightn't actually like to step inside and have a real look around.

Because the night his father dropped him off in the Ford and told him that he'd be back in an hour, "just as soon as you've had the opp*atun*ity to get acquainted with Miss Emily" (oh Lord, a name from a movie script), he hadn't had a real look around at all. He'd assumed, from his father's fussiness and formality, that Miss Emily was one of the rich old biddies who'd stood by Frank despite his total failure, some old lady his mother couldn't abide, some rich woman his father and now he had to toady up to because she might someday leave them a little something in her will. And the "surprise, son" his father talked about receiving would be a pinkie ring. A stock certificate. A fountain pen for college.

The house his father took him to was a plain small frame job (no wonder he was so willing to believe ill of the blue-trimmed house) in a neighborhood of downtown Charleston that was neither here nor there, too far from the Battery to be swell, too close to the Battery to be poor. The woman, the Miss Emily who opened the door, was old enough to be one of his lay teachers at school, but not old enough to be what you'd call *old*. He'd seen before he ever got past the front door that the lace rimming her handkerchief was ripped, that her skin was pitted, that there was something else entirely on his father's mind. For one horrible minute it occurred to him that his father had a sweetheart, another family: and he wasn't far wrong.

"Miss Emily?" Her eyebrows were moon-curves, brushed up artistically at the ends. Her maroon lipstick cracked at the corners. She could have been one of his classmates' mothers, in a modest silk print dress with a wide patent-leather belt, where she tucked her handkerchief. Matching patent-leather pumps.

"Thas right." She didn't trouble herself to strike up a co-
quettish pose. If his father had taken him to a Belle Watling, to
a whore with a low-cut red satin dress and a bottle of gin in one
hand, he would have *gotten* it. This was more like going for a
private tutoring session in music or Latin, and he didn't even
know that he didn't get it.

"My father dropped me off?"

Not even a hint of amusement in her brown eyes: "Oh," she
said. "You're *Frank's* boy."

"Yes ma'am. Bill Rooney."

He stuck out his hand. She was kind enough to ignore it.

"Well come on in, honey, but it's early, I told Frank eight
o'clock. He thought you might like to get here before the
crowd, but I swanee I said after eight."

It was seven-thirty, still light outside. He could hear the
smack of a bat against a ball up the block.

A party, then? She fussed over him a little, and took his
hand to lead him into a dark modest double parlor: big rubber
plant in the corner, a potted palm at the narrow window, a
braided rug whose rose-and-tan simplicity would have meant
home to any Charleston boy. He sat, accepted her offer of a
whiskey. He'd been drinking for a year now, though his father
didn't know it.

She disappeared. He waited. Her gilt-framed prints appeared
to be classy anyway: his mother would have disapproved of
flowery Italian semi-nudes; but Brother Peter in biology class
would have called them *full of the physical beauty God granted
us as the first gift. Never forget that. A gift, and so not intended
for giggling over.* He did not giggle.

Finally two plain girls with brown weedy hair (one head
curly, one straight-haired) came in together and smiled at him
(the curlyhead bold, to match what the curling iron had done,
the straight-haired one evasive). They both wore flimsy satin

party dresses and the straight-haired one appeared to have no bosom whatsoever under her girlish bodice. She could have been someone lately released from the Home for Juvenile Correction: Girls Division. Instinctively he felt for his wallet, and in the move toward the back of his pants—perhaps it was the way the flat-chested one leaned toward him as he made that gesture—he understood exactly what this was all about.

"Miss Emily says we should show you the ropes," said Curly Hair. Straight Hair found this hysterical, and choked into her own pocket handkerchief, but Curly Hair was a cheerleader preparing to introduce the new kid around the cafeteria. "The others'll be in soon," she said. "You're early. Unless of course you'd like"—she tittered a trill that you couldn't call *bitter* exactly: maybe empty—"unless you'd like to get started right quick and settle for a smaller selection. Anyway just make yourself at home. *Any*thing we can do."

"Who do I pay for the scotch?" he said. The second he understood, he wouldn't let himself be subjected. I reject you both, you trollops. You reek of whoever had you last night. What did his father think: that he could *shame* him into this one? Frank had been hounding him, since he skipped the spring dance, about the naturalness of a boy seeking a girl's company. Was this what he meant? Did his father think that he'd be so embarrassed to turn them down that he'd follow the one with the curly dark hair (curly dark hair on her arms and on her upper lip too, and black stubble probably on her legs) into the bedroom *so as not to hurt her feelings?* Well, well. The truth was close to that—he had to hand it to the old lecher, counting on his manners in this situation. He wavered. It was a terrible thing, after all, to be the age these girls were—what, a year or two older than he was?—out of the public high school, and rejected by a chubby Billy Rooney.

He rose and swallowed down the liquor, then let the ice

cubes click around the empty glass to indicate his lack of concern or hurry. He had kissed three girls in the last three of his eighteen years, and one of them, Helenann Bogan, had told him to quit that fresh stuff or she'd knock his block off. He had been dreaming of her cold cleavage for months.

"It goes on your *bill,*" said the juvenile delinquent. She might as well have added *moron* to the end. "The bill your daddy's paying."

"Perhaps you don't understand," he said, Brother Peter's tone and inflection issuing from his own mouth. "I'm asking for my bill right now."

The whores looked at each other and managed to swallow their giggles. He saw at once that they were younger than he was, sixteen and seventeen maybe. He saw too that his father—to arrange all this, to have this special *display* put on for him—was a regular customer, that his father climbed into bed with seventeen-year-old girls while he, Bill, was left home to comfort a sobbing mother. To think of lying with a girl after his father finished. A sudden swelling of admiration for his mother: *she* got it. *She* knew where his father went.

Oh it was debasing to even think about the bulge of their thighs over their dirty cotton wartime stockings, though he spent the next year imagining his way right up past those thighs, berating himself for not taking the chance when he had it; and sometimes, especially after he had left home and gone on up to school, he thought for a minute drifting off to sleep that his father knew no other way to show kindness. That it had been, after all, nothing but an attempt at kindness, and not the tacky picture that would fix in his son's mind forever the measure of his failure and hypocrisy. To think of Frank going down on one knee for the Consecration.

He had been so loath to look straight into those girls' faces that many times the next year he thought he recognized them on the Carolina campus, heart-shaped faces looking for a date. Looking to hold hands and walk through the quadrangle.

That night, though, he had let pure fury—VENGEANCE IS MINE, SAITH THE LORD—and his mother's honor carry him through the night. His father had said he'd be back to pick him up, and Bill spent an hour wandering through Charleston, hoping to head off the car, ready to split his father's head open the way he'd split a watermelon. After an hour of circling on foot it was clear that he wouldn't find Frank without going back to Miss Emily's. (Oh God, after the fact it was even more pathetic that his father wanted him to call her *that*. Didn't his father know, as every boy at Bishop England knew, even boys who didn't go to the spring dance, that only swabbies, desperate before they were shipped off to war, went to prostitutes? And for God's sake, did he think that the mayor and all his old pals at Harvey's would show their faces at a sad place like that? The ripped lace on her handkerchief. Her cracked lipstick.) For long stretches of his walk, he saw flashing like hallucinations visions of his mother's fleshy arm and the curly-haired girl's fleshy unseen thigh. He tugged at his hair the way the Marx Brothers did, and thought to laugh at himself. Then back to feverish fury at his father.

Later, he told Dolores, who did not wear dirty cotton stockings because she did not wear, had not, through the whole war, she said, worn any stockings at all, that he had passed his father's test, though not to his father's satisfaction. She gave him a peculiar pursed-lips look, one that gave him pause: did *she*, a sweet Catholic girl who would only be giving herself to one man in her lifetime, think he was stupid for not having taken the opportunity? Would she have preferred an experienced man, a man whose hands had run over the length of a *whore?* But no, she must have been vexed with him for even telling the story when what they should be thinking of was what they, two virgins before they met, two babies for the love of Mike, could do in concert.

Maybe he should not have told her that his father was testing him, since testing was, after all, her own specialty. Dolores had been testing him since the night he'd met her. He'd stumbled too—she wanted to know if he didn't think that personalism wasn't better than distributism? Personalism? *Personalism?* Well didn't he think some of these Southern writers, this Faulkner especially, was going to go over the top? And he'd had the bad sense to say that he hadn't yet read any Faulkner but the one story he'd started in *The Saturday Evening Post* (oh he'd never compete with a Fordham boy, much less the goddamn flannel-trousered Ivy Leaguers who came slumming through the clubs on a weekend). Didn't he think Kant too disdainful of simple human feeling? He hadn't read Kant either. He hadn't taken a philosophy course in college and he couldn't hardly call Religion I, II, III, or IV at Bishop England a philosophy course, though they had in senior year thought to mention the Great Religions of the World.

He could see Dolores wavering with her little tests: sometimes she did what he intended and took his bluntness, his admissions, as charming, so different from the academic pretensions she—even at her third-rate college—was used to. And of course if he sat down at her mother's piano, once he was safely introduced into that strange narrow little household, he could do no wrong. The one thing besides piss standing up that he could do better than she could.

Other times, though, she sucked in at her cheeks and *didn't feel like talking*. She was embarrassed all the time—embarrassed that she had not stood up to her mother and gone off to a good school, embarrassed that she bought her clothes on the Grand Concourse instead of at Best's or Altman's—and he could see, when she tested him, that she was deciding whether to be embarrassed by him. *That* he would not tolerate, not after all the years of Frank's disappointment. If he saw her drifting off in the direction of shame, he pulled her back by the shoulders and kissed her hard, Clark Gable style. He had a natural talent for it: who would have thought? When he could get her to quit talking, when he could get her to quit thinking, he could convince her. He could convince her in bed. If only she hadn't slept with him the very first night: that was enough to plant the idea that she'd closed off her options. Because what else could a Catholic girl like that, a girl who drank too many martinis and let the piano player take her to his hotel room, think? They were as good as married in the eyes of the Church. Sometimes he could see her forcing herself to be civil the way he'd forced himself to comfort his mother.

And then she was pregnant, and her options really were closed.

And his options were closed too. Didn't she know that her tongue was acid and that sometimes when she spread that makeup on her legs rather than wear darned stockings he was shamed too, shamed that she couldn't be more like the other girls?

It was a hell of a thing to spend a lifetime with a contemptuous woman. He only wished sometimes that she would be contemptuous of him without pause, that she would bar the doors as securely as Regina had barred the doors against Frank. He only wished that she would not warm to him if he sat down at the piano after two weeks, or decide after a hard party meeting to drink a beer with him and then—three beers down the road, mercy, just like the old days—seduce him before they were even sure the kids were properly asleep. He only wished that she did not possess a sexual split personality, because it made *him* crazy, and it left her pregnant. Pregnant again, when she was pushing forty and they already had more than they could handle.

He did not, after all, turn down the road to the blue-trimmed house, but circled instead until he was back at the intersection that would lead him onto the beach road. The night was thick with chill. He turned on the heater fan, but it was on the fritz: oh Lord, could you please bring me a new car before the day I die? A new heater fan anyway? A new way to sing the blues.

He waited at the stoplight by Coot's Store (groceries through the left door, liquor through the right) where high school kids paid old colored winos a quarter to go in and buy them a pint of bourbon. The light changed to green and as he made his turn he had a start: the car pulling up to the red light, a car making its way back from the beach, carried a redhead in the passenger seat who could have been Dolores's twin sister. Sitting next to a man whose face he hadn't had time to recognize.

It was impossible, now that he'd pulled away from the little cluster of lights back at the Coot's Store intersection, to see anything but a black sedan stopped on the road behind him. It couldn't have been Dolores (though if the driver had been a woman he wouldn't have thought twice about tooting and waving, because he would have assumed that Dolores was out on the islands with do-gooders and their frozen turkeys). But Dolores out here with a man? At dusk?

Oh now. Oh now, be *sensible*. For a split second he'd thought that Dolores (hadn't he, not but a second before, labeled her a sexual schizoid?) was running around. But he didn't really, not in his wildest dreams, think that Dolores—Dolores McGillicudhy of the Catholic Worker, Dolores Rooney of the Rosary and daily Mass—would cheat on him. Running around was something Marine wives did, or mysterious skinny waitresses down at the new bowling alley. Nobody he knew, male or female, not since his own father, and his father of course had to pay for it.

Passing someone with that shade of hair. But it was night. And Dolores hadn't let her hair loose that way since the summer.

He couldn't seem to stop himself; he slowed, so the sedan could catch up, so he could get a good view of the woman in the black sedan from his rearview. Then a slow-moving station wagon pulled out of a packing shed and separated him from the black car. Behind it a little Volkswagen pulled out of Island Esso, and then a third car fell in line: a conspiracy of slow-moving vehicles stretching out on the beach road. The mystery car was lost somewhere back in the night behind him. The dark car was lost.

Oh Dolores, oh sweetie. There was his news to give her, and the sherry, and by now his dinner would be waiting for him on the table. A solid glutinous ball of rice, the overcooked meat-and-cornflakes loaf. Jesus, she was a terrible cook. Just terrible.

One more glance in the rearview. Now the lights behind him skipped along, and he was leading a parade back to town.

He thought he might rummage through the attic after supper, and see for himself, without asking Dolores, if they'd held on to all the old baby furniture. Later he'd set sour Andy to work sponging it down with Pine-Sol. They'd have to tell the children soon and why not tonight, when he could pair announcement of the pregnancy with the news of a big commission? Tomorrow he could write to Maggie, a note from his office, a note he'd pass on to Dolores, who would append clippings from her beloved *Catholic Worker* and the Due East *Courier* and the most strident of the Charleston editorials, editorials still calling—in 1963, in the year of inevitability, the year when the handwriting was not only on the wall, the wall was tumbling

227

down—for the South to stand firmly behind segregation. Dolores would mean for Maggie to understand that Tim and Andy were still being called *nigger lovers*. Dolores would mean for Maggie to congratulate herself that she'd escaped the South. He had long since stopped carping at his wife when she stuffed the envelope with incriminating clippings. He had long since accepted that Maggie wouldn't settle here.

And Tim would never stay in Due East. But maybe Andrew, past his pimply resentment, would open up a law office: Rooney & Rooney, Law Offices and Real Estate. Real estate advisers? Maybe Kate would find herself a good Southern boy with a sailboat. Maybe this mystery child would want to learn to hunt or learn to be a nabob.

He was back over the bridge and into town. The polio banner was still flapping in the breeze, and he did not even stop to think that one of his own children might succumb. There was a certain symmetry to leaving town with Sharmayne on his mind and coming back with suspicions about Dolores (St. Dolores. His father would say: "My God Billy that's *womanish* to fret over nothing. Quit your worries.")

But then symmetry, and worry, were what marriage was all about.

□   □   □

"Care for a cigarette?"

Seeing that they were coasting into the intersection and the first stoplight along the beach road, Dolores had already roused herself from the torpor of the ride; but she was grateful just the same for Tom Prince's outstretched hand. His cigarette case was sterling, and popped open with a tidy *click*. She made herself look up and away from the silver case while she pulled one out for herself: just a schoolgirl again, gawking at another schoolgirl's family china. Pretending she daily plucked cigarettes from cases, and not crumpled packets, she had her eye on the intersection when the family's old station wagon pulled out from Claire's Point Road.

"Hmm." She pointed as the Plymouth slid away down the beach road toward town. Looking older than ever. She wouldn't have been so conscious of its dilapidation, not even sitting in a new rental car with a padded dashboard, if she hadn't just that moment been handed a sterling-silver cigarette case. She would have *liked* the old station wagon's disrepair—theirs was a family with bigger concerns than late-model cars. "Our car."

"I guess you were right," Tom Prince said. "I guess your husband was out showing property." Now Tom was wary, tapping his cigarette against the steering wheel while he tried out the first conversation since the Awful Moment in the beach parking lot. "How much does land out here go for?"

She didn't have the faintest notion how much land out here went for. "We'll have to ask Bill tonight how much the prices have climbed."

"I guess real estate's a tidy living in a pretty place like this. I hear there's a lot of talk about resorts, about developers coming down. Your husband talk about making a big killing?"

She couldn't help it: the image of Bill, hat pushed back on his head, making a big killing with developers at Ralph's, sent her giggling. "Oh, no killings yet," she said, and then—had she no sense of loyalty?—"but it's a tidy living." And kept a smile going, because it was the messiest living possible, which struck her suddenly as not so bad, not half so bad as the thought of Bill wheeling and dealing. And it occurred to her that Bill, out of view now, couldn't have been showing property tonight, because he was alone in the car. Probably going out to see a new listing, before he showed it. Though he rarely had anything out toward Claire's Point; the farthest rental house was two miles closer to town, in the shadow of the water tower. No: he had never sold or rented out here.

Tom Prince, having started this conversation—real estate bored the living daylights out of her—seemed determined to keep it rolling. "I can certainly see coming down here to sell land."

But *she* hadn't come down here to sell land. Who could have said what incited the flush that was spreading upwards from her neck? Annoyance at Tom Prince for being so perky? For asking for figures in dollars and cents? The sight of that busted taillight on her husband's car? Andrew McGillicudhy said, when she was small and complained of her tiny room, that she was a selfish girl. Couldn't she see that the size of her room was a badge of honor, a sign that she was a child of the working class? She'd already told Bill that she was sure she could work the taillight into next month's budget and that meanwhile they should all look on it as . . . *As what?* Bill said. *A beacon of honor?* He'd made her laugh, after all these years, at her father's words: exactly what honor did broken shards of red plastic bestow?

She was grateful sometimes for Bill's ability to live in the real world, to remind her that there was nothing shameful in replacing a broken part.

Tom Prince ground his cigarette out.

Poor guy. First she'd humiliated him in the parking lot, and now she hadn't even answered him. And there wasn't anything shameful in a reporter—he was *supposed* to ask questions—inquiring about local real estate prices. She was so judgmental, Bill said. Bill was right. Bill, all alone in that car tonight, driving out by the Friends Center, where he'd have no business, and the fort, which didn't interest him, and the brothel. What in God's name was he doing?

"Sorry," she said. "I'm drifting, I guess. You're right—a lot of people come on down to sell land. Quite a debate going on over development. You know, the old biddies who want to keep the marshes for themselves. And some of us who'd like to see jobs come in. A lot of people in Due East need *jobs*."

Too much passion, once again, in her voice. Actually, she sometimes took the side of the old dames—you wouldn't want to put too much on these islands, and the universality of bad taste guaranteed that any development would be tacky development. But what it would mean to some of these tenant farmers, some of these men who couldn't read well enough to dream of taking the civil service test, if they had a paycheck coming in week after week: even if the work was no more meaningful than mowing somebody's golf course, even if that golf course grass was a color green that God Himself had never imagined.

"What can these salt marshes stand, in terms of building?" He seemed to be trying to engage her in some sort of debate, while she—for the first time she could remember in years— flirted with the idea that her husband was driving alone not because he'd been showing land (he never showed land after five o'clock!) but because he'd been out at the brothel. That Bill was out tomcatting on these islands the way other men in town did. If Bill had actually resorted to a prostitute. After all these years. After all those stories, the telling and the retelling of his humiliation at his father's hand. Bill might just be going through a middle-age crisis, with the new baby coming: he might, after all this time, have thrown off all his own beliefs for one little afternoon dalliance. Or maybe he was a regular. Maybe somebody of J. C. Smalls's ilk had introduced him out there and—

She could imagine it, but it was ridiculous. *She* could imagine it, but Bill probably couldn't. Her spirits sagged. Such disappointment at the thought of his virtue. What was the matter with her? The thought of her husband peeking in at a whorehouse down a dirt road, working up the courage to rap on the front door, gave her again the urge to giggle.

"Why, what's so funny about that?" Tom flashed her a grin. Sweet fellow. "I think folks would get a big kick out of seeing alligators. Sends a shiver right up *my* spine."

Alligators? She hadn't heard a word.

"Oh, I wasn't laughing at you." She laughed again. "Not laughing at you at all." She was so transparent, even to herself: what could you call a need like that, a need to have a man say *I won't let you tie me down, you can't control me?*

But what would have flashed through Bill's mind if he had seen *her* sitting next to this strange young man in the dark? Her husband was a hulking big man, and when he was angry he colored sunset rose, from his dark receding hairline down to his big gesturing hands.

"I'm glad you got the chance to see the beach," she said to Tom Prince. The palmetto frond was forgotten: he grinned at her, and reached again for the cigarette case, and she forgot for a moment about the busted taillight and the meat loaf that would embarrass them all.

BREAKING BREAD

Kate couldn't have said at exactly what point she decided that the Snake Man was not raping the girl in the trailer, but surely it was long before she reached her father's office. Surely it was long before this fall night deepened into darkness.

Now the streets of Due East were night streets. Her father's office was dark too—even if she'd gone to Rooney Realty looking for help, Bill would not have been there. She should have known that all along; her father always shut the door at five o'clock. He would be home then, and on a Thursday her mother would still be home too, and together they were fingernails on a blackboard.

In any case, she would not be asking either one of them for help. She had decided the Victim was not a Victim at all. Pedaling along toward the Point, she was not embarrassed—she would save that up for Tim and Andy's return—but she pumped hard. If she didn't hurry then her long-legged brothers would beat her home, where they could lord her mistake over her for the rest of her life.

She felt nothing but the hot strain on her thighs as she pushed the pedals. She had probably decided that the girl was not a Victim somewhere on Union Street, somewhere near the junior high: the very junior high where she herself pulled blood clots from squirrels with tweezers; the junior high where the P.E. teacher, trying to contain the resonation of his voice in the big gym, asked them please oh puhlease not to stuff up the toilets with their personal products. She had probably decided the girl was not a Victim when she remembered Andy saying *I've seen him plenty of times.* Did they watch the Snake Man, Tim and Andy, the way they pored over those magazines?

Past the Golden Apple she waved again to the cook, who was sucking in his last cigarette before supper was served. When he waved back, his cigarette trailed smoke the way the fighter jets from the Air Station trailed exhaust. She took the corner so fast that her bike nearly toppled.

But then at the head of O'Connor Street she hit the brakes: an ambulance loomed, parked just off the road. For a split second she thought it had stopped in front of the Rooney driveway, but then she made out in the dark that it was next door, at the Rapples'. Ambulances in Due East were big winged wagons with a place for bodies in the back, the same as hearses; this one, white and abandoned by its driver, still twirled the red light that pushed it through traffic. The driver's door had been left ajar.

She crossed herself, a reflex; but now that her family was safe, she could barely summon a prayer for the Rapple woman. This would be her third miscarriage. The turnip woman—why

234

exactly Dolores called her that, Kate could not have said—was doomed.

Oh she was a terrible person. Other girls would have said *oooh* at least at the thought of young Mrs. Rapple, plain Turnip Rapple, lying on a stretcher, bleeding. Bleeding to death, maybe. What was it like, a miscarriage? Terrible pain in your groin? The worst: she herself had already had a shameful bladder infection. Did you see the baby before it was all over, its little glassy eyes? Or was it still a blob? There were plenty of gravesites for infants, at the Episcopal church and at Our Lady of Perpetual Help, but she'd never seen one for a baby that hadn't yet bulged out its mother's belly. Maybe they just threw it out with the rest of the hospital trash, the grits that didn't get eaten.

It was hard to know whether to pedal on or to wait where she was. She couldn't say how she knew for sure that Mrs. Rapple was having another miscarriage, or even how she knew that the gray-skinned neighbor was pregnant. But she did know. Her father said women, knowing those things, were witches. So she was a witch now too.

Finally she decided to pedal on ahead and risk the meeting with the stretcher. Sure enough, as she began down the block the Rapples' kitchen door swung open and the ambulance men carried the woman out toward their hearse just as she was passing. Even in the dark the sheets shone white and moony, but there was nothing dramatic: no blood. Mrs. Rapple did not call out or wave or even moan when she passed, and Kate—should she stop? should she whisper her regrets?—continued her furious pedaling. There was no telling what proper ambulance manners a good little lady should follow.

Safe in her own driveway, she stood astride the bike, out of respect, while they heaved Turnip Rapple into the back of the ambulance. Her own house was dark save for the kitchen light.

She shivered—her mother said, last time Mrs. Rapple lost a baby, that it was hard to know God's will, that maybe some women weren't meant to bear children. But this was the third time. This was beginning to seem cruel.

Awkward waiting—she should have said *some*thing, she should have whispered *sorry* as she passed—she lingered in the front yard until the ambulance careened off down O'Connor Street, the driver ringing out his siren with abandon. Then she headed inside and flicked on the light in the vestibule, in the hallway, in every room she passed through. She called out *Momma* as she went, but she'd known from the empty driveway and the stillness of the house that no one was there. At least they'd gone out together in the car. The worst was when her father was here alone, waiting, and no one knew what church chore Dolores was up to.

Creepy in the empty house with an empty house next door. Where was Mr. Rapple while all this was going on? Riding home, she was able to force herself blank of feeling, but now she could see the Snake Man's eyes peering in at every window. The Snake Man's snake eyes. He could have slithered along behind her, through town, without her ever knowing.

She backtracked from the kitchen and in the parlor cut on the television, an old monstrous console. They had been the last family in Due East to get a TV, the very last, and her mother had only succumbed when it was pressed on them by Father Sweeney on his way out of town. The priest's old castoffs, and now her mother talked back to it the way they all did, to Everett Dirksen and to Barry Goldwater and to the President himself. She was reduced to pointing, the way their father did: look at that Shriver, he seems decent; or *oh*, what a handsome man Belafonte is, so graceful, arm linked with Dr. King's.

She turned the old set on good and loud so the Snake Man, crouching in the dark outside, would know the house was filled with family watching the evening news. Captain Sandy and the Weather: she hovered over the controls. This meant Huntley-Brinkley next.

Still it was hard to sit. Poor Turnip Rapple. She'd probably be a mean mother anyway, the kind who made a child scrub the sheets when she wet them. Now she paced, looking for the Due East *Courier*. It was Thursday, and Franny Starkey's name should be in the paper for winning a yellow ribbon in the rooster-crowing contest at the fair. Franny was the only girl entered: *Don't you get it?* Stephen Dugan said. *It's a rooster-crowing contest.* Still, Franny won a ribbon after all and she'd like to push the article right into Stephen Dugan's face. If she could ever look at Stevie Dugan's face again. If Mrs. Rapple would ever forgive her for not saying something when they passed in the night.

No *Courier*. There were bills on top of the piano, and a Savannah paper. David Brinkley's dry cynical voice pressed on. She glanced at the screen. The Kennedys were landing in San Antonio (that was odd; she'd *known*, earlier in the day, that she should have called on St. Anthony). Ordinarily, especially with her brothers out of the house, she would have sat on the edge of the big old armchair, chin on her hands, and soaked it all in. Texas, though. It was hard to get interested. Lately—maybe it was her mother's derision, though she couldn't believe herself that disloyal—the photographs for her scrapbook piled up before she had time to paste them in. Lately she watched the television screen from across the room. Who'd want to go to Texas? That was someplace the Snake Man would have come from, someplace where they choked out those thick accents and called girls *shug*. Doubt crowded the room again: what if Andy was wrong about all those girls?

Oh, once you made up your mind what was right it was useless to torment yourself. What were you *supposed* to say to a

237

woman on a stretcher anyway? *Sorry you lost the baby?* She wished her father were there to hear her examination of conscience and to say, with complete dismissal:

"Oh Jesus Mary and Joseph. Oh shite and onions. Forget it!" (He had borrowed *shite and onions* from Dolores's father, a man he'd never met. That phrase was her grandfather's legacy, hardly all Dolores would tell, except that Andrew McGillicudhy was blacker-haired than Bill, and taller; and that he'd walked out on them, on poor Grandma, who didn't even know how to type. An irresponsible man, Dolores said: that was all. Just irresponsible. Kate would have settled for his faithless presence though, if he was the kind of man who yelled *Oh shite and onions* around the house. She would have set her tall black-haired irresponsible grandfather on the Snake Man.)

The Kennedys still danced on the screen, but she retreated to the kitchen to peer out the back window there. If she could be disloyal to a girl in a trailer, if she could abandon her neighbor as she lost a baby, she could be disloyal to the Kennedys waving to the crowds in San Antone.

After she adjusted her eyes, she was staring into a crowded night. There were shadows in the dark: Due East was a town of dogs roaming, of cats and squirrels and coons. Birds were always flitting (and sometimes they came right into the house, which forced her sensible mother to reveal her only superstition: a bird in the house, a death in the family. Last week a plain sweet wren appeared on the ledge over the bathroom cabinet. They could all see that it had flown in through the open window, open because the screen had fallen out and her father had never gotten round to hauling it back upstairs; but her mother turned egg white just the same and begged Tim to shoo it out: a death in the family. And just look—the bird had flown off toward the Rapples'; there was the death.)

Now, from her safe kitchen, she was looking out on the last

bird of the night, another wren sailing across her own back yard
and into the Rapples'. Down the block the Mansards' ugly gray
hound dog was howling out an evening serenade. It was getting
on to seven o'clock, past suppertime in most of the houses on
the Point, most of the houses but hers, where her mother was
occupied with more important things. Getting on to seven
o'clock, and the houses—the houses but for hers and the Rapples'—were occupied and safe. There was no Snake Man in her
yard, no Snake Man in the night. Tim and Andy would be
along.

She seemed to have forgotten her fear all in a moment, a
moment of staring into the dark. She slipped from one mood to
another lately without noticing: one minute she would be purple
with fury and then, before she caught the transition, bug-eyed
over a boy. Hadn't she just done it over the girl and the Snake
Man? Hadn't she thought one minute that she must save the
girl; and then the next minute, somewhere on Union Street,
hadn't she decided that her help wasn't needed? She didn't
know when she realized that Mrs. Rapple wouldn't have wanted
her to stop, not while she was losing a baby.

She left every light switched on downstairs, and turned the
volume up higher on Huntley-Brinkley, just in case, but as she
skipped up the stairs she knew that she would leave the top of
the house unlighted. If she meant to get any time in for herself,
she'd have to fly.

So she flew, up the last few steps and into her room, turning
the door lock as she landed. Then, remembering the afternoon
and her brothers' intrusion, she piled books up against the door
as further protection, her dictionary anchoring the pile. Her
room still smelled of the ammonia Lily used when she wiped
down the walls: sharp and safe.

She peered through her bedroom window, one last look into
the night: no bikes down the street, not yet. No Mr. Rapple

banging on the door for his absent ailing wife. She would have time to put her clothes back on when she heard Tim and Andy clanging through the front door.

Now she pulled the old window shade down as far as it would go, far past the sill. If anyone ever saw her. Sometimes she dreamed that her brothers had nestled their borrowed camera (borrowed from Father Berkeley!) in some corner of her bedroom to catch her in these moments, but that was crazy. And besides, since she'd started keeping the lights off, their hidden cameras (couldn't you just see Andy as Allen Funt?) wouldn't register a thing.

She opened her closet door where Maggie had, years ago in an uncharacteristic self-conscious moment, asked their father to hang a full-length mirror. It was a cheap aluminum-framed glass, distorted the right way, thank goodness, so that she looked long and skinny, so that her white thighs stretched out into possibility.

Dark though the room was, she still checked its corners, even got down on her hands and knees to look under the bed, before she took her clothes off. She peeled off her cotton underwear—they came in pink-flowered packages of three at Friedman's. Mr. Friedman always hired a woman to discreetly handle that end of the store, that end of girdles and stays and underwires—and double-checked the piles of books barricading her door.

Not a soul in the house. Still no sound of her brothers on the street. She could hardly believe her luck (but didn't she deserve it, after all the scares today? No: she wouldn't think of the scares or of how deep the gloom was in this old room with its yellowed shade pulled down against the moon). Often she got just to this point, this point of sliding the elastic down her narrow hips, only to hear the front door slam. But tonight she was in solitude, and even in the dark she would be able to make out her own dark shadow in the mirror when she stripped naked.

There. She flicked the underwear across the room with her foot. Motionless, she stared at the dark mirror and after a time could make out that she was as white as a plucked chicken. She'd never be a surfer girl, glory be. She knotted her hair up atop her head but then, remembering a photograph of Isadora Duncan, let it flow loose again. Before she'd started this Ritual Dance (well, that was what Mr. Digby would have called it, and she couldn't think of a better name herself) she'd had a recurring dream: she was out in Franny Starkey's back yard, surrounded by thousands of Franny's little brothers and sisters; or she was up at the Communion rail, and Stevie Dugan was serving Mass; or she was in front of the French class, pulling down the screen for the filmstrips of Monsieur and Madame Thibaut. In all the different versions of the dream she was fully dressed from her neck to her waist, a veil on her head and crisp white gloves on her hands—but from the waist down she was stark naked. Since she'd started performing the Ritual Dance, her two halves equally naked, the dream had disappeared, banished with the Dance.

And she was not a dancer in the normal sense of the word. Oh, her mother had seen to it that she and Maggie had their years of froufrou costumes and tap shoes at Miss Spicer's School of Dance, so they would not be so very different from all the other little white girls in Due East; but she had never dreamed, the way other girls did, of the day she got her toe shoes. This year the gym teacher defended the C minus he gave her on the grounds that Kate was *unusually lazy with her body.* ("But you've kept her off the honor roll," Dolores said, reasonable, unthreatening. "She had A's in everything else.") She and Franny had downright flunked the modern dance presentation, and they hadn't even had the nerve to do the striptease they intended, down to their gym bloomers; instead they descended into silly giggles and fell on the floor, helpless, their shawls and boas burying them, while the theme for *Peter Gunn* circled round and round the record player.

Now, though—fair and full-bellied, with spidery arms and legs—she was a Body Artist. She moved on tiptoe and dug into bureau drawers, pulling out Maggie's old nylon scarves, Maggie's old mantillas and her own Communion veil, a glorious bandeau of what she had once believed were real pearls, a pouf of gossamer floating out beyond. One after another she draped the headdresses, removed them; draped the scarves, removed them. Naked, she was elegant, her breasts twin corsages: white roses. Mr. Smolinski begged her pardon for the C minus. If only he'd known what she was capable of. If only he—coarse ill-bred football player that he was—had given her the artistic freedom she required. Hers was an Artist's Revenge.

And revenge on Stevie Dugan. She imagined him begging for a further glimpse, but she tied Maggie's brown scarf (a brace of pheasants flying across the silk) tight around her middle. The point of its triangle licked her thighs, and she gave him no mercy. If she looked over her shoulder, squinting, she could see her naked backside, the scarf's knot breaking the middle of her back. Her tight buttocks flicked in the mirror, providing their own light. There. On your knees, Dugan. The Blessed Virgin beamed down veiled and pacific from the wall; and somewhere underneath her image on the dresser, buried in the piles of undershirts and nightgowns, was the poem her mother had copied out for her after she'd found her dancing naked around the room:

> *If I admire my arms, my face,*
> *my shoulders, flanks, buttocks*
> *against the yellow drawn shade,—*

Who shall say I am not
the happy genius of my household?

A headlight slid across the window shade, and she leaped to her pink-flowered cotton underwear before the light was extinguished in the Rooney driveway. Stretch pants on. Ribboned undershirt to hide her nipples. The half-ironed blouse: no. A pajama shirt. She wasn't feeling so great. She'd have to get to bed (to the mirror, to the Dance) early tonight.

She lifted the shade a half inch and, expecting the old station wagon, was taken aback by a strange black sedan parked in her driveway and a strange tall young man circling the car to open the passenger door. He was wearing a tie, but his shirt sleeves were rolled up (there was Kennedy style now, apparently, even in Carolina). By the combined glow of the streetlight and the yard light she could see that he had a good high forehead like Bobby Kennedy's too. (Her father called him Bobby, as if they washed down beer together every night at the K. of C. Bobby was even more saintly in her father's eyes than Jack, mainly, Kate supposed, because of all those children.) This highbrow had a short haircut, though, a crew cut like those white Freedom Riders, and his glasses gave him a serious professorial look. Was he coming to teach at the new branch of the university? A Peace Corps worker coming down to look over the new training center? Oh, the times sure were changing, and changing fast. She loved him already.

She watched him swing the door open and hold out a gallant hand for—

drumroll; it would be somebody elegant but snappy, maybe in trousers—

she watched him swing the door open and hold out a gallant hand for—her mother. What was Dolores doing driving around with a good-looking man half her age? They were a Hollywood couple alighting from a limousine on Oscar night. Her mother wore a midnight-blue sweater over a plaid jumper, and in the dark, her bare legs chalky white, her feet slipped into a pair of Maggie's old flats, she could have been a schoolgirl. From above, Kate watched her with wonder: for the past two months she'd thought her mother was reaching those years from which the mother you knew would never return, but here she was, a girl again in one night. She had let her hair down loose, and Kate realized that she hadn't seen it that way since summer. The mist had fluffed it full and wavy, and as Dolores shook her head back and forth, laughing with the man, it brushed her cheek. Oh. These past few weeks, these weeks of fatness and grayness, Kate had believed that women all eventually grew mustaches and sagged and faded, until their flesh truly was a disgrace. Now her mother alighted from the car and held a young man's hand.

A sharp stab of pain in her gut, from what she'd been thinking: that her mother *belonged* with a young man like the one standing down below in the driveway, escorting her home in a decent car; that her mother had only been ageing because she lived with Bill Rooney. She watched Dolores stare full into the man's face. It wasn't that she, Kate, didn't love her father, or that she, Dolores, didn't love Bill. She knew what was required of her. They knew what was required of them. Dolores would have called her swoony fantasies *trashy romance*, and Kate would never have dared utter them. But her mother looked so light, walking up the front step. Released. This morning her father had pushed Tim into the counter, where he'd shaken the coffeepot loose from the socket. Someone could have been scalded to death. And Dolores had said in a voice she must have meant the neighbors to hear, because Kate had heard it upstairs in bed, a controlled deliberate loud voice: "If you ever harm one hair on his head, one hair on any of their heads, I will not hesitate to call the police." There had been no other sound downstairs, no sound but that of her father leaving; but Kate had been able to picture the scorn on his face: that the mother should shame the father this way, in front of the son.

They were already through the front door, the man and her mother. She would not be going downstairs with a pajama shirt, not with *that* man in the house. She went to the bureau and began again the long search through clothes that were never right.

□ □ □

Dolores slapped shark fillets around the kitchen counter, considering how she might cook them. J. C. Smalls had finally done *some*thing right in his life: when Bill stopped by the Smalls house that night, to inquire if they might have had word from her (as if she'd have left a message with either half of that yahoo couple), J.C. had presented Bill with five pounds of newly filleted shark from a ten-foot mako Buddy Miles and his friends had caught that morning. So the Rooneys, needing supper for their guest, were presented with exotica—exotica for them anyway. And Tom Prince had acted suitably impressed, especially after that shark conversation on the beach.

The Rooneys were regular lilies of the field, and if God chose to provide them with shark, it was her business to figure out how to cook it. Oh praise be, that she wasn't crumbling cornflakes into round steak. But she had no idea where to start. Other Due East women—women who whipped up oyster bisque or deviled crab and had stacks of sweet little ramekins for serving the latest recipe from the parish cookbook—would know how to proceed, but she was lost. She'd been brought up on stews, on pot roasts and chickens: anything that Rose McGillicudhy could toss in with carrots and potatoes and turnips, while she was off to the church. Her mother would die of hunger before she'd let so much as a nugget of shark meat pass her lips.

Bill, God bless him—though for once in his life he had every cause to be furious, driving all the way out to the Friends Center to look for her—was restrained and matter-of-fact, as if he brought in a load of fresh fish every night and had the kind of social life that required him to make evening social calls to his closest friends. Fingering the thick white flesh (sauté? bake? bread crumbs? onions?), she prayed that he would keep up this new understated host act. Just now he and Tom were in the parlor, where Bill had dragged out from the back of one of the bookcases a nautical chart to show him where the shark had been hooked. As if he knew about such things: Dolores suspected that he put his finger on an arbitrary spot, and then began talking riptides and spring tides, whole tidal basins. Bless him for acting as if nothing were out of the ordinary when he walked in tonight lugging the fish and found his wife sipping wine with a reporter from the New York *Times*.

The children, all three of them, were in the parlor too, hanging on Tom Prince's every word. Not too many words so far, from what she could make out, but a lot of deep belly laughs as he let them do the talking. Tim and Andy, picturing quotations in print, were tripping over each other to give Tom a fair picture of Due East High School's attitudes toward the court-martial, integration, rock and roll. And Kate, quieted by her favorite words, New York, was staring up at him bedazzled and lovesick, her hair twisted into submission at the back of her neck, her feet bare to show off toenails painted in Hearts on Fire. Poor Kate: stabs at normalcy. Her little toes were grubby and stubby, and now she'd splattered them with a sunglow even less restrained than the color of her hair.

Her husband came smiling into the kitchen, and she said: "Oh Bill," almost startled at the high-pitched tremulous sound of her own voice. His open face, the way he'd rolled his own shirt sleeves up by now, shamed her: she'd no right to go off like that, without any word. He was like a big bear padding around the kitchen, fingering his own buttons, tickled to be playing host.

"Seems like a nice guy," Bill said, aiming for offhand. "But Dolores, next time leave a fellow a note."

"Oh I'm sorry." She was as fluttery now with her husband as with her guest and in a stage whisper she said: "Bill, how the hell do you cook shark?"

He threw up his hands, but he must have been feeling the wine, the way he fairly glowed at her. He pictured himself, maybe, gathering musicians around a couple of quarts of beer. Reporting on the reporter tomorrow morning at Ralph's. "Don't you worry now. I s'pose you just put it in the oven the way you would any piece of fish. Throw it under the broiler, huh? Lots of butter? I *told* you J.C.'s a decent fellow. Looky there, he's even gone and cleaned it for you."

"Well bless him. What would I have done otherwise?" She reached her hand out to touch his forearm. "Wouldn't you have thought after all these years in this godforsaken place that I would have learned how to cook a piece of fish." She was feeling the wine herself, letting *godforsaken* slip out.

His hand came down atop hers—he hadn't heard it then— and there they stood, peaceful, glad for once of each other's touch, until Bill said: "I'm sorry I lost my temper that way. This morning."

She took a deep breath. She really had to get this fish underway. And rice, she guessed.

He squeezed her flesh, and it rankled. "But I do—I lose my temper, and when I do, you can't just bless me out that way in front of Timmy, hear? You can't just strip me jay naked that

247

way in front of my son. You don't talk like that about the police. You know full well I wouldn't hurt that boy."

Oh the weight of his hand resting on hers had been perfect. A little moment of peace between them. She had no desire to bring back what he'd done this morning, the way he'd shoved Tim, that stripling who hardly needed a shove when he could have been blown over if Bill had felt inclined to puff. She had no patience for it, none; she despised herself for tolerating as much as she did, but she knew, and Bill knew, and Tim himself knew, that it would never come to more than the hollering or the raising of a hand or—the most it ever did—the shoving, the grabbing him by an ear. The humiliations. Bill'd had no way of knowing that the cord would be grabbed or wrenched free, no way of knowing that hot coffee would go spraying all over the room, that they would all catch their breaths, or that Andy would have time to say, before any words were out of her own mouth: "You could get arrested for that." It was Andy's dripping disgust that forced her hand, and she was shamed at that, and shamed that she didn't send her sons out of the room when she laid down the rules once more for Bill. But she hardly wanted to be reminded of it now.

Bill took her silence for some sort of acquiescence and maybe, after all, it was: hadn't she grown to the age of thirteen in a house where Rose made it her business to smile false agreement with a big blustery man?

"Anyway," Bill said, "I almost forgot. Looks like I've got a sale on Max's place. I went out and got you a bottle of sherry to celebrate and look there, the bottle's just sitting on the counter worrying itself sick about when it's going to get drunk with all this wine flowing. Oh sweetie."

That eagerness: now he was behind her, squeezing her shoulders: she hadn't seen him this hopeful in months. He loosened his grip, then went dancing around the kitchen, looking for all the world like a big heavy Tim, pouring the sherry into a jelly glass and ignoring her when she tried to signal no, the wine was enough for now.

"I can't drink too much, Bill. You'll have me sick before the night's out. And you know, the boys are so red-eyed. You think they're guzzling out of the bottle when we have our backs turned?"

He was back to her side, to pat her belly.

"Oh, they're fine. Don't worry. Don't worry about anything. The sale on Max's'll buy us worry-free months, Mrs. Rooney. You won't be sitting up over the bills tonight, sweetheart. You just put plenty of butter on that fish"—now he gave the fish an affectionate little pat—"that little sucker's met *his* maker. Buddy'll be on page one of the *Courier* next week. And you just drink that sherry down, Lorey. *Good* for the baby. I'm getting on out of here to entertain our company."

And he waltzed out of the room, a carefree man she hadn't caught sight of in six months. Sweet Bill, soon to be father of five. Going to entertain *our* company.

Rice down from the shelf, carrots from the refrigerator: carrots with Rose McGillicudhy every evening, carrots boiled beyond taste. She swallowed the sherry down after all, thought of butter and cinnamon, and saw that the carrots did not look so bland anymore lying on the counter. Broil the fish! Of course! With lots of butter: Bill got through the practicalities of life far better than she did. And Tom, opening the car door for her earlier, had produced from the back seat a loaf of Italian bread he'd bought at the bakery that morning—she hadn't even known that the little shop where they bought garish birthday cakes with pastel icings six times a year baked daily bread. It took a stranger in town.

And tonight they would break bread with their plain fish

and their plain rice and their plain carrots, and they would even have wine to go with it. They would be provided for.

Lilies of the field.

☐   ☐   ☐

Bill said: "So where're they putting you up, Tom?"

Dolores was handing around the plates, the square hunks of fish shrunken and overcooked, and Bill jumped in to cover the china's cracks and chips with conversation. He filled the wineglasses again too, while Tom said that he was staying in town at the Oaks, the new brick motel on River Street. A practical place to put up, but not especially classy. Thank God for small favors. Less need now to apologize for the lack of luxury on O'Connor Street.

"And how are you filling up your nights, once the court-martial's done? —Oh, I guess you're back typing up your stories, hunh?"

Tom fluffed his napkin out (glory be, Dolores had found clean white napkins somewhere), sipped at his wine, and said: "Well actually, I try to phone the story in pronto. Then if I've got a long evening facing me I head over to the library in town until closing time." He ran his gaze around the room, bestowing eye contact on each of the Rooneys. "Funny how we develop these habits. I was just the same way when I started Yale, down every afternoon to the library. Fending off the loneliness of a new place, I guess."

At the end of Tom's speech Andy sputtered into his napkin, spritzing out the wine-and-water Bill allowed his children once they rounded the corner on the age of twelve. Usually you could count on Andy to be the sobersides at least, to have *some* sense of what was decent. Maybe Dolores was right: tonight he must have been sneaking more out of the bottle than Bill was aware.

Puzzlement fixed itself on Dolores's face. (How could she forget? This was the sort of thing you just had to cover over.) "What's so funny, Andrew?"

And Andy, *dammit, couldn't he just swallow it at this point,* said: "Oh you know. Daddy's old bet."

Now Tim was laughing too, and Dolores and Tom were sharing the puzzled smile, and only Kate and he had the sense to look mortified.

Tom seemed to know he was the butt of a joke, but he was a good-natured butt. "What old bet's that?" he said, and Andy, out of control, answered:

"Well, Daddy says ever since he met Momma she's been introducing him to guys who went to fancy schools. And he says he'll make you a bet. If they went to Harvard, they'll be awshucks about it, and they'll just say they went to college in Boston. But if they went to Yale, he says—" *He says.* When he, Bill, was sitting right there feeling his receding hairline radiate more heat than Dolores's tongue when she was being a shrew. "He says if they went to Yale, they find a way to work it into their conversation before five minutes have passed."

"All right now, Andy. You *know* I wasn't talking about the kind of remark Mr. Prince just made. He had to tell us he went to Yale to make sense . . ." His own sentence hovered.

But Tom Prince had a good laugh and said: "Andy, you almost got me. But I've been in the house forty minutes at least. I guess your daddy lost the bet that time around. Oh Lordy"— where on earth had he picked up that crazy accent?—*your daddy, oh Lordy*—"I guess I'm going to have to keep an eye on myself. Keep a lid on, huh?"

Well didn't Tim and Andy eat it up. Yale and the sense to laugh at himself. Dolores was beaming, Katie back to that sickdog devotion she'd been casting at the fellow's feet. Why did he, Bill, have to be the one to come out looking bad? He made a conscious effort to stifle a dislike that was growing. He had liked the man at first. Dolores had brought home a normal, unpretentious (he'd *thought* anyway) sort who might give them some inside news. There was an initial moment when the man's self-possession had seemed to him a mirror of his own self-possession as a young man, back when he gathered his company around him in a hotel room; but now that Tom Prince had an answer even for Andy's laughing at him, the confidence was not nearly so attractive. Before dinner was done Dolores would get out a balance sheet, profits and losses. Too bad she hadn't defied her mother and gone to a better school. Too bad her husband hadn't even thought of going to a better school. Great that this kid Tom Prince had, though. The same thing had gone on years ago with the Mansard boy.

"If you've been down to the library in the afternoons," Bill said, "you've probably run into one or the other of my children. That's why they squint so much, huh, Andy?"

Oh sweet Jesus, Dolores wasn't lowering her eyes already, was she? Two minutes down at the dinner table and already he'd said something to embarrass her.

Tim said: "Not our fault. Mother sends us."

The three children groaned in unison, an act they had perfected, though they usually didn't have an audience for it.

Dolores brightened at this turn of the conversation, and Tim said: "You have to be careful what you say at the dinner table, Mr. Prince, 'cause she might have you run look something up."

And Katie, rolling her eyes: "That's right, last year when our sister was here Momma thought it was a good idea to hear a poem before dinner, so every night one of us had to recite."

"Off the approved list," Andy said, and Kate went: "Ugh."

Dolores loved it. "Oh well," she said. "Maggie made a funny story of it in her college application. And at least it'll counteract those horrible inspirational things Mrs. Lovelace gives you to memorize. Mrs. Lovelace," she said to Tom, "teaches English out of the *Reader's Digest.*"

Andy stood, wobbly, and said: "Poor soul, the center of my sinful earth . . ." and Tim, not to be outdone, got up from his chair, picked up his glass, twirled it around, and recited: "In a wife I would desire . . ." The two of them, red-lidded, had definitely been at the wine bottle.

But Dolores was tickled. "Tim! Don't you dare, don't you *dare* go on with that one."

Tim sat back down and groaned. "Oh, it was on the approved poets' list. And I memorized the *whole* thing."

Tom Prince leaned forward, breaking his bread. "I think it's *fabulous* you do that. Great fun to recite."

Great fun. Oh this was going to be a long evening after all. Already the wine had gone sour in Bill's mouth.

"It's torture," Kate said. "It's worse than when my brothers bug me." She twisted her face into a good imitation of Tim's. "'Who's your boyfriend, Kate? Who do you love?'"

"It's true, Katie, that your brothers torment you even more than I do, but I must point out that it's *whom* do you love," Dolores said.

Moans all around. "See what I mean. She tortures us. This September we had a dry spell, so Momma actually made us all read a story called 'Dry September.'"

"Oh, all mothers have their means of torture." He winked at Kate. "But I don't know this story, Kate. Tell me about it."

"Faulkner," Andy said, with wonderful drunken derision. "It's been a whole memorial year since he died."

Now Tom snapped his finger, pretending he knew the story after all, and Bill knew his own patience wouldn't hold much longer. "Faulkner. Of course," Tom said. *Of course.* Oh the liar.

Timmy said: "We don't have that kind of violence in Due East. Lynchings and such. I think that whole part of the country, Mississippi, Alabama, I think that's a different South. Course we've got pockets of that stuff even in this state, but still—"

Bill could have finished Tim's sentence for him, since he'd taught him the concept: "But still, there's a line drawn down the middle of South Carolina, and it just isn't like that here. Along the coast."

"No," Andy said, sarcasm oozing. "We just have Marines marching a few good men off into the sunset."

"Well, I don't care," Kate said. "I don't care much about 'Dry September.'"

Bill had *told* Dolores that stories fit for Tim and Andrew were not fit for Katie. Stories of rape and lynchings for an eleven-year-old.

"I think the man's highly overrated," he said, not having actually read the story or any of the novels either, for that matter. Couldn't get past page one, which made his opinion— based on whether one man could communicate to another— cleaner and purer. "Nobel Prize? The good Lord knows who'll get it next." Kate stared down at her plate, and the boys too seemed suddenly interested in their food.

Jesus the fish was terrible. Incredible you could dry out something this thick. You'd think Dolores had taken it down by the Savannah River Plant and let it wither in the rays of atomic power. As if reading his thoughts Tom said: "I never would have thought shark would be such a *tender* fish."

Embarrassed—no, excruciated—silence. Kate chomped on the tender fish with a vengeance.

"My congratulations to the chef."

The chef looked ready to run weeping from the table—*she* knew what it tasted like.

"Yeah, Mom." That was Tim and Andy in unison, hollow and stoned, the two of them.

"So." He didn't mind jumping in: he'd been trained for the role. "So how's about we raise a glass in honor of our guest and do what the priest does when he throws a party. How's about we . . ."

". . . Celibate."

He and Tim had developed near-perfect timing on the line, and Tom Prince took a second to react. Then he appeared to think it was hysterical, mouthing *How about we celibate* and shaking his head. "Highest form of humor, as far as I'm concerned."

"Oh, these two can provide you with the lowest form too," Dolores said. "Bill's father was an old-fashioned Southerner who believed jokes were the key to all social relations."

"And they *are!*" Bill said.

"But your dad used to tell the worst jokes," Dolores said.

"Absolutely," Bill said. "Roosevelt jokes for a good long while."

"That's right. Remember? The Roosevelt stamp?"

"Oh Lorey, that one's old as the hills. I've heard it turned on every President since Hoover, and they were probably telling it before Hoover too. You know that one, Tom? About the presidential stamp?"

He fully expected that this Tom Prince would pretend he'd heard the joke too.

"No, I can't say that I do."

"Well, I heard a new version of it not but a week ago. My father told it about Roosevelt, but now they're turning it on Dr. King. One of my customers—"

"I don't know, Bill."

"Oh now, Lorey. You're the one brought it up. *Got* to tell it now. Only the man who walked into my real estate office told it this way: 'I heard the Postal Service has sent out word that it won't be issuing a stamp of Dr. Martin Luther King after he goes.' And of course I play dumb, like I've never heard it, and I say: 'Oh, why's that?' " Dolores was really squirming. Okay to tell the joke about Roosevelt, but not about her beloved King.

" 'Why,' says the man, 'the Postal Service won't issue a King stamp because they're afraid people'll spit on the wrong side.' "

Dead silence. Even Tim and Andy.

Finally Kate looked up, world-weary, and said: "Daddy, that's disgusting."

"Oh Kate, it's political humor. I tell you, I've heard it told about every President since Hoover. That's how this conversation started—your momma was telling Mr. Prince here the kind of jokes my own father used to tell."

You'd think the rest of them were all sitting on hemorrhoids.

Then Tom Prince began a low chuckle, which escalated, and all of a sudden the faces brightened. Now it was funny. But no —Tom said:

"That was a pretty bad one, but I'm just thinking of the Pope jokes I've heard since Kennedy took office."

Bill felt his own skin prickling. With great deliberation, he said: "Sorry. Political humor's one thing. But I draw the line right there, at religion."

Tom Prince was unflappable. Still twittering a little at the remembered joke, he said: "Oh, I agree with you. Completely."

And Andy said: "I believe I've heard a joke or two about a *preacher* in this house."

Bill laughed. "Tom, we're going to have to send this Andy of ours to law school. I swan, he has a legalistic mind. But listen now, Andrew, a joke about a preacher is a joke about a *social* issue, whereas a joke about the Pope concerns a *religious* issue. Religious issues just aren't for joking over."

"A fine distinction, but an important one." Bill glared at Tom for backing him up, or for making fun of him, whichever it was. It was impossible to tell, when a grown man looked sixteen years old, whether he was making fun of you. Too close to your own sons. Tom's open face—small nose, sharp jaw, medium coloring of the Protestant variety spreading down from a cheery high forehead and out to big schoolboy ears—could have been indicating complete and sincere agreement, but Bill doubted it. So, evidently, did Dolores, who had gone beyond being shamed to being saddened. She was beginning to slump over her plate: a worse state. Much worse state.

Now it was Tom who jumped in to cover the silence. "But you can understand why people would make jokes about the Pope, even if they respect him. After all, he's the strongest religious symbol we possess, in the Western world anyway."

A little huff from Bill: "I'd say he's more than a symbol."

"You're right. You're absolutely right." It was hard to tell if the man's smile or his constant ingratiating agreement was more irritating. "I guess if we were talking symbols, we'd be back in the political arena where we started. I suppose it would make a lot more sense, for example, to talk about Martin Luther King as a symbol, since people are making jokes about him. Or J.F.K. Kennedy as a symbol of the liberalism so many Americans thought died a final death with Stevenson."

Bill leaned forward, and so did his sons and even his daughter, but this time he was leaning forward with anticipation. Political talk. A pleasure.

"Again," he said, but he was no longer flustered, and so his cadence slowed, "I'm sorry to say that I have to disagree with you. Strongly. President Kennedy is not a symbol. He is a living breathing man and as such he's a leader, not a symbol at all."

To his surprise, Dolores said: "I have to agree with Bill there. He may symbolize certain issues to certain people—a number of people around here, I might add, think he's a symbol of all that's wrong with America—but it's dangerous to work living human beings up as more than they can be. He's not a saint after all." She blushed: at agreeing with him?

Tom Prince smiled wide. "No, no he's not. He's not a saint, and Martin Luther King's not a saint, but—"

Now Kate piped up. "They could be one day." Oh her sweet face. If only God had graced her with Dolores's pale freckles, instead of the dark crowd she entertained. What a sweet, sweet face. And she *did* believe he was a saint, that the two of them were barreling down the road toward canonization. St. J.F.K. St. Martin Luther King. "You don't know what states they'll be in when they die."

"Good point, Kate." Tom Prince beamed at her, and Kate's very freckles colored. "Maybe you're right. Maybe politicians can't be symbols while they're being politicians. But can they be symbols after they die? Is Lincoln a symbol, for instance?"

Bill hesitated. He was certainly being trapped. "I s'pose that's easier to swallow."

"All right then. Could we use the same distinction with religion? If the Pope is not a symbol, how about Mohammed? Or Jesus?"

"I can see you're not a religious man, Tom."

"Not *religious* perhaps. But I consider myself as spiritual as the next fellow."

"Oh." He couldn't resist, despite all the furious eyebrow-raising going on all around him. "Spiritual. But you see no one with a religious inclination would ever dream of calling Christ a symbol."

Dolores was livid. "But Bill, surely you can see what Tom's driving at."

"The wafers at Communion, then," Tom said. What a persistent little rodent: he had his teeth in it, and he just wouldn't let up. "Would you allow that Communion wafers are symbols?"

"And I thought we were talking about stamps! No, Tom, I

most certainly would not allow that Communion wafers are symbols. Communion wafers—which we rightly call *hosts*, you see—are the body of our Lord Jesus Christ."

"Bill, it's hard for people outside the faith to understand. If you could talk to Tom on his own terms—"

"What terms are those? Spiritual?"

"Bill." Oh she spoke to him as if he were a naughty boy. No more rudeness, Bill.

"Well you answer him, Dolores. Would you call the Communion host a symbol?"

He didn't like the way she hesitated. "Yes," she said, "if I were having a discussion with Tom, as I am, I might begin by agreeing that Communion is a very important symbol."

That was it. Enough of this sycophantic talk. All he'd wanted in the first place was a chance to tell his wife the good news, but instead his wife had driven all over the county with a reporter from the New York excuse me *Times* and then invited Mr. Yale to dinner without once consulting her own husband, who'd been worried sick about her. Dolores could write a book: Ninety-nine Ways to Belittle Your Husband. He didn't mean to be known as Mr. Uxorious around town. He swallowed down the bottom of his wineglass, slammed his fist on the table, and said:

"Well, Simon Peter denied Christ three times. You've only done it once."

Dolores stared at her dry fish and did not breathe a word. So she was playing the usual game: he was wild out-of-control Bill, and she was the long-suffering wife. He wasn't even worthy of reply. They'd probably appear, the two of them, in the New York *Times*, anonymously of course, as the picture of a couple whose marriage was falling apart. Maybe Tom Prince would write them up as a North-South couple whose lives had been twisted into one long philosophical argument. Didn't she have any idea what she was doing in front of this man? A reporter!

"Well, I've certainly sent this conversation way off track," Tom said, glib. Oh, glib as a senator buying votes in a country store. "I must say, though, that I'm delighted to find such a full-bodied wine down here. Your Due East has everything."

"Yes it does," Bill said, steady for the minute at least. "It has everything including people who still believe in the body and blood of our Lord Jesus Christ."

Now there was a little trio of voices imploring him, Dolores pleading *Bill* and Kate and Tim moaning out *Daddy*. Only Tom and Andy appeared interested in what he had to say: the two of them, out to see exactly how he would trap himself with his own words, appeared delighted at the prospect.

Well, he'd see that they got their satisfaction. "I'll tell you something else, Mr. Prince. Down here in the South we still have men who see fit to walk off from their own supper tables if they feel their religion has been insulted. And I feel—" As he stood he discovered how drunk he was. He, a man who put away a half dozen beers without remembering he'd drunk them, realized in rising that he wasn't accustomed to wine and that it had loosened his tongue and maybe even his senses. The way Dolores hid her face in her hand, the corner of her mouth peeking out to plead with him, might have stopped him if he hadn't swallowed so much of this pretentious New Yorker's wine. If he hadn't finished off the sherry. If he hadn't started in at five-thirty. If he hadn't had so much to drink, he would have recalled the way he and Dolores had put hand atop hand in the kitchen, or the way, as she settled into the pregnancy, her face was resettling itself, like a room set right after Lily had passed through. He did remember. But he was past stopping himself.

"I feel my religion has been insulted." The sentence came out just above a whisper and, hearing its dignified melancholy, he thought the lowering of his voice a good dramatic technique. His audience, however, did not even watch him as he hit stride leaving the room (he wasn't stumbling down drunk anyway). They looked away as he left: Dolores with even her mouth covered now, Tim staring red-faced at the ceiling, Kate and Andy in a face-lock. On the way out he reached over, as if he were going to grab the back of Tim's chair, and gave his son's right ear the slightest of cuffs. A glancing blow, really: just a reminder that his father was still his father, not an invisible source of shame.

They all looked away but Tom Prince, whose shrewd eager gaze turned and followed him, until he could feel it pressing, hostile and triumphant, against his retreating backside.

□   □   □

Dolores rapped on her own bedroom door, an action she could not remember taking in all her years of marriage. She'd already spent an hour downstairs cleaning up with the children, after it became clear that even Tim and Kate didn't have the will to keep up a dinner party after Bill's crazy outburst. (What were they *talking* about? *Stamps?*) They'd whisked Tom away and got the kitchen cleaned up in record time. Tom had been very understanding of course, had even made little jokes about the kind of things *he*'d said under the influence of a good wine. Once, he said, he told a professor at Yale that he was an old windbag, and the children had tried to grin at that. It had been agony for all of them, and he hadn't even waited for Dolores to unwrap the cellophane from a Sunbeam pound cake before he made his escape. He was probably back in his motel room making notes on the episode for a novel he intended to write someday, or making long-distance calls to a sophisticated friend, to some girlfriend, telling her about this remarkable night. They

were probably collapsing in giggles about it right now ("Down
here in the South we still have men who see fit to walk off from
their own supper tables").

She couldn't help connecting the dinner fiasco with the fiasco in the car: she'd used poor judgment in both cases. God
knows she'd used poor judgment thinking that her husband
would be able to restrain himself in the face of someone who
reminded all the Rooneys of what they were not.

She was weary of it, and more. "Bill," she called as she
rapped. He'd been cowering up here in the bedroom for the
hour they'd all been trying to forget the incident.

No answer.

"I'm meeting with Mae about the Thanksgiving turkeys tonight."

Still no answer.

"But first I'm going over to the motel to apologize properly
for what's happened. I won't have Tom Prince going off thinking—"

For once, she couldn't think of how to end a sentence she
was directing at Bill. Tom Prince would go off thinking something so accurate that surely it was better not to articulate it.
But it might help her own pride (oh it was hard to visualize
rapping on Tom's door) if she spent a quiet dignified five minutes explaining (without somehow justifying the rudeness) the
pressure Bill had been under, the mistrust of Catholics he'd
lived with all his life. If she could only explain, lightly, she'd be
able to file Tom Prince away and forget his visit within a month.
By next year they'd have another baby, and they'd have another dinner guest, and Tim would remind them of what had
happened and they'd all have a good laugh about it, Bill loudest
of all.

Bill loudest of all. He was, to her surprise, opening the bedroom door and facing her in his stocking feet, his shirt rumpled

and escaping his pants, to say: "Oh, I did it this time, didn't I, Lorey? For God's sake, don't let anybody serve me wine like that. Straight to my head. *Straight* to my head."

But he didn't look drunk in the least anymore: his flush had cooled, and now he looked abashed. He was jealous of Tom after all; but the anger she was tending needed more heat, not cooling.

"You'll have to see yourself to what you drink, Bill," she said; and remembered how, when her father berated her mother, he lowered his voice the way a schoolteacher does, his own dignity paramount. "Meanwhile I'm getting out of here to see to my errands. It's late."

"I'll drive you," he said, and touched her with a conciliatory paw. "But sweetie I wish you wouldn't make things worse by groveling over at a *motel.* I'll call him in the morning. I swear I will." Already he was leaning against the doorframe in his relaxed, expansive K. of C. way, as if they were gossiping about local marriages or tallying up the cost of the spring baseball picnic.

"I don't want you calling him," she said, and was aware that her three children, in their bedrooms, were listening to every word of the exchange. She shook her husband's hand off her arm. There was an uncanny silence in the hallway. She should have stopped, she knew that; children should never hear their parents belittling one another ("Rose, you might think that running out to the priest makes you holier than the rest of the neighborhood, but don't forget about whited sepulchres"). But instead of stopping, she heard herself revving up: "Do me a favor, Bill. Do us all a favor, and please don't pick up the telephone to call that reporter. Don't make things worse."

Bill's spine stiffened against the doorframe. "Jesus Mary and Joseph, Dolores, what's he to you? After he's denigrated our religion? A sniveling little *Yale* man and his feelings are suddenly more important than your own husband's?"

"Oh," she said, and could have spat. "I wasn't aware that someone who was capable of humiliating his entire family at the dinner table was capable of feeling."

He looked as he did when he went to grab Tim, his very ears twitching with frustration, but of course he had never grabbed her, and he never would. She found herself watching the pulsing ears, the thick gray hairs that sprouted now from within those ears.

"Dolores," he said, "I do not want you driving to some man's *motel* room to deliver any apologies. I won't stand for it!"

Her father would have said: "Then sit for it, you ninny," and if she'd used the line and cracked even a quarter smile she could have cut the tension with a regular butcher's knife. The tension, though, was exhilarating, and it had already built enough to explode into release, buckles and snaps and garters loosening all over her body. "I understand perfectly, Bill. I understand that you do not even trust me—pregnant as I am. What a despicable thing to focus on. A motel room."

She sounded as snitty as Andrew. Worse. She sounded as bad as Kate, petulant and defiant and childish—which was just what she was accusing Bill of being—and the truth of it was, she hadn't even been so hell-bent on going over to talk to Tom in the first place. Really it was more in the line of a threat; hadn't she been hoping that Bill would offer to talk to Tom himself? But Bill's ugly slurring of the word *motel,* accent on the first syllable in that hokey Southern way, sent her flying down the stairs, leaving Bill, the big bear caught in a pair of headlights, staring after her.

And as she took the stairs she could consciously feel herself unfastening the last of the tight stays of her conscience and preparing to squirm out of them. What a strange and recognizable sensation, though it was one she hadn't felt for many years: room to wiggle her hips and let her good big breasts float free. She was light-headed, and hadn't had a drink in an hour. She grabbed the car keys without feeling their weight in her hand.

In the yard she floated, as she'd floated that afternoon, and was reminded of Mrs. Rapple sitting out on her front steps. Kate said their neighbor had been taken away in an ambulance again. Poor woman. Now she could not even make herself remember what Mrs. Rapple looked like, except that her smooth purplish skin resembled a turnip's.

She was beginning to speak to herself in silent full sentences: *It was awkward enough on the beach* and *This is just pure crazy childish revenge.* She even said *This is a time for prayer if ever there was a time,* and remembered stern Teresa of Avila; but as she turned the key in the ignition she did not after all pray, but instead stretched herself out behind the steering wheel.

As she pulled out of the driveway she thought to look up at her daughter's room, and—as if the mother were transmitting brain waves again and had summoned the daughter—there was Kate, perched on the narrow windowsill, staring down at her with a look that Dolores imagined, in the dark, was disapproving. They were supposed to have told the children tonight about the baby. *Baby.* Now she got a tight hold on the steering wheel: what a crazy carried-away notion she'd just had, that she would go to Tom Prince's motel room, that he would want to seduce her. Kate, from the looks of her above, thought her mother was up to no good. Tom Prince had seen right away how sharp she was.

If she circled back around the driveway, and ran up the stairs, she could take Kate along with her on her rounds, as a bodyguard, a chaperone, someone who saw to it that she got over to Mae's house to go over the turkey list and not to a motel room at all. On the way home she could tell her daughter about the baby, and in the telling she would begin to accept the child herself.

But she didn't circle back around the driveway. She was still running on the adrenaline from her argument with Bill, and instead of heading to Mae's house, way back over in Moonlight Bluff, she drove the car to the Oaks Motel on River Street and announced her presence in the front office. There would be no question that she was sneaking around behind her husband's back; she wanted it clear that she had legitimate business to discuss with the reporter from the New York *Times.*

She did not recognize the clerk, whose hair was short enough to make him an off-duty Marine, some corporal from the Air Station. She had been so pleased, her first years in Due East, that all the faces along River Street were unchanging and familiar ones. Now she was pleased that it was a stranger who greeted her, a stranger indifferent to whatever she might do in a motel room with a reporter.

Tom opened the door in a sleeveless undershirt, an article of clothing she wouldn't have pictured him wearing: it was Bill who always wore an undershirt. He was flustered—"Gosh, I thought you were the clerk. He stops by sometimes at night when he's bored. Come in, come in"—and he was pulling on his rumpled white business shirt before she had time to stop him. The hair under his arms floated tawny and stringy; his chest, over that silly front dip in the undershirt, was hairless.

"Oh no," she said, standing in the doorway the way Bill had stood in theirs, feeling herself ready to collapse right back into the frame. "I didn't mean to bother you so late. I just came by—"

"Nonsense," he said. "Don't be silly. And don't stand out there in the chill air. Come on in and have a brandy. Can you?"

He flicked the television off (she'd envisioned stacks of books on the dresser, or maybe the clack of his portable Royal) and sat her down in the only chair. The bottle was right, but surely a newspaperman would be drinking scotch, or down here, bourbon—not expensive cognac.

"My word," she said, and was horrified. Now *she* was doing it with the accent. "You didn't bring those glasses down to Due East with you, did you?" His own snifter was nearly empty, and from a drawer full of socks he was pulling out another.

"Heck, no. I asked the clerk for paper cups one night, and got him in here to share a drink, and next day he comes back from the P.X. with these made-in-the-Philippines glasses. Can you beat that? I told him he's got to take them back when I go. A reporter packs in a paper sack."

She laughed and pointed at the full-size suitcase on his rack.

"Oh, all right. Caught again. You Rooneys have a good eye for pretension, don't you?"

She did like him.

The brandy poured into the glass with a good *glub*. "He offered to get me more than brandy glasses, let me tell you. He offered to get me—and here is a direct quote—however many pretty women I thought I could handle."

She reddened just as he sat on the edge of the bed, facing her.

"Hey, I didn't say *yes*. But I thought I was in a seedy detective novel for a minute."

"Oh, of course. I didn't suspect you." They both forced smiles. "Listen, I didn't mean to interrupt your evening here. I really just dropped by because that was such a dreadful scene at the house and I wanted to—"

"Don't you dare say you're sorry one more time, after all that carrying-on. You were absolutely charming, and you fed me a good meal. And look, I for one don't think your husband was so outrageous. I thought it was *good* to see a man with such a firm fix on his religion. That's disappearing from this country, you know. The ground's shifting under everybody's feet, but he intends to keep his balance."

This was the moment when she should identify herself as a Catholic too. *You must always defend your faith:* she'd spent a lifetime hearing it, and not just from Bill. Even her father, who couldn't keep the faith himself, had counseled her to "remember Peter's agony. Don't ever deny what you believe in."

She said: "Bill's religion is his life."

"And yours?"

Her religion? "My *life?*"

"Yes—what's your life besides feeling guilty about not doing enough for the civil rights movement?"

He was only dusting her with a light tease, but she could have choked anyway. This was like one of those teenage dates with a neighborhood boy saying: "So, you like the Yankees?" when what you really wanted him to do was give you a slow wet kiss.

"That's a pretty big question, Tom."

"Twenty-five words or less."

"I guess it's an ill-defined life, then. First the children."

"Oh, your children are great. Great fun. Tim'll be fine at Columbia—I think that's a good choice for him. But I could see you biting your lips when he told me."

She smiled. "I can't picture him on a college campus, not when he's sixteen. Right now he's not your standard fifteen-year-old."

"Oh, there's no such thing as a standard fifteen-year-old. It's one long humiliation, fifteen. College will be a relief. He'll establish himself as the boy genius."

"Bill doesn't want him to go off." Why was she telling him this?

"Thinks he's too young?"

"The idea of Tim at a good school bothers him." Oh, she

was completely disloyal—but she didn't stop. "He doesn't want Tim to pass him by. Bill dropped out of college himself to be a musician."

"That's it."

"What?"

"I—pardon me, this is probably way out of line—but I found you an odd couple tonight. I *like* Bill, I really do admire that sort of brash say-what's-on-your-mind way of operating. Really. Don't look at me that way. But it seemed to me there must be more of him, something he wasn't revealing, that would have brought you together. Now, this really *is* out of line, I hardly know you, but I can see you falling in love with a musician. I just couldn't see you falling in love with that heavy-handed proselytizing."

Oh really, she should disabuse him; she should tell him he surely was out of line and then she should back right out the door. But he leaned forward on the edge of the bed, trying to get a good look at her in the stiff armless chair, and there was that same innocent eagerness she'd seen when he first approached her on the bluff. He was only trying to figure her out.

"Bill was a good musician," she said. "He was a happy man when I met him—happy, I think, for the first time in his life. He'd escaped his family, you see."

A long silence. Two sips of brandy. She had to be careful with the drinking. But it was softening already the hard edges of her betrayal—if Bill knew she was sitting in a motel room drinking brandy.

Tom, jellylike, slipped himself down the edge of the bed (he must have been drinking since he left her house), then settled in at her feet, where he stared at the chest of drawers as if it were a cozy fire. The two of them maintained an easy silence. She watched his right shoulder tensing through the thin white shirt: not one of those broad shoulders that would have excited a woman, just an ordinary man's shoulder of an average size, a shoulder tightening a little as the quiet wore on. She wanted to reach over and touch it the way she sometimes wanted, in a Charleston antiques store, to stroke the arm of a brocade couch. She didn't know anything about this man. She pictured her father, picking up blowsy Lorenes and Pattis in bars, then sliding down beds to sit at their feet. The whole world was charming when you were drunk.

"When you said your husband was happy when you met, I guess you meant he's not happy now."

"I guess I did."

"And, excuse me, but I think you meant me to know that you're not happy either."

There was no need to answer. They sat in the quiet of his motel room, the two of them waiting each other out. What changed when you were drunk was the way you gave up the struggle: one minute it was impossible that you'd consider such treachery; the next it seemed silly to resist in the face of such innocent questions, such innocent possibilities. Those college years spent listening to the rantings of boys in Union Square (was it politics? or did they just want to get laid?) came rolling back at her: she'd been good all those years after Timmy, but tickled just the same that a bearded Trotskyite was trying to seduce her and three of her convent school friends at the same time. The Catholic Workers were so much more reliable: they would be faithful family men. But then she had followed Bill back to his hotel room.

Tom edged closer on the carpet. Tonight all the awkwardness of the car and the beach was smoothed over with brandy, and he had just made the first move with that line: *You're not happy either.* A line you picked up out of a phrase book, *Endearments for Seducing the Married Woman.*

"You even have a sad name."

Oh he was shameless, and she was shameless enough to smile back at him. "My father was sure he was Black Irish: you know, part Spanish. He thought *Dolores* had an exotic sound."

You're not happy either. It was the kind of line Walker Mansard had used on her, trying to wear her down, trying to persuade her to get out of her marriage while she could: Walker thought she'd go off with him on some avant-garde adventure, when she knew perfectly well that fifteen minutes after he'd introduced a pregnant mother-of-a-toddler adulteress to his family on Long Island he'd realize *his* big mistake. And even if she had been in love with Walker Mansard, she couldn't have walked out on Bill while she was pregnant with his child. Unhappiness wasn't even part of the calculation. Bill had done nothing wrong. He was only himself.

She felt Tom's leg against her shoe: had he shifted his weight? She was a girl again, a girl who flirts with the neighborhood boys she'd never dream of introducing to her friends, certainly never to her family, boys who had nothing more than dark eyes or rough stubble on their chins to recommend them, boys who would stick their tongues deep into your mouth and their hands deep into your blouse, and wouldn't recognize you the next day.

But Tom, instead of titillating her with a hand that twirled her buttons and sent a little thrill up the center of her spine, would titillate her with the word *unhappy*. Oh, why blame him? She was the one who'd shown up at his motel room. She kicked off Maggie's flats, and he reached out a hand to feather her bare foot. She could stop right here. Once she'd put her babies to sleep by holding their feet, and now she was letting Tom Prince tease the same fine line of nerves.

"So cold," he said. "You have a lovely cold foot." He'd had so much brandy that the words slid out honeyed. Then he let her foot flop down and took off his glasses; folded them up

271

carefully, the way a drunk man *would;* and stretched to set them down atop the dresser. She could stand right here, and take her leave. Tom's ears were huge flaps in the glare of the overhead light. She could see her father standing at such a dresser, singing a corny song and twitching his big backside. Funny, how Andrew McGillicudhy thought he had to marry his Lorene and his Patti, how he had to be faithful in his infidelity.

Tom eased back, drunk and happy, stroked her foot again, and looked up at her with sappy pale eyes that made her want to just hoot. What pleasure he took, just from being young: and what pleasure she was taking, in this moment, from watching him. What did those boys in Union Square say—that it was base selfishness to own someone's body? Just now it sounded right and funny and full of goodwill. Spread it around. Love thy neighbor. Oh Lord she was dead drunk. She heard ringing that old church phrase: mystical body. She was floating in a warm pool that brought her closer to her own father and the Wobblies in Union Square and even Bill, even Bill who'd once taken such delight in her eagerness, the way she now took delight in Tom's.

But here she was, one foot in the water—one foot now being tickled—holding back. Was Tom holding back? Had her father held back? Did any man, any man but Bill Rooney, ever trouble himself over an act of love? *In a wife I would desire*—even her innocent goofy Timmy—*what in whores is always found.* And what was always found in whores? Her memory wavered, under the influence. *The lineaments of gratified desire.*

Tom would find her breasts enormous. He would get an extra charge out of making love to a pregnant woman, a married pregnant woman, though in the morning he would wake with a hangover and a generic spiritual guilt. He might drive by her house in the morning to try to assuage it.

Even drunk she knew she wouldn't be home when Tom Prince drove by. Feeling the first swoon of dizziness—she'd bolted that brandy right down—she pictured Kate looking right through her tomorrow. Bill would never know, and her boys would never know, but her daughter would look right through her glass heart. Sober, she hadn't even been sure she liked this man; drunk, she only knew that he resembled her father and her cousin and her husband and her sons, that men were only looking for lovely uncomplicated gratified desire.

And so was she. Right now, letting him hold her bare bony left foot, waiting for him to lean over—to fall over, probably, from the looks of him—she was watching herself loosen the last bent fastener on her conscience, the one she hadn't even known was still in place.

She was looking down on this scene from another plane, watching this motel room as if she were perched somewhere at ceiling height, as if she were a camera. She was warm up high, where heat rises, warm with goodwill and desire. It was pleasant to be so far away from the action: it was easy. An easy lay.

She—the woman down there anyway, the one still living in her flesh—slid down off the hard-back plastic chair and settled in next to Tom on the scratchy rug. She didn't even wait for him to pull his arms around her, schoolboy fashion: she rubbed her palm against the sparse gathering of his stubble, a woman of the world, and watched the brandy glass topple behind him. The last drops rose into the air, a sweet perfume for the two of them.

NEVER DIE

Dolores would never do such a thing. It was only his mother's training—be suspicious, believe the worst—that made him dream such nightmares. It was his own fantasies tormenting him, not even the possibility that Dolores would betray him: his own fantasies and, face it, the image of Dolores's full white pregnant body, which hadn't lured him even in the old days of the first pregnancies and now, flabby as it was around her thighs and backside, came close to repelling him and would for another six months. How could he debase them both by suspecting her? *The Way of Perfection* sat right on the night table.

"TIMOTHY."

Tim's head appeared in the doorway instantaneously, as if he had been waiting outside for the call.

"You rang?"

"I want all of y'all in bed now." He himself appeared to be lounging in bed, the paper spread around him, when what he was doing was trying to banish an image of Dolores in that smug boy's arms. Oh, she wouldn't. She'd be shamed to let a kid see those pocked wedges of flesh. A kid not much older than Tim, staring at him purse-lipped and exasperated.

"Dad, it's ten o'clock."

"Don't you sass me."

"Dad, I've got to figure out what to do about my English project. I was going to ask Mom—"

"Your mom's not here to ask, so I don't s'pose it'll do you any good to haunt the hallways waiting for her. Now get to bed."

Tim had the nerve to shake his head in disbelief and then to loiter there in the doorway, as if he were waiting for handouts.

"Also, Tim, it might occur to you once in a while to take your old man's side when there's a stranger in the house. Maybe your momma'd be home right now if you had."

Tim's face blew up like a blowfish's, but tonight he stopped himself from talking back. Tonight he merely shook his head again, in the same wild disbelief, and backed out of the room.

Bill folded up the paper, again, again, yet again (oh Lord it was the way his mother taught him to fold a piece of toilet paper for maximum efficiency), and then, horrified, unfolded it just as carefully, smoothing out the front-page article. The segregation school was going gangbusters; inside there was an editorial endorsing it, and another taking potshots at J.F.K. To hell with newspapers. To hell with the Due East *Courier* and the New York *Times.* Now he crumpled the paper in a ball, so Dolores wouldn't be able to send it to Maggie after all, so she'd have one less piece of dog doo to rub his nose in.

□   □   □

The worst of it was that Dolores was whistling as she pushed open the front door, and still whistling as she climbed the stairs: "Heaven Can Wait" snaked out of her mouth before she heard the notes. She gathered a handful of skirt; she was sure there was a damp stain in back, a damp stain that meant she'd have to face her family frontward to say her good-nights. And still she was whistling. She had been whistling in the car too, all the way out to the Claire's Point turnoff. Little snatches from God knows where, "In a Sentimental Mood," "Body and Soul." She had even stopped at Coot's to buy a single cold beer, and had drunk it down before she reached the bridge coming back into town.

It was just past ten-thirty—she hadn't been gone two hours —but already the lights seemed to be out in Kate's room and even in the boys'. Usually she had to flick the switches herself to get them off before midnight.

She crept into her own room, head first. Bill was in bed, pretending to be asleep, and she positioned herself sideways at the dresser so he wouldn't see a small wet circle on the back of her skirt. She had her eye on him in the dim lamplight when he rolled over and said:

"Mae called to ask where you were."

She didn't even have to pause to think of a reply. She put her hand on her hip, "Sentimental Mood" still gliding through her head, and raised one eyebrow high enough for it to say *Oh Bill. How could you think such a thing?*

"I knew she would, Bill. But I had to work that anger out. I just drove around and around, all the way out to Coot's and back." The truth of it was that she'd driven out to Coot's so the gas gauge would register lower. She'd been in the motel for an hour: long enough to cheat on her husband and bathe at the sink, and now she couldn't stop whistling. A succubus. Hadn't she almost twenty-five years ago climbed out of her cousin Tim's arms and reappeared in front of the radio in Aunt Brigid's living room grinning like a fool?

"Lorey, I don't like you driving all over the county like that at night. The Lord knows who's going to climb into the back seat of that car." A pause, and then a comic-strip gulp before he got the next question out: "Did you go over to that reporter's?"

"No Bill." There was a position on her dial midway between matter-of-fact statement and hurt denial, and she had tuned it in right on the mark. "I only said that out of anger. I wouldn't shame you showing up there, Bill."

He sat bolt upright in the bed. He must have been tensed there for hours after he chased the children to bed, imagining his wife where she really had been, in bed with Tom Prince. Well, not in bed: she'd been on the floor, where she deserved to be, pretending to be the sort of woman who sneaked out to motel rooms every night of the week.

"Come here, Lorey," he said, and held his arms out in a gesture that wasn't so much possessive as it was defining. She went to him without hesitating, because if she had hesitated she would have recoiled, and there was to be no more of that in this long pregnancy.

He pressed tight against the small of her back, and she could feel the fast thud of his worry. "I didn't really think you would," he said. "Not *hardly*. And God knows, Lorey, I wouldn't suspect you of doing anything untoward if you had gone. You know that sugar, don't you? You've been a saint through all this worry."

She stretched her own weightless arms out until they circled his neck and then she kissed the top of his head, her cold lips pressed against his warm skin. Sweet trusting Bill wore a padded suit like an astronaut's, protecting him from what she'd gone and done, and there was a thick plastic visor drawn over his face: he wouldn't even let himself smell the strange scent of motel soap on her skin, or the cognac on her breath.

Guilt was hovering somewhere in the corner of the room, kept at bay by the last beer, and here she was whistling while her padded protected husband held her tight. When she was thirteen, she couldn't even make herself read through one of the cheap hidden detective novels her friends pulled out of their book bags. It was just too easy to imagine herself the cool dame in the feathered hat who pulled out a revolver and plugged away. It didn't even take any imagination to see herself stabbing her father right through the heart. So cool a liar: she'd even fooled herself, all these years. Maybe the beer was too much. She was beginning to tilt, a little wave of nausea licking at her.

She was supposed to be praying, and instead she was hearing music. Would prayer allow guilt to sit down right beside her on the bed? Like one of her children when they were small. Like her own small self on her father's bed in Inwood. She drew back and looked at Bill's pink-rimmed eyes, at the fleshy stubbled cheeks, and his thick curling eyebrows, and she said: "I love you Bill." The nausea drew back. She was looking through a long lens at his innocent trusting face. She hadn't known she would say *that*, but it seemed the least of her lies tonight. Once she had spoken, she went back to humming as if she hadn't missed a beat. Bill would drift off to sleep with the music lulling him.

Then he loosened his hold on her and eased back on the bed, just as she had thought. She let her own hand rest on his hard fat belly and found it steadied her in this dizziness. Bill steadying her. Who knew what was possible, after all these years? She herself was certainly dead drunk, a state of consciousness she had not been aware she could reach. She was incapable of guilt or prayer or holding herself still. She was brimming with music, with whistles and lullabies and Mozart and Ellington, music that would keep her awake all the night, music that would join the swooping tingly liquor to keep the guilt at its proper distance. Prayer? She put her head to the pillow, but it floated up, keeping its own time.

□   □   □

The lamp had been out in her parents' room for an hour, maybe more: it seemed to Kate that the dagger of light underneath their door, the one that pushed under her own door, had been dim a whole nighttime. She had tried saying the Rosary, but there was no keeping track of the decades in her state: the prayers were like lengths of moss on the trees outside her window, dangling down vaguely.

When she went out into the hallway, she could hear her parents' heavy synchronous breathing; asleep, for once, they worked in rhythm. There was no need to tiptoe on her way to Timmy's room. She and Tim always knew when the other was awake: they beamed mysterious signals to each other. They would glide back down the corridor together, and never disturb the heavy paired breathing of her parents.

Sure enough—Andy was scrunched in the corner of his bed, his sheets knotted cords, but Tim was wide awake and debonair, propped up on one elbow to wait for her arrival. In the dark her brothers' plain square room was bare as a tomb: plaid cafe curtains and a Blessed Virgin Mary were the only decorations. No baseball trophies for the Rooney boys. It reminded her of her grandmother Rose, of Rose's order, of the way she whisked magazines away into pink plastic trash cans before anyone had a chance to read them. She always expected to smell her grandmother's smell—mothballs and talcum powder—in her brothers' tiny room, but instead she smelled dirty socks, even on days like this when Lily had worked at banishing the odor.

Tim put a finger to his lips, but there was no need. They had done this routine half a dozen times during a year of sleepless nights for the two of them. Tim never slept: he was always waiting in those worn flannel pajamas with the missing button halfway up his chest. Sometimes he forgot to close all the snaps on the bottoms.

She waited for him to rise and then led the way back down the little hallway to her bedroom, where he would sit on the edge of the bed until she could fall asleep. The first time, he had caught her sleepwalking and trying to crawl in with him, and he had propelled her by the elbow back to her own bed, where she woke while he was trying to drag the covers up. Now she came to him awake. Her brother took on a different personality at night, a priestlike manner (old, wise, kind); and she wore a different nighttime personality herself. There was no one to see her in the dark with her brother Tim.

They did not signal each other until they were back in her room, and then Tim closed the door—slowly, slowly—with a careful authority that he did not possess when the sun was shining. Suddenly (oh it was just like the hypnosis scene in some corny old movie) her eyelids were very very heavy; and she almost thought she might fall asleep before she breathed a word.

But he sat at the edge of the bed, wide awake, and folded his arms while he waited. She propped herself up on the pillow. If Tim hadn't been reading all those psychoanalysis books, the books her father kept snatching away, she wouldn't have known that he was just practicing on her. It didn't matter. At night, she would have just as soon confessed the naked dancing to him as to Father Berkeley.

They sat quiet awhile, not a word yet exchanged between them, and Kate flipped over on her back. Through the window fronting the street, she saw a dim moon out past the oak trees. "Did you hear what she said to Daddy?"

That rolling wave on the mattress would be Tim stiffening. "She was just embarrassed. She just wanted to explain to that guy so he wouldn't write up some stupid article about Southern families."

"Not that."

"What then?"

"She's pregnant." She had lain in the dark for two hours, feeling the sickening swell of her own belly at the thought of her mother's secret, good as a lie.

Tim shifted again and moved closer, until he was almost leaning over her. He was such a goofy-looking guy, even in the dark: he reminded her of one of those overeager cartoon faces, Bugs Bunny or Daffy Duck, ready to splutter. "Kate," he said. "You didn't know, did you?"

She could have spluttered herself. "Oh don't tell me *you* knew."

He watched her.

"Did she tell you? Did they tell everybody but me?"

"Hush Katie, they didn't tell anybody. But she's been so—"

She's been so *pregnant.* She's been so fat and white and sleepy and moody and ugly and old. "Is she sick."

"No Katie, she's *pregnant.*"

"Tim, for God's sake, I mean is she sick like Turnip Rapple, is that why they didn't say anything?"

That stopped him, but he waved it off: "They didn't say anything because they don't know how they're going to pay for it. They didn't want to worry you."

"Ha." She shot spittle through her front teeth, and would have shot it across the room if anyone but Tim had been there to witness it.

Then more silence, Tim easing back and staring at the door-

281

way while she turned her back to him and watched the window. Fall night. If you looked long enough you could make out the clouds pushing by.

Finally she said: "You can go now Timmy. I can get to sleep."

"Sure." He didn't move.

"Really, you can go now."

"You sound like you're 'bout ready to burst into tears."

"I am not ready to burst into tears." She let a soft whimper escape.

"Listen, Kate, it won't be so bad. Be company when Andy and I're gone."

"Oh, I wasn't even thinking about *that* anymore."

"No? What you thinking about?"

"Well to tell you the truth I'm thinking about that girl in the trailer."

"Oh Kate for*get* the girl in the trailer."

"I should've helped her."

"Oh criminy Kate." Bill's word, criminy. "You're worried about Mom, can't you see?"

"That's not what I'm worried about. I'm worried about that girl. What if you and Andy're wrong? What if he drags girls there and cuts them up?"

"Katie they were *fornicating*."

A word with sharp edges that dug into her just below the ribs, and then dead center through her belly button. She started to cry, good mean silent crying, and willed the tears to stream down until they rolled across the sheets and soaked Tim's pajama bottoms.

"Look, I'm sorry"—" what did *he* sound so angry about?— "but that's all that was happening and you can't get all hysterical about it. I've seen your list, Kate. I know you've got *fornicate* on it. That's just what happens in the world."

Oh the moron.

"It's *Mom* you're worried about, don't you see that?"

She knew she was sniveling and didn't care. "She doesn't love him."

"Well."

"You think she does?"

"Well."

"Momma went to that man's motel room. Tom Prince."

"No she didn't. Good *grief.* Katie, what are you talking about?"

"She did, I know her, I know her better than you do. She went to that man's motel room. And for all you know they were fornicating too."

"Oh dry up Katherine Rooney. How can you even say such a thing? That's really disgusto, when she's about to have a baby. Can you *see* Mom doing that?"

Well of course. Clear as she could see clouds bumping in the night sky, or Tim's flat white belly where the top snap of his pajama bottoms had come undone. She could see the reporter who looked like Robert Kennedy with a crew cut pulling up her mother's plaid schoolgirl skirt and resting his hand on her thigh. She could see her mother leaning over to kiss a man who didn't get drunk and make fools of the family. She could picture herself in the scene almost as clearly as she could picture her mother: whichever one of them Tom Prince had chosen, she would have said yes. It was an OVERWHELMING FORCE, though she, of course—well he wouldn't expect her to—wouldn't have got any further than the kissing.

"You don't know everything Tim."

"I know our mother. I know I wouldn't say something stupid like that about her just so I could be a maniac."

"I'm not a maniac."

"Listen to you."

"You think it feels good to cry like this?"

"I think it makes you feel good, yeah. I think it makes you feel like a big shot, like Daddy when he's yelling. Go ahead, wake up the whole house."

She was bawling by now, and rolling her fist into a ball.

"Stop hitting yourself like that."

It was an old trick: banging on her thigh.

"Stop hitting yourself like that, Katie, and get some sleep."

"I'll never go to sleep. I'll never go to sleep."

She didn't accelerate all the way to this hysteria often—she wouldn't have dared pull it around her mother, who would have shrugged her shoulders and told her to stop her nonsense—but once she got it up to speed, she wasn't entirely sure she could put on the brakes.

"That girl could be dead right now. That girl could be cut up in the woods lying in a pool of water."

"Katie I swear to God I'm going back to bed and tell Daddy to get out his belt, you don't shut up."

She found the brakes, and the crying decelerated until it was only a hiccup.

"Now hush."

She hiccuped. "Timmy don't go." She burrowed under the pillow. Behind her the mattress rolled as he decided.

"Timmy don't go, I'll never get to sleep. I know she's okay. Please don't go."

And to make him decide she removed the pillow from her head and rolled herself in a compact ball. She held her breath for thirty seconds, facing the window so he wouldn't think she was begging. She wasn't a maniac.

And soon enough he lay down beside her and let his hand fall down on her shoulder, then lift again, mothlike, until it lay next to her hair.

"It's okay, Kates."

284

DID HE THINK SHE HAD APOLOGIZED?

She sniffed. "G'night Tim."

Then his hand lighted on her shoulder again. "You're safe now. Go to sleep."

And she did, for a while, because her brother was priestlike, and he was keeping watch.

◻   ◻   ◻

Four o'clock: the sweetest dreams before morning. The Rooneys dreamed in the old creaking house on O'Connor Street.

Andrew's dreams were always orderly and, like the papers he wrote for school, focused on a single theme. Earlier tonight he had dreamed he was invited to dinner at the rectory and the cook brought out a trussed chicken.

His new dream opened with an image that he himself had seen through Father Berkeley's camera: his own dirty feet, in a dirty pool of water close by the trestle. The dim pool of water expanded until it was a regular swimming pool, all white concrete below. Andy was on the diving board, waving to the crowd (politicians mostly: he recognized Nicholas Katzenbach and Sargent Shriver; his mother, standing apart from the crowd, smoked a cigarette and watched him with narrowed eyes). Andrew was bouncing on the board, up and up and up, but the dream was stuck, a piece of film caught in sprocket holes. He strained to bounce higher, high enough to dive, up and up, again and again and again. In the deep end his father held out his arms to catch him, but his father, of course, couldn't swim. Sargent Shriver poised his hands to give a polite round of applause. His mother waved the cigarette, signaling him, but now he could only take baby bounces on the diving board. They were at the country club, and Andrew could not make the

285

board lift him up. All around the edge of the pool blond tan surfer girls laughed at his teensy-weensy bounces. In bed Andrew Rooney, who like his parents lived by the sea but could not swim, curled the sheets around him until they resembled bandages, and he became a mummy.

Tim dreamed he was locked in the top of a Steinway grand piano, the only physical object he'd ever seen his mother crave. They'd been in Savannah, and the way Dolores stood on the sidewalk, drooling at the piano inside, would forever define for him the word *lust*.

Kate, who had rolled over until she was close to smushing Tim and who was responsible for his dream that he was suffocating in a piano, was dreaming rapid-fire images: a saxophone; a hurricane lamp; her father's belt; the sunlight, white-hot off the water. Now she was at the Canteen, dancing the shag with her brother, and when he whirled her around her wide skirt lifted and her underwear showed, only *she wasn't wearing any underwear.* The bed shimmied and shook with her shame, and next to her Tim dreamed the piano strings quivered until he plucked them into calm.

Dolores dreamed a sound—oh maybe there was an image to go with it, but if there was it was just a corny movie image from these corny times, the beating of a war drum in a Western. The sound was what possessed her: TimTimTomTomTim-TimTomTomTimTimTomTomTimTomTimTom. She woke with cotton mouth, bewildered and possessed of a childlike fright, and after she realized that she was in Due East, not in Inwood, she remembered that she had been drinking. She'd drunk so much she'd probably made the baby drunk too, and done God knows what to its innocent trusting soul. Now that she knew that she had been drunk, that she was drunk still, she knew that she would remember soon where she had driven in the old station wagon and why she was left now with this sharp fear for the baby, for the baby and for Timmy and for Kate. For a moment, lying on her back next to her husband, she had the distinct impression that she was occupying someone else's body; but then she realized that she was only mimicking the quick decided hand motions her mother used to make in the evenings, in the easy chair, after Andrew left them. She was only fingering an imaginary pair of Rosary beads, and she had already passed three decades.

Bill was not dreaming with the rest of his family: his first vision of the night had caused him to give up dreaming altogether. In the early dream, he was ringmaster of a carnival, his children and his childhood friends and his River Street friends all dressed up as clowns and freaks and acrobats and even cigarette girls (Dolores and Coramae and Sharmayne) strutting through the stands. Now he was the Pope: Pope Bill of the Carnival. Glory be. Tim came by on stilts, taller than even the Pope, and vaguely threatening. They did a comedy routine: Tim asked the question, and he was to deliver the punch line. The question was:

What's the difference between a President and a Pope?

Bill leaned forward to catch the punch line. But no—*he* was supposed to tell the joke.

What's the difference between a President and a Pope?

Even the cigarette girls, high in the stands above him, hissed when he couldn't remember. He leaned all the way into his dream. He leaned until he was dizzy.

He didn't know the answer. He just didn't know.

He didn't know the joke. Sweet suffering Mother of Jesus, he did not know the joke.

□   □   □

At five-thirty in the morning Dolores gave in to wakefulness and rose: for a while, in bed, the physical hangover was only a drug's pall stretched out over her, while underneath its dark shadow she wrestled with her memory. Now, standing—or trying to stand anyway, one hand against the old dresser, wanting to retch and climb back into bed simultaneously—the panics of body and mind merged. Poisoning. If she was poisoned, then the baby was poisoned too.

She dragged off to the bathroom. If only she could throw up the wine, the sherry, the cognac, the beer—the volume of it, the variety—but it was too late for that anyway. The poison had already gushed through the umbilical cord to the baby, and every throb she felt in her head the baby would be feeling tenfold. Dr. Black always said *Hey, a glass of wine's good for the little peanut,* and she'd believed it too, raising a beer to her lips when the sun went down and imagining with pleasure the cartwheels the little one would turn. She'd always been careful before, careful to stop at a bottle of beer, a glass of wine.

Now when she drove off to Charleston or Savannah, to find an anonymous priest to whom she could confess the adultery, it would be hard to name adultery as a mortal sin at all: not when she balanced it against the sin of poisoning an unborn child. Her well-lighted picture of the motel room embarrassed her with cheap shame, but her hazy memory of the drinking terrified her.

In the bathroom she ran water and felt Tom Prince's innocent mouth, rough and inexperienced, come down on her own again. She felt herself, after a long dry moment, slipping her tongue across his narrow lower lip. His drunken deadweight was pinning her to the scratchy motel carpet, where he flailed over her and she swung her hips into the slow bump and grind she'd once thought would please her cousin Tim. One of the painted dolls in a carnival's girlie show, an image she'd remembered from God knows where. The water ran on, and she felt in its hesitant flow Timmy's gentle touch after she'd undulated that way for him. When she was a girl she had closed her eyes and imagined herself wearing the tight sweaters and scarlet lipstick of her father's barstool admirers, the ones who squeezed Andrew's thigh with their glittering dark fingernails. Last night she had closed her eyes and imagined that she was a girl.

The faucet shrieked when she turned it. Back to her bed, to try to lie still for the baby's sake. In the hallway her sons' doorway was open and she stopped, as if gazing in on them would steady her. Andy slept in his underwear, the sheets twisted around him, and in her state she could have wept at his sinewy legs, dark-haired and adult. What was he dreaming, to twist himself so?

She leaned in past the doorway, wanting to take in an image of Tim too (drunkenness made your arms and legs go liquid over your own sons, made you picture them small and struggling). But Tim's bed was empty.

A clutch of fear, not at Tim's absence—Tim would be curled in the armchair downstairs, staring at a piece of music or the paper—but at how she had failed him, how she'd given birth to one son who had to rise before dawn because he couldn't sleep and to another who twisted himself in the sheets like a toddler with his bad dreams. More than one way to poison a child.

Now she looked in at Kate, imagining she would find reassurance there. But when she pushed open the door she saw a twitching fretful Kate, who had kicked off her sheet and pulled her nightgown waist-high, leaving her plump white fanny exposed.

And worse.

Flat on his back, next to his sister, the top snaps of his pajama bottoms undone, his proprietary arm flung across his sister's back, was Tim.

She held on to the doorknob and heard one of Lily's lines

ringing: *I like to die,* Lily would say if she walked in on this scene. *I like to faint dead away.* Kate and Tim. Dolores and Tim. She would have knelt down by the doorknob and wept, if she'd stopped for another minute to think about it, but as it was she followed a different mother's impulse: she skipped to the bed, where she intended to pull Tim up by the ear and drag him downstairs for an interrogation.

Tim had wakened though, at the sound of the opening door, and he was up before this Mother Superior of his could bean him. He sat and, swinging his arms down, sidestepped her as she reached the bedside. Then—wonder of wonders, mercy of mercies—he motioned her to hush, as if she were the one acting out of the ordinary. He backed out of the room, taking charge, having her follow, so they wouldn't wake Kate.

Her cousin putting a finger to his lips as footsteps passed in the narrow corridor. He never once had to say *We won't tell a soul.* Now, even before she hissed the question to her son in the hallway, she knew that this Tim didn't know how to lie.

"What were you *doing* in there? Wait. Come downstairs. Come downstairs this instant."

She led the way, charging though convinced of his innocence, the poison in her veins burning itself up in sweet crazy anger, anger that licked out at her cousin and her father and that pretentious ingratiating newspaper reporter. Together she and her son clunked down the stairs and into the kitchen.

She set one hand on the kitchen table, one on her hip, and the dizziness and headache and nausea vanished with her purpose. She could feel the reporter's smooth hand, tenuous on her thigh.

"Now. Timothy Rooney. What exactly were you doing in your sister's bed?"

Tim grinned—he *understood* why she was so upset—and

then twisted his face into goony protestations of innocence. "Oh Mom. She couldn't get to sleep."

"Tim Rooney, you are fifteen years old. You don't go sleeping in your sister's bed because she can't get to sleep. And button those snaps, for God's sake." Tom Prince's taut belly, when he slid off his pants. The way he turned his white backside to her when he tugged off his boxer shorts.

Now Tim reddened, and narrowed his eyes, the way she did hers to show anger. His snaps clacked into place.

"What do you mean, she couldn't go to sleep?"

He barely raised his head to answer her. "There was some carrying-on before you *left* last night."

He had Andy's sarcasm down just exactly right. He was furious with her, livid that she thought he might have laid a hand to his sister that wasn't an innocent hand—and how *could* she have thought it of this one, this Tim with his droopy drawers and his hurt? She hung her own head, imitating him. She hadn't even thought of it, not really: she had only seen herself in the curved sleeping forms of her children. There was no way to properly tell him how sorry she was.

And Tim, seizing the moment of her silence, said: "She knows you're pregnant now," only this time he took care to concentrate every word into adolescent drops of acid.

This spinning she felt was not from a hangover. She hadn't even told her own children she was pregnant. Miss Social Conscience, who didn't even give her year at a soup kitchen. Mrs. Civil Rights, too diffident to go out to the Friends Center and offer her help. Mrs. Faithful Wife, knocking on motel doors. Mrs. Understanding Mother. She was a fraud, through and through. And Bill said: *You've been a saint through all this worry*.

Oh Tim.

"Oh, Timmy."

Now she went to cradle his head the way she'd cradled

Bill's, but Tim was standing and taller than she. Her arms ended up around his waist, where she felt him stiffen. She let him loose then, and stepped back, but still he stared down, the way he stared at his guitar when the Daydreamers played in the talent contest down at the high school.

"You smell like liquor and cigarettes, Mom," he said.

And then her older son ran from the room the way he had when he was three or four or five, and Dolores held herself up at the kitchen sink, the only holding her son would allow her. Tom Prince was reaching out a hand to hold her down on the scratchy carpet beside him, but she—giggling; giggling!—was rising to bathe at the sink and then drive out into the dark Due East night. Then she was whistling. And then she was comforting her husband with lies. She was a woman who said the Confiteor when she slighted a neighbor, but hid away from prayer when she'd committed adultery. She ran the brown water, same as every morning, and stared at it spitting down into the chipped stained porcelain, until it ran through clear.

□   □   □

Bill Rooney woke to the smell of coffee and the bump of the front door closing: Dolores was off to daily Mass, and this time she hadn't roused him to make sure the kids got down to breakfast. He'd felt the dip in the mattress all night while she shifted back and forth: her wakefulness was due, he knew well, to the strange brew of alcohols she'd stirred up last night. He'd smelled brandy on her breath at the end—she hadn't been driving out to Coot's at all, but sitting down, probably with Father Berkeley, to cancel out what she saw as her humiliation at his, Bill's, hands. *I wouldn't shame you, Bill,* she said; but that was exactly what she set out to do when she left the house last night. Maybe she'd even been drinking the brandy with that god-awful brownnose of a reporter, Tom Prince—though he doubted it. He doubted she would have gone back for more humiliation once the first serving was spooned out.

Thank the Lord she was pregnant.

And why in God's name didn't she think of the baby when she poured it down her throat like that? They said alcoholism ran in families and that was all he needed now, to see Dolores fall apart in that self-satisfied way of hers, sitting on a barstool and imitating dear old Dad. Bad enough she was lying to him, but for Christ's sake, he didn't want to hear his mother's high-pitched voice issuing from his own mouth, needling and whining. He'd never interrogate Dolores.

Now the front door clunked again and Bill, stuffing the pillow under his belly, snuggled in to wait for Dolores, come back to say goodbye. But no: a minute passed, and another, and then from the back yard underneath his window he heard the scrape of metal as a bike was disentangled from the jumble vine of Schwinns.

Merciful Jesus, have pity on us down below. It was, what? Seven-thirty? He pulled the alarm close and found himself five minutes shy of the mark, then bounded out of bed to holler out to Tim (only Tim would be dressed at seven-thirty in the morning) to come inside and fry up some bacon for the family instead of rousing the whole neighborhood. "C'mon now" was already out of his mouth before the window was raised, but by the time he'd stuck his head out into the cool clear day the bike was leaving the back yard and the rider was not Tim at all, but Kate.

"C'mon now, Katie."

The bike disappeared around the side of the house, and his attempts at calling it back were pitiful. She had *heard* him. He shook his head out into the good day, breathed in the good air, and felt himself swelling with the relief of morning. He was going to make him some money today.

"TIMOTHY."

He called his son's name into his own bedroom, and then for good measure he called it into the hallway:

"TIMOTHY MICHAEL ROONEY."

"You rang?" Tim stuck his head out of the bathroom, the Brylcreem still wet above his widow's peak and his face covered with shaving cream. He was dressed in undershirt and shorts, the way he must have pictured the fellow in the shaving ad. The gobs of shaving cream struck Bill as less pathetic than usual—this, after all, was going to be a lucky day. Dolores was off to Mass: *not* the behavior of an adulterous woman.

"Your little sister just went tearing off on her bike. She say anything to you?"

Tim shrugged his shoulders, one at a time, in especially guilty fashion.

"Come *on*, Tim. Out with it."

"I dunno. Honest."

Dolores would have bitten off his head for using that tone of voice.

"Well, is she going off to somebody's house for breakfast? She doing one of those dissections again?"

Now Tim was wiping the shaving cream off with a grimy white towel, dispensing with the shaving part of the operation altogether. *"Dad.* I don't *know."*

"And where's your mother this morning? She *always* sets out breakfast before she goes."

"She set it out. I s'pose she's gone to Mass the way she does every morning of the week."

"Well she didn't say goodbye to *me."*

Tim was dragging on tan pants pulled off the damp floor. "Maybe that has something to do with last night."

"I'll thank you to keep a civil tongue in your head, Timothy Rooney. And I'll have you know your momma and I are not fighting. Mr. Know-It-All."

What was that head-cocking Tim was pulling now? And he was scrambling into his shirt.

"What are you in such a hurry about this morning? Where's your brother?"

"Andy's still in bed. I think maybe I know where Katie went. I think I'll just ride out after her."

"Then where's she gone?"

Tim brushed by him with not so much as an excuse-me, and by the time Bill was watching him sit on his bed to pull on brown suede oxfords—oh he *wished* Tim didn't have to look like such an old man. If only he would wear loafers or at least a decent pair of sneakers—his son said: "We were out shooting by the trestle yesterday. She must have left something out there."

"Something what? Andy, get your rosy behind out of the sheets."

"A notebook. I think she left a notebook out there."

"Why don't I believe a word you say?"

"I don't know, Dad. She left grapefruits and sugar buns on the table."

"What? Oh your mother. Timothy, for God's sake please call your mother Mom or Mother or Momma or even Dolores. But do not refer to her as *she*, hear?"

"I hear you Dad. Father. Daddy. Bill."

"And get back here and tell me why your sister would run all the way out to the trestle at seven-thirty in the morning to pick up a notebook. Peter and Paul, those woods are full of lunatics, all we know. Tim, I am talking to you. Tim, get you back here this—"

He retreated to the hallway, not to finish, but to be absent when smug Andrew saw that he could not summon any of his children back.

"You better get yourself some rags on your back time I call back up here, boy."

Argh. Downstairs he went, to wash out the tired false sound of his voice with the bitter coffee—Dolores would *not* measure it, no matter how many times he asked. And what was this weird meal? The grapefruits were put out in segments. Nobody ate grapefruits like that. And the sticky buns were cut up in narrow precise strips. My we were dainty this morning: still feeling the effect of Mr. New York Reporter, perhaps? He popped a grapefruit section into his mouth and it sizzled out its bitterness onto his raw tongue.

There was still a hammering of suspicion in his head, and he wouldn't have it.

"*An*drew. Get down here for some breakfast. You are the last one left home and your momma's going to be here any minute now to see you off."

She still did that. She didn't go take a walk or stop to chat: after all these years, Dolores trotted home from Mass to see her nearly grown children off to school.

A masochist, he popped another grapefruit section in, and heard Dolores's step at the front door. His throat constricted, the way it had when she was twenty and told him she was pregnant, and he found himself rearranging the grapefruit sections on the plate, until they formed the spokes of a wheel.

□   □   □

Kate was lingering on River Street, deciding whether to inquire at the office or to snoop around the maid's carts, when she heard someone else's bicycle humming up River Street. A spy in a war movie, she flattened herself against the side wall of the

Oaks Motel and watched her brother Tim speed by. He looked straight at the brick she hugged without seeing her.

So her father had sent Tim after her, and Tim believed she'd gone to the trestle. A shiver of satisfaction settled in her spine. Tim had convinced her—he'd really convinced her—that the Snake Man was only fornicating, not raping, but still he believed she had gone out to the woods.

The sight of her brother filled her with resolve. She nudged the kickstand to her bike, settled it on the sidewalk, and entered the Oaks Motel office. A plump grandmotherly woman sat like a nesting bird, feet tucked up beneath her, in the armchair guarding the front desk.

"Why good mornin', darlin'," the clerk said, her eyes still on the lobby's big television and the morning news: there was the same shot of the Kennedys she'd seen last night. Her spine still tingled pleasantly.

"What can I do for you this morning, sweetheart?" The woman did not look her way.

"IcametoseeMr.Prince."

Now the woman turned a blue-eyed gaze on her that was sharper than Kate would have expected. Her hair was rinsed blue too.

"What's that, honey?"

"I-came-to-see-Mr.-Prince-the-reporter. Could you tell me his room number, please?"

"Mr. *Prince.* From New *York.* " The blue-haired woman rose but glanced back at the screen with regret. "I saw him out here buying the paper at the crack of dawn. I don't believe he's still in his room, honey. He'd most likely be out to Parris Island by now."

Seven-thirty. But she had been sure she would catch him before he left. She'd lain quiet in her bed from the moment her mother grabbed Tim to holler at him in the hallway until six-

297

fifty, when Dolores left for Mass. Then she'd dressed with care —white pullover, clean for once, God bless Lily and her Clorox, and black knife-pleated skirt—all the while planning exactly what she would say to Mr. Thomas Prince. *Was my mother here last night Mr. Prince? Just say yes or no.*

The grandmotherly clerk had made her way back behind the desk, and was lifting an operator's headset. "I'll just give his room a little buzz. In case he's there after all." It had not occurred to Kate that a motel clerk would think it the most natural thing in the world for a little girl to show up asking to speak to a reporter. She'd been prepared for a grilling.

"Aren't you a Rooney, honey?" the woman asked, waiting for a response to her ringing.

"Yes ma'am."

"I knew it. It's that hair. I remember when your momma first moved down here, you could see that blazing head of hair coming all the way up at the head of River Street."

"Yes ma'am."

"And which one are you, sugar? I can't keep all of y'all straight anymore."

"I'm Katherine."

The woman peeled off her headset. "Well, Katherine, I'm sorry to say Mr. Prince has done gone out to do his reporting. But I could tell him you stopped by. You could leave your telephone number."

Kate knew she was making a face.

"Is it real important?"

Kate considered.

"No ma'am. Well I guess so. My momma sent me to fetch the pocketbook she left in his room last night. When she came by to get interviewed."

"Oh my word."

She saw her mistake, but how else was she to get into the

room? Already the blue-haired lady's blue eyes shone with anticipation.

"So Mr. Prince has been doing some interviewing off the base."

"Well, I think they just dropped by to get a pen or something. They were at our house all night. With my father. Mr. Prince was interviewing my mother *and* my father."

The woman cooed her understanding. "Oh *I* see. Well let's us think about this. I don't imagine Mr. Prince would object if I just walked you down there to see if your momma's handbag isn't right out on the dresser. I know he'd understand how a lady just can't get by without her purse. We won't snoop, will we?"

The woman seized up her keys with relish and flittered out through the lobby onto the breezeway, where the clear November morning washed the concrete with light. The bay out beyond could have been a sheet of ice.

"Down this way, sugar."

Kate trudged on behind. What did she expect to see in Mr. Prince's motel room? Why had she given her mother away?

The woman clicked the door open and rushed to enter and flick the switches for the bedside lamp. Its thin paper shade gave off a dim glow, enough for Kate and the clerk to take in together the handsome plump brown bottle on the dresser. The bed itself was smooth, still made up but for the blanket which had been wrenched free and now lay crumpled on the carpet over pillows. The room was otherwise orderly: a few cuff links on the dresser, a paperback detective novel, a glossy magazine in the trash. Two balloon glasses perched atop the television. Two.

The woman whirled around to give Kate her sharp look. "I don't see a pocketbook," she said, nearly making a question of it. Then she leaned over for a perfunctory search in the dark corners beyond the dresser. She even ventured further, into the bathroom, but she did not ask Kate to join her.

And Kate had seen enough. She stepped outside to wait in the bright light while the woman poked around. It wasn't the sight of the two fat glasses, or even the blanket crumpled on the floor. She'd known when she saw her mother alighting from the dark sedan last night. She'd known when she heard her mother whistling on the stairway. She'd only needed to step inside the man's motel room and feel the coolness of her mother's presence, the pleasant clear order Dolores had bestowed on the room she was in last night.

I wouldn't shame you, her mother had said to her father. She'd heard that clear denial right through the hallway, right through the night.

It was a good thing Tom Prince wasn't there after all, because she would have cracked one of those glasses over his head if he had been. Couldn't he see after that lousy meal how totally hopeless her father was? Maybe she could call the New York *Times* and get them to send him home. Maybe she could call and say a New York *Times* reporter had tried to rape her. Or kiss her or something.

Now the desk clerk was locking up behind her, and when Kate whirled around the woman gave her the sharpest look of all, as if she could see her trembling. "You tell Miz Rooney to come by later and we could go through the room together. Or maybe Mr. Prince will hand-deliver that pocketbook to her today." Kate was sure that this blue-haired little old lady was smirking. Smirking.

"Yes ma'am," Kate said, forgetting already that she'd made up the lost pocketbook. She was picturing what she would say to Mr. Prince if he came by after school, while her father was at his office. She was picturing herself pulling out the carving knife to point it at Mr. Tom Prince's lousy flat belly. She was picturing her mother in the background, helpless for once and sad that her daughter was called to such a bloody defense. So very sad that she'd gone and done what she'd gone and done.

◻   ◻   ◻

Running the lines of their silence was worse than running a gauntlet. Andy and Bill, who both preferred solitary confinement to each other's company, did not so much as grunt or glance at one another at the breakfast table. They popped thin strips of pastry in their mouths, then sucked at the grapefruit, and watched points just beyond one another's heads before they slurped up their coffee. Katie usually kept the conversation going at the breakfast table, and if she wasn't chattering then Tim was picking an argument with his dad and sparing the rest of them any effort. Now the two talkers had run off: what on earth had possessed them, sneaking out of the house at the crack of dawn and leaving this sad breakfast party? A chill ran through her when Bill said they were gone, but she calmed herself with the memory of Tim's face, resentful that she didn't trust him. She would have to trust the two of them now. She would have to get through breakfast with Bill and Andy.

Finally Bill said: "You all right, Lorey?" She was an old lady leaning on the counter again. The walk out to Mass was supposed to have cleared her head, and her isolation in the pew at Communion time—she was the only worshipper at daily Mass not receiving—was supposed to have shocked her back into prayer. Instead she'd kneeled alone and remembered an overheard conversation at the Piggly Wiggly, one old lady complaining to the other that she wanted food "as bad as one of them niggers up in Harlem wants heroin." Look what she wanted. Moments on the floor, spasmodic encounters over the

years with men—with boys—when she pretended she was someone else entirely.

It was cold that morning in Our Lady of Perpetual Help,
and she had thought once again that she was inhabiting someone else's body. A woman whose soul was mismatched with her
body could not pray, no, not even recite. Sidling away from
Father Berkeley after the blessing, she had resolved not to think
about her hour with Tom Prince. It was done. Over and done.
This would be the last time: what could she do but make that
resolution again? The last time in her life. She pictured her
father's profile, false tears streaming down as he whispered *mea
culpa.* No breast-beating for her.

She would not even allow herself to think about poisoning
the baby because that too was done, finished, and if she'd damaged the little one she'd have a lifetime to nurse it through its
troubles. Now, through all this mold covering her brain,
through this panic and this false strange body, she was beginning to picture the baby for the first time. She was beginning to
imagine a boy and even boys' names. It was time to name a
baby after Bill. A sweet William to wipe out her night with Tom
Prince.

"Not really, Bill," she said. "I don't feel great."

And she let him rise and help her along by the elbow, an
invalid, until she was sitting with them instead of standing and
waiting to serve. A Mary, not a Martha.

"I'm not *that* bad," she said when he pushed her chair in,
and she managed to smile, but still she was grateful for his
strong arm guiding her down. Grateful for the table anchoring
her. She was lowering herself into the chair with a pregnant
woman's slow ungainly caution. She was beginning to imagine a
pacific family scene, Maggie home from college and the baby
spooning up mashed bananas.

Andy gave her a peculiar stare and Bill, seeing it, said: "Your mother's pregnant, Andrew. We're going to have another baby."

Dolores could see that this chill message came as no surprise to Andy, that all three children knew. Her son reached over and squeezed her hand, as if to let her know that she needn't worry about how *he*'d take it.

"The common response, Andrew," Bill said, "is *Congratulations.*"

She returned her boy's squeeze. The child was fourteen years old. This was his mother, having a baby.

"Congratulations, Mom," Andy said in a monotone, and now she gave him double squeezes, triple squeezes.

Tim chose that moment to come crashing back in through the kitchen door, and Bill—on a mighty roll—said: "Sit yourself right down there, Timothy. You can be working on your sorry excuses for this behavior. But right now we want to tell you that your mother is going to have a baby."

Tim wouldn't meet her eye either. It was as if both her boys knew where she'd been last night, knew how Tom Prince had kissed the back of her neck and the bottom of her spine, as if they saw it in the wrinkles on her skirt or the lankness of her unwashed hair.

"Congratulations, you guys."

Bill grunted.

"That's *great.*" Tim pulled his chair out with the same false heartiness he projected in his congratulations, and the size of his gesture sent Bill and Andy staring out past each other once more.

"Five kids!" Tim wouldn't let up.

"Where's your sister?" Bill said.

"I don't know," Tim said, everything still oversize.

"She wadn't down at the trestle?"

"Nope."

"Trestle?" Kate was the only one who swam, and there was always the chance that she'd leap off after one of the boys down there.

"Oh Lorey now don't worry. She's fine. Tim, you two are grown boys. I don't hardly know *what* you're doing playing around in the woods like babies. Now your little sister's got to run out there after you."

"Speaking of babies, when's the baby due?" Tim said.

"DON'T CHANGE THE SUBJECT ON ME."

Dolores watched Tim and Andy exchange raised eyebrows. She could not bear it, not her two resentful sons and her missing daughter and the knowledge of what she might have done to the baby. Family peace. She could not bear Bill, not for another minute, much less for a lifetime. Cuffing Timmy's ears that way. In front of a stranger. What would he do to a son born too late in his life? Oh she could remember the early drinking years, the long silent nights and the contemptuousness when Bill picked up one of her magazines and then let it slide from his fingers, to rest where it fell. The way he embarrassed the young mothers in the discussion groups, squeezing their bare arms until the finger marks rose purple on their skin. Walker Mansard strolling across the green. Family peace. Some other young man coming into Due East five years from now, or ten years from now, all her resolve dissolving in a glass of bitter whiskey. Confiteors for the neighbors, empty barren panic for her own family. Already she felt tugging at her the fatigue that would come with another baby's sleepless nights. Already she could see Bill, the beer weighing him down, sleeping through the baby's cries. She lay her head down on the table, right smack in the middle of this sad breakfast.

She felt Tim—or Andy?—stroking her loose hair, and the light touch roused her. It was Timmy.

"The baby's due at the beginning of May," she said, and sat

herself straight up. Despair was the unforgivable sin, not adultery. Through the door she caught sight of a redhead bouncing along atop a bicycle in the back yard and she grabbed on to the image as if it were a rope that would pull her back to her children.

"Katie's come back."

"Gonna tell her?"

"Of course we'll tell her." Bill stretched to watch, through the window, his baby dismounting the bike. "We told you, didn't we?"

"Dad. We already knew."

That, strangely, tickled Bill, and he swiveled around to grin at Tim. "That so? And does our Miss Katarina know?"

Tim nodded, grave. "She does."

Bill laughed aloud, at himself probably, for thinking he could keep a secret in this family. When Kate finally trudged up the old kitchen steps, one dawdling step after another, Bill let her have it, double barrel, before she was fully in the door:

"Katherine Rooney, where in blessed Jesus's name have you been running off to? We've got big news for you, little girl, and you up and disappeared on us."

Kate shrugged and took her place at the table, bringing the eye-averting that had been going on to a climax by managing not to look a single one of them in the face.

"Don't you want to know what the news is, honey?" Bill poured on the syrup.

"Mommy's pregnant," Kate said, and Dolores watched her daughter's bottom lip swell out purple and resentful: a little girl, still. Her dark freckles were a mesh across her face this morning.

"Is that why you left this morning?" Dolores jumped in before Bill could. She saw her daughter perched on the window-sill, watching her drive off to a man's motel room.

"No."

"D'you leave something out by the trestle?" Tim used an exaggerated cagey voice.

"No."

Andrew said: "I bet she just wanted to get out of this hellhole."

"Andrew, do not tempt me."

Kate sat catatonic and stubborn, and Tim finally passed her the plate of sticky buns, only one thin sliver left, and said:

"Hey Kate, we'll be a *big* family now."

He sounded so jolly and false that Bill laughed out loud and even Andrew cracked a smile. Kate, though, wouldn't budge, not even when her father said:

"Now *you*'ll have someone to torment."

Rebuffed by his daughter's stony slouching body, Bill shrugged and reached an arm out to touch Tim's shoulder. "Better hurry, son. You'll be late." Dolores didn't think she'd ever heard him call Tim *son* before.

"C'mon now, Andy. Katie. Time's a-wasting."

The boys rose and barreled off to collect their books, but Kate kept her vigil, scrunched down low in her chair, staring out the back door. Her father leaned down close and said, low enough so his sons in the hallway wouldn't hear him:

"Don't you worry now, Katie. We'll keep you safe and sound. There's *plenty* to go round."

Kate grimaced. "Oh Dad. That's not all we ever worry about. That's all *you* ever worry about."

Bill grabbed his chest, stabbed through the heart, and staggered around the table wounded. Still he got no rise out of Kate, so he made his way back behind her chair and dropped his arms down over her shoulders. Kate tugged at his fists, hanging on to them, and closed her eyes.

"So where'd you run off to this morning, baby?"

Now Kate opened her eyes and stared at her mother, as if

Dolores would know the answer to that question. There was nothing to do but throw her hands up—you've got me—and feign ignorance. Kate was eleven years old looking out into the night, guessing what her mother was about to do. Dolores saw herself at eleven on a barstool, one hand on her father's thigh to match the other female hand, on the other thigh.

"I love you Daddy," Kate said to her father, and reached out once more for his big hands. "I love you forever and *ever.*" She drew one of the hands down to press it against her cheek. The ferocity of that last word was not aimed at Bill. Dolores watched her little girl hating her. Sleepless nights. Bill's resentments. Kate's knowing.

"Time to get moving now, Kate," she said.

Her daughter glowered.

"All right now," Dolores said. "Let's get you off to school." There was no use hoping for forgiveness. Just now she must force herself into false businesslike briskness and hope for some return to order. She rose to clear the plates and hurry her daughter off, and Kate radiated the contempt of a slow rising.

She would get through this day the way she had gotten through every long day of her marriage. Thanksgiving and Christmas and a baby coming. Tim would need her to edit his application and pencil through the self-deprecating lines. Father Berkeley would need somebody who could actually read the Aquinas and carry on a conversation that was not faked.

Prayer would not come today, or next week, or maybe for the rest of her lifetime, but she could at least shape her day around imagining prayer. Imagining that Kate would forgive her. Imagining that she would forgive Bill.

She could force herself out of the house early this morning, woozy hangover and all, so that she would not be there when Tom Prince drove his black sedan by, to offer his regrets.

□   □   □

Katherine McGillicudhy Teresa of Avila Rooney slogged through the school day, the old brick building as oppressive as the heat rising up through the morning. Mr. Smolinski was in an especially foul mood after lunch, and sent the boys out scrimmaging on the back field while he faced the sixth-grade girls in his little shorts and Bulldog T-shirt. The girls huffed back in their navy-blue uniforms. Their one-piece suits could have been designed as modest convent issue: the drab tops all angles and order, the bottoms puffing out into bloomers. Designed for humiliation. Finally, after he'd run them through more sadistic calisthenics than they'd had all year ("I said hold that leg in the air to a count of *fifty*, missy"), the gym teacher sent them back to the locker room, where they languished, glistening.

Kate and Franny were late running up the back stairs to Mrs. Lovelace's class and Franny said that since they were going to get three demerits anyway, they might as well just spend the hour in the girls' bathroom. She pulled a flattened cigarette out from her satchel's side pocket: filtered temptation.

Kate looked at it longingly—today she'd try *heroin* if somebody offered her a needle and she wasn't about to let Franny, who was wearing her skirts shorter and shorter, get a jump on her—but was saved from a decision by the sudden arrival of Mrs. Lovelace herself on the landing above them. She rushed down past the girls, her mouth puckering as she tripped along on her bowed and low-heeled pumps.

"Come along now, girls," Mrs. Lovelace sang. "Go along now, Frances. I'll be up di-rect-ly. Assignment on the board."

"Who pinched *her* behind?" Kate walked on silent until she was sure Mrs. Lovelace was out of earshot. Franny was getting D's in English and bragging on them: she would have been getting F's, but her father was assistant principal.

The last ones to arrive, they entered a class of semi-controlled bedlam. A few earnest girls in front were busy copying down the poem Mrs. Lovelace had written on the board in a sloping schoolgirl script:

> *Out of the night that covers me*
> *Black as a pit from pole to pole*
> *I thank whatever gods may be*
> *For my unconquerable soul.*

"Jesus H. Christ!" Franny said. "Don't tell me we have to recite *that* crud out loud."

"You have to recite that crud out loud," three boys answered in unison, and Stevie Dugan said:

"That's right Fanny, you got to memorize it for tomorrow, only *you* have to say it this way.

> *"Out of the fright that covers my face*
> *Pink as a pimple from ear to ear*
> *I can't for the life of me figure out why*
> *Boys run from me in fear."*

Franny delicately removed her bubble gum and flung it at Stevie Dugan's forehead, where it held for one glorious moment before it toppled off.

"I hate you, Stephen," Franny said, with great dignity, and then sat herself down in the desk with her feet up in the air, a long slice of pink thigh showing for his sake.

"Hey, Katie, look."

Carlene Perkins pointed out the long window fronting River Street. Carlene was one of the cool blondes with padded bras; the other ones, this year, were named Darlene and Charlene. Franny said her father, who did the scheduling, thought it was hysterical when he put them all together. Mrs. Lovelace put Carlene and Charlene in the desks by the window—her class was on the second floor, with a good view of the bay—so they'd stare out all dreamy and lovey-dovey at the glassy water and quit their chattering in class.

Kate stared out down below and saw nothing in the water to interest her. Three sailboats in the middle of the day—that was how warm *this* November was—but even the sky was erased of clouds.

"No, look," Carlene said, and pointed again, lower this time.

To her horror, Kate saw that her father stood on the sidewalk opposite the school.

"Looks like your daddy's looking for you," Carlene said. "What'd you do?"

"I dunno," Kate said, and went to kneel by the long window and focus on her father, looking up at the junior high windows. He couldn't possibly know that she was behind one of those windows, that she had a class on River Street just now. By now a crowd of five or six girls had joined her to wave at Bill Rooney, but he could not see them in their dark interior.

A row of boys formed behind the girls to see what was going on outside. There was no mistaking Bill Rooney. He crowded the sidewalk, all alone as he was, and he seemed to be performing, gesticulating up at the window and then swiveling around to face the bay, face in his hands. He was jacketless, his starched white shirt a banner. Oh God. Had he started drinking in the middle of the day? If he'd lost that big sale. If he'd dragged out another bottle of wine. If he'd dragged out the wine that *reporter* brought.

"He's crying," one of the boys said, indifferent.

"He is *not*," Kate said. She could feel her cheeks heating up as hot as the day, as crimson as the thermometer on the United Way billboard downtown. Her father could not be downstairs, drunk and crying, in the middle of the day. It was not possible. When Mrs. Lovelace came in, everyone would be lined up at the windows, pointing at her father, and then Mrs. Lovelace would send someone out to see—she'd send *Kate* out, of course—and her humiliation would be total and final. No hope at Due East Junior High School from that point on.

"Ooh, Katie, is *that* your dad?" Charlene. Or Darlene.

Below, Bill pivoted again to face Mrs. Lovelace's class, an avid audience. Now she could see, not from any tears splattering down his florid cheeks, but from the way he'd scrunched up his face like a bawling baby's, that he certainly was crying. She'd never seen her father cry before, though she'd seen him bellow until his very forehead surged. The entire class had gathered behind her to watch her father crying down below on the sidewalk.

How could he have walked toward the junior high knowing what it would cost her? He might not have known that she'd be by a River Street window, but if he'd stopped to think he could have figured that *someone* would see him, someone eleven or twelve or thirteen years old, someone who could know now for certain, if they hadn't guessed it before, just exactly how strange the Rooneys were.

"Oh God I hope nobody's *daid.*"

Kate couldn't have said who breathed that fear—some fluffy voice sounded it out—but she dismissed it. The only two things that could make her father stand on River Street, miming his grief to a whole school, were her mother losing the baby (and her mother didn't go and lose babies, she wasn't some Turnip Rapple) or her father finding out about Tom Prince and Dolores. Kate's eyes watered. Her father had found out about her mother's faithlessness. He'd found them together. He'd found them embracing in the kitchen after they thought he'd gone to work. He'd got out the carving knife, the very knife Kate had intended to use on that good-looking snake herself.

Someone sensed Mrs. Lovelace in the doorway behind them all and they turned, in groups of two and three, to face the teacher.

"Mr. Rooney's out—"

"Sit down, please." Mrs. Lovelace, lady that she was, forced her voice out low and sonorous. No screeching in *this* English class.

"But Mr. Rooney's—"

"I asked you all to sit down, please."

Kate could have kissed the jellied black spit curls that plumped themselves against Mrs. Lovelace's forehead, or buried her face in her teacher's prominent pointed breasts. Mrs. Lovelace, God bless her, was not in the least interested in what her father was doing on the sidewalk down below.

"I'd like you all to prepare yourselves for an announcement. Mr. Starkey will be speaking to us in just a little minute," Mrs. Lovelace said, and ran her fingers down her girdled pelvis. Fluttering and tittering feathered through the class, but Mrs. Lovelace raised a ladylike index finger to halt it, and rolled back and forth on her low heels.

Now Kate's panic spread and diffused. An announcement? Her father waited on the sidewalk. The class waited for the crackle of the p.a. What was it then? War? Were there hidden missiles in Cuba after all? They would be asked to squat under their desks, which they wouldn't even remember how to do since Kennedy did away with the practice, and she'd never have a chance to fling herself into her father's arms, her father who had come for *her* before he'd gone even to rescue Dolores. Soon they would hear the drone that meant the fighter jets were leaving the Air Station in formation—the same drone they'd heard all through the Missile Crisis, the drone that would swell up to roar and pop and screech in the lovely blank sky over Due East.

Stevie Dugan flopped his hand through the air, but again Mrs. Lovelace raised her finger, and then pointed delicately to her own ear. *Listen. Listen.*

It took forever for Franny's father to come on over the speaker, and when he did there was—first time all year—not a trace of static. There was something else in Mr. Starkey's voice, though: a catch?

"Boys and girls," he said—catch—"I have some sad news to give you this afternoon." This was it. The missiles were headed their way. They would be the target, Due East dead center, loaded down as it was with bases. Oh her mother had been right all along. Thurmond and Rivers and the rest of their segregationist military gang couldn't have made them more vulnerable if they'd painted a red circle around Due East.

But here was Mr. Starkey's gentle soothing voice again, after another catch: "Our President has been shot. President Kennedy has been shot. I'm sorry, boys and girls, he is"—catch —"he is no longer with us. Let's take us a moment of silence."

Silence? The classroom buzzed and crackled. Mrs. Lovelace hung down her head, and the obedient girls up front followed her example, but a current of giggles passed through the center aisle.

Then the familiar static of the address system spluttered into the room again, and Mr. Starkey said: "Due to this terrible —*event*—we're going to send you all on home. The buses will be here from the high school in five minutes, so if you're a bus student you can start lining up on the breezeway. If you get to school on your own you can go ahead. Go ahead on home now. That's all."

The low cheers and whistles started up when the assistant

principal said *send you all on home now* and bubbled still despite Mrs. Lovelace's warning raised palm.

Is no longer with us? Kennedy?

She saw across the room that Franny sat rigid at her desk and crossed her legs at the ankle, ladylike, for the first time in her life. Behind her, Stevie Dugan wept recklessly and rested a hand on Franny's shoulder. Of course the three of *them*—Starkey and Dugan and Rooney—would be grieving.

"Is he *daid?*"

The rest of the class had erupted into carnival time, a stunned slow sweep of confusion and jubilation. Someone shot the President—why, half the boys in this class had threatened to kill him themselves.

"This mean they won't integrate the high school next year?"

Mrs. Lovelace drew herself up and sucked her girdled belly in further. "Boys and girls, we don't know *what* this means. We do not know what this means. Now, I have made no secret of my own sympathies, but it is not seemly—sit right down there, Wyatt, or I'll sit you down myself—it is not seemly to carry on celebrating when the President of the United States has been shot dead. What did I just say, Wyatt?"

"You said when the President of the United States has been shot dead. Miz Lovelace, Mr. Starkey said we could go now."

"YOU'LL GO WHEN I SAY YOU CAN GO."

Now the class froze in shock: Always-a-Lady Lovelace had raised her voice. She was chewing the insides of her cheeks and pursing her lips, guppylike, and it appeared that she—Dolores said she must be the strategist for the Due East Republican Party, because all their press releases were accompanied by lines from *The World's Most Beloved Verses*—might even let a tear escape from beneath her baby-blue marbleized glasses.

"Boys and girls?" Her low dignified voice was back again. "Someone has been *killed.*"

Mrs. Lovelace shook her head, turned her back to the class, and breathed deep dignified sighs. Finally she signaled them to leave, and the class filed out behind her. Franny did not even look back for Kate—Stevie was ushering her out the door, whispering fierce sympathies—and Kate moved over to the window. Her father was still standing below, staring up at the windows though now streams of children gushed out from the doors front and side.

"Katherine?" Mrs. Lovelace said.

"Yes ma'am."

"I'm real sorry. I know what this means to your family. To your momma."

She nodded.

There's such a thing as too handsome, Dolores said about J.F.K., but she'd run to the television set quick as any of them if he was on, and moon over him longer than she did over Gregory Peck. The night he gave the Alabama speech she crossed herself three times: he redeemed himself just as the *Catholic Worker* had her all riled up about this Vietnam business.

But my father. There is my father on the sidewalk down below crying his eyes out over a man he wouldn't have even *voted* for if his name had been Pulaski or Goldstein or Jones. There is my father, who doesn't even know what's going on in his own household, thinking that this is the worst thing that could happen in the world.

She too was crying: she wondered if Stevie had not known either that the tears were streaming down. She could cry forever. She hated him. She hated her father for showing up to shame her and make her carry his own grief.

Mrs. Lovelace had moved across the room to rest a hand on Kate's shoulder the way Stevie Dugan had rested his hand on Franny's. A week ago Kate would have shrunk back from the ladylike silky feel of it.

"You know your daddy's the one alerted the school. He came running over from his office. I saw him downstairs, and I says: 'Let me send her down to you, Mr. Rooney,' but he says: 'I think I'll give her a minute to collect herself, Miz Lovelace. She's going to take this hard.' He said you kept a scrapbook of the President, honey?"

Kate froze. She was picturing the little boy and the little girl.

"Look," Mrs. Lovelace said. "He's waiting for you right downstairs. Who's that down there with him?"

Kate looked. It only got worse.

"My brother. He must've got off the bus here. He must've come to fetch me home too."

Now the two of them weaved on the sidewalk, Tim and her father probably weeping still. Two old men bracing each other. Oh the whole school knew they belonged to her as they filed by. Carrying on like that. Sentimental fools. As if nobody else's heart was broken. As if anybody in Due East cared two cents whether John Kennedy lived or died. Tim had his arm around his father's shoulder as if he could all alone hold his old man up.

And where was her mother now, while the two of them came for her? Burying her face in that reporter's chest? Being all dignified and still not able to make up her mind? She hated them both. The two of them, the three of them, the four of them.

"You better get on down, sweetheart, before he comes inside and y'all lose track of one another."

Kate nodded and moved off. What strange comfort Mrs. Lovelace was. What strange shards of light burned in the Due East Bay.

Down the stairs she trudged alone, the shame of loving Kennedy and her brother and her father consuming her. She was a ball of fire. She dragged her sweater along the floor—oh God, she'd forgotten to go to her locker—and pushed the big front door open.

There they were still across the street, Bill and Tim, statues now, their dignity regained. Dignity regained now that everyone had passed them by. Now that it was too late.

She would not look up as she walked toward them. She could not bear the thought of reaching them, or even drawing near. How brown the grass was on the school's front lawn: oh yes. They'd had a dry September. You could see worms roping their way through the stubble. They'd cut up worms in science, before they took their scalpels to squirrels. Now she was on the sidewalk across the street from them and had no choice but to look their way. But they were not watching her. Now they stared out in two directions, oh elegant and cool, two guys shooting the breeze, two jazz musicians waiting for a cab. They were not watching her, Tim and Bill: they did not want to shame her after all.

How tall Timmy was growing. He'd shoot past his father by next year and maybe then they'd finally buy him pants that covered his bony ankles. Oh those Hush Puppies he wore. How he could even bear to climb on the school bus Kate did not know. And how old Bill looked in the bright light: Tim's old man. Old as Dolores.

"Daddy," she called. "Over here."

And her father lifted his arms the way the priest did at the Consecration, as if they were only greeting each other after a brief separation. The sun shone down on the thin patches of his hair, and his big belly strained against the white buttons of his white shirt. He was older now than her grandfather had been, dying. Old as Kennedy, almost.

She crossed the street though she hadn't looked for cars. A car would pass through her today. Out in the bay the toy boats sailed on, their white sails innocent of the news. Her father spread his arms.

He was crying again.

Oh if he would never die. If he would never ever die.

◻   ◻   ◻

Father Berkeley called Dolores with the news and she cried out: "Sweet suffering mother of Jesus," the very line her father had spoken with such bitter sarcasm. "Oh Father," she said. "How can this be." But it was she who ended up comforting the young priest. "We'll pull ourselves together, Father," she said—and when he said that it would be Dr. King next she answered: "It very well may be."

She turned the television on, but even before the volume coughed itself up she had blackened the screen. A shot of the hospital. She retreated to the phone to call Bill, but his office line rang on and on, into the day. Bill would want more comforting than Father Berkeley, and here she had spent the morning wandering the back streets downtown, where he could not reach her. The woozy morning had trembled on, but now she was steady, steady with this terrible news from the outside world. Her mother's calm when Andrew gave them the news.

Hartley Dinkins from the Democratic Party called, his voice bright with excitement, and she contained herself while he listed what telegrams they should be sending. Then he said: "Johnson'll be *much* more palatable down here. *Very* much more," and Dolores said: "Good Lord, Hartley, do you think we should shoot off fireworks tonight?"

It was almost two o'clock. Soon the children would be home, and she would have to tell Kate. She had learned of Andrew's death coming in from school too, and she could still remember her mother's smugness: "The first thing I have to tell you, Lorey, is that life goes on. Life goes on." Terrible the things you held against your parents all your life, the way you savored them—and what had she said to Father Berkeley by way of comfort? *We'll pull ourselves together.* Ah well, mother and daughter, mistresses of the cliché.

She found herself in her bedroom, though she did not remember climbing the stairs. She had opened the closet—looking for what?—and now was staring at Bill's white shirts, stiff with Lily's starch. What was she thinking? On a shelf above the rack of shirts was a shoebox full of letters and cards, and underneath lay her grammar school missal. She had come to look for the prayers from the Mass for the Dead, but now she could only stare at hanger after hanger of Bill's identical white shirts. The look of Tom Prince's starched shirt, rumpled on the floor.

Through the window she caught a glimpse of another shirt— and this one was not white at all, thank God. It was Andrew in a green shirt, walking in the back yard. So they had let the schools out when the news came that Kennedy was shot. She would not be the one to tell them after all.

Andy was circling aimlessly—no, now he was headed toward the back corner, where Timmy kept the shrines. They'd gone to weed lately. She pictured herself flying down the stairs, holding Andy in her arms, though he hadn't let her do that since he was eight or nine.

She did start down toward him, but did not make it back through the house. The front door opened before she was halfway down the flight, and there were Tim and Bill and Katie, their noses red-tipped and their eyes as puffed as adders. If only she could cry the way they did: Tim, seeing her, had started in again. If only she did not feel so stiff reaching a hand out to Bill and saying: "I heard. I heard the news." She must reek of what she had done.

But Bill spread himself around her, circling down with his

warmth and his welcome flab and his rapid heartbeat, and he held her so tight that her eyelids flashed bright orange light. When he released her she saw that Katie and Timmy were afraid to look at her, and she squeezed one hand from each the way she'd squeezed Andrew that morning.

"We could say a Rosary," she tried, but they stared up at her with wide-eyed derision, and Tim finally cracked a smile. They wanted to watch television, to see for themselves what had happened.

"Some lunatics in this world," Bill said, all his bluster vanished. Andy had come in somehow from the back, without their hearing him, and they all settled in front of Walter Cronkite. Her family, her Bill and Tim and Andy and Kate. Steady again, she was traveling a different track, and went back to the kitchen to try to reach Maggie at Mount St. Martyr's. She needed to comfort her eldest—she dialed again and again—but the switchboard rang busy for forty-five minutes: all those Irish families, up and down the East Coast, trying to reach their daughters. She could picture the carrying-on in the dormitory rooms.

Back in front of the television, her family still leaned forward in their chairs, as if this were a ball game and they might still affect the score, as if they could change what had happened through sheer will. They had no memory of last night. Dolores told them she was just walking out to get some air.

"You come right back," Bill said, without looking away from the screen: not a question but a demand. She said she would.

And then she walked out into the light. It rushed down clear as water, but it had lost its dreamy glow. All morning she'd been walking the back streets in this light, and a half dozen times she'd tried the Rosary, but the hangover reached out its shaking hands and squeezed the neck of the prayer. She had been pretending that she was avoiding Tom Prince, but Tom Prince would have been out at his trial all morning. She had been pretending that the Rosary held some meaning for her. There was no end to her delusions.

She walked toward the old pecan tree and saw it in sharper focus: the chips of bark crusty, like the dried icing of a forgotten birthday cake, each strand of moss announcing its presence. She leaned her hand against the tree and felt the soft old bark yielding. Yesterday she was leaning her hand against the old live oak on River Street, watching a boy struggling along the bluff. Three hours ago, she was wandering Due East, loath to come home, and thought what she had done would stun her family. Just now she could walk into her living room naked with no effect.

When she was a girl, when she and Rose didn't hear the news about her father in time for a proper burial, she found the graveside prayer in her missal and recited it every time she passed Lenehan's: "Grant, O Lord, we beseech You, that while we lament the departure of our brother, Your servant, out of this life, we may bear in mind that we are certainly to follow him." She'd heard her voice go childlike when Father Berkeley gave her the news, and she'd felt a childlike current coursing through her: she'd caused it, this murder, with her own drunken carrying-on.

Looking out past the tree, she realized that they should bring some food over for that sad ungainly Mr. Rapple, whose grief, after all, was closer to home. Now she would not have to drive off alone to her Confession—there would be a big memorial Mass for Kennedy in the Cathedral, and her family would line up to hear their penances there on Saturday night. There was a cheerful young priest assigned to the Cathedral who knew something about the War Resisters League; they would all have to keep a closer eye now on Vietnam. She should have been keeping a closer eye all along. She should have been pushing Hardly Thinking to make some statement about the integration of the high school—good night, Hartley, what are you sitting on your hands for?—and soon. *Right* soon, Hartley: she'd slip that in when she called him back about the telegrams.

Just now there was Maggie still to reach. There was a baby on the way and—oh God forgive her, the way she dreaded the cheery calls—her mother to telephone up in Inwood. "Like your father," Rose would say of Kennedy. "A big good-looking Irishman."

Just now there was food still to fix for the four inside and for Mr. Rapple too. She turned to go back in, but Kate wandered out the front door and, morose, sat herself down on the front steps. Dolores waited by the tree and finally, after a long exaggerated sigh, Kate said:

"I had a nightmare last night."

"Oh dear." Dolores steadied herself and, seeing Tim running from the kitchen that morning, did not go to put her arms around her daughter. "I thought the bad dreams were leaving you alone for a while. Want to talk about it?"

Kate looked at her mother, at the tree, back at her mother, down at the step below her.

"No."

Dolores let her huff and puff and then said:

"Sometimes it helps."

Kate looked up to the heavens and said: "I had a nightmare you went off with that man."

"What man?"

"That newspaper man."

She didn't even pause to take in a breath, but still she made it light: "Oh Kate now. I wouldn't do that." Then: "Dreams are. . . ."

"Dreams are *what?*" Andy's sour inflection.

"Never mind," she said, and almost could have laughed. "Your father would kill me if I started telling *you* about Freud."

Kate brought her eyes back down earthwards and stared long and hard at her mother.

Dolores watched herself walk into the lie she dreamed would protect her daughter still. "Kate, I wouldn't do anything to hurt your father."

Kate was tugging at the pleats of her black skirt as if she'd like to rend the cloth in two.

"Oh Momma, go on inside, Daddy's all blubbery. Make him quit."

Dolores waited.

"You don't even call him Bill. *Your father.*"

"I'm going in right now," Dolores said, "but you, Miss Rooney, must keep a civil tongue in your head." She could still pretend to be the mother.

Kate reached her hands out at her mother's words—oh miracles never ceased—and Dolores gave them a good tug. The television would be on through the night. She'd bring her daughter into the kitchen to work beside her, to have her close for a while, while she still could.

But when she started up the steps her daughter swung past her, into the yard, and mumbled as she went. "I'm going for a ride."

Dolores, hand to hip, tried to hold her back. "Oh Kate. *Today.*"

Pained indignation. "It's not like I'm being disrespectful. I mean, if he's dead, he's dead. I can't bring him back sitting in there next to Timmy being a weirdo."

"All right, then. Maybe a ride will do you good. What time should we look for you?"

"I dunno. I'm just going to the trestle."

"The trestle? Back through the woods?"

Kate's only answer was a single raised brow. Oh *Mother*. It wasn't just that she'd reached that age: now she had an afternoon of anger to kindle in the dark woods. Slumping through the yard, her shoulders weighed down with Kennedy and Dolores, she left her mother behind.

"You be careful in those woods, Kate."

But Kate was already out of sight, and maybe she was out of hearing too. Dolores heard Bill bellowing from deep within the house:

"FOR GOD'S SAKE TIM I WOULD LIKE TO WATCH THE TELEVISION WITHOUT HEARING YOUR PRIVATE DIRGE ON THAT SHRIEKING FIDDLE,"

and she looked round the yard at the moss and the decay and the light pushing down through the branches. She waited until Kate and her bike came tearing around from behind the house, and she waved at her daughter's disappearing back as if her child had not seen a thing the night before, when she looked out the window into the dark.

So she would not have her daughter beside her while she cooked after all. She saw the piles of potatoes and carrots her mother had set out for her to peel. Maybe it was not the Rosary she should have been trying to say all morning, and maybe it was not the Confiteor either. Memory was the only prayer she was capable of.

Now she could see herself, small as Kate on the bike, lying rigid in her bed after her father was gone. Rose's thick white arm lay beside her, and her mother's scapular swung down from her neck to brush the sheet. The close damp air of a New York summer pressed down on her, and she imagined seeing her father in the street with his Lorene.

Lorene would be a peroxide blonde, her black eyebrows tweezed thin and angular, her breasts sharp points. Andrew and Lorene would be snuggling even as they walked, Lorene's narrow high heels clacking along on the sidewalk. Dolores imagined calling them softly from a doorway. She imagined their drawing near, her father's mouth yielding a small smile of surprise and pleasure. She imagined a knife in her pocket, and Lorene's eyes widening.

Then her father died, and the vision died too. Now she lay in bed and saw her father strutting down Broadway, solitary and handsome, his coxcomb gleaming in the morning light. Coming out of a store, she would reach out to touch his arm, and he would say: "Mother of Mercy, you're a grown woman!" He would be able to see, just from the swing of her hips, that she had been with a boy, and he would not be able to look her in the eye. "Can you forgive me, Lorey? Can you ever forgive me?"

And she, a woman of the world now, would answer her father with a squeeze to his hand. "Oh, now, Dad. It's not such a big thing after all, is it? That pious stuff drives *me* crazy too, you know. Makes me want to run right out of the apartment sometimes myself." Andrew would stare at her in wonder, and his eyes would fill the way they had when he said his *mea culpas,* only now his tears would be real.

Now was that memory, or dream, or prayer? Dolores Rooney watched her daughter's white pullover flapping as she rounded the corner of O'Connor Street, and she saw too her husband's white shirt flapping in the wind out at the beach, that year when he was so glad to be with her.

She climbed the steps to go back inside her house, to be with them while she still could.

DATE DUE

Demco, Inc. 38-293

127390